Praise for *Winter Range*

"In the stretch of Montana that causes most visitors to bump up the cruise control, even lock their doors against all that emptiness, Claire Davis has stopped and let the land, the sky, and the people into her story the same inevitable way rain soaks into that parched soil. *Winter Range* follows well in the tradition of Ivan Doig's *English Creek Trilogy,* Larry Watson's *Montana 1948,* and Nicholas Evans's *The Horse Whisperer.*"

—Pete Fromm, author of *How All This Started*

"*Winter Range* re-creates the heartbreak and quiet joy of life on the snowbound prairie of eastern Montana with an authenticity that is pure gold. Claire Davis's novel is one of the very, very best ever written about Montana."

—Mary Clearman Blew, author of *Sister Coyote: Montana Stories*

"The beauty of Davis's language reawakens us to the magical possibilities contained in the simplest of words."

—Kim Barnes, author of *Hungry for the World: A Memoir*

"This original novel introduces gothic to the high plains of the modern West. Claire Davis is a fine writer and *Winter Range* will keep you glued to the edge of your seat."

—James Welch, author of *The Heartsong of Charging Elk*

"In vibrant language, Davis offers a darker vision of modern cattle ranching, where lost opportunities, isolation, greed, and self-pity can too easily degenerate into self-justifying irresponsibility and violence. An interesting examination of the complexities of our relationship to those upon whom we depend most for our survival."

—Laurie Hendrie, author of *Remember Me*

"*Winter Range* is absolutely engrossing, a vivid thriller, and a look into the degree of absorbed selfishness which results in merciless conduct. I stayed up all night with this one."

—William Kittredge, author of *Hole in the Sky*

"*Winter Range* moves with an elemental force. . . . [Davis's] writing has tensile strength, a quirky grace, a wise humor. Claire Davis is an important new voice in the literature of the American West."

—David Long, author of *The Daughters of Simon Lamoreaux*

"Brilliant, beautifully written . . . Davis's skill brings wintry Montana alive."

—*Kirkus Reviews* (starred review)

"Penetrating and heart-wrenching detail . . . Davis has pictured the region and its peoples with such credible vividness that her images speak for themselves."

—*San Diego Union-Tribune*

"Haunting and remarkable . . . staggering."

—Ken Fuson, *The Baltimore Sun*

"The drama heats up. . . . Davis's writing is as clean and uncluttered as the Montana horizon."

—Ginny Merdes, *The Seattle Times*

Claire Davis

Picador USA   New York

Winter Range

www.picadorusa.com

Picador® is a U.S. registered trademark and is used by St. Martin's Press under license from Pan Books Limited.

Frontispiece courtesy of PhotoDisc Inc.

Book design by Victoria Kuskowski

For information on Picador USA Reading Group Guides, as well as ordering, please contact the Trade Marketing department at St. Martin's Press.
Phone: 1-800-221-7945 extension 763
Fax: 212-677-7456
E-mail: trademarketing@stmartins.com

ISBN 0-312-26140-3 (hc)
ISBN 0-312-28425-X (pbk)

First Picador USA Paperback Edition: October 2001

10 9 8 7 6 5 4 3 2 1

In memory of

Clara and Glenn Davis,

whose love was an act of grace.

And for my son,

Brian Wroblewski

Acknowledgments

I want to thank Judy Blunt, my guide through the heart of these range lands and its people, for her generous gift of time—the numerous nights at her kitchen table, staying up too late, drinking coffee too strong; to Robert Sims Reid for believing in this work and lending me his expertise in the law. My thanks to David Long for his friendship, his selfless mentoring over the years. To Robert Wrigley and Kim Barnes, in whose home, high above the Clearwater River, I wrote this book—thank you for your love and support. My thanks to Mary Clearman Blew for her friendship, her generosity, and to Phil Zweifel, who started it all so many years ago. I also want to thank Sally Wofford-Girand, George Witte, William Kittredge, Mark Clemens, Keith and Shirley Browning, Rudy and Gail Martin. I want to extend my gratitude for the support of the Idaho Commission on the Arts and Lewis-Clark State College.

Finally, thanks to Dennis Held for his support through the years of work, for helping me realize the idea.

Winter Range

Chapter One

T he sheriff, Ike Parsons, stood at the curb, zipped his coat closed to his throat, and knocked the snow clear of his hat. A truck rolled past, hit a glazed patch in the street, and did a little sideways slide and jiggle. The driver ducked his head to the sheriff as if apologizing, and then the truck straightened and moved on. It was a year of big snow for this small town, in the corner of Montana, eastern edge of what was known as the hi-line to the locals—a corridor of high desert, along old Highway Two, bisecting the northern tier of the state. Just a jump from Canada to the north and the Bearpaw Range, the Little Rockies to the distant south. Dry land farm and ranch country—wheat, cattle.

Parsons tucked his hat over his ears, tugging the brim to a beak above his nose. The snow fell haphazard out of the bright blue overhead, papered alike the streets and hydrants, hats and shoulders of his fellow townsfolk. Across the street, the vet Purvis was angling his way over a snowbank, cutting a diagonal toward Ike. He was a tall man in his early sixties, graying, but like many out here, ropy-muscled and fit from dealing with livestock. He hopped the curb and a foot dipped under him so that he bobbled a moment and the sheriff snatched him under an arm and steadied the older man.

"I meant to do that," Purvis said.

Parsons shrugged. "And I meant to let you fall on your ass."

The two men grinned. Purvis looked up, dodged a clump of falling snow, said, "Ain't this a sight? Once in a generation."

Come spring the land would be rich with water, and with any luck it would signal the end of seven years of drought, but now, late winter, it was snow, burying the streets. Just outside of town—a flat-open slab of white over hardpan and scrub, a scattering of sage and cactus and greasewood punching through, a skiff of tumbleweeds dashing over the icy surface, swooping about in the wind.

"You off to work?" Purvis asked.

Ike stepped away. "My day off."

Purvis fell in alongside. "You get those? What the hell's the law coming to?"

Ike shook his head and a clot of snow flopped down from the brim. "World's gone to the dogs, I guess." Parsons glanced in a storefront window, sucked his stomach in. At forty-two he was still a solid man, but softening at the edges and he did not take kindly to it. Too many sedentary hours behind the desk, too many miles on the roads.

"So, your day off—what you got lined up?"

"Hardware store." Ike shoved his hat back, tugged at his hair. "Steve's for a trim. Get lunch. Find my wife." Ike tipped a finger to his hat as Lucy Mattick ducked past. Some few people lived in town, but most, like Lucy, drove in once a month, or twice, and their families had done so for two–three generations, so that everyone knew each other as well as the vehicles they drove in. A far cry from his former life as a police officer in Milwaukee, Wisconsin, where, with any luck, he was able to keep all the faces anonymous, and where, on his old beat—downtown to the near north side, the projects rambling down Cherry and Vine, the entrenched North Avenue—there were more steel bars over doors and windows than in a jail.

Lucy walked with her shoulders braced forward as if against a headwind. Her son Joe scuffed behind at about ten feet—a sullen teenager who'd already been into enough trouble to look the other way as he passed the sheriff.

The vet doffed his hat, said, "Morning, Lucy." And after she'd passed, he leaned into Ike's hearing. "One damned fine-looking woman, that Lucy Mattick. But nervous."

"Purvis, don't you have some sick animal to go look after?"

The older man shook his head. "Think *I'll* take the day off," he said, "think I'll just keep you company till you find Pattiann. See if I can't talk her out of a home-cooked meal later." He grinned at Ike. "*She* likes me, you know."

They crossed the street at the courthouse, turned right toward the mercantile. A good-sized town, by western standards, seven parallel blocks east–west, four north–south around a central square. Building fronts were brick and wood, two-storied with western faces, free-swinging shingles, and hand-lettered signboards: post office, grocer, mercantile.

The bell over the hardware door saluted their entry. Ike found his way between tall shelves of pipe joints and plungers, nuts, bolts, and chain, samples of barb and insulators. The fir floor dipped in the center of the aisles where a hundred years of boots had worn a groove. He found a new float for the toilet, a spare ball and chain just in case. And damn but he hated this business of home repair, hoped he had the right parts, already dreading his awkwardness in the confines of the tank, at odds with balls and washers, how easily undone he was by overflows. At the counter he paid for the parts. Purvis lifted a cigar from the display case and tipped it toward the cash drawer. "On my bill," he said. The young clerk smiled and nodded.

Back in the street, Ike squinted against the white light of sun on snow, the spangling of chrome and windshield. He took a deep breath, caught himself hoping for a glimpse of his wife Pattiann, her red hair as bright and buoyant as the air itself.

At the end of Main Street and Third, Purvis lit his cigar, took a great puff, and hummed as he released the smoke. They stopped to read the signboard on the Unitarian church: *Here today* . . . In the sky behind the Unitarian's stunted steeple, Ike could see the grain elevators where birds convened and squabbled. No songbirds for this place, nothing fancy, just starlings—black on black so deep the sun couldn't shine bright enough to light their feathers.

Across from the courthouse was Steve's barber shop. Purvis stepped in ahead of Ike. Five men were spread out among the row of seats against the wall and the sofa backed to the front window. Ike's father-in-law Bill was seated on the sofa, neck clean-shaven, his dark hair clipped close and scalp pinked as a shorn sheep. Pattiann sat kitty-corner to him, her booted feet raised and resting on the low table that magazines were rifled across. When Ike entered she smiled, lifted her face to him.

"Jig's up, Pattiann," Purvis said, walked over and gave her a smacking kiss on the lips. "Sheriff's here."

"Oh good," she said. "You got the handcuffs, honey?" She smiled at Ike, a toothsome grin.

Her father was extending his hand to Ike, and a deep flush moved up his neck and over his face. He looked over at his daughter. "I don't know that a father needs to hear this," he said.

Pattiann snorted. "Really? And what about those dress spurs hanging on your bedroom wall?"

"Those, Missy, were your grandfather's," Bill said, his color rising.

Rob, Pattiann's brother, seated in one of the three barber chairs, fended Steve off with a hand and sat forward. "Believe he's right, Sis. The spurs were Grandpa's. But the lasso next to them is Dad's."

Purvis knocked the ash from his cigar into a sink. "Used to be I knew a few lariat tricks myself."

Steve leaned over, flushed the sink clear with cold water. "You know an ashtray when you see one?" he asked. Steve was a long-shanked man with a ripe, pear-shaped belly. A birdly man who had a peckish way of combing and cutting, his elbows winging over the heads of bibbed customers. "You here for a cut Sheriff, or to shoot the bull like this other bunch?" he asked, his scissors stabbing the air toward Aaron Wolfgram, Wes Long, and John Fonslow.

Wes clucked his tongue, said, "Well, now I *am* hurt. You hurt?" He turned toward Aaron, then, "You, John?"

Both men nodded.

Ike slung his hat up on the coatrack.

Steve eyed Ike's hair. He nodded, satisfied. "A trim," he said, pointed to an empty barber chair, wagged his finger in Rob's direction. "And you could take a lesson. Sheriff here may be the only man in town hasn't come in asking me to salvage his head after some botched-up, ham-handed home haircut."

"That's 'cause the only way Pattiann's likely to cut anything is with a livestock clipper," Rob said.

"Well," she said, "I like to go with what works. Why, the other day, when I was doing my legs . . ."

Ike eased into the chair, enjoying the men's laughter, the pride in his father-in-law's eyes as he cocked his head to a side and winked at his daughter. There was no getting ahead of Pattiann for long. She could keep the best of them treading water. Steve flapped a bib over Ike, and the cloth billowed down slow as a sheet over a bed. Ike leaned back, the sunshine warm, reflecting brightly off the pin-striped cloth. Steve bustled back to Rob and Ike let the men's chatter fall about him. Let himself enjoy this moment in the company of his good friend Purvis, the friendly town men, Pattiann and her family. He let his gaze drift to where Patti-ann lounged, a booted foot crossed over the other, wagging a slow three-beat rhythm, waltz time. Her head tipped back and her red hair, kindled in the wide swath of midmorning sunlight, lit the ocher wall behind her. And on the wall over her head was the gallery of old photographs that Ike loved next best about this place, next best to the friends and jokes and tall tales. The row of photos, framed with handwritten notes Scotch-taped below and alongside—the who and where and when of each.

Pictures of the town's boom era, 1910 through 1917, when in that narrow window the high desert was blessed with years of water and the dry lands became great waving prairies of grass: blue grama, needle and thread, redleaf sedge, bluestem, buffalo, plains muhley and barley. A savannah of green under a breakneck blue sky. And there were the rush of homesteaders, Midwesterners mostly—farmers, merchants, newlyweds, and mavericks, greenhorns all, clutching full-color brochures, and ready to cash in on their own free three hundred and twenty–acre parcel of land. A little bit of paradise. A homestead of their own.

And then the rains ended, this little bit of paradise, after all, being part of the Great American Desert.

Damn but they were a scrappy bunch, their wagons and trucks strapped high with furniture like a presage of the Great Depression caravans. Young men trailing mismatched teams, a hobnob collection of this and that they'd mustered up, or brought along. Ill-prepared, ill-informed, downright lied to by the railroads trying to people this great wasteland. A photo of the train depot—a clutch of men and women in fine but rumpled clothing, an unlikely crop of parasols blooming overhead. Ike's favorite picture was the front of the old boardinghouse, a line of men in cocked bowlers, waistcoats, and bow ties, arms over each other's shoulders grinning into the camera, ignoring the sweat, the heat of the day. And others. Women with bibbed and knickered children in front of tar paper shacks. Or women in long dresses, in the field, great shocks of wheat bundled under their arms. And what Ike thinks most telling, perhaps, is their gaze, not the brash head-on stare of the men, but a distant kind of seeing, their focus directed somewhere clear of the camera's lens, some other place on the far horizon. Some other time.

And truth was, most all of the locals were descendants of that raw-boned, greenhorn stock, savvy with the accumulated breaks and mistakes of three and four generations. It was true of Bill and Rob. Pattiann was a third-generation Montanan—a rancher's daughter raised to be a rancher's wife who had instead married a Midwest boy turned sheriff. Sometimes he marveled that she chose him. But what choice had he given her, really, appearing out of nowhere with his hat in hand, *Pattiann, will you marry me?* Like some orphaned calf. How that must have appealed.

He shut his eyes, drifting in the warm sun, the bantering, the soft chatter. He and Pattiann had been married three years now, had known each other for two years before that. He met her in a night class in criminology at the university back home in Wisconsin, the one and only semester Ike had ever agreed to act as a visiting instructor. She sat in the back of the classroom, by the door, on the edge of her seat as though she might bolt.

The first time they made love was in his single bed in an efficiency apartment. He'd turned on a portable cassette player to cover the neighbor's TV. She took off her blouse, and he said, "I'm a lot older than you." She slipped the bra straps from her shoulder, and he said, "I don't think cops should marry." When she shrugged out of her jeans and panties, he shut up. Afterward he said, "We probably shouldn't be doing this." She offered her bed the next night.

She earned a C in his class. She might have done better, but she never got assignments in on time. Six months later, she had left to go back home. Montana. A place, at that time, he could hardly conceive of. A place she'd talk about only reluctantly. A year later, he'd followed.

He heard the chair next to him tip forward with a squeak, and opened his eyes to see Rob stand up, then duck his head to glance in the mirror as Steve whisked his shoulders with a small hand broom.

He caught the tail end of a conversation between Wes and Aaron. The words "stubble," and "field," and then, "Well, if I ever turn that stupid, shoot me, put me out of my misery." This from Aaron, who ran a tidy ranch, great-great-grandson of one of those early homesteaders. Then silence. Pattiann was staring down at her lap, her hands capping her knees, and her father Bill was turned sideways on the sofa, looking over his shoulder and out the front window. He seemed distracted or uneasy. Purvis came out of the washroom, wiping his hands on a paper towel that he tossed into a basket under the sink. The stub of his cigar was clamped between his lips and he knocked a full inch of ash into the porcelain sink. He scooted over to Pattiann, out of the range of Steve rinsing the bowl once again, with a great splashing gesture.

"You must be wondering what I'm doing here," Purvis said to her.

She patted his hand, her lips twitching to a side. "My guess is you need a haircut or a home-cooked dinner."

"You know," he said, dousing his cigar in the clean ashtray, "if just one other woman knew my heart half as well as you—"

"You mean stomach."

"Whatever." He waved his hand in front of her. "I'd snatch her up."

Rob grabbed his coat off the rack, threaded his arms into the sleeves. "Knew this guy—Phil Zweifel was his name—trail cooked for us one season. Best chow I ever ate."

7

"Well," Purvis said. "He still around?" He laced his fingers behind his head, grinned up at the ceiling. "He more than half ugly?"

Pattiann pumped him in the ribs with an elbow. Bill stood and gathered his coat and hat. "I am taking my leave now, while I still have a high opinion of you all." He tipped a finger to the group, leaned over Ike in the chair, studied the right side of Ike's head, the left, returned to the right, and asked Steve, "That look even to you?" After which he backpedaled for the door. The bell chimed and a cool whiff of snowy air brisked in and was as quickly snuffed as the door clamped shut behind the two men.

Steve was fussing over Ike's right side now, and Pattiann was laughing into her fist, while Purvis named off a list of dinner favorites. Ike basked in the warm sunlight coming through the wide windows, the soft laughter and chatter making him drowsy with pleasure. The bell rang again, and then again as more men filed in while others took their leave. Greetings were exchanged, news of weather and livestock, bad jokes and good-natured ribbings. He studied how his wife joined in the banter, how easily she moved in and out of this most male arena with wit and grace. He watched the faces around her light with humor. He knew them by name, their spouses and children, and a good number of them, their histories. The scissors snicked in the air beside him and there was a crow of laughter and in the far corner a pocket of quiet conversation. He watched the give and take between the men, the conversations, the gestures, all the delicate connections between strangers that make up community, family. Sometimes, he thought, it was unaccountable. How we found ourselves so far afield from our expectations. And even more surprising, how right it could feel. He lifted his gaze, and outside the large window in the waning light of morning was the weightless fall of snow.

Chapter Two

A set of headlights picked out the indigo road ahead of the white-on-blue Bronco, sheriff's insignia on both door panels. Inside, Ike popped his knuckles, cracked open the side window. Below the full moon and peck of clouds, the swale of land sprawled flat and blue as far as the eye could see. He drove slowly, headlights a rogue star moving countercurrent to the swarm overhead.

The night was cold, startlingly clear. He kept his down jacket open and the shearling earflaps slapped up on his cap. The air stung his nostrils so that he pinched them twice to keep from sneezing. He was watching for the Mattick boy, reported missing by his mother. What had Purvis said about her the other morning? A fine-looking woman but nervous. And yes, she was—chewed her nails to the quick, chewed the quick till it was bloody—but that didn't mean she hadn't cause. Joe was a troublesome kid, but mostly petty stuff, more irritating than anything. And chances were they'd find him by morning, holed up with a friend or in a shed drunk on Thunderbird. Still, he felt compelled to check.

Jackrabbits paced him, white, long-shanked, mule-eared, and hurtling down the headlights with a sudden veering and then a small *whump* under a rear tire, and the Bronco would shift like an old man accommodating a full stomach before settling back onto its course. Lucy'd said Joe had a friend out this way. The fence line scrolled past, and in the distance he could see running forms. Coyotes, he thought, but slowed anyway.

He pulled the Bronco over, switched off the headlights to let his eyes adjust. His concern was the boy wandering drunk in the cold, trying to make it on foot. The radio was on scan, picking up the county's cross-chatter. So far, all he'd heard was a lot of useless talk from Harley, a whey-faced deputy who was dating the dispatcher. In the morning, he'd have *another* talk with Harley. Wished his young deputy would marry the girl, nothing quenching chatter as quickly as marriage.

Though, to be fair, Pattiann had never been given to unnecessary speech. And marriage only made her predictable in small ways—her rowdy hair in the mornings, or the way her shoelaces came untied and she would tie the right before the left whether it needed it or not. Marriage had not answered the look she shot him at odd moments, her eyes narrowing while the focus drifted and he wanted to know what or who it was she saw. In those times, it was like living with a stranger. But maybe that was true of all women. A Goddamned mystery. Their nature, secret as the womb. Damned confusing. Still, it would be good for Harley to marry. It settled young men down, wised them up, taught caution where the job couldn't. He stretched back in the seat, the springs creaking.

Out in the field, blots of black moved against the snow—cattle. Through the cracked window came their plangent lowing, a sound he could not hear without being reminded of his father's farm, and the barn—two-storied oak plank with a fieldstone base. And perhaps his belief in the orderliness of the law came from being a child of the fifties in a central Wisconsin farming community, with trim stone walls where fields were plowed in days instead of weeks. Just the other side of the fence, cattle huddled, ropy tails to the wind.

He stepped out, crossed the road. The fields were crisp with moon-light, flat to the horizon but for drifts and mounds that gave the land-scape an ingenuity it lacked in summer. The winds had crafted the snow into waves and skiffs of powder snaked through the troughs, or lofted off the crests in fine whiffs like sea spume. Ike's skin burned with the cold. It was not something he could explain—the way this land humbled and terrified him. The cattle made soft grunting noises. There was one horse, and it nickered, a sound like chestnuts knocking in a pocket. It walked with a nodding gait, then leaned over the fence, its breath frosting whiskers and the eyelashes over the round dark eyes. It was a piebald, face wide and white. Stark as honesty. Ike reached over and the horse nosed the gloved hand, then offered its head.

He'd seen winter-poor stock, but these might be the worst. Ike ran his hands over the horse's wither, down the ribs, fingered the dips between accordioned bone like a knacker. He reached through the barbs, thumped the horse on the chest. He gazed over the small clot of cattle, looking and not looking for the boy.

Land, more land and more of the same. The year he'd first come west, he'd find himself imagining roads quartering the vast sections, homes sprouting in suburbs, malls convening on the highways. It would happen, he believed. Not that he wanted that change, no, but you couldn't stop a train by standing on the tracks.

He peered into the dark and saw the coyotes, blackly silhouetted, body heat rising from their backs like smoke from snuffed candles. There was a bark, an answering yip, and they loped away.

Curious their being so near house and herd. Ike hoped to get another glimpse, but close at hand there came a bawling sound and one of the cows staggered. The animal rocked like a boat anchored in choppy water, then dropped. It tried to lift itself, and failing, rolled back with a grunt. Ike glanced down the road then at the barbed wire. None of his business. He eased between the fence wires, caught his pant leg on a barb, and cursed his clumsiness. Alongside the cow, he settled on one knee, hands against the spine to roll her to her feet. The animal's nose drooped into the snow. He pushed, but it would not be roused. He knew the way it would happen: the animal too weak to rise, the snow drifting up over the hide. In an hour, maybe two, the cow would be shrouded. By morning, it would be a mound–like any other in the field. Ike braced his legs and tugged at the head, its eyes large and black, an odd intelligence in them, as if resigned to the way the body fails. He stopped with the head between his hands. He released it slowly.

A mound. Like any other in the field.

The horse nudged at Ike's jacket, and he elbowed it aside. He waded over to a drift, whisked the snow clear, and ran his hand down the outline of a cow. He looked over the acres of mounds and drifts. As he walked farther in, the horse followed, nosing at his hair, its breath friendly on Ike's neck. Every now and again, Ike lifted from his task, resting his arm over the horse's back, grateful for the company, to stare across the distance to where Chas Stubblefield's house watched over them, lights dim in the windows like a well-banked fire.

Chas Stubblefield liked to believe himself a self-made man. His daddy had preferred to think him a kid, right up to five years ago when Chas turned twenty-eight and his father had died at seventy-nine. Chas stood over the stove, his shadow skittering across the walls as the overhead fluorescent coil sputtered its blue-white light until he reached up and ticked the bulb. When it stopped fluttering, he turned back to the counter, prodded the steak with a fork. His stomach griped. He dropped the meat into a cast-iron pan and watched the edges crimp. Through the back porch windows, the quartered cow, silhouetted by moonlight, hung from hooks. Torso tall as a man. The best cuts nearly gone. Didn't matter. Tomorrow or the next day he'd bring in another, hoist it, skin and quarter it. As long as the cold stayed and the cattle kept dying, he had all the food in the world. It was all a meat locker now. He lowered his face to the pan, inhaled. Meat. That was what was left him.

Accustomed to living alone, he ate with con..picuous relish, a swath of meat through potatoes and gravy. He swabbed the plate clean. He was not a man normally given to waste, but encouraged to these ends by men he'd trusted. Such as Taylor at the bank. Best friends as kids. But Taylor had put distance between them these days with his three-piece suits and immaculate nails.

"We've known each other a long time," Taylor had said at their last meeting a month ago. Chas took note that for all Taylor's high-handedness, there were no windows in his office, and the bathroom was far down the hall. He wondered if Taylor rutted with the secretary in there, skirt hitched up and nylons hobbling her ankles, like he'd taken the girls in the back of Chas's pickup as teenagers. Taylor, always the one the girls chose, and it was Chas, the awkward one no one really cared to know, who was reduced to chauffeuring them down some bucketing road deep into the breaks where Taylor would assure them, "Old Chas don't mind," and, "He won't look." Though he had watched the first couple of times, through the rear window, saw the buttocks rising and falling, a breast flattened in a mouth, but for the most part, Chas would stretch out across the seat with his boot heels hooked on a window, hopping one cigarette off another, convincing himself it made no difference to him, convincing himself he needed to be alone because he had a future in mind with no room to accommodate anyone else. Just then.

"A loan. Just enough to tide me over," Chas had said. He was pieced together in clean jeans, white shirt, and string tie. He'd taken a scissors to his blond hair and the ends looked chewed over his forehead. It gave him a boyish appearance. He sat straight.

"You needed to unload some livestock, Chas. There isn't another soul here didn't see this coming."

"My dad survived worse. I come from a long line of survivors." He shrugged.

"Your daddy made it because he had *half the herd*." Taylor wiped his forehead with a handkerchief, folded it into neat squares, and lifted a cheek to tuck it in a rear pocket.

Taylor leaned over his desk, the blotter under his elbows the green of freshly minted money. He rested his hands on the desk, screwing his wedding band up to the first knuckle and down. He shrugged the cuff on his wrist. He slumped back from the desk, as if coming in from a long day. And, of course, it was hard work, this turning away, ignoring old ties: *I knew you when.* Hard work. *A real piece of work.* Taylor stood. He sighed, put a hand on Chas's shoulder. "You already got a payment coming due. You understand? Much as I'd like to, I can't. . . ." He crossed over to the door. "Sorry, Chas."

But Chas stayed seated, a smile on his face—sweet and quirky. "We done then?" He lifted a picture of Taylor's wife from the desktop and squinted until his blue eyes were a slit. "You remember we used to run the back roads? Stinking drunk until even God wouldn't claim us?"

From the doorway, Taylor nodded, taken by charm as easily as he had always been—the first misled and the last disabused. Seeing what he wished to—that Chas was the young rube he'd always been, and bad things did not happen to bankers in the light of day, in their offices.

"And all those times in the back of my pickup?" Chas asked. "I remember," he said, "her dimpled ass."

"Get out."

"You two should come out for dinner. I got steak and more steak."

Taylor stood in the doorway. "Don't come back, Chas."

That was one short month ago when his cattle were the other side of desperate, back when Chas still believed salvation was for the asking. He ran water over a dishrag and the rag turned slick and the counter clouded with each swipe.

He could still smell the steak. And something else. Yes. The house still smelled like the old man his daddy had become. Isn't that the way? All the shed hair and bloody noses, farts and cigarette smoke, the stink of old shit and bad breath stayed on in the wood, the furniture. Sometimes it was like living in another man's skin.

Pattiann woke to the sound of the downstairs door opening. She turned on the bedside lamp, letting her long copper hair shield her eyes from the first light. Their house was on the edge of town, a white two-story bungalow with narrow clapboards and green trim that could have been lifted whole from the Midwest, a concession she'd made in buying this particular house, knowing how its familiarity comforted her husband. She greeted Ike on the stairwell. "I'll make us coffee," she said, and led him back to the kitchen. She was dressed in flannel pajamas, throat buttons open, socks—winter sleepwear of choice. She bent to the sink, sloshed water through the pot and ground fresh beans while he told her about searching for the Mattick boy and what he'd found instead. He told her how after uncovering one carcass he'd gone on to another,

another, and another, and stopped only after he no longer had the stomach for it.

The coffee dribbled into the pot, dark and strong, the fragrance thick as humus. She kept her back to him. What to say? She turned to him. He was changing—his skin aged, his hair hinting at salt and pepper, but his heart? Still in the right place, warm and so easily damaged. Some days she had little tolerance for it.

She set him in the chair, poured them coffee. He sipped the strong brew. "It's been a hard year," she said.

"No," he said. "This is a slaughter."

When she did not answer, he stood and left. She counted his steps, five to the first landing, turn, and the last five. She heard him cross overhead, past the small hall table with its Chinese-lacquered box, a Christmas gift from his mother, past the family photos on the wall: a portrait of her father and mother. More pictures: her brother Rob, wife and kids. A picture of Ike as a kid—buzz haircut, eyes pinched against the sun, behind him the barns of the old farm. In the next picture is his mother, her smile short on patience. His father always behind the camera except for the one small print that shows him glancing over a shoulder, surprised in the act of milking. He's a slender man, with a face gentler than his wife's, a softer version of Ike's own. It was Pattiann's favorite picture: the young man caught with his own camera in the intimacy of milking.

She closed her eyes, heard the soft thuds as Ike sat on the bed, releasing one shoe, then the other. Setting his gun in the bedside table drawer. She rinsed the cups, unplugged the coffeepot, and turned out the lights. In the dark, she felt her way along the Formica countertops, coming to know this place as she had known her father's house—late at night after long hours of calving, feeling her way to the bathroom where she washed in the dark, feeling competent and discovering the aches in her arms and back strangely comforting—as if finding the smell of blood, the dark house, the land and animals, were all pieces that completed her.

She'd heard about Stubblefield's trouble, early on, from hired hands at her brother's. "Goddamned cattle are starving," they said, and, "Flopping dead like flies." And she'd heard about it again the other morning, at Steve's shop. But they were rumors, after all. You didn't tell the law rumors, particularly if the law was your husband. She'd waited like everyone else for the issue to resolve itself. And it would. Painfully. This sort of thing shamed them all, and no one liked to hear about it. She kept her hand on the banister, wound her way up to the second floor, down the hall.

And as for Chas? She was startled by the glitch she felt in her breathing. This would finish him with the community. Light seeped from around the bedroom door. She braced herself. Tried to think of what she could say to Ike that would make this reasonable. Or acceptable? She was tired of apologizing for the intractability of the land, its people, for the distances that wore at him, the endless driving. She reminded herself: he had followed her here. Landless and loving and too damn good to be true.

She sat on the edge of their bed and waited for him to come out of the bathroom. He would leave a slough of water on the sink that he would ineffectually mop up. She still thought the small mess endearing. He returned, toweling his neck, his face, as if he could rub it clean of the windburn, clear down to the Midwest shine.

"This sort of thing is rare," she said, "but it happens."

He looked at the towel, at his hands. Sometimes, at night like this, they would cramp from the long hours on the wheel. When he looked up, she was composed on her side of the bed and he wanted something else from her. "If you'd seen it," he said. But she didn't answer. He knew he was being willfully naive, for of course she'd seen it before, other places, other times. Hard winters. He knew how he looked to her: foolish. He hated that. He balled the towel and pitched it into a corner. "You ranchers act like nobody can understand anything out here but you. You act like I don't live here."

He wished he'd kept silent, that he'd come home to find her frowzy with sleep, when her lack of presence was a thing in itself, so utterly distinct from the woman she was by day—a force to be reckoned with. It was the way she had been raised. She could string fence, pull calves, cook for a crew of ranch hands, balance books, and take insult if you thought that exceptional. She took gain and loss with the same levelheaded shrug. Sometimes Ike believed she could lose anything but her way.

She snapped off her bedside lamp. "Sometimes, Ike, you *don't* live here. You're still back on some little farm where corn can't help but grow and the cattle die fat and happy."

He hated that, too. The way she could ambush him, put him back where he belonged.

"There's no pleasure in it," she said, snugged her feet under the covers and rolled over. "No rancher wants to see his stock die. You're taking this too personal."

She looked small in their bed. She was thirty-three years to his forty-two, and slimmer than when they'd first met. Weren't wives supposed to gain weight, grow complacent? And wasn't there something comforting in that? Not Pattiann. No soft edges in her old age; she'd chip them off herself, if she had to.

"They're *his* cattle," she said.

And that was the problem here, he thought, their inherent belief in property as a "God-given right." For them the law protected property, didn't infringe on it. She'd settled under the covers. He slipped into the far side, reached up, and drew aside the curtains. Her breathing was shallow, but it would soon change; she always fell asleep so easily. Even on a fight. He could hear the wind sheering around the corner of the house. He craned his head back and saw the snow in sloping ledges on the mullioned windows. Moonlight fired the iced glass, spread onto the sill, the headboard, his body. He looked over to where Pattiann lay on her side, the rise and fall of the bedding, her body adrift, and he was hit with the familiar fear that he'd missed some *thing* that could not be regained. He put his hand on her hip. Never let the sun set on your anger—his mother's creed, sparked, he thought, from that childhood dirge, *If I should die before I wake,* as if death were the consequence of sleep, or the dark. Pattiann's hand shrugged out from under the quilts and covered his, an abeyance for the night and that was enough.

Ike sat at the counter of the Dig-In Diner, still mildly peeved with Patti-ann. He picked at his sandwich as if it were a bone. The single-roomed diner had a wide thermopane that looked out on Main Street where men tugged hats against the wind and women herded children ahead of them. There was counter seating for eight where Ike sat, three chrome and Formica tables behind him and two window booths hoarded by teenagers on hot summer nights, the underside of the tables lumped with gum. Roy, the owner, worked the grill; his wife Mary made salads, desserts, and kept the place as clean as weather and working cowboys allowed. Today's special—meatloaf sandwiches and split pea soup. Ike left a two-dollar tip for Fran, his waitress, who rented an apartment in town so her kids could go to the only school in two hundred miles, sixty miles distant from where her husband worked their ranch, where she spent her weekends—weather allowing—restoring order. He stepped out onto the diner porch. He rolled the brim of his Stetson, a hat he tended to hold more than wear.

Lucy Mattick's car was parked across from the mercantile. That morning her son had surfaced, hungover and with sixty unaccounted-for dollars in his pocket, of which his mama relieved him and delivered to Ike's office in a plain white envelope. "I ain't saying he took it," she said. "But you hear someone lost some money, misplaced it, maybe, you give it back. No trouble."

Ike stopped at Coker's feed mill. It was one of those queer blue days with a mist of snow falling through bright sunlight. Next door, the steel-sided grain elevators marched in an imposing row. He parked his Bronco alongside the loading dock, hefted himself up the boardwalk. Sunlight streamed through the bay doors over stacked bags: hog feed, chicken, sheep, dog, horse, rabbit, cat, cattle. To the left, through the store window, shelves of coat conditioners, hoof varnishes, salves, calf and colt formulas, tack. A young clerk, apron rucked up between thighs, stocked shelves. Overhead a country tune buzzed through a blown speaker in the warehouse and the wind gusted and eddied. Down the feed rows, tucked beneath and between the pallets, were bits of silver paper with chocolate-colored cubes displayed like party favors. He angled through the building and out the back door where he found Sam Coker seated on a bench. When he saw Ike, he shrugged. "Rats," he said. "Rats, cats, skunks." He offered a cube to Ike. "Poison. Smells just like those French chocolates." He looked smug. "Rats are fools for chocolate."

Ike wondered how he had arrived at such insight into the rodent mind—this curious little man with droopy trousers and suspenders. "Won't own a belt," he'd once said. "Pinch your gut. Won't own a wife, either," and left the town to wonder if the same reasoning applied.

"Chas Stubblefield?" he said, answering Ike's question. "Gave him barley cakes on credit a couple months ago. Told him to make it last." He clapped his hands over ruddy ears; his thin hair looked sprung in the wind. "He's going down and taking a bite of me along." Then he seemed stricken with the indelicacy of his words and he picked at Ike's sleeve. "Don't go spreading it about."

Late afternoon, Ike drove past Coker's again, saw the big bay doors battened against the wind. He turned down the street bordering the cemetery with its small stone chapel and a rick of brush where black-birds huddled. He drove down residential streets quiet on this a work and school day. He slowed past the vet's pole barn clinic, a horse and cow drowsing in separate holding paddocks, then turned onto the high-way, and although the land looked flat, it was the sheer scope of dis-tances that leveled the eyes instead. A half-hour or an hour between ranches and connecting roads. The intersecting county roads had lad-dered signs with names scrawled on the crossbars: Macley, Zito, Har-rington, Forman, Maresca. An hour out, he turned down Beaver Creek Road, Pattiann's family's ranch at the far end, five miles of ranch road, dead-ending on the Missouri Breaks in their thirty thousand–acre spread with all but nine thousand leased from the Bureau of Land Manage-ment. Here she could locate her way by a boulder in the field, or the stunted juniper, having named them, as children of this place did: Indi-anhead cliff, painted rock, the old Jonas tree, as if naming gave the thing substance, though what it really did, he suspected, was give the *people* substance for the span of their or their children's memory. A small place in history. And who could deny the need for that where the land so easily swallowed accomplishments, so blatantly wore its age in the bones of the prehistoric inhabitants lumped in the hardpan?

Stubblefield's spread was near the end of the road, just after the turn-off onto private road. Ike stopped on the shoulder. The piebald horse paced the fence and cattle huddled in small groups. Chas stood at the water trough. A rifle, a Marlin, lever-action .30-.30, was propped against the tank. He was bending over one of the cows, a surprisingly reverent posture, an attentiveness Ike found familiar—his own father had done this, moving among his cows, leaning into their guts to hear the rumbles or silence. Chas watched as Ike approached.

"Who died?" Chas asked.

Ike stopped. And then he nodded. "Must seem that way to folks when a sheriff stops—somebody dead."

Chas was a man of medium height who carried his weight in his chest and arms. He wore a Stetson punched low over his forehead, the brim dipping toward the nose he scratched with a gloved finger. He looked clean, his clothes laundered. He waited patiently.

"You got a problem," Ike said.

"No," he said, and his eyes were the unperturbed blue of the sky. "I don't have a worry in the world. Bank's got about two hundred," Chas said. "And more every day." He prodded one of the weakened cows with an elbow.

"You out of feed?"

"Out of money. Out of credit. Out of luck. All I got left is patience. I got patience to spend."

"Sell some of them."

Chas tugged on his hat. "Why you could be my own father come back from the dead," Chas said. "You're that farsighted." He clapped his hand over the spine of a cow and the animal shuffled away. "Not enough meat to pay what I owe and nobody to buy. No. These animals are going to die." He turned away, lifted a sledge, and brought it down on the skin of ice in the water trough. He knocked the ice loose and sifted it off the surface. When he turned around, he looked surprised to see the sheriff still waiting. He wiped his hands on his jacket.

"What do you want? You think it's me doing this, you're wrong. Talk to the bank. Let Sam at the feed mill come out. Let all of them come see it up close. Come spring, let them *smell* it." He picked up his rifle.

"This isn't about the bank, Chas. This is about you."

Chas winged the rifle stock up under his arm, barrel swinging around. Chas was smiling again and shaking his head as though he were just another of the stunned cattle. "Maybe what you mean is everyone wants everything neat and odorless, you, Taylor, and Coker . . . and you got the law to make it so. But these animals are mine." He raised the rifle to his shoulder, drew a bead on a cow. Then he turned his face toward Ike, his cheeks dimpling, and Ike caught a glimpse of what the man must have looked like as a boy. Then he fired. The animal stood a moment, blood spraying an outline of its forequarters in the snow, a curiously liquid sound in the frozen landscape, and then it dropped, its eyes still open as though contemplating life with no regrets.

"I can shoot that cow because it's mine," Chas said. He raised the rifle, levered another bullet, aimed it at another cow. "This one. That one. You tell me what difference it makes if they're shot, pole-axed, or starved." He lowered the rifle. "They're meat and meat," he said, leaning into the sheriff's face. "You just think they're something else."

Chapter Three

C lear and simple, Ike believed there was an order to the world—a
sensibility that man could comprehend: boys became men, the
moon followed the sun, stars were birthed and collapsed, environment
determined its inhabitants and their numbers. And order—the need for
it—inspired law, both moral and social. What bothered Ike in Stubblefield's case was the manner in which the animals were suffering, the
waste. Ike thought of his father measuring feed into bins, the cows yield-
ing a marvel of milk. He ate meat like a sacrament.

Not that Ike was the sentimentalist his father had been. No. What it
came down to for Ike was respect. We were human, with the ability to
construct order, to make choices, and a conscience that demanded we
bear the consequences of our actions. It raised us above the animals. It
was a matter of humanity. Dignity.

Bullshit.

It was the cow dropping, the grunt as it hit the turf, and Stubblefield's
smile.

Ike crossed town on foot. He turned down a block, crossed through
the cemetery, and out the other side. He found Purvis working on his
'57 Chevy in the garage connected to the clinic. A good vet but an
unlikely mechanic, who believed he could master anything if the problem were presented in the correct frame of reference. When they'd first
met, he'd endeared himself to Ike by comparing a fouled carburetor to
an impacted anus. Ike had asked if the exhaust wouldn't be more like an

anus, after which they'd retired to the house to mull the problem over whiskey. It was clear to Ike the Chevy would never run properly as long as Purvis was under the hood. It was equally clear Purvis knew as well.

The Mattick boy was on a stool, stripping electrical wire. He was a handsome boy, dark, and Ike supposed that's what fed the rumors about the Indian blood. The boy was a heller and folks were apt to seek an excuse for whatever dark inclinations moved within them, preferring to believe there was good blood, bad blood, and what constituted bad blood often came down to what skin color wasn't yours. So damn much out there you *couldn't* know: weather, disease, government. It inspired a reductionist kind of thought—find a name and face to place the blame. The boy shifted on the stool.

"Ike," Purvis said. Coming out from under the opened hood, he offered his hand. "Come to help?" He pointed to the boy. "You know Joe?"

Joe's eyes passed over Ike's face, rested briefly on his badge. Guilty, Ike thought. Of what he didn't know, but suddenly he worried for his friend Purvis. This boy was trouble in the making. Ike pointed to the car. "What's it this time?"

Purvis wiped his hands down his coveralls. "A problem with the synapse," he said.

"Careful or that synapse is going to electrocute you," Ike said.

The young boy snorted and looked away.

Next to the car was an enameled tray with wrenches and sockets lined up on a surgical towel. Joe set the snips down. "I got to go. Back tomorrow, okay?" At the door, Joe hesitated. "You won't do anything," he said, waving a finger toward the wires.

Purvis smiled. "Tomorrow."

The door heeled open against the wind. The boy eased himself through and the door blew shut. Outside the walls, the wind whistled—a constant with all that land and no purchase for the wind, no mountains, or forests, instead, the elements of land and heaven skittering loose, chaff, sticks, stones, rain, hail, snow, and sleet, bearing down and down until buildings canted and what few trees there were grew one-sided as a limp. People rode their animals or stood in the fields pitched forward until it was a part of them, ligaments shortened, tendons stretched. Even in churches, halls, and homes, still they leaned in bodies remade by the fervor of wind.

There was the patter of corn snow on the roof. Purvis watched the door. "Joe's a good boy," he said. "He worries too much, though. Thinks I might hurt myself." Purvis motioned Ike closer. "What happens if I hook this up here?"

"Epilepsy," Ike said.

Purvis nodded, set the wires down. "I need a drink."

"I'm on duty."

"Didn't say nothing about you drinking. Make you some coffee."

They crossed through the pole building with its pens and chute where people dropped off livestock, and at the barn door a head catch arrangement with side panels that swung out of the way. Inside the heated building, block and tackle hoists ranged on the overhead beams to remove the dead, or drag unconscious animals clear. Along the wall were stacked portable corral panels. In one corner, hay bales loomed fragrant and stacks of rubber pans teetered against bedding straw. At the far end was the surgery—a concrete floor with a center drain. Boxes of sterile packing lined shelves on one wall. Cabinets stocked with antibiotics, tranquilizers, anesthetics that could reduce a thousand-pound animal to cataclysmic dreams, or dust and bones. Art consisted of diplomas and an anatomical chart of a pig done by Purvis during his van Gogh period.

They crossed through a connecting passage to the main house, entered the kitchen transformed into a small-animal surgery, then into the living section—kitchenette, dining, and parlor all in one, with a bed and bath off to the side. Ike thought it eccentric, even for a bachelor. And what woman could live with this? Pattiann. Put it on some land and Pattiann could. She'd welcome the challenge. Her pioneer great-grandmother had raised five boys in a tar paper shack not much bigger than a one-car garage.

They sat at the table, pushing aside dishes and dog-eared magazines.

Purvis poured Ike a cup, which he used to warm his hands, having learned long ago about Purvis's coffee. Purvis ran his thumbs down a glass of whiskey, took a sip, and swiveled in his chair. "I know what this is about," he said. "And it isn't as bad as you think. He's a little misdirected, let's say."

Ike was beginning to believe he was the last person to have found out. "Misdirected," Ike repeated.

"He's young. We worked it out. He's coming over two days a week." Purvis crossed his arms over his chest and rocked back. "If he shows any aptitude, I'll send him to a good pre-vet program." He studied Ike over his glasses. "Trouble with the law is it doesn't recognize potential."

"What the hell are you talking about?"

Purvis rocked forward, braced his hands on the table. "What are you talking about?"

"Stubblefield."

Purvis ducked his head. "Oh shit." And it came out that Purvis and Harley had had breakfast at the diner with Harley mentioning the sixty dollars found on the kid, and Purvis admitting he was "missing some money." Eighty dollars Purvis had "sort of forgotten and left on the table in the garage." Which money just "up and disappeared" after the Mattick boy and a friend stopped by to admire the car. Purvis had asked Harley not to make an issue of it.

"They bought a case of the dry heaves—twenty of the eighty—with wine, cigarettes, and donuts. Couldn't ask for a more fitting retribution, could you?"

Ike sipped the coffee. His stomach quailed and then stilled. The lull before the storm. Christ. "Maybe I ought to go out and heal some cattle," Ike said.

Purvis shook his head. "You wouldn't like it. Prolapsed uterus, mastitis, hoof rot. Makes me wonder why I left small-animal practice." He finished the whiskey. "No. Poodles were the worst. Can't take a decent shit. You got to pick the hair off their ass and squeeze their rectum." His fingers pinched the air and Ike's buttock flinched. "Do you have any idea how many years of selective breeding it took to produce an animal that can't take a crap?" His hands spread open before him. "So now all I got to deal with are cows bred too young to bulls too big. Or steers dropping dead from heart attacks in the feedlots for the marbleized beef market. I should have been a mechanic."

"Purvis, I don't give a good Goddamn about constipated poodles or fat cows. I'm talking about respect."

"Respect."

"For the law."

"Right and wrong." Purvis poured another shot. "You're so single-minded. Say I bring charges," he said, and waved his hand, "and I won't, but say I do. He's a minor. He goes to juvie, gets a record and community service. So instead, the kid helps me–knows more about engines than either of us. Hell, third son on a ranch–he's been tinkering on the damn things since he was a baby. He keeps me from electrocuting myself. I'm the only vet for a hundred miles. That's community service, and I save the citizenry some taxpayer money."

"Purvis, you're a real hero." And even as Ike joked, he suspected it was true. There was something large and generous in the old vet. His stomach clenched, a stabbing in the gut. "But you can't make coffee to save your life," Ike said. "I'm going to have to use your bathroom–no, I don't need you to squeeze my rectum–then we're going for a drive. Just you and me."

It was midafternoon, and from where Chas stood in the door of the mercantile, he could see the sheriff's Bronco pulling away, tires sluicing a rooster tail of grit and snow. He stepped into the street, watched the turn signal *blink, blink, blink.* The vet was in the passenger seat.

Chas had come to set matters right. Explain things to the sheriff. But even as he'd stood watching them pull away, he knew there were no words that could detour the events of today, or tomorrow or yesterday. He felt doomed, and there was a relief in that, as if his head had just rolled free of his body, taking its imponderable weight with it. And maybe this was what death was, when the soul fled the body.

But what did he know of that? What his mother had told him? *Unto thee O Lord, do I lift up my soul.* Daughter of a Baptist minister, a tall, earnest woman who favored the psalms: *O, keep my soul and deliver me . . .* Who, of certain evenings, would retreat to Chas's room, settle herself bedside with her long brown hair knotted as tightly to the back of her neck late at night as it was first of the morning. An educated woman who picked through the handful of books she had salted away, a woman who favored the lyrical, whether it was the psalms or Milton, Dante . . . *for I put my trust in thee.* And she would read to Chas, her voice rising and falling, but so softly, a patter of sound like rain on the windowsill, that he would quiet his breathing, hunch forward to hear the words as insubstantial as the things they spoke of: the fall from grace, love, redemption. The soul.

No.

More memorably, it was what his father believed. It was the spring of Chas's tenth year, a hot day in May, and they were branding and cutting. Chuting young calves through the corrals narrowing in a bottleneck where Chas branded them and ending in a calf table with an iron gate that vised over their necks. Chas's father stood on one side of the table. His left hand clamped the squeeze catch and the restraining bars pressed into the calf's side. His right hand, large and pale as a slab of cooked pork, held the knife. He depressed a foot pedal and the table tilted, the locked-in calf keening over onto its side, and then Chas looped the catch rope around the calf's upper hind hoof, pulled it back, exposing the testicles, bearing down with his weight to keep the animal from kicking. His father ran a slit from the underbelly of the sack to the top and stripped the small balls out with a pinch of thumb and forefinger. A few cautious knife strokes frayed the cords, and then he swabbed the empty sack with Lysol-water. Then Chas flipped the table upright, loosing the animal. Now and again, his father would swipe at the sweat under his hat brim.

Chas goaded another calf through the chute. It balked. Chas kneed it in the rump, hot, dirty, and angry at the calves with their rolling eyes, dull hooves, and burned flesh. The calf reared in the pen and trapped itself sideways. His father turned, asked, "What the hell's wrong?"

"Just scared to the soul," Chas said, shoving the animal clear.

His father had spat into the dirt. "And suppose you tell me what a soul is, boy?"

And for all his mother's talk—of winged insubstantial things, a light in the hollow of your chest, or a thread tangled in your body like a second intestine tying you to God—he could not.

The calf was locked in, the table careened, and the animal lay supine. Chas's father slit the sack and held out the matched balls. "Here's all the soul you'll ever see. The only afterlife there is. Animals fuck. People fuck and anything worthy of regard is passed on to the offspring." He drew the handful close to his eyes. "Think on it. My daddy living in me, and his daddy and his daddy before him, and me in you." He tossed the testicles into a bucket. "Or not. And that's as much of an afterlife as this youngster's ever going to know."

The sky was clear overhead, and even in the stink of the stockyard Chas could smell the sweet tang of sage. Magpies squabbled on the rail and a few stock flies buzzed in the offal bucket. And that was as much soul as his father would credit any creature. He'd never been a generous man—least of all in opinion.

Chas walked back to his pickup. There was nothing to keep him in town. And then he spotted Pattiann, the sheriff's wife, striding down the walk. She was dressed in a long gray coat and jeans, a bright spark of hair escaping a watch cap. The only real color among the shabby buildings, drab sky, and slowing snow. When he thought of her, if he thought of her at all, these past years, it was of the heft of that hair and how it used to curl around his hand with a life of its own. He unlatched the cab door, stepped out, and aimed for her. Would she be pleased? After all this time? Probably not. They'd managed to avoid each other so thoroughly. But then it only seemed just, after all, the sheriff at his place and Chas with the sheriff's wife. Why not? Might as well be hung for a fool as a coward.

They took the highway west. Purvis stretched out on the seat, his arm looped over the backseat. A standard-issue shotgun racked next to him. Ike thought he looked as amused as a child by a ride in a squad car.

"You going to tell me where we're going?" Purvis asked. "No. Don't. A little mystery in the afternoon is good for the soul." He pulled his coat open, the snaps rifling. He shrugged a cigar from his shirt-front pocket, slipped off the cellophane and rolled open the window. "Nothing like a good cigar after whiskey unless it's whiskey after a good meal and a good woman waiting at the end of it all. Speaking of which, how's Patti-ann? Good, good," he said, as if he'd given Ike time to answer. "I was pleased that little girl took up with you. Get her out of the damn ranching business."

He lit the cigar, looked out the side window. "This way of life's going to end. Mark my words. Another fifty years, the fences'll be down. The government will reintroduce bison to the plains with a command to be fruitful and multiply. Tourists will pay to be trampled. Wolves, elk, antelope, movie stars—they'll press the prairie flat with their numbers. 'Home . . . home, on the range, Where the deer and the antelope play,' " he sang.

Ike flipped his Stetson into the backseat. "Purvis, I knew you'd smoke your stinking cigars like I knew you'd talk my ears off, and I came prepared to pay the price. But I draw the line at singing."

Purvis drew on his cigar and leisurely released the smoke. "So I suppose you want to know why I became a vet."

"No."

"It's a vocation, like a call from God—"

"The Mattick boy—he get this call too?"

Purvis waved off the question. "Heard it while riding an eight hundred–pound sow on my daddy's farm. Southern Illinois. I was nine."

Clouds rankled in the east, a high wide billowing like the thunderheads of summer, but overhead was blue sky, and Ike flipped his sunglasses on, the snow and the world turning deeper, more vibrant, the light polarized and somehow more true so that the distant cuneal hills were compressed, and the plains became dimples and swales, gullies and hollows, brushed blue and bluer, cobalt and indigo.

Purvis was speaking of his childhood, of hogs, and his father's farm that would eventually perish under rising land prices, and corporate farming.

"A prize sow, a prime specimen of Yorkshire cultivation, ears like the wings of a dove, shanks broad as the hills that spawned her breed, a nose of absolute grace. My father's pet. He'd have called it daughter if God and my mother could have abided it. Naturally, I hated that pig." He rolled an inch of ash into the ashtray, clenched the cigar between his knuckles.

"We had cows," Ike said.

"Lucky you. Pigs stink. It's a natural fact. Even the pearly pink ones. My brothers and I rode them every chance we had, though my father forbade it. But it's human. That old saying you only hurt the ones you love? Doesn't say half enough about the ones we hate.

"It must have been a hundred degrees the day I took it into my head to ride that sow. My brothers cornered her and I hopped on. I rode her like a bronc. She spun and bucked, torqued and trotted. Scraped me along the fencing. But she never squealed. And I never let go." He held his hands up. "My knees locked over her belly and she ran so hard, I didn't know who rode who anymore." Purvis was laughing, wheezing like that winded pig. He wiped his eyes, took a deep breath.

"When she began to stagger, I believed I'd won. And then she did the only thing left her. Her hocks buckled up and her snout shoveled a three-foot-long trench. She lay there, eyes open, sunlight pinking through her ears. Dead. In the mud—spiteful—getting the last word in after all. And maybe fear of my father had something to do with it, but more than that I knew I had killed her—you know, that instant when you *see* you'll never again be who you once were? Life, even for pigs, is no small matter. Call it shock, or my first reckoning with an irrevocable action, but when my brothers took off, I hauled that head into my lap, clamped her mouth shut, and fit my lips over her snout. I blew into that pig like God blew breath into Adam. I blew into that pig, and I blew and blew, even when lights swam in my eyes. Until I passed out. And that's how my father found me, passed out in the pig yard."

Purvis leaned his head back, took a haul off the cigar, and smiled. Ike exited the county road, past the old Grant homestead, foundation drifting, razed by rodents from the inside out. It was a half mile of silence before Ike gave in. "Well, did you save it? The pig?"

"What do you think? I was a snot-nosed kid with pig dirt in his mouth. Of course I didn't." Ike started to laugh and Purvis clamped a hand on his arm. "No, you don't laugh at this part. This is a matter of the miraculous and it requires respect. In all my father's grief for that pig, he still found it in him to love me. And though I learned I could kill, I could not resurrect. A heady and humbling experience, as the miraculous commonly is. But it was clear what I wanted from the rest of my life, it just required I set my sights a bit lower than bringing back the dead. So, where we headed?"

"Thought you wanted to be surprised."

"All my life, I've opened presents before Christmas. Can't keep a secret either."

"Chas Stubblefield's." Ike watched to see if that registered, but the vet was resting his head back on the seat again, eyes closed, mouthing the oily cigar stub.

"Knew his father," Purvis finally said. "Avery. Avery Stubblefield." Purvis eyed the cigar stub regretfully and stobbed it out in the ashtray. Ike picked it up and flicked it out the window. Purvis grinned. "My father used to say, you can't hate a man. You can hate the things he does, *but you can't hate the man*."

Purvis leaned against the side window, crossed an ankle over his knee. "There's all kinds of mean. I've studied this. I've known men mean to their wives who can love a Goddamned mangy dog. I've known men who sing in church and rob their neighbors blind. It's as if people can't bear to be all of one thing—good or bad.

"But Avery . . ." Purvis shook his head, settled deeper in the seat.

They were nearing Stubblefield's, the road flat and straight as a razor slice. The snowbanks were gritty reliquaries—bones and skin, slivers and fragments of jackrabbit, skunk, deer.

"You believe the sins of the father can be visited upon the son?" Ike asked.

"I believe in the process of distillation. You can cook and cook a thing, reduce it, skin and bone, until you find the thing you desire. With Avery for a father, I believe Chas must have spent a lot of time in the pot."

Ike pulled over onto the shoulder across from Stubblefield's lot.

"Why bring me?" Purvis asked.

"I need a second opinion."

He leaned with his back against the window, staring across the seat at Ike. "Is it bad?"

Ike opened his door. There was roughly the same grouping of animals as on his last visit. He felt strangely relieved to see the piebald horse. "You tell me," he said.

That morning, Ike had waited for Pattiann to say the first word. She suspected he wanted an apology. Some teary response. Not a chance. Pattiann almost felt sorry for him. At twelve years of age, Pattiann's old horse Jubilee had died. It was the animal she'd learned to ride on at three, had hung on to her over younger horses, a sense of loyalty perhaps, or that streak in her that would not let go what she believed was hers. It was a clear, sweet day, land trampled green, the reservoir blue as an eye. Branding time, the neighbors and family gathered, calves milling in the corral, irons hot on the fires, and in the middle of work the horse had simply folded under her. After her father had touched an eyeball for response and found none, she unbridled the horse herself, unbuckled the chin strap, and dragged it from under the head, pried the bit from its teeth. Her father watched, offering a soiled handkerchief, for although he strove to inspire stoicism in his children, some part of him believed a lack of tears unnatural in a woman. Her mother knew better. That evening, at bedside, her mother had asked, "Will you cry when I die?"

"Would it do any good?" Pattiann had asked in return.

Her mother had laughed at that, straightened the bedsheet, snugged it between box spring and mattress, then kissed Pattiann goodnight. Turned out the light.

She studied the barber shop window, snatched a quick glimpse of her hair, embarrassed as she so often was by its . . . *redness*. She waved to Steve sitting in his own barber chair, reading the paper. Steve waved and then the paper fluttered up over his face again. It was a good morning, she decided. Never mind Ike's picking at his eggs and slopping his coffee only to wipe it up with a dish towel, even though he knew that that would anger her. *Because* he knew. But she'd ignored it, finished her own breakfast in silence.

She checked her pocket for the grocery list. She hurried on, feeling, oddly enough, guilty. Her silence had pushed Ike, as she knew it would, and she admitted some small pleasure in that. She'd confounded her father with her composure more than once.

When she looked up, she saw Chas Stubblefield crossing the street in her direction. She thought to turn away. Instead, she smiled politely.

He tugged his Stetson down on his brow. "Afternoon, *Mrs.* Parsons—Pattiann?"

"Chas."

"That's encouraging. You can still speak to me."

"No reason not to."

"*Some* might find reason. We didn't part so well, did we?"

Pattiann straightened her shoulders, while Chas shifted from foot to foot, each smiling, but at a point over the other's shoulder. "Well, I have to go, Chas." Pattiann fished out the grocery list and started to leave, but he caught her sleeve.

"Thought we might talk. But if you're in a hurry . . ." His voice was apologetic, and he hung on to her coat. "Been a rash of that this morning. Drove all the way in to speak with the sheriff," Chas paused, "but he's gone with the vet. That mean anything to you, Pattiann?"

Across the street, Kathy Grieger looked at them briefly before turning back to her own business. Cars drove by, pickups. Pattiann cocked her head toward Chas. "I can't help you."

He shook his head. "You think I'm going to ask you to talk to your husband. You think I'm going to call in old friendship—"

"That's history, Chas."

He flinched, and it made her feel petty. He looked vulnerable and she found that embarrassing. Foolhardy.

He released her arm. He turned away, stepped off the curb.

She was tempted to call out, apologize. No excuse for incivility, not in public. But chance encounter or not, people would improvise scenarios. *Saw Stubblefield cozying up to the sheriff's wife. Those two? Again? His cattle dying out there, the whole damn shooting match from what I heard—*

In the grocery store, she took her time, browsed the breads, tipped each egg in its cup, broke one and felt compelled to buy it. When she finished shopping, he was waiting at the door. "All right," she said, tucked the bag of groceries higher on her hip. "One cup. I'll buy."

Ike and Purvis stayed roadside. Chas's pickup was gone and Ike wondered where he might be. The piebald strained its neck over the fence as if they were old friends.

Purvis studied the herd, squinting into the snow's glare. His breath chugged. He rocked back on his heels, eyes skimming the drifts and the nearby patches of brown where coyotes had scavenged, a hank of fur, bone splintered like greenwood. Then he shuffled back to the truck, and seated himself. Ike offered his open palm and the horse licked it for salt.

Forty-five minutes into the return ride, when Purvis started speaking again, it wasn't about the herd. "Why the law?" he asked. "Was it like a call from God?" He was fading to a silhouette against the early darkening. "I've often thought the law's like the priesthood. A contemplative life on the applications of morality. You mete out punishment: three Our Fathers, a Hail Mary, two years in jail, and grant absolution."

"I don't deal in punishment or absolution. That's for the courts."

"You don't turn away sometimes? Give a warning instead of a ticket? You don't judge the perpetrator by means and motive and intent?"

"You saying I should forget this?"

They turned east onto the highway, heading into the early moon. In the rearview, Ike saw the last of the sunset, a slim band of red and umber hazing into the darkness. He tapped the high beams on and waited for the first of the inevitable jackrabbits.

"What was your father like? I imagine he was a principled man."

The fields lapped into the horizon, snow dunes cresting under the moon. It could be a lake, broad and handsome, and the cruiser, a skiff troweling through. He thought of his childhood. "Back home," Ike said, "a lake bordered our farm. Nothing big, just a pockmark with a swamp on one end where ducks and mute swans nested. Our side was rocky. Couldn't dive in. Had to tread water until you were exhausted. So, my father got this idea. He was a man of ideas." Ike raked his fingers through his hair. "You remind me of him sometimes. You and that Chevy."

Purvis grinned. "But principled."

"Yes," Ike said.

"I knew it," Purvis said.

"His idea was to build a beach, but this was midwinter and the lake was closed in ice. I was ten. I spent three successive Saturday mornings with him in our old stake truck at the quarry—a mountain of sand crusted six inches thick with frost and snow. Pickax first, then by the shovelful we loaded the truck. Oh, yes, come summer, my father said, we'd wade to our knees in sand. At home, he backed the truck onto the ice and we shoveled it out. He'd say, 'You watch, the ice will melt, the sand will drop and we will wade in our wisdom.' " Ike dimmed his brights, slowed. Deer stood off to the side of the road. A buck, two does.

Purvis's head reclined against the headrest. His eyes were closed and he was smiling. It could have been he'd drifted off to sleep, dreaming of home and bed, or of the good woman he was always pining for, but then he asked, "Did you get your beach?"

"Come spring the ice melted, all over that lake, except for the hundred or so feet insulated by sand. And then the winds came up and blew it to the middle of the lake, a huge dirty iceberg. It sank in sixty feet of water. We watched it. We were up in the pasture clearing rocks." Ike tapped the wheel with his fingers, glanced at his side mirror to where the sun had set, now pearling gray. "He laughed until he had to sit down—right there in the dirt. He laughed until I thought he'd gone crazy. All that work for nothing. I told him so. I was a practical child."

"Surprise, surprise," Purvis said.

" 'It's not every day you catch the Lord jesting,' my father said." And this was, Ike thought, the essence of his father—unaccomplished dreamer, undaunted in the face of midwestern icebergs and a scrub rock farm, one of God's good fools. Ike could smile about it now. As a young boy, he had walked away disgusted. He could still imagine how his turned back must have looked to his dad.

"He still alive? Your dad?"

Ike shook his head. "Died of a heart attack when I was eighteen. He'd sold the farm, oh, a good two years before. He got a job at a factory—Allis Chalmers—working on turbine engines. I think he'd have preferred the tractor division. He died on the assembly floor."

"Sometimes God's jokes leave something to be desired. So, you went into law enforcement?"

Ike nodded. "It was a job. Turned out I liked the work. Went back to college, got a degree in criminology, moved to Milwaukee, worked in the police department, taught a night class, met Pattiann"—he grinned over at Purvis—"lived happily ever after."

"You off work yet? I could use a beer."

Ike nodded. "I'll call in."

"So, why take me to Stubblefield's? You knew what you'd seen. It's a formal complaint you want?" Purvis rapped his knuckles on the side window. He watched the land slide by in the dark. "Nights like this, I know why God bothered with eastern Montana."

"It would make it official," Ike said.

"But you *could* file it yourself." He looked over at Ike and waited. "Cowardice is an unlikely virtue in a sheriff, don't you think?"

"I prefer to call it caution."

"I'll bet you do. It's an issue of property. Nothing else puts their backs up like property. Fact is, whoever calls the alarm on this one's not going to be popular. And you're elected. You got to consider that. I understand. As for me. They haven't much choice, have they? And I've been here longer." Purvis looked down into his lap, mumbled something. He had the look of a man about to flip a coin. Then he turned to Ike. "Give me *your* reasons."

"I'm in office because they voted out Art. You know it, I know it." The old sheriff, impeccable in his appearance, had been slovenly with the law. He was a native Montanan. A tall, silver-haired man who did not gain weight and so had developed appetites without restraint. Stockpiled snack food—Fritos, donuts, chips, and crackers; lotions he swabbed on his coddled skin, colognes that lingered in the squads to this day. He'd had a taste for young girls as well, it turned out. But Ike had come into his office, asking for a job, and the man heard out his credentials and gave him one. He must have thought Ike traitorous for running against him two years later. But Art Anders was a rogue cop, an outlaw in even the kindest terms.

"I'm the outsider here—I mess with a man's cattle, they'll take that seriously."

"Still strikes me as cowardice. And that's not your style. No. It's something else."

Ike kept his silence. This could be a pleasant drive in the moonlight, a good friend at his side, the Bronco casting off miles of clean road, past the solitary prick of lights where ranchers and families settled down to meals, their cattle watered, fed, and lulled into believing by the good life—the vale of stars overhead and the wide land—that the slaughter trucks never roll for them.

"It's gotten personal, hasn't it," Purvis said.

Pattiann slipped the bridle over the horse's head, tweezed the ear through the leather eye. The roached mane bristled in her palm. The barn was empty. Earlier, her brother had come upon her while she was currying the mare. Rob gave her a loving knock on the shoulder before slouching off to another of the chores that kept him moving all day and tossing in his sleep. He was of medium height, shorter than their father, with the width and breadth of chest and shoulders their father had had when young. Rob's arms were wedges that split shirt seams. And like her father, he was a man who got over things quickly. He ran emotions like running hurdles—impatience, anger, love.

He did not ask why she was there, though he must think it strange, leaving her husband and home to drive out at all hours. But he would not ask. What she would say might be more than he cared to hear. And Pattiann credited her brother for his discretion and his generosity that had nothing to do with guilt. It wouldn't have occurred to him there might be cause—this ranch, now mostly his, was to be *all* his on the day their father would decide to hand it over. She was the eldest, but he was the eldest son, and that's the way it was.

She led the horse out into the yard, ran her hands through the cinch strap, raised her knee into the horse's belly, and pulled. The horse farted, and Pattiann secured the cinch. They walked past the house through the squares of light that wicked from windows, pausing to hear her niece practicing the fiddle. Pattiann's father played too, though less now with age crabbing his fingers. It pleased her to think of her niece learning the instrument, that plump girlish hand curling around the wooden neck. She was trying a jig, and Pattiann could almost see the way it used to be, her father on the fiddle while a young Rob—in his father's boots, tops over his knees and hat falling across his face—clowned and danced for their mother as he would for no one else, not then or ever again.

Across the fields, due west a mile and a half, was the main house, where her parents still lived. She clucked to the mare, picked her head up, and urged her down the utility road, along the fence line. At the gate, she released the come-along latch, swung it open as they rode through, and kicked the horse a quarter turn to close the gate behind them.

She wore a fleece-lined denim jacket, jeans, lined leather gloves, and a canvas navigator's hat with the earflaps snapped beneath her chin. The horse minced in the snow and she slapped its flanks, drew back the reins until the walk flattened out. They left the road, wading into the snow;

heat rose through the horse's shaggy coat and its breath was a rapid chuffing like the trailings of a steam engine, its heart stoked.

She'd come for silence, solitude, but for another reason as well—to reassure herself that the herd was safe. It all had to do with Chas, their talk over coffee.

"You didn't expect to find yourself here," he'd said, "with me. Maybe the last thing you expected, huh?"

"It wasn't an idea I woke up with." She looked off across the diner's tables, toward the door and the street beyond where even now, had she been wise, she would be walking homeward with a sack of groceries in arm. "It's been a long time, Chas. You're not in town very often."

"And if I was, would you notice?" He stalled her off with a hand. "I don't mean to make you uncomfortable. You got to understand, I'm not in the habit of friends." He shrugged. "Making or keeping."

"What do you want, Chas?"

"Just this." He waved a hand around the room. "A cup of coffee. Some time away from everything dead or dying. Someone to hear my side. Someone else who's got something in this world to gain or lose in the hearing."

"And you think I have a stake in this?"

"Don't you?" He looked genuinely confused. He shook his head. "I just want *you* to understand. For old times' sake."

Her cup was half empty, and she covered the top with her hand when Fran skimmed by. Chas tugged at a shank of blond hair fallen over his forehead, an old habit she'd once found endearing, and it was strange how familiar the gesture still was, and how she had to squelch the urge to comb the lock back from his face with her fingers. Emmylou Harris sang on the radio in the kitchen. Acquaintances, friends came and went, politely and observantly ignoring the two seated in the back booth. She felt weary. This was an old business she'd long thought herself done with, and here he was, playing on her sympathy. She sat straighter. "What's to understand?" she said. "Too many cattle, too little feed, cash, and equity."

"No. Yes," he said. "Of course." He leaned back in his seat, the coffee mug cradled in his hands. "They came to me, the banks. Drove out to my spread shortly after my old man died. Wanted to set all the business straight, what debts I'd inherited—few enough. 'Your daddy was not a person to take advantage,' they said, 'of opportunity.' "

"I've heard this song and dance," she said.

He pursed his lips, blew out his cheeks with a sigh. "They walked my place and *showed* me what it was capable of. And of course, I'd dreamed that very thing myself, all those years ago as a boy, when I imagined the ranch mine. More land, more cattle spread over the hills, the hills greener.

"Machinery. Work. A few good years. All it would take was money, they said. Jesus, I was fresh-faced." He shook his head and laughed, then stopped abruptly.

"I was set up. A patsy."

Pattiann leaned back into the booth. "No," she said. "It's not that easy. The bankers believed, too. They're businessmen and they believed there was a profit to be had. They don't make money out here on foreclosures. Imprudent, maybe, their advice, but not intentionally bad."

"Imprudent." He snorted. "You've changed. I never knew you to be so *careful* in your opinions. God damn," he said. "It was like a fire, those bank loans." He stared over her shoulder. She lifted the cup to her lips and sipped, set it back down.

"Starts with a spark," he said. "Sure your hands strike the match, but the spark—it's an independent-minded thing. Sets about its business of living, feeding. Ever set a fire, Pattiann?" He was studying her, watching her hands, her eyes.

He brought his cup back up to the table and perched forward on the seat. "How one minute you think it's in hand and next thing it's eating everything around you until there's nothing left but you and by now it's a whole lot bigger than you, than anything you imagined. It's eating your house, your cattle, and it'll take you too, you know, but still you stand there holding your hands out to it, like it might just warm them." He leaned back and stirred his coffee; the spoon chattered against the sides. There was an intensity in his eyes that bore through her into the

41

booth behind her, the wall, and the streets beyond. She knew what he meant. She understood how things went out of control, how easily, even naively, we tendered our own downfall.

The mare shifted her hindquarters, cocked a leg. They had stopped in one of the near pastures. In the dark, the cattle were a pale smudge, a fog of breath and body heat. They had congregated like the spokes of a wheel, their heads forming the hub. In another month or so, they'd be brought in for calving. Pattiann gripped the pommel and eased her numbed feet up out of the stirrups, then to the ground. She tossed the reins over the mare's head, ground-tying her. Pattiann walked to get the circulation in her feet started again. The area had been roughly plowed so that feed would not get trampled into the snow. Horses would paw and forage. Cattle wouldn't. There were dark streaks where Rob had lined out long running cuts of hay so that the cattle would not bunch and injure themselves.

When the needles in her feet turned to a warm flush, she pulled herself back up into the saddle, pocketed her feet in the stirrups, and goaded the animal forward. The land comprised long dips and rises, deceptively flat to the naive eye. She followed the trampled path.

Coyotes howled in the distance, yips and yodels, the love of that sound a heresy all cowhands shared, even knowing what coyotes did to calving herds, the sickly, the wounded, the very young. The mare balked, but Pattiann gigged it in the ribs and scolded. The mare's head complied with a droop.

There'd been nothing overtly threatening in Chas's conversation. No tactless reminders of their time together—back when they were young and headstrong as range animals.

The herd was dozing, their bellies full. Barring catastrophic weather, and you could never exclude that possibility, Rob and her father would do well this year, this abundance of snow turning to much-needed water. The families would thrive. And even as she was thinking of him, Rob's oldest son rode up. "Evening, Pattiann," he said. All wisdom and courtesy at the ripe age of fourteen.

"Your papa send you, Justin?"

"No, ma'am." He snugged his horse closer, let the reins drop, and picked out a wad of chew, a vice he enjoyed well out of his parents' sight. He offered her some, a solemn gift, which she declined.

"I'd have a smoke if you had one," she said, knowing he didn't. It had been a long time since she'd wanted a cigarette, and having said it, she knew the young boy would find one and keep it pocketed, somewhere, so that he could oblige her in the future, and whether she ever asked for another or not, it would be there. He was that kind of boy.

"Thought you might like some company."

And that was like him too, giving her the hour of privacy before checking on her. Justin, with his child's body and man's heart, could not be rebuked. He leaned over the other side of his horse and spat.

"So, where's Orion?" she asked, although she could have picked it out on any given night, even those stumbling drunk nights as a young woman and she believed she felt a yearning for that again too—that sweet, unreasonable state.

The boy raised his arm dutifully. It was a ritual they both enjoyed—pinning the heavens at fingertip, naming the constellations. His finger riveted Orion, then his arm dropped. "Leo?" he asked her. She raised her arm. "There, there, there," she said, and outlined the stars. The horses' heads lowered, their eyes lidded, breath evening out. They shifted from foot to foot, while the cattle, crowded for warmth, sank to their knees as if in genuflection and drifted into sleep. Pattiann felt the fierce joy she found only in these odd moments, outside her usual life, and then she remembered Chas's parting remark: "Your husband and I should talk. Only common courtesy. Don't you look a steer in the eyes before you shoot it?"

And then he was gone, out the door, down the street and into his pickup. And Pattiann was left to wonder what he meant and who he believed was holding the gun. She looked at Justin, nailing constellations, the elaborate sweep of his arm, and she felt frightened again, as though Chas were there with them, and in a way he was, her cheeks burning now as they had at the diner, at the shame of it—his dying cattle—his failure become hers.

This was a community that knew each other's families and histories and shared the same jokes, and one person's grief became another's. Shame ran deepest. All of them were stung by Chas's shameful act, the cruelty of it, because that worked at the fabric of their lives—these animals, this *way* of life—all of it dependent on a basic respect for what was given into your hands, and for the first time she wondered if her own hands would have been any stronger.

The cattle drowsed. She heard the chuffing of their horses, the squeak of saddle leather, and despite the cattle calmed in sleep, their shadows pilloried in the snow by a steady moonlight, she sensed events in motion beyond their control. She watched the shining face of her nephew, followed the pointing arm, and it seemed to Pattiann that the stars overhead turned perilous.

Though Ike had gotten home late, he'd only had one beer with Purvis, the remaining hours spent on paperwork in the office. He came home to find the bedsheets spread back, pillows plumped like airy pastries. He'd apologized, but she'd dismissed it, saying she'd been at her brother's and it was only a matter of luck she'd gotten home first. But would he have thought to prepare for her? He doubted it. Kept a meal warm in the oven? Probably not. Be honest. No. Not that he wouldn't, should he *think of it,* but that was the rub; it just wouldn't occur to him, those small attentions that were more a part of her, not because she was a woman— no, she would not be accused of that, no girlhood lessons on how to temper or please your man—but because it was her nature to trust action over words.

They ate a quiet dinner, then Pattiann ran a bath for him. She sat tub- side, soaping his back, and seemed mildly amused by his erection, though she declined his offer to join him. Instead, she waited in the bed- room while he dried off. Another woman might have put on music. But Pattiann preferred the quiet, the jounce of bedsprings, and that was fine to his way of thinking. She was naked on the bed, a book, *Dry Land Ranching,* spread open in her lap. A candle flickered in the window.

"Pretty dark to read," he said.

She turned a page. "I don't want to appear anxious."

He looked down at himself. "I could use something myself, maybe a *Life* magazine." He measured his erection like a trout, and as he drew his hands upward, they moved wider apart. "Full spread."

She held her thumb out in a painter's measure, notched her knuckle with a nail, shook her head.

"Your perspective is screwed," she said, and he lay next to her.

"And the rest of me?"

"In good time."

They laughed, and when they leaned together to kiss, they bumped heads. And this was the best of it, holding each other as laughs turned to small talk until that dissipated like the weather they grumbled about. They held each other as friends. Their toes fidgeted under the sheets and she lay in the crook of his arm, her red hair spread among the peppered hairs on his chest. When they made love, it was Ike taking her each step, beyond her own surprised embarrassment—as, after all these years, she was still reluctant to lose that fine control she held over her emotions, slow to bare them, or perhaps trust them. He laid his hand on the hairs that furled into the ditch between her thighs. He eased her legs apart and touched her here, and here, watching the focus in her eyes come back from that place she always went to, come back to him, the iris opening even as she had, and he cautioned his own impatience, kissed her in the hollow of her throat, amazed as always at how soft that flesh felt to his lips, and when at last she reached for him, it was with an unfamiliar gesture, kissing the tips of his ears, drawing his fingers to her mouth, and when her own hands clasped his arms, his shoulders, buttocks, he entered her with a sweet quiet and held still to feel her close around him and he wondered how it must be to open yourself like this to another person, to take him into your body, and the vulnerability of the act was both appealing and appalling, and he moved slow, and then quicker, enjoying how her skin moistened like the bed of a leaf in early morning and how the white span of flesh between her chest and neck flushed red, and when at last she came in a cry, his own orgasm caught him like a blow to the spine, a jolt rising from his groin through his chest and arms carrying him over that brink where he let go, as he would in no other part of his life, the order he so carefully maintained.

When he slumped to his side, he took her with him down into the deep folds of quilt, the candle guttering. When they parted, it was to spoon her back to his belly, his right hand tucked under her breast and eyes closed to the reassurance of his breath in her hair, and while they slept the wind continued its low complaint over the house and into the fields, and snow fell from the starless sky, great dollops of snow that broke the wind's back at last in bundling sheets, blanketing the land, crowning fenceposts with top hats and transforming coyotes, cattle, and horses into snow creatures, and in all that land the only movement was of smoke lifting from chimneys, snow falling from the sky.

Chapter Four

C has dug the book out from under his old bed, a youth's bed, still blanketed and pillowed as if waiting for its occupant to step back across the years and rest his head. He flipped the yearbook open. There was no writing in the book, no well wishes or jokes, the only signature his own printed on the fly of the front cover. He always printed. He believed printing gave nothing away.

He flipped to the senior class, and found Pattiann. She wore a crew neck sweater, her hair in a flip with a shelf of bangs across her forehead. No smile, her lips narrowed, clenched. In her eyes, he believed he could see her old wildness. He found it intriguing that she seemed softer now— steel gone malleable. He flipped past the school clubs and activities pages—she wasn't there, as he wasn't, another similarity, a kinship. But then there were the rumors of her drunkenness, her promiscuity, and he believed no one better appreciated the power and efficacy of rumors than he, nor how they pale against the truth. He tore the page out and folded it around her picture. He put on coat, hat, muffler, and gloves, and opened the door.

It had snowed, a wet, heavy snow that cleaned the air, submerging fences, the land, until even the calling of cattle was muted. The overhead casters rumbled as the barn door rolled back. Starlings racketed off the eaves. He was struck by the static colors of the pickup, the barn, sky, fields: red, gray, blue, white, and then the sudden chattering flight of black. And it seemed if ever there was a time to curse God, it was at this moment, with starlings reeling overhead, and a woman's picture cozied in his pocket, this was the time to curse Him, His benevolent, malevolent face. He loaded a couple of the too few remaining feed sacks into the pickup, switched on the hydraulics, and the plow whined into place. He set the blade and cleared a lane to the pasture. He plowed a space for the gate, pulled through, closed it behind him. In the field, he opened a twenty-foot corridor, and the cattle in the far corner swung their heads like bell clappers and bellowed. They stumbled in single file, one or two trying to run, crowding him while he opened the sacks. Some of the cows fell to their knees, some butted heads, some stood dazed in the background. These he roused with kicks to the shanks. He chipped ice from the trough and ran new water. The last of the rationed feed he reserved for the piebald, his father's old horse, that stood its distance. The horse nickered when he approached and ground the feed in the bucket with its teeth.

He hauled bridle and saddle off the back of the truck while a few cattle hung their heads over the truck bed huffing the chaff to the far corners with strangled breaths. He saddled the piebald, cinch strap looping long and trailing. He roped a pickax to the cantle. When he mounted, the horse staggered and planted its feet wide. But it moved off well enough, and they set out at a slow walk, skirting the heaviest drifts, wading up to its canon bones through the wet snow.

An hour to cover a half-hour's journey. They stopped at the reservoir, and though he saw no living cattle nearby, he chose to believe some might have survived on scrub. He ground-tied the horse and fetched the ax, teetered across the bank's edge on snow-covered ice. A crease ran down the center—like a wound, like a woman's sex—where he had picked the trench two days past. He set to work, absorbing the blows with his muscles, feeling useful again with this pain. He thought of his talk with Pattiann. She'd listened, her heart driven by the same needs as his—land and cattle—and had despaired of the same failure: she was a woman, he was incompetent. He drove the pick: water sloshed over his boots, a sulfurous smell. He moved down.

They'd been so young the first time. Seventeen? It was late summer, in the field, wheat buckling in the wind, his knee cocked against the sky, and the sky a black platter overhead so near he believed he could raise up on an elbow and touch it. Closer, it seemed, than Pattiann staggering over him, tipping a bottle up, up until almost gone. The bottle he'd bought with the money he'd been saving for a new pair of boots. But it was worth every cent to see her, so much more than he'd dared imagine all those times he'd watched her driving cattle, or across the school corridors. Or listening to the other boys talk—none of what they said deterring him, but rather believing the thing that drove her drunk from one boy to another was the same emptiness he'd so often felt. And when he'd seen her at the dance, he'd sidled up to her, and when she turned to find the boy she'd arrived with, instead she found him—all one and the same to her in those days—and he was grateful for that.

He'd struggled with his jeans, the zipper, the condom that seemed easy enough when he'd practiced all those times, alone. She kicked her jeans aside and he halted his fumbling to take it in, skin and wheat and stars. He tried to roll the condom down, like a sock on a foot, but his penis was unsteady, wavering between rampant and retreat, and the rubber ring tweaked and pinched, tweezing pubic hairs, his breath in winces. She was standing over him, straddling his torso, and he said, "Oh yes," and then, "Just a minute."

He was still on his back when she mounted him, and the condom she'd flung like a spent snakeskin dangled from the trampled edge of wheat. A wind sock. And then Pattiann had him in hand and then inside of her, and sex was as much a thing as he'd imagined. He'd seen sex before—Taylor with his procession of girls in the back of the pickup—and from a small boy on he'd seen sex among the animals, and heard about it from friends in jokes, mostly about sheep, and so this is something he'd never admitted to anyone, how he'd masturbated as a young boy, imagined nestling his crotch to the woolly behind, lanolin waxing his belly. Because it was what he could picture back then, never this. But now it was happening and shocks rippled down his legs so that his toes curled. Her breasts swung over his face. She was lovely and he made himself breathe. I could marry her, he thought. Make this right. He let himself imagine this. He was that young and foolish. He was that drunk.

She was on him, rocking, and then something changed, the tenor of the stars or the complications in the way her hips cradled him because it began to chafe and she was grinding down as if she'd reduce him to rubble. She kept him inside her in a distracted way so that he became embarrassed, fearful he would shrivel inside her.

"Let me up," he said, but she wasn't listening, her eyes closed, a clicking noise in her throat, and she began to ride him up and back again. He understood then that this had nothing to do with him, and was it then he'd promised to change that? To make her see *him* as someone.

"Let me up," he said again. But she'd turned sweet, and so he wasn't sure he meant it, though by then he was sore and getting sorer, wishing she'd come, or he would so that he'd be excused like a young boy from the dinner table.

It ended as it began. She was suddenly standing over him and he was startled to see his cock still full and poised, and while he couldn't bear the thought of risking her again, he was already anticipating the unaccomplished ache that would settle in.

She stood contemplating the stars through the bottom of the bottle, holding the mouthpiece to her eye so that when some liquid dribbled down her cheek, she swiped at it and licked the hand. "Big Dipper," she said. She swung the bottle west, "Big Dipper," oriented the bottle on him, his penis, "Little Dipper." She dropped to a squat, and the suddenness of the action tilted her off her feet, landing her at his side.

When she lifted herself from the dirt, she struggled to put on her jeans, hopping one-legged, falling, scuffling in the dirt. "Damn stupid," she said.

He watched as she struck off across the field alone. Her daddy's field. Where she'd insisted they come. She reeled her way through the wheat like a haywire combine. He thought to follow, but instead walked back to the road, to his pickup parked down by the coulee where he sat with the door open to the cooling night, contemplating the act of sex, the stinging rawness of it.

They were meant to be together.

He'd believed that way back then. And he was startled to find some part of him, after all this time, willing to forget how she had cut and run, willing to believe that again.

He stepped farther out onto the ice. He'd had plenty of women since. Some few from town or neighboring ranches. Nowadays, he mostly drove to Lewistown, or Havre, dressed in his best, prosperous with distance. He met them in bars, paid the motel bill up front.

He preferred the dark where they were one and the same, this one, that one, skinny, tall, fat. Their skin yeasty beneath his fingers. And in most he found relief, for at least a little while. More than men, he thought, women carried God inside them, ejaculated His names in orgasms, oh Jesus, oh God, oh Christ, oh sweet Lord.

He niched the trench deep and the water wept over the snow, yellow, as if hounds had pissed the length of the cut. He fastened the pickax across the back of the saddle and mounted, his leg swinging over the point, nestled his feet in the stirrups, and nudged the horse. He followed the trail they'd cut and returned in shorter time to see the sheriff's Bronco pulled alongside the highway. The door swung open and Parsons was crossing the road.

Chas unstrapped the pickax, carried it to the truck bed, and leaned it there. He returned to the horse for the saddle.

The sheriff called, "Stubblefield." Then again, "Stubblefield." Chas glanced over. He looked stocky in his sheriff's jacket and Chas wondered what it was Pattiann saw in the dark of their bedroom and if she too cried, *oh Jesus*. He felt strangely privileged thinking of them like that, as if he could see them as they couldn't see themselves. He thought of her picture in his pocket, the raw-boned younger Pattiann, and then he thought of her now and saw her marriage to a landless man, an outsider, for what it was, a penance.

"All right if I come in?" the sheriff asked.

"Hasn't stopped you before." Chas slung the saddle over the tailgate. "You got a warrant?"

"This isn't court business." The sheriff shut the gate and strode to where Chas was unbridling the horse. The sheriff laid a hand on the horse's back, rubbed at the sweat and salt streaks. It was a proprietary laying on of hands and Chas paused until the hand withdrew. That done, he slapped the horse's neck and the animal pivoted, ran a few steps with a coltish kicking.

Ike laughed, and it seemed to Chas the sheriff's eyes went softer. And Chas knew then that he was already a gutted man. The sheriff would have it all—meat and gristle. Chas tossed the bridle into the bed.

"I could buy that horse off your hands."

Chas pulled his Stetson down so that the brim of his hat cut short the sky and all he could see was the white below and the horse. "If I was selling."

"You could use the money. I'd pay a fair price."

"Fair." Chas sank his chin on his chest. "Buy my cattle, too? The ranch, my truck, my tack?" He lifted one foot at a time. "How about these old shit-heeled boots?" He looked up, saw the way the sheriff's eyes grew guarded. Chas laughed to put him back at ease. "Why don't you tell me what you *think* is fair?"

Parsons looked relieved. "I'll go nine hundred."

Chas glanced up into the sky, watched the first edge of a new snow-fall tumble toward them, slowly, from feet up, or miles, he couldn't say, but it was coming at him with the inevitability of hard luck. "Then you're a fool, and I don't deal with fools." Chas started to walk away, felt a hand on his arm. He shook it off.

"Another few weeks there won't be enough money to save that horse. Nine hundred now," Ike said, keeping his distance, "could buy enough feed to pull some of the cattle through."

Chas looked over at the milling cows, knowing that this was all the herd that might be salvaged, and if there were any cattle left standing in the backcountry it was just another grudging gesture of Providence, too little too late.

"I'm just trying to help—"

Chas felt for the picture in his pocket. Found, instead, a coin, a pill of lint that rolled between his fingers, but no picture. Lost, he realized, somewhere back on the trail, moments ago, no years before, actually. It didn't really matter, did it? Chas walked over to the truck, raised the pickax overhead, and sank it into the truck bed with a clang so that the handle stood upright like a masthead. "You can open the gate. Close it when you leave." He started the truck. He waited, windows shut, staring out over the hood past the sheriff, who swung the gate wide, and driving out never looked back to see if Ike closed it after him.

Ike spent the afternoon in the office on reports, then to the courthouse for three DUIs and a break-in while marshaling crews to deal with stranded cars on the drifting county roads, in the middle of which he'd dispatched Harley to a domestic squabble. The snow kept falling. Late afternoon, while Ike was wolfing down a tuna fish sandwich, coffee, and an eclair in his office, he'd asked Troy, the desk sergeant, if Harley'd checked back in.

Three hours. No word. They tried the radio. No answer. No phone. Ike hauled on his jacket, snatching the address from the counter. "Call if you hear anything." And then he was out into the cold, the eclair and tuna fish swimming in his belly, and he was thinking about the dinner Pattiann would already be cooking, which he would probably miss and maybe just as well, because he wouldn't be able to eat anything anyway for a long time. Fish and custard. Good God. He turned on the lights, and the town's snowy face was stricken blue with each sweep. He accelerated past his house even while wanting to slow and pull in, her tenderness last night still with him like an aftertaste.

When he hit the highway, he kicked the Bronco into four-wheel drive. He was headed to Tom and Emily Millan's trailer home, eighteen miles south down the highway, five miles east on gravel that might or might not be plowed. He cruised by a vehicle in the ditch. The driver was standing alongside his car, smoking a cigarette, disgusted with himself probably, the weather, the sheriff's car that blew past. Ike called it in. He thought of Pattiann and how she turned in his arms, her breasts rolling onto his chest, her legs hitched about his groin. He let in fresh air. What did it say about a forty-two-year-old man who finds himself lusting like a kid again for something as simple as a good fuck with the same woman he's slept next to for years? Was he that easy?

He slowed for the county road, skidded, and steered to compensate. Farther down the highway a plow approached, its headlights fuming in the snow while sparks off the blade fired the undercarriage with a cobalt light. It would be a long five miles, and Ike drove slowly, trusting the road was straight.

The snow drove at a hard angle into the windshield. To a side, a column twisted into the air; it whirligigged across the road, buffeting the front end of the Bronco, and then was gone. For not the first time that day, he questioned what this place had to recommend itself, the long burn of summer, when the land fried to tinder, or spring when the roads turned to gumbo—six inches, ten inches deep, compact clay saturated to a vast wallow. Flash floods that drove burrow owls, deer mice, and prairie dogs shooting for the surface and curled scorpions into balls to roll like pennies down culverts, turning the high desert into an ocean, inches deep, that glutted reservoirs, rushed over the jumps and breaks— a confluence of water, mud, rocks, and small mammals—down to the Missouri and its tributaries.

Though he believed none of the seasons had the better of winter, whose storms varied like a catalogue of ailments: sleet, wind, whiteouts, arctic freights.

He turned into the Millan drive. In a makeshift corral, two horses and a handful of cattle. Harley's cruiser was pulled up alongside. The trailer door was cracked open, and somewhere behind a television yammered, canned laughter. To a side stood Tom Millan, a man in his seventies given over to long underwear and semizipped pants. He held a gun to his own head. His wife Emily stood in front of him, in a pink housedress and matching mules. She had a kitchen knife in her fist. Jesus H. Christ.

54

Ike walked to the side window, stretched up on toes to look in. Harley sat on the sofa. His gun was drawn and resting on his knees. Ike could swear Harley was watching the TV. He looked sour.

When all else fails, be polite. Ike knocked on the door.

"Come in," Emily called.

Harley lurched to his feet, and Tom slid the gun to his temple. "I'll shoot," he said.

"You do, I'll cut my throat," Emily said, and the wattle of her neck shook.

Ike stopped, kicked the snow from his feet, and stepped in carefully. Harley had dropped back into the sofa, though his gun was still out. "Put that thing away, Harley. We got enough weapons here already." He turned to Tom, took in the phone cord pulled from the wall. "Would someone like to tell me what's going on? Tom?" he asked.

The old man looked away.

Ike turned to Emily.

"The IRS. They say we owe seven hundred dollars from 1994," she said. "For seven hundred dollars he's going to blow his head off. Like it's worth it, you old dope." She pointed the knife at her husband. "I tell him, fine. But he's not leaving me to deal with the mess."

Harley sighed. "So he calls us, thinking we'll take her off his hands so he can get on with it. She won't leave, he won't drop the gun—"

"So you pull yours?"

"I thought—" he said, and stopped. "They could have—" He waited.

"Why don't you go radio the folks back home. Tell them we're fine." Ike took his coat off. "Warm in here. Didn't think it of you two—a domestic squabble."

"We ain't fighting," Tom said.

"The heck we aren't," Emily said.

Ike lowered himself into a chair, a vinyl and chrome thing that wobbled. The kitchen was a four-foot galley papered in old calendar pictures: canyons and gorges, steam-fired locomotives trundling over trestles. Their dishes were a secondhand mix. There was the sweet smell of starch and the ironing board was still out. These people lived by their own scratch and scrabble. A small retirement fund maybe, a few head of cattle, some chickens. What could the IRS want of them? What needs of this community, or this nation, would be met by that piddling amount, $700, still more money than these two had in the world right now? He felt guilty, as though his role as sheriff gave him some part in this. "We could talk to an accountant; Ben Johnson would do it," Ike said.

Tom's spine stiffened, and the gun skidded to the hairline. The old man's hand whitened. "Number shifters. Next thing you know I owe him, too."

His hand was shaking. And Ike feared a mistake might happen. "All right," Ike said, his hands inching closer to his own gun—*getting as bad as Harley, what are you going to do, shoot the old man?* "Just give me a minute," Ike said.

Tom nodded, eased himself into the chair across from Ike, rested his elbow on the table. The gun pinned to his temple took on a deadly steadiness. "A pound of flesh. You mail it to them, Sheriff."

Then Emily seated herself and there they were, the three of them. It might have been a stage play, theater of the absurd—the old man with the gun to his head, his wife with a knife, and the sheriff.

Emily leaned toward Ike. "You tell me if you think seven hundred bucks is worth killing yourself and your wife?"

"I'm not killing you," Tom said. "Just myself."

"Yes, you are." She reached over, patted her husband's free hand as she must have comforted their children many years ago. "It would kill me," she put the knife down, "and wouldn't need this to do it, either. Forty years together and this is what I get." She turned to Ike. "My husband kills me. It'll be on his soul."

"Hear that, Tom? The IRS won't even sneeze at losing seven hundred dollars. Who wins?"

Tom closed his eyes and beneath the thin lids his eyes fretted and he sat so still that Ike could almost believe he had fallen asleep except for the sighs—one, two, and then two more. When he opened his eyes again, he lowered the gun, his hand shaking. "Cripes." He pushed it across the table to Ike. "One year I take a lousy part-time job. Pays a few bills, buys some good meat for a change, maybe a new set of long johns, some things for Emily. Two thousand dollars and now they want seven hundred back that was gone and spent years ago.

"I don't bother them. No welfare, no handouts, no gimme, gimme, gimme. I was in the war." He shook his head.

"How about this?" Ike asked. "You pay them five bucks a month for the next one hundred and forty years and the hell with them."

Tom was nodding. "I could do that."

They talked awhile longer, about the government and their grown children and the weather outside. Emily sliced thick slabs of homemade bread, doled pats of butter on them, and set plates before the men. "Where's the mercy?" she asked. "Where's the milk of human kindness?" She looked around. "Where's that other young fellow, maybe he'd like some bread?"

Harley would not be coaxed back in. Ike ate, though lunch still warred with his stomach. When he left, he took the handgun. "Next week, I'll bring it back."

Tom shook him off. "That's all right, I'll pick it up next time I'm in town. I got another." And Emily closed the door softly as Ike stepped out into the yard. He nodded to Harley, started up his own vehicle, and pulled out.

Nearing the town limits, Ike called Harley over the radio and told him to stop at the diner. They took a side booth. Harley wasn't talking and Ike felt talked out as well. They drank a half cup each.

"I nearly pulled *my* gun," Ike offered and stirred his coffee. Black coffee. His stomach already felt soiled.

Harley looked up in surprise, blushed. "God damn," Harley said. "Those old fools."

Ike reached under his jacket, shrugged his gun to the side. Some years were enough to give men a load of wisdom, but Harley, at a tender twenty-five, hadn't seen that year yet. That was clear. It was beyond Ike to instruct him, but Ike had no doubt it was coming. Today, tomorrow, next year or the next, somewhere down the pike a semi was rolling and painted on its side was the message: *Here to break Harley's heart and make him a better human,* and Ike didn't envy Harley that moment of impact. He hoped it would come while Harley still had a young, tough hide. It had happened to Ike the year his father died: the world had gone out of true, and it'd seemed to Ike that all the orderliness of his own world had finally hinged on a man with skinny legs and a weak heart. "This wasn't one of the Millans' better nights."

"Jesus."

Ike laughed. "But still," he took a sip of coffee, grimaced, "it was a hell of a gesture." More than Ike had managed with Stubblefield, his ploy to buy the horse at double its worth. But sometimes, Ike believed, that was all you were left with, the gesture.

"How'd you get the gun away?" Harley slopped coffee on the table, swiped at it with a napkin. "I tried everything. The old man ripped the phone out. I couldn't leave them to go radio in—"

"By that time, Tom was looking for a way out." Ike finished his coffee. "Damn, they're a prideful people."

Harley cleared his throat. "You going to tell them"—he nodded toward their office—"about tonight? About me?"

"Yup."

"Shit."

Harley left and Ike stretched his legs under the table and gripped his belly. He ordered an Alka-Seltzer and Fran dropped two tablets into a glass of water, seated herself across from him. She was Pattiann's age, or close to it. She looked worn as Pattiann rarely did, but Fran had three children, and children were something Ike and Pattiann had discussed at length long ago and rarely since. "I'm not ready," she'd said, and truthfully speaking, Ike had been relieved, believing that if ever he'd been ready, it had been years before, when he was younger, some green and earnest years he'd overlooked taking care of his mother, taking care of his career after his mother had remarried and moved on, and then Pattiann had come after he'd despaired of marriage, used to dating women who had tried commitment and found it stifling, or could not bear the prospect of their husband wearing a gun every day. And he'd seen enough cop marriages and divorces to understand their fears. When he'd met Pattiann, he'd expected the same. He was wrong. And when she'd left the Midwest to return to Montana, she'd said, "I love you. But I can't stay." It had nothing to do with him but everything to do with *home*. He'd followed a year later, just showed up, got a job in the sheriff's department. There were days of late, he admitted, when he thought they should have had children, might yet. A daughter, maybe. A son. He glanced up. Fran was shaking a finger at him.

"I warned you about that lunch," she said.

"What is it about women makes them love to say I told you so?" The seltzer was expanding in his gut.

"Being right, I suppose," she said. She slipped her shoes off, rested her heels on the bench next to him; her feet were narrow. "You'd feel better if you belched."

He belched, nodded. "Maybe it's because they're always stating the obvious."

She loosened her collar button. "How you suffer." She closed her eyes, sat dreaming a moment.

She was beautiful, her face slack and clean, the dark under her eyes like soft thumbprints, brown hair escaping the hairnet. To a stranger, she might look frail, and that would be a misapprehension. Just maybe Fran held reserves deeper than Pattiann or Ike, because she'd risked children, and, so that her children could be schooled, lived a life separate from her husband's, even though she was a young woman, and he found himself thinking of her, alone, in restless nights turning to find comfort where there was none—her husband sixty miles away dreaming of the next day's ranch chores. He shook his head, looked down at his hands. He belched again.

Fran smiled. "Did Stubblefield find you yesterday? Came by early afternoon, asking for you. Came back later with Pattiann."

His stomach clenched. He looked over her shoulder to the darkened picture windows where the diner was reflected—the fluorescent lights, stools, and counter, the couple at the booth, elbow to elbow with their reflections, lifting twin sandwiches to lips, the young woman turning her head, hand wavering toward the glass as if she meant to reach into the reflection. "I was out of town in the afternoon," he said.

Fran eased a foot over her knee and massaged it. "With Purvis. Word gets out. I was a little surprised to see Pattiann with Chas. Been awhile."

But Pattiann hadn't told Ike about seeing Chas. He thought about the previous evening, the dinner, bath, the way she took him into her.

Fran settled her feet back into her shoes. "Been years, so I was kind of surprised to see them together.

"I always thought Stubblefield was trouble. Never could see what Pattiann saw—Chas kept to himself mostly." She tapped the tabletop with a fingernail. "They were wild, those two." She looked up at him. "But you've heard all this?"

Ike shrugged and smiled. "There's little I haven't heard before," he said, which was mostly true, for Pattiann had spoken of her own troubles, her drunkenness, her anger, but never in detail. Never any particular man.

"Thought so," Fran said. She kicked back in the seat. "They were into pranks, general rowdiness, like the time they painted Browning's dun mare in camouflage and it took that man with his lousy eyes a week and a half to find her out on the range. Though I never believed Pattiann capable of meanness—did see her lay Chas flat one night with a bottle upside the head, and never had a doubt he deserved as much. You need any more?" she asked. And for a moment, Ike thought she meant of the history, until he noticed her finger pointing at his coffee cup. He shook his head.

"Her dad hated Chas."

"Not a good catch?" Ike asked.

"Not as good as she got," Fran said. Her smile dimpled and she winked.

"Ah, but he had land."

She wrinkled her nose. "And look where it got him. Land without sense." She rolled her eyes. "Might as well own a horse without feet."

"He doesn't strike me as stupid."

She sat forward, plumped a fist in her back, and stretched. "It's as much intuition. Something that can't be taught. Maybe it's an astuteness that he lacks. Or maybe he's just a sonofabitch."

She leaned forward. She smelled of soap, and hamburgers and fries. "It's just that Pattiann did all right by herself, and I guess I'd hate to see her mess that up."

Ike waited, but he could see Fran had crossed some line and was regretting it. She fetched her order book out of a pocket, flipped out the bill. She patted his hand and stood up. "Seltzer's on me."

Ike drove past their home without slowing. The lights were on. He mulled over what Fran had told him. Quite a surprise. Pattiann hadn't mentioned a word about Stubblefield. Ever.

He drove just to drive, and ended up where he'd known he would. He stood roadside. The lights in Stubblefield's house were out, but smoke puffed from the chimney. The truck was parked next to the shed. What had he thought to do? Roust Stubblefield? Ask what he and Pattiann talked about?

It was so still. The land and house and even the stars seemed frozen in place. The cattle were a darker piece of the night, as though the evening had congealed in solid fragments on the snow. Ike pulled a pail from behind the seat.

The bucket swung at his side, loaded with pellets and grain he'd bought at the mill that morning, back when he'd believed this whole mess could be resolved with the purchase of a horse. He watched the house to see if Chas had the second sight that told him someone was out there. Ike had had it while working the city beat, and he wondered if it was an acuity that fled with disuse. All *he* could feel was the wide night. All he could hear was the cattle blowing in their sleep, the *plock, plock* of the horse ambling across the packed snow. The house was still, and he imagined Chas deep in sleep, or sitting in the dark with his feet propped on the woodstove while embers popped and dimmed. The horse nosed the air, snuffled, and banged its muzzle into the feed pail.

This was what he'd come for—the simple act of feeding this horse. What this horse had come to mean he didn't understand yet, but Ike knew he must go through with it. He'd keep it on its feet with feed at night, and then once the animals were confiscated, he'd pay for the piebald's keep until he could buy it at auction. Maybe, in the next few years, he and Pattiann could get a few cattle, more horses—and land—her own small spread. Not that she would ever ask. No. And wouldn't it be better unasked for—a gift? Life would go on. Standing in this doomed place, he felt it was essential he believe that.

The night drew closer, the stars squandered in the black canopy, and the horse snorted in the pail, lipping the sides, the bottom. When finished, the horse swiped its head on Ike's arm in a long leisurely scratch. It nickered, then stood watching the distance over Ike's shoulder as if dreaming of buffalo grass, blue joint, silver sage and cats paw, a swale of fescue to bunk in, the smell of green and greener: a feast of air.

Ike's arm hooked over the horse's neck, fingers scruffing behind the ears. He looked at the house, and it seemed unchanged, although Ike sensed something. He watched the field, the calm night, the sleeping cattle. The horse stretched its neck over the barb, hooking a straggle of mane as it lipped at Ike's sleeve.

Ike walked to the Bronco. He sat behind the wheel and shut the door with a thud. He tucked his hands under his armpits to warm them. Stubblefield's yard light was off and the yard was a haphazard clutter of disabled cars and pickups, old farming equipment, a warren of waste. Little enough to admire here even in the forgiving dark, but Ike believed he could understand Stubblefield—stumbling deeper into the tangle of hope and luck with loans, believing each wrong step was the right one. Not so unlike those last years before Ike left Wisconsin, marking time, hoping there would be more in his life than the usual suspects, the faceless crimes, the succession of wounded—not joy, he couldn't hope for that, but some contentment perhaps, just the ability to lay aside the day's despair, go home at night to the sound of his own footsteps in the rooms, and not hear the echo as loss.

Ike snicked the key into the ignition, turned the engine over. He wanted to be home. He'd felt stung to hear secondhand of Pattiann and Chas—their meeting. Their *history*. This was a complication he hadn't counted on, would not have dreamed of. Though he knew something of Pattiann's trouble as a young woman, he didn't have the details: *Wild,* she'd said. *A lot of drinking. I got around.* And he would no more have considered asking for the details of her sexual past than she would have considered asking about his. And that seemed natural enough. The safest path. Until now. And what did he want now?

He turned into Stubblefield's drive with his headlights off, idled a moment. In the deep of the porch, he saw a spark, an ebb and glow. He waited. Then again, the glow and ebb, an ember hopping in the dark. Then the cigarette arced out over the porch and onto the snow. In the shadows something moved, the door opened and closed, and Stubble-field was gone. Ike hit a switch and the front of the house was washed with light. He rolled the vehicle back onto the highway and was gone.

Chapter Five

S tubblefield drifted in and out of his house with a new aimlessness that disoriented him at odd moments so that he was uncertain what task followed another, or even what hour of the day or evening it was. He'd find himself standing on the threshold of his bedroom, or hovering over the kitchen sink trying to remember why he was there. He had never appreciated the length of a day, until he'd run out of work. He plowed the feedlot as though there were bales to put down, and chipped the ice from the reservoir. What little feed was left, he rationed to the horse and the few standing cattle, enough to keep them upright—a week? Maybe. Did he care?

Avery Stubblefield would have. He'd never wanted to give Chas the ranch. Wouldn't have, except he'd died before he could sell it off and move to Arizona where he'd planned to finish his life withering away to a shank of leather. But there he was seized up in bed, already in his winding sheets, his heart squeezing in his eyes and telling Chas, *Get me to a doctor.*

And Chas took that old man up into his arms, carried him out the door fully intending to get help. But on the porch, he stopped. The old man had no more substance than a bird. The moon was a spit of light in the west and the yard lamp out front burned a hole into the night. Each time a pain hit Avery, Chas could hear the old man's leg bones grinding in their sockets, the old body knotting and breath coming, but so thin, so far gone, it was as if Chas could see right through the sheet and bone to the knotty pine floorboards. Was it then, Chas wondered, that he came to know what was just? Chas willed the heart to clench, and it did; the old man's eyes strayed, one up, one left. His bladder voided. Chas raised his head to clear his breath and the stars were a rapture; the cattle knelt in the grass lowing over their cud and his father's piebald horse loped the length of the fence. All this and more would be *his*.

The old man's breath piped, and the space about them grew still. He set his father in the dirt, went to the truck and turned on the radio, tuned in the national ministry and cranked the volume. He dragged the body up under the yard light. And to give Chas credit, he'd waited at his father's side, the long hours it took before taking himself off to clean up and go to bed.

And perhaps that was where it had started wrong. The land never properly given. Perhaps Avery's ghost lingered, a skinflint in everything but grief, even now. Tonight, Chas went out of his way to drive past Pattiann's old home. Smoke lifted from the bunkhouse chimney, the hay mows in the feed yard were tall and solemn with snow. He doubled back, drove into town, past Coker's mill, doors bolted on the feed. Chas slowed at Coker's house where he thought he saw Sam's shadow on the drapes.

Chas stopped at the filling station where he bought ten dollars worth of gas for the truck. In the back of the truck was a five-gallon can of kerosene from home. He drove to the bank, parked in front, lit a cigarette, and waited.

He fired up the engine. It choked, sputtered, and caught. No traffic. His truck wavered in the street-front windows, awnings clamped shut. The diner, concrete block with cedar trim, CLOSED sign in the window. He circled the square. The grocery, one bank of lights lit, the grizzled guard dog napping behind the glass door. Past the courthouse—white, squat as a mortician's slab. Past the sheriff's quarters, two lights burning. The parking lot: a car, three squads, and a pickup. A bank of dirty snow. He drove on. The vet's with horse trailer backed up to the loading bay. Barn lit. The sheriff's house. Lights out. Driveway empty. He pulled up to the garage, left the motor running. He thought of Pattiann: her snorting laughter, how she used to chew the inside of her lip when anxious, the way she used to balance on his hips. He thought of the sheriff, offering to buy that broken-down old piebald.

No one home. And me come to visit.

The clapboard house sat like tinder. He pressed his forehead against the window, humming a tune whose name he could not remember.

He turned back toward town, left at the junction, one mile, swung a hard right down the gravel lane. Taylor's house. A sprawling two-story affair. Lights out. Chas parked off the road a quarter mile down. He walked back; the can of kerosene hung like a plumb bob from his arm. He stepped lightly. No stars. Clouds thick as smoke damped back down a chimney.

As he walked the road, the small birds that inhabited the pines shifted on their perches and snowshoe hares squatted in snowy depressions. There was darkness and the air smelled as if it had been peeled clean, and here and there a bed of animal musk, a whiff of woodsmoke, wet bark, the streambed choked with snow and ice, and Chas believed he knew as animals did a world brighter in detail for lack of sight, and that the musk of him was a thing still traveling the road behind, trailing like a spirit.

He walked the plowed driveway leaving no prints and found the front door locked. He circled to the back and that door opened. It was cooler inside, cluttered with smells: gas, oil, and cat piss. His eyes adjusted and he picked out the hood of a car, two bicycles hanging from the ceiling, their front wheels crooked like mounted heads. He crossed to the door connecting the house and opened it. A night-light was on next to the stove. The kitchen was clean, counters cleared, table scrubbed. Chas stepped onto the threshold. The stove's digital clock notched a luminous green moment and another. He stepped forward and the floor creaked. There was a thin yapping overhead and Taylor's voice, "God damn it, shut up," and the dog did, and then mumbling, then silence.

Chas backed into the garage, easing the door shut. The car sat humped in the dark and Chas slipped into the driver's side. A big car, new. He imagined starting the engine—the computer dinging to life and a seat belt wrapping across his chest as though he were precious. He checked the ashtray, no butts. The interior smelled of cologne. Leather. No vinyl for old Taylor. He'd come a long way from those days in the back of Chas's pickup.

Chas stepped out of the car, removed his glove, and unscrewed the cap from the kerosene can. He leaned in, tipped the can, and emptied it over the front bench seats, the carpeted floors. Splash and gurgle. There was a thick oily smell in the garage now. He could have used gasoline with its quick hot *whoomp* of conflagration, but kerosene burned slower, dirtier. He stepped back, fished in his pocket for his glove and lighter.

Paused. It was all too easy.

He thought of Taylor falling back into dreams. That easily. When had Taylor suffered his last sleepless night? Chas cocked his head to a side. There was a lesson to be learned here. He slipped his glove on, tucked the lighter in his pocket. Looked around the garage one more time and passed back through the door where the night waited.

Chas drove home rejuvenated. He drove past the sheriff's home, honked and waved as though someone were there to receive it. He passed Coker's and turned onto the highway. Like a kid he gunned it so that the headlights wheeled a circle on the empty roadway, and another, and then the truck was bumped up against a snowbank like a compass for home. He engaged the four-wheel drive and relaxed as the road drew him away, and behind him the town with its sleeping, careless people vanished.

The elderly woman at the table had been a stunner in her day. Proof was in the old photograph on the table in the living room—Martha in jeans and boots, cowboy hat, brim hawk-nosed over her face. There's a quirt in her hand, at a jaunty angle to one hip. She looks like trouble standing next to a large raw-boned bay. Hard to believe she would shrink from five foot three to four foot ten, her back humped, spine collapsing, bone to bone. Always small. But not like this.

No one would have actually *called* her small. She was a presence, an only child who refused to be spoiled, though her father tried, and her mother let him because of all the miscarriages since. And finally surgery settled the question once and for all.

Did Martha know this? Too young, surely. And yet after the surgery, when her mother took months to recover and Martha came in from the range, wild and headstrong as her father had encouraged, she settled herself in to cook, clean, and tend. Ten years old and she did well enough, though she was a failure at breads. She bulldogged the dough on the counter, her arms and hands smelling yeasty even in bed. The chickens grew peevish on the hard loaves and still she worked. There was nothing to explain it, and her mother moved from the bedroom to the sofa while her father moved his cattle farther out to range, distancing himself from the commotion of flour.

When did it end? When did that prize-winning loaf first appear? Martha herself could not say. But somewhere in the span of a year her attention turned inward. It came finally like a gift, that reserve of quiet, and the day indoors came to be as wide and various as the open range she'd loved.

Her mother got strong and Martha rejoined her father working the range when he needed the help and her life took on a pleasurable wandering between house and fields. She raised bread and cattle with equanimity, and when at last the neighbor's son came to court, she studied his eyes and hands as if that were all there was of the man. They married, and her father, as an old man, died happy, having seen the properties joined and a son-in-law to tend the herd he'd started.

The stuff of family history. Pattiann perched on a stool a little ways from the table. She caught a smile her mother aimed at Ike across the table, a small wink, as intimate a gesture as Martha was likely to give. It surprised Pattiann, the affection between her mother and husband. Martha turned to listen to her husband Bill, who sat at the head. Pattiann's brother sat across next to their mother. Her sister-in-law Harriet shuffled dishes into the dishwasher. At a stool next to Pattiann, Justin was braiding a hackamore, working the bosal, the noseband that, when fitted to a bronc, cut the wind until the animal behaved. The braiding was her father's craft, taught to his grandson as he'd taught it to Rob and Pattiann.

The boy was configuring an eight-string braid over a core of rawhide, half-inch by two yards in length, cured and twisted for endurance. The eight ends of outer braid, soaped and pliable, splayed over his lap. His fingers caught each up, turned it under, released it to his other hand, and moved on. He was deft. Such a serious boy. As a young woman, she'd imagined evenings like this at the ranch—though she'd always imagined it her home, her son. She'd never imagined a daughter.

"Place is changing," her father said. "Look at Bozeman. Christ. People lived there three, four generations, bought up, moved out. Livingston. For Christ's sake. Used to be a town you could get shit-heeled in—"

"Bill," Martha said, tossed a look toward Justin.

Pattiann's father leaned over, his elbows thumping the tabletop. "You think he ain't heard worse? You heard worse, son?"

Justin turned a rawhide strand under. "Yes, sir. Heard the price of tit's gotten out of hand, so to speak."

Harriet slammed the dishwasher closed. "That's Odell, isn't it? You been hanging with Odell."

Rob quietly changed the subject. "Won't happen here, not like there—"

"Well, this is still a Christian household, isn't it?" Harriet cut in.

"You got any more coffee, Harriet?" Martha asked, attempting to rise. Harriet waved her off.

"Sit. Anybody else?" There were nods and shakes and the conversation moved on.

Sometimes Pattiann felt sorry for Harriet. She had married Rob just after high school, had Justin during Rob's first year at Montana State: agribusiness. She was town people, her father an accountant. Pattiann suspected conversations ran differently there—sentences carried through, ideas completed. Not the starts and stalls, the dodging of issues, silences saying more than words. Ike had never had a problem catching on to the elliptical nature of these conversations, their wariness, but was often unwilling to partake. He was bullheaded. Curiously, she loved that in him for its familiarity.

"Wolves," her father was saying, "cannot be confined to one place, unless it's their hide tacked to a wall."

"Read somewhere, long time ago," Rob said, "Wilt Chamberlain had a blanket made of wolf snouts."

"What's to admire? He didn't shoot them, did he?" Bill asked.

"Don't know I'd want to sleep under it," Rob said.

"Point is, the world's gone to hell and suddenly it's our fault—as if this ain't the least altered place on God's good earth." Bill dared each in turn to contradict him.

"Maybe that's it," Ike said. "A toehold. Some ground to turn around on."

Bill rubbed his jaw. "For some hundred years those big city folks been sitting in their own crap. Now they wake up surprised to find their bottoms dirty. So what's that make us? A place to come clean 'em off in? Missile silos, nuclear dumpsites, toxic landfills. Ain't nothing we done to this land they wouldn't do worse given half a chance."

"Will Angela play for us tonight?" Martha asked. The fluorescent light buzzed overhead. The coffee had cooled and on cue, they heard Angela in the living room tuning.

"You bring your fiddle, Dad?" Rob asked.

Martha pushed her chair back, braced her hands on the table. "He'll say no, but of course he did. Justin, it's out behind the truck seat. Now, you excuse me, I'm going to creep off, settle into the softest seat in the living room while the rest of you plead and beg this old coot to play until he finally breaks down and does exactly as he'd planned to all along." Her steps were crabbed.

Bill looked stricken. Martha patted his arm as she walked past him. "Sometimes, dear, the bullshit gets just too deep to wade through."

He smiled at her tweaking, laughed deep from his belly, said, "You heard her. Start begging."

Pattiann stayed in the kitchen with Harriet. She could hear her father's voice rasping in the living room. Then more tuning. There would be coffee at the end of it and some cake that Harriet had stashed out of reach of Rob and the hands and the kids.

"You need help, Harriet?" Pattiann asked, picked at a length of damp rawhide, thinking she should take it up again. Make a braided quirt, like the one her father had made for her mother as a fifth wedding anniversary present. The one her mother held in the photograph. The leather felt good in her fingers.

"No," Harriet said. She turned to Pattiann, her hands dropped to her side. She looked faded in the overhead light, the table cleared, sink clean, her hands empty. It wasn't that Pattiann didn't like Harriet, but she'd truthfully never felt much need to make a friend of her.

"I'd like to ask you something." Harriet rushed on, "I'm thinking of moving to town with the kids. Justin starts high school next fall. But Angela wants to stay in school here, stay on the ranch, though the change might do her good."

"Might," Pattiann said.

"It's Justin. You heard him tonight."

"Won't be any less of that talk in town."

Harriet shook her head. Lowered her voice. "It's him falling in with *them* all the time. Without a chance to think differently."

Them. Pattiann's hands stilled. It was *us* and *them* and Harriet clearly saw Pattiann in her camp. Pattiann dropped the rawhide strip back onto the bench. "What's Rob say?"

Harriet pulled a chair up. "He doesn't want me to go."

"He'd miss you."

Harriet nodded. "And who'd feed the hands, do the chores?"

"Other men survive."

"Who'd take care of Martha? I'm over there two, three times a week keeping their house up."

Of course. She could see it, Harriet stopping to visit and later on, after Harriet had left, Martha would find the wash done, or some dusting, or a floor scrubbed, or meals in the freezer, and neither would say a word to each other about it, or to Pattiann. Least of all Pattiann. If Harriet moved into town, it would be three households. "I could help," she said. "Come out every few days—"

Harriet was picking at her sweater, pilling the fuzz and gathering it into a nest in her lap. "I didn't mean that. Rob says Justin can make it on his own in town. Get a place, a part-time job, just like he did at Justin's age."

Just as Pattiann had. Moved out from the only place she knew or understood into town. And how frightening it had seemed back then, at fourteen, just off the ranch. All the noise, the cars. The town kids who bawled as she went by, calling her "new stock." She spent the first months ducking, or fighting. She lived in a one-room apartment, over the mercantile. Worked as a waitress part time, minimum wage for lunch money. Home weekends and holidays. How she'd hated it. Grew up fast.

"It's easier on boys," Pattiann said. "Justin'll be fine."

Harriet's breath hissed. "That's what Rob says. I didn't argue when he had Justin out on roundup and branding before he could keep his drawers dry." She stood up. "It's not like I knew what I was getting into."

Pattiann should say something of comfort, but she wanted, more than anything, to change the subject. She didn't want to know her brother's life wasn't what she'd believed it was. There was laughter in the next room, then the sound of a fiddle. Angela, a little unsteady, off pitch. Another fiddle joining, slowed from its usual pace. It was a kindness her father was capable of, but rarely showed. He was not a patient man.

Harriet's eyes studied Pattiann's, looking for some imagined sisterhood, assuming another woman would understand, a woman from town, as if Pattiann's ranch history were an aberration in some larger, more meaningful story. She sighed. "I'd better get the cake and coffee ready." She stood and turned away. She worked quietly at the sink. Her body looked as if it had sustained a blow.

Pattiann drove, and it was a treat for Ike, being the passenger, kicking back in the buzz of coffee and the leftover glow of Jim Beam while the road slipped by. Snowing again. It fell in clumps, a giggling clumsy descent. White on white. Not a break for miles, no barns, homes, trees. White, more white. A person could get lost out here. A person could go mad. But at least it wasn't blowing.

"I miss trees," he said. "Deciduous: chestnut, maples, hickory, oak— something to turn color in fall. Something to stop the snow, the damned wind."

"The wind gets to everyone," Pattiann said. "*Something* gets to everyone here." She turned onto the plowed highway, disengaged the four-wheel drive. "I need to spend more time at Rob's."

Ike snorted, leaned his head back and closed his eyes.

"With Harriet. Help out at my folks'."

He cracked an eye open. Pattiann didn't go to her old place, Bill and Martha's. Rob's house was as close as she got. It was why the family gathered there now, with Martha's frailty, too weak to entertain, supplying the excuse. Typical. Don't mention it, just move the gatherings. He waited.

"Justin's entering high school come fall. He'll need to move to town."

Sometimes there was just no following. They conversed as if they were herding cattle, circling, driving in, backing off. Listening was a Goddamned art. They dodged real talk with jokes and silences, as though words were blunt objects in their hands. He opened his jacket, turned the heater down. Ahead of them, the snow pitched into the headlights, the fields were a billowing white and seemed to glow as if the earth beneath were lamp-lit. They hadn't seen another car on the road, which suggested to him that people were staying in. His pager hadn't beeped. Another good sign.

She cleared her throat. "We got that spare room downstairs. I was thinking Justin could use it. He'd go home some weekends, holidays, summer."

And this was a surprise. He reached down, turned the radio on, swung the dial listening for a weather bulletin. "A kid in the house makes a difference. Loud music. You'll have to close the door when you take a bath." His mouth ticked into a smile.

She was watching the highway, hands fixed on the wheel.

74

Ike sat straighter. Packing snow, wet and heavy. There would be heart attacks in the morning—the elderly town man shoveling his sidewalk. The older rancher who walked too far out into the deep drifts, or seized up while cutting a path to the shed. How were you supposed to know? "We haven't talked about children in awhile," he said.

Pattiann nodded. "Have we avoided it?"

"I don't know. You go from day to day. You don't think of it." He paused. "Maybe I have avoided it."

"You'd make a good father," she said.

They were passing Stubblefield's. The lights were out. No truck in the drive. Ike leaned against the glass. There was the lower corral and the field, the few standing cattle, maybe fifty head. Skinnier by now. The piebald horse, holding its own with Ike's help. And Ike wished he'd brought grain. They could stop and the horse, its back hi-hatted in snow, would trundle its way to the fence, dip its muzzle in Ike's palm. Pattiann would be startled by their easy familiarity. He'd confess how he'd been feeding the animal. He'd tell her how he'd tried to buy the horse. She wouldn't laugh.

"I don't know," he said. "I'm not around much. Things can happen to a man in my job." Ike sat up away from the window. "My dad was a good father, I guess. But damn, he *loved* the farm. Silos packed with silage. Calves in spring. Milk pouring from teats. Bulls mounting cows. No artificial insemination for his cows." He looked over at Pattiann. She was watching the road. "He was a sensual man. Does that surprise you?"

"No." Pattiann laughed.

"He used to embarrass the hell out of my mother, the way he'd moon after her. There couldn't have been a more unlikely pair. She kept the farm going, the bank off our back. She shipped the cows out when they went dry. Sold the veal calves. My father—he'd have kept them all, the sick, the old, the worthless, and starved us doing it." And that, Ike knew, would be beyond Pattiann's comprehension. Sentimentality past the age of six.

"Did he hate her for it?"

And what surprised Ike was that he hadn't wondered the same thing.

75

He took out a cigarette, tamped it on his watch. He lit it and took a deep breath. Air whistled through the window he'd opened to a slit. After the rendering truck would pull away, or the veal calves were loaded on transports to the slaughterhouse, his father would hide out in his study. He'd come out three, five, twelve hours later—when he was good and ready to. Then he'd fold himself behind the wheel of their old Rambler station wagon and drive off. He'd be gone for days, a week, leaving the farmwork to Ike and his mother. His mother never made any move to find out where he was or what he was doing.

When his father returned, he brought flowers. He told jokes, took to his chores as if he'd never abandoned them. "No," Ike finally said. "He didn't hate her."

By the time they hit the outskirts of town, the snow had eased. Ike thought he could make out a new opacity in the cloud cover, a thin umbrus of light that might be the moon. It was late, and he wondered if he would hold Pattiann in his arms, beneath the bedroom window, under the light of moon on snow. If she would respond. He wondered if it was the talk of children that prompted his interest.

"We could try it with Justin," Ike said. "If you'd like. Might be nice to have a kid in the house." Watching her face, he had the feeling that it was the possibility of enjoying it that frightened her.

The next day, late afternoon, Ike found Chas sitting in a booth at O'Brian's. Ike seated himself across from Stubblefield, who didn't bother looking up. There was an empty shot glass next to a coffee cup.

That morning, Ike had been over to Taylor's to investigate the vandalism on his car. Taylor looked hard rode. Insisted it was Stubblefield. "You got any reason to believe that?" Ike asked after inspecting the car.

"Turned him down for a loan."

"That something new for you? I expect you've got more than one person pissed." Ike glanced over at the doorway, saw Taylor's wife wavering there. "Excuse me, ma'am," he said, though she did not look offended. She slumped against the doorjamb, her hands pushing at the hair tightly pinned back from her face. She was a handsome woman, though this morning it looked an effort. He told Taylor they'd keep an eye on his house and check out Stubblefield.

The bar was dim; a thin edging of sunlight squeezed under the drawn shades. The length of the walnut bar was gouged where the clientele scored the wood with the edges of quarters, or silver dollars in the old days. Nothing personal or intimate to the act, one hand taking up where another left off. The back bar reared up through the dropped ceiling to the old pressed-tin ceiling, oxidized from smoke, too fussy in those modern sixties for the management's taste. A Goddamned shabby place, but you had to admire them clinging to the 1960s while the more savvy towns conjured up the 1880s and cashed in.

Chas looked rested. His hands were scrubbed and he held the coffee cup as if his fingers were sensitive. "Your phone out of order?" Ike finally asked.

Stubblefield grinned. "You know, funny thing, I get these letters from the phone company, next thing the damn phone don't work. Good thing I didn't pay, hey?"

Ike tried again. "You all right, Chas?"

He looked over Ike's shoulder. "Is it snowing yet?" And when Ike shook his head, Chas went on, "It will. Just won't stop this year." He leaned back. "Like in the ninth circle of hell. That's the *Inferno,* you know. Read it. Read *Paradise Lost,* too. When I was a kid. Those two books up there on the shelf butt-ending the Bible like last-minute scripture. My mama's books.

"But there's this ninth circle of hell, and it's all snow and ice and shit with sinners buried up to their necks in it." He waved a finger to the bartender Barry and pointed to the shot glass. "You?" he asked Ike. "No? Anyway, I have this dream last night, and there I am buried up to my neck in frozen cattle, hooves and eyes and teats and balls, and I'm thinking it's so fucking cold, ain't there supposed to be fire? What burns hotter, fire or ice?"

Ike wasn't in the mood. "Last night, someone broke into Taylor's garage, poured kerosene over the front seat of his car." He watched

Stubblefield's eyes, waiting for a flicker, amusement, nervousness. Nothing. "He and his wife were asleep in the house at the time."

Barry brought the drink and refilled their coffee. Chas saluted with the glass and gunned the shot. He sat back. "So there you go," he said. "It could have been worse. Seems to me whoever did it was downright Christian."

"Taylor thinks it was you." Again Ike waited.

"Well, I am a Christian. I think."

Ike stood up to leave. "I don't have time for this. I'm watching you, Stubblefield."

Chas reached across the table, grabbed Ike's wrist in his hand, held tight. "You come in here to talk, or what?" His hand relaxed, drew back around the coffee cup.

Ike thought there was something in Chas's eyes, so that Ike hesitated, thinking to see at last a side of Chas he could understand if not trust.

Ike sat and Chas asked, "You meet Pattiann back east? Your family from there?"

Ike didn't like the sound of his wife's name in Stubblefield's mouth.

"They farmers?" And when Ike nodded, Chas asked, "Dairy?"

"Sixty head."

"So'd you lose the farm or what? You didn't want it?"

"We sold it, just before my father died." Ike opened the last two buttons on his coat. "The sale kept us comfortable until I got work."

"Comfortable. I like that thought. With the police."

Ike eased back in his seat.

"I knew there was a reason you got elected. I mean an outsider and all, but you'd been here a couple of years, married Pattiann." He stirred more cream into his coffee. "You come from a farming background, had all that experience, a diploma, and you didn't diddle none of the ranchers' daughters like the old sheriff used to. You'd think that sorry old sonofabitch would have known. It's like a rule: *You don't diddle the ranchers' daughters.*"

"Or mess with their property," Ike added.

Chas crooked his head and laughed. The afternoon light shone hot on the shades, a warm amber glow that deepened the gloom in the rest of the room. The bell over the door jangled and the first of the early evening regulars stepped in.

"Don't fuck with the daughters, or property." Chas wiped his eyes and straightened up. "So why you doing it? We both know I'm going down either way—quick your way, or slow mine."

"As slow as the cattle?" Ike asked.

"Just so." He held his hand out over the table, ticked one finger down, another and another. "One piece at a time. Come on, Parsons. You never seen cows die on your father's ranch"—he corrected himself—"farm? You don't know all things have their seasons?" Stubblefield straightened his fingers, rubbed his palm across the table. The skin of cream trembled in his cup.

Ike rested his head on the backstop and turned to look at the bar where Barry sat talking with old Charlie Sandovar who'd lost his wife and only son in a car wreck. It had been Ike's first year here. He'd had to go tell him. It was one of the difficulties working with so small a population. You knew the face of the wounded and they were always there to haunt you. And then there was Chas, a whole different kind of spook, asking the question Ike wasn't comfortable with himself. Why? Because animals were suffering? That's where it'd started. But now? Had it gotten personal? Slippery grounds for a man with a badge and a gun. But Chas was in the wrong, after all, and it was Ike's *job,* and enforcing the law wasn't arbitrary, turning a blind eye when it was convenient or things got too uncomfortable. And then, between one breath and the next, it seemed to Ike as if he were missing some *thing,* some reasoning outside of logic essential to the heart of his work, a dim reckoning that was almost physical, like the memory of taste or smell.

Conversation at the bar picked up with the *ding* of the door opening. Chas was watching him. Ike shook his head, weary with the only answer he could find it in himself to offer. "Stubblefield, what I'm concerned with here is the law dictated me by the state of Montana. You break it, I'll nail your ass. I don't care if it's for starving cattle or vandalism." He stood to leave. "Keep clear of Taylor."

Ike was almost out the door when Chas called, "You say hi to Pattiann for me?" Stubblefield waved to Ike's back as he stepped out and then raised a finger for another shot. "There'll be a tip in this for you, Barry," Chas said.

The crowd was picking up, two more people at the bar. Chas took a sip of whiskey, and followed it with cold coffee—a lousy chaser, but free. His mind slowed; his limbs jigged. He paced himself, keeping track of drinks like a loan payment. And they were. A dip into the small store he'd set aside. Not enough for much of anything, just a little something, good-faith money. But there was no good faith in this world, only sheriffs, feed suppliers, and bankers . . . driving kerosene-soaked cars. He snorted and eased further down into the seat, pulled out a pack of cigarettes. Chas flicked back the cap of his old lighter, thumbed the wheel. There was a spark, a flame, and the smell of lighter fluid. He lit a cigarette.

A mistake mentioning Pattiann. Making the sheriff angry. But he'd sensed it was what was sitting between them, and wasn't it interesting that she should sit, a phantom third party at the table, that each begrudged the other. What the hell, he was going down, anyway. Wasn't nothing going to stop it. He took another sip to keep the spin in his head going, the buzz, the lovely stall before the fall.

Smoke trickled off the burning cigarette, script in the air. He heard the *ka-chink* of change, the whirr of the jukebox selection, and then Willie Nelson was singing "Blue Eyes Crying in the Rain." The door opened and another body shuffled in. He ordered another shot.

Barry dawdled, served two, three other folks first, but when Chas called a second time, spread a five-dollar bill on the table, Barry delivered. He made change, hovered. "You sure you can afford this?"

Chas shrugged. "Can't afford not to."

He sipped the shot. The door opened and it was darker outside than in. Chas guessed that it was a weekend, maybe. Or Friday. Payday. Maybe. The bar was filling with groups of men, a few couples, a cribbage game set up at a near table, men slapping cards, *fifteen-two, pair is four,* at the pool table a young kid sighted down the cue. Chas wet a finger in the shot glass and wrote his name on the murky tabletop. When he looked up, Purvis was standing next to him.

Chas grinned. "This a house call?"

Purvis pointed to the empty seat across from Chas. "You waiting for someone to come and play catch-up?"

"I'm waiting for the floor to open and swallow everything but me, this handful of change and barful of drinks."

Purvis set his beer down and seated himself. "Don't see you out much."

"Yeah, well," Chas said and downed the shot. "We're a private people. Come from a whole line of folks nobody's ever seen or heard of."

Purvis shrugged. "Knew your daddy."

"You count yourself a lucky man?" Chas tipped his empty shot glass, rolled it in a circle under the palm of his hand. "You really here to talk about my old man?"

"I've seen your cattle."

"You and the sheriff, and anybody who hasn't, has heard—old lady Carver drives by in her Studebaker like she's still queen of the 1940s, sees a cow drop on my place, and next thing people in two counties know my herd's dying. And soon as they hear it's starvation and not disease, they breathe a little easier and turn the dogs out to watch the hayricks. Maybe one of them sonsofbitches comes along in a pickup with a load of hay, shuffles his feet at my door, and says it's the Christian thing to do—ain't much, mind you, 'cause times are tight and he's got his own, and it's been a bad stretch of years, but it's the least a God-fearing man can do. And so I show him the gate and tell him to take his charity with him." He raised his shot glass to Barry for another drink.

Purvis took a swallow of beer. "You need to put those cattle down, Chas. Way it is, they're suffering and not likely to be brought back."

"No," Chas agreed. "But that's the point."

Purvis looked confused.

"You think I'm the only one had a hand in this? Tell you what, you get Taylor, Sam Coker out to my spread. You get them to shovel shit and blood for awhile—and I'll think on it. That'd be a sight, hey?"

"Christ, Chas." Purvis thumped his glass down on the table, a skud of foam rose to the lip. "I don't give a rat's ass about any grudge match between you and them. And I don't give a good Goddamn about what all went wrong, or some sorry-ass song about how you tried your best. Those animals are suffering and you can stop it now. It's the decent thing. Before the law steps in."

"Parsons." Chas smiled. "He's got his own agenda."

"I'll help you do it, Chas."

Barry delivered Chas's drink, then stood there, as if reluctant to take another of the dwindling bills on the table. Barry's head was back-lit, his face in shadow so that it was hard for Chas to read the pity he knew was there. Chas turned to Purvis. "You want to help? Buy this round."

Purvis slipped out of the booth. He handed Barry money for the drinks and walked out the door.

"Now that's what I call Christian," Chas said and sipped the whiskey. He settled in, parsing out dollars and cents to last the night, or for however long it took. He drank until the edges softened. The jukebox played the same tunes over and over, but Chas found himself humming along now. The overhead light turned liquid the faces at the bar. Bottles were stacked on the back bar like a firing line among barrel-bellied jars in which floated pickled pigs feet, sausages or eggs in a rusty brine, and on first glance it reminded him of the traveling freak show he'd seen as a young boy in Havre, with its array of jars: jellyfish, a two-headed eel, six-legged frog, a lamb with a leg growing from its stomach—phantasms of heavy metals, inbreeding, and mythological creatures hatched of taxidermy. And the finishing touch: on a creaking turntable, one human fetus floating in alcohol, making its own slow revolutions in the fluid, butt cheeks bumping against the glass in pale eggish ovals.

He would order one now, he thought, an egg, if he could, and he rested his head against the seat cushion and listened to the talk: football and kids, cattle and crop forecasts. He saw old Jerry Tallwell canting on a barstool and suddenly Chas had a clear picture of him, a year or two distant, heeling end-over-end in a combine while the blades still thrashed, the wheat and dirt rising skyward in a plume. And then Chas found himself in the latrine, the urinal clogged with plugs of chew that rose and floated as he relieved himself and even in the dark and stink he *was* relieved, with the music thumping at the door, the voices raised in laughter so that he laughed too while fumbling with the zipper. And when he made his way back out to the bar, he saw his table cleaned, found the last of his money tucked in his pocket. He was sidetracked by the black-haired, middle-aged, recently divorced daughter of one of his father's old cronies, and though he could not come up with her name, she was offering to buy him a drink, and then she was leading him in hand through the maze of tables, past the politely turned backs of the other men, and out into the dark behind the bar.

Chapter Six

Ike sat in Judge Costello's home study. The judge thought the situation unfortunate. "It happens," he said, wheeling back his office chair. "Back in the snow of '49–'50, the whole state stank—cattle putrefying in the fields." He shrugged. "This Stubblefield . . . a bad judgment call. Pride goeth before—" The judge was a small man, made smaller by the mahogany desk, his head so bent that Ike could see where the black hair tint had leached onto his scalp. "Haven't you ever made a bad call?"

His legs were delicately crossed, one argyle sock shucked down around an ankle. "And they are, after all, *his cattle*. Our constituents are particular about what belongs to them and who fools with it. They've mortgaged their house, their land, barn, and equipment for the cattle. They got ledgers in their heads saying what cow birthed what calf and when, and sometimes they can trace it clear back to their grandfathers' stock. It's awful personal.

"The rains don't come, prices drop, the wife fools around, but they can still run their finger down a book and tell you what quarter this steer is in and how long till market." He wagged his head but the hair didn't move.

"Ike, nothing happens on this earth hasn't happened before. They are used to dealing with it their own way. The man's an anomaly and there isn't a member in this community won't condemn him for it, won't hesitate to turn their back when he comes around. But you take his cattle away and who do you think they're going to turn on?" The judge dug out a small sheet from a bundle of loose papers on his desk.

"Now I got attorney McLeod's memo, but I don't think she's committed to this. Says given a choice, the county generally ignores this sort of thing. Too expensive, no chance of recovering the expenses. I could talk to her."

"What isn't dead is dying," Ike said.

"Yes. He's a fool."

"With a gun," Ike added.

"That's not against the law," the judge said.

"But starving livestock is," Ike added.

"Only if it's brought to the attention of this court."

The late afternoon sun shone through the French doors, and the judge's hair gleamed blue. There was the smell of fried chicken coming from another part of the house. His stomach growled and he had paperwork to do. Ike stood. "Consider it brought."

The judge sighed, nodded slowly. He offered his hand across the desk to Ike. "I'll get the paperwork started. We'll meet in my chambers with Stubblefield, see if we can't clear this up outside of court." He walked Ike to the door. "Gets any untidier than that, no one will thank you for it."

Ike stood at the stove next to Pattiann, lifting pot covers and peering in. Purvis had invited himself to dinner, walking the mile and a half to their house through a mixture of rain and snow to stand in the back doorway, dripping onto the hooked rug. Pattiann toweled his hair and face, an intimate gesture she bestowed on no other guest. "He's such a great shaggy dog," she'd once told Ike.

"You need a wife," Pattiann said.

"You find me one can stand me."

"Amy Schumacher?"

Purvis ducked his head. "If I offered her my heart, she'd eat it."

"Purvis," Pattiann scolded.

He raised three fingers in front of her face. "That we know of. She's a widow maker." He bobbed out of Pattiann's arms and over to the stove next to Ike. "Spaghetti?"

"Lasagna," Pattiann answered, "once I put it all together. So why don't you two pour me a whiskey ditch and let me work?"

Ike and Purvis sat in the dining room while pots clattered in the kitchen. Sometimes Ike could see Pattiann as she crossed to the pantry. He thought how comfortably ordinary a thing it was—this time spent anticipating dinner, his wife's shadow flirting in the doorway. He rolled the glass in his fingers, sipped the drink, and listened to the ice cubes clink. Purvis sighed. "She could almost convince me to marry."

"Worked for me," Ike said.

"That's not the way I heard it," Purvis said. "Heard you had to follow her fifteen hundred miles and take hostages."

Ike smiled and lifted his feet onto an adjoining chair. "No hostages."

A kettle banged in the background. The oven door yawned open and clamped shut. Pattiann brought another setting for the table, lit candles, and slapped the overhead light switch off.

"*Miss* Pattiann," Purvis said, "candlelight?"

In the doorway, she looked over her shoulder at the pair. "Covers a multitude of sins."

Purvis nodded. "You should have married someone handsome."

"The bread didn't raise properly," she corrected and strolled back into the kitchen.

"What, you don't think I'm pretty, Purvis?" Ike asked.

"There ain't a light that forgiving." He scuffed at his drying hair. "Got a call from Judge Costello today."

Ike waited.

"So you went and did it," Purvis pushed. "Got an order on Stubble-field."

"You make it sound like I shot my best bird dog."

"My daddy used to say—"

"Christ, Purvis. None of your homespun wisdom. The man's gone off half-cocked, it's time I put an end to it."

Purvis tipped back in his chair. He looked older than he needed to. "Heard about Taylor's car," he finally said. "Think Chas did it?"

"I think he's capable of it." Ike tipped the bottle, refilled his glass and Purvis's. "I don't want to find out what more he's capable of."

Ike looked up and Pattiann was standing in the doorway. The kitchen light on her hair was a pale red corona. He knew Pattiann didn't want to talk about Stubblefield's troubles, and in that way she was a barometer of the locals, her disapproving silence.

Ike patted the chair next to him but Pattiann stayed where she was, caught in the half-dark where he could not read her face, just the shape of her breasts and hips, her feet planted on the threshold. She ran her hand down a kitchen towel draped from a jean pocket, a nervous gesture. She was a woman any number of men might have fallen for, still would, but he was the lucky one. And what were the odds of that?

Purvis rocked his chair forward, landed his elbows on the table. "Judge wanted my opinion. Three days ago, I might have kept hands off. Now, I think maybe you're right. Up and down I hear talk, folks taking sides. People feeling sorry for him. Think he's gotten a drubbing from the bank. Nothing they enjoy more than to bad-mouth banks.

"My father bought everything with cash. A man made by the Depression. Never got past it. 'When the banks closed their doors,' he'd said, 'they gave back the people ten cents on every dollar. But come time to collect, they'll empty your pockets—a dollar ten and more for every one you borrowed, and there's no door you can close against them.' " Purvis rolled the glass in his hand. "People carry a grudge a hell of a long time.

"And I think Chas has grudges to spare." He sipped the whiskey. "Pattiann," he called to her in the doorway. "Where's dinner?"

"In the oven," she said.

"Good." Purvis slapped the place next to him. "Bring your pretty little good influence over here and set it down next to me."

He poured her a fresh drink. "What I like about you—you got that lasagna timed? good, good—is that you smell like God intended woman to." He inhaled deeply. "Sausage and onions and Roma tomatoes."

"Christ, Purvis, you make every woman sound like a deli?" she asked.

He wrapped an arm around her shoulder and buffed her cheek with a kiss. "Only the best. A vet makes more money than a sheriff."

"That much, huh?" Pattiann shoved Purvis's glass a little farther out of reach.

Ike laughed. Pattiann could nose-lead just about any man she met. Years of dealing with ranchers and cowhands and other stiff-necked animals.

"Rejected again," Purvis said, snagging his glass.

"You expecting sympathy?" Ike asked.

But Purvis was puffing out his chest. "I can take it." He turned back to Pattiann. "So what do your folks think about Stubblefield?"

Pattiann took a long, slow drink, started to rise. "I should check the meal."

Purvis snorted.

Pattiann sat back down. "They don't think much of him, or his management of finances. They don't like to see cattle starve, but they've seen it before." She looked them both over.

"Their own cattle?" Purvis pushed.

Pattiann looked slapped. "Not in my recollection."

"Never happened," Purvis said. "Never will. Because there's something infinitely more decent in your father and most of the other folks hereabouts than in Stubblefield. Money might have started this, but it isn't money keeps him from putting those animals out of their misery.

"No," Purvis continued, "he's in the spotlight, and where most people might duck with shame, he's taking a bow."

"That's a little rough, don't you think, Purvis?" Pattiann asked. Her lips were pinched. "Don't you think there's more to it?"

Ike watched out of the corner of his eye the way her back straightened, her chin tipping up and elbows braced—a fighting stance. He felt the glow of the candles and talk and whiskey fading. He felt irritated and was surprised to realize it was directed mostly at Purvis, his turn of conversation, and Ike wondered what that said about his own silences these days, his avoidance of the problem, about what the town was thinking, or even how Pattiann felt about it all. About Stubblefield.

Purvis pushed back in his chair. "Well, *of course* there's more to it. More than I or Ike, or Stubblefield himself can fathom. I don't mean to reduce the thing it is—a tragedy—but neither will I choose to ignore what I sensed when I ran into him the other night at the bar. And maybe it was just the booze, or my own faulty intuition, but I believe he's pleased with the suffering of his cattle, the discomfort of decent people, and even the clumsy offer of help from a country vet. You know," he said, shook his finger, "I have seen animals worry a healing wound because they *like* the taste of blood."

They sat in the fulsome air: garlic and roasted tomatoes, a peppery backbite of basil. The candle flames wavered as the furnace fan kicked in and Purvis's whiskey glass cast a watery circle of amber light onto the white dinner cloth that he fingered as if it were a stain. They did not look at one another, until Purvis cleared his throat.

"Had an interesting case the other day," Purvis said. "This rancher comes in, wants me to do a vasectomy on him. Says all the doctors he's talked to want an arm and a leg along with his nuts. I tell him I'm not a physician, I'm a vet. All I do is castrations. He says, 'Hell, if I'd wanted that, I'd do it myself.' "

Ike laughed. Pattiann sat quietly a moment, then smiled at Purvis. "Is that supposed to provide a lesson about Stubblefield's problem?"

Purvis smiled back evenly. "Doesn't it?"

She patted his hand. "Purvis, it's a good thing you're a vet and not a preacher."

The conversation moved more easily after that, like breathing after a hard swim, though there was one small glitch when Ike asked about the Mattick boy. "Fine," Purvis said, his eyes evading Ike's. "Promising." And he'd said no more about it. Purvis ate two large plates of lasagna and was offered and accepted a ride home. He carried his belly in both hands out the door.

When they went to bed that night, Pattiann was fidgeting, punched her pillow, slid a leg up over the quilt. She sighed.

Ike raised on an elbow. He ran a finger down her exposed leg, and the limb jerked. "Something wrong?" he asked.

She turned toward him. "Dinner was all right?"

"Purvis ate like two men."

She waited a beat in the dark. "About Stubblefield," she said, "I have the feeling you expect something from me. You and Purvis both."

Ike kept silent.

"Which is curious, because, you see, Chas seems to expect something from me as well. I saw him, you know. Last week. Had coffee with him."

Ike nodded in the dark. "I'd heard."

"What else have you heard?" she asked. "Never mind." She pushed the covers back and sat up. "Nothing that isn't true, I'm sure. Chas says he just wants someone to talk to. Someone else with something at stake."

"Like?"

"My marriage, maybe."

Ike nodded.

"This could get ugly," she said.

"It already is," he answered.

"Not between us. Not yet."

"But you see that as part of a natural progression?"

She sighed. "I think it's a distinct possibility. Don't you?"

Ike laced his fingers behind his head. "I'm disturbed that Chas seeks you out, thinks to use you. That it took you this long to tell me."

Pattiann sighed. She tucked the quilt around her legs. "Chas and I started out as kids together, both of us wild and holding grudges. The first time Chas stopped over at my folks', we were eighteen. He arrived in his best pair of jeans and a clean short-sleeved shirt—buttoned to the neck—entered the house, hat in hand, hair slicked back, a good-looking young man. It damned near broke my heart . . ."

And Ike could believe that, remembering the way he'd been fooled by Chas's smile, how young it had made him look, how strangely vulnerable, and how Ike had thought, just maybe, there was something in Chas a person could like, could call friend.

"My dad met him on the stoop, stopped him before he ever got past the door. Looked him up and down like he did breeding stock at a sale. You could see it—I know Chas could—the way my dad backed up even as he offered his hand. Took one look and judged Chas like meat on the hoof, too shallow in the chest maybe, or weak in the haunches. My father built his ranch on the accuracy of his eye, and Chas sure as hell didn't make the grade." She stroked the quilt, patted it down like a temperamental horse. "Which was reason enough for me to stay with Chas, at least early on."

"And later?"

"It's hard to imagine now. Never mind that I don't want to think of it, and a lot of it's just gone. I can't deny there came to be more than just willfulness and spite on my part. A genuine . . . regard."

It was dark in the room and Ike wished he could see her face. He tried to read the pitch of her voice, but that felt as if he were trying to catch out a suspect. "Regard. Makes it sound like you two were shaking hands." She laughed and leaned into him. His arm snugged around her and she turned her face into his chest, kissed the narrow spot where his arm conjoined his chest, a light airy touch that allowed him to breathe again. This is what saves us, he thought, these gestures deeper than reason.

"I never loved him. Even back then, when I thought up any number of reasons for the things I did, that was never one of them. He was there. He was lonely and hurt. And so was I." She snugged down deeper next to him. "I wanted his anger." She exhaled deeply. "To sustain mine.

"Purvis is right." She tugged the quilt up under her chin. "About Stubblefield. The cattle. They're an end to his means," she said.

Ike looped a strand of her hair over his hand, stroked it between thumb and forefinger.

"You know that look in Stubblefield's eyes?" she asked.

He wasn't sure he did. He quieted his hand a moment and waited.

"Vengeance," she said. She turned, positioned herself in the crook of his elbow. "And it scares the hell out of me." She was quiet a long beat.

"But you know the really crazy part?" He felt her head turn up toward him. "Something in me still feels like his friend."

Early morning at the courthouse people arrived one at a time, holding coats closed against the wind. Sidewalks were shoveled and the two-foot mounds on either side had taken on the glaze of a newly frosted donut. Chas was sitting on the steps so that people navigated around him as if he were a stone gargoyle. He'd been in the building already, while it was mostly empty, radiators just then clanking and hissing to life. The secretary, a middle-aged dowd in a black dress, raised a powdered face and told him the judge was readying himself in chambers, asked, would he care to wait? He turned on his heel and walked out. Chas had dressed for his appearance. Wore his mucking boots.

He sat with his head pitched forward, so cold that the nerve endings in his cheeks ached. When the door at his back opened and the dowd's voice called, he didn't turn, but stared out over the square where pigeons squatted in a gazebo while a hawk wheeled overhead.

He heard her descend the stairs, her breathing labored, and then her hand was on his shoulder and he swatted it away as if it were a fly.

Her hair had blown loose, the ends yellow as straw and thin as a gleaned field. He stood and passed her, letting the door racket on its hinges. Her stubby heels clacked counter to the chunk of his boots, and when they arrived at the office, she hurried ahead, alternately tugging at her skirt and hair before opening an inner door. "He's here," she said, then ducked out.

Chas scraped his boots on the threshold, ignored the judge's hand, and took a chair in the center of the room.

The judge seated himself. "Good to see you, Chas," the judge said. The vet sat in a corner. Parsons watched from the side of the room, his eyes connecting with Chas's. He nodded and Chas thought there was something new in the sheriff's posture, something different. As if a new distraction had set in. Chas smiled back, ignoring the judge. "You the cat that swallowed the bird, Parsons? You think you can do it in one bite?"

"Chas," Purvis said. "Don't make this—"

"Shut up," Chas said.

The judge stood. Chas turned his smile on him.

"We're doing you a favor here, Mr. Stubblefield."

Chas laughed.

"I expect you to return the courtesy," the judge said and picked up a sheaf of papers. "Got a complaint here, that you have neglected your cattle to the point of abuse. That said herd is dead or dying, offending all sense of human dignity and posing a serious health risk to the community. Now we're just here to try and resolve this with as little embarrassment to you as possible."

The room was warm. He could smell his boots heating up, a sweet, rank odor. "Where's Taylor?" Chas asked. "Coker?"

The judge set the papers down. "Sheriff Parsons filed the complaint and Purvis here has verified the problem. It's common sense, man. Simple decency. You have got to do something about those animals." He leaned back in his chair. "Would you like a cup of coffee?"

"You got any whiskey?"

The judge sighed. Purvis was rolling his head on his neck as if it ached. Parsons walked over to the window overlooking the courtyard.

"That hawk still out there?" Chas asked, and Parsons looked skyward, nodded.

"This is what we'll do," the judge cut in. "We agree, neighbor to neighbor, that you clean up this mess or hand it over and we do it for you."

"And if I don't agree?"

"You go to court, lose the herd, you pay court fees, a fine, and jail."

"I can't pay no lawyer."

"I'll appoint one."

"I can't pay no fines."

"You go to jail longer."

Chas thrummed his fingers on his pant legs. Books lined the walls, gold-lettered spines. He guessed they were law books. Tomes of the quick and the dead.

"You considering what I've said?" the judge asked.

"I'm considering the quick and the dead," Chas said. "And the quick are quickly enough dead, so I guess it's all one and the same thing." Chas stood, dusted his hands down his pants. He looked around. He walked down the row of bookcases, finger bumping the spines like a stick on a picket fence, the soft *tha-bump, tha-bump.* He knocked into the back of Purvis's chair, kept going until he'd stopped short of Parsons at the window. "I never been here before."

"We didn't bring this on, Chas," Purvis said.

Chas turned on him. "No. You're just the warm bodies that operate the machine, and it's a Goddamned complicated piece of work, that machine. Parsons here's just a grease monkey and you"—he pointed to the judge—"you turn the key. Like to keep your hands clean, don't you?" He stepped back into the center of the room. "I got to go," he said. "I'm a busy man."

The judge was standing with an effort. Chas thought to walk over there, behind that desk, and pinch the bony elbow in his own strong hand—help the old man understand that for all his books and robes and wide desks, what he *really* was was just so much flypaper even as Chas's own father had become.

"Is that it then?" the judge asked, his voice rising.

"Unless you got a gavel or something you want to pound." Chas walked to the door, opened it, and stood with his back to them. When he turned, they were each held to their private occupation: the vet with his mercy, the sheriff with his law, and the judge with his clean hands. "I'll think on it. Let you know in a day." He shut the door behind him. The secretary was still out. Hiding maybe.

When he stepped into the wind again, Taylor was waiting, coat collar turned up, hands muffled in his pockets. His face was puffy, his eyes wedged in skin, as if he hadn't been sleeping well. There was a pleasure to this, Chas thought.

"Stubblefield," Taylor said. "You sonofabitch. I'm onto you."

"You drive here, Taylor?"

Taylor's hands balled in his coat pockets. But they were soft hands tied to weak wrists and scrabbly arms. Chas kept his own hands loose at his sides. Didn't feel the cold for calluses. He almost pitied the poor fat fuck.

"I got a gun, Stubblefield. You step foot on my property again, I'll kill you."

"Ain't that the way?" Chas asked. He looked out over the town square, people shoved down the sidewalks by luck and wind. Like so many cattle. He turned his attention back on Taylor. "Man gets a gun, next thing you know, he's turning it on his friends." Chas stepped past him. "Gun's a dangerous thing, Taylor. You don't want to keep it loaded in the house. Who knows, that little dog of yours might take to playing with it and blow a hole clear through its ass."

Taylor's face had gone tight. "Maybe I'll just get a bigger dog then." He raised a fist out of his pocket. Chas snatched it on the rise, turned it back.

"Easy," Chas said, twisting it. He let go.

Taylor looked chastised. A whipped dog himself. "Chas, damn you, it's not my say who gets money and who doesn't. There are guidelines—"

"Well, why don't you take those guidelines to bed with you, see how much sleep you get."

"Don't come near me again, Chas."

"Taylor." Chas shook his head and leaned into Taylor's ear. "I didn't search you out." He whispered, "You put yourself at my door, and as Jesus once said, you just got to knock to enter the kingdom of heaven." He backed away, cupped a hand to his ear. "What's that I hear? Someone knocking?"

He stepped clear of Taylor and strolled off, the wind at his back as if they were old friends.

Maybe it was the paperwork that put Ike in a bad mood, an unending stream of reports and requests, a chore he had dreaded but had never fully comprehended when he ran for the office. An eight-hour shift at the desk made even driving the back roads in snow appealing. Or maybe it was spending the morning in a closed room with Stubblefield and his stinking boots. And of course, it had everything to do with his talk with Pattiann, her confusion over her loyalty to Chas. The last straw was Harley dropping in late with a battery of excuses that came down to his lollygagging with the dispatcher.

Ike handed him a radar unit, told him to set up in Dodson—there'd been complaints about speeders on the main road out of the small township. An hour there. Three hours on radar. An hour back. It would keep him out of Ike's hair and off the dispatcher's desk the rest of the day.

Harley looked down the radar gun tube. "What the hell am I supposed to clock up there this time of year? Birds?" Harley followed Ike back into his office.

Ike sat in the chair, eyed the mound of papers. His mood grew blacker.

"That new kid, Dan Roehe, could take it. He ain't doing anything."

"Harley," Ike said, took a deep breath and waited.

"Well, this is a damned snipe hunt." He waved the radar gun at Ike.

Ike closed his eyes. He was hungry and he could smell manure on his clothes, as if the stink of Stubblefield had taken residence. When he opened his eyes again, the gun was limp at Harley's side. "How far you want to press this issue, Harley?" he asked.

Harley gave a sullen nod and walked out of the room. He shut the door softly behind him though, and Ike gave him credit for that.

Ike took his work to the diner. Fran settled him into the far booth. "You look like varmint bait," she said.

He plopped the papers on the table. "Your tax dollars at work."

"You'll want the chicken. A green salad on the side—keep you regular. And a nice glass of milk."

"How about you take my temperature and write me a note?" he crabbed. "I'll take the meatloaf special, heavy on the gravy, extra mashed potatoes, and all the black coffee you can pour."

"You want an eclair to finish you off again?"

"You give your husband this much shit?"

Her face whitened and she took a step back. She turned away, turned back, and settled into the seat across from Ike. She folded her hands on the table, looked him in the eye. "My husband eats the meals I freeze, calls Fridays to make sure the kids and I can get home for the weekend, and when I can't he drives the twelve miles to Jolene Peck's trailer home where he's taken very good care of, I'm sure."

She raised her chin and her fingers locked tighter so that the knuckles shone. A country jig piped from the kitchen radio and a pot clattered, an oven door closed. A customer dropped a couple singles on the counter, some change, stood, and took his leave.

"I'm sorry," Ike said. And he was, and he was at a loss for what more to say. He looked at her hands, the fingers curled in a tired fist, and he wished he could say something, do something. He wondered how a man married to her could look at another woman. And he wondered at how easily life is altered—one day he's living alone, working in a big city police department, grabbing the meatloaf special night after night. And suddenly he's here, in this small-town diner, trying to edge his way around Fran's heartbreak. Trying to feel his way through Pattiann's mixed loyalties. In another life, he could have been Chas with his world collapsing about him. Ike closed his eyes. Fact was, he *understood* the pity Pattiann must feel for Stubblefield, but he could not *feel* it. He looked across at Fran. "He's a fool," Ike said. "Your husband."

"No. He's a practical man. Most particularly when it comes to his *needs.* And I," she pointed a finger at herself, "am a practical woman. I've got three children. Whom I love and who love their daddy. Cripes, you really needed to hear this." She tapped a finger on the stack of paper— "Like you haven't got enough crap to deal with"—and she bustled out of the booth.

"Meatloaf?" she asked.

"Chicken," he said. "Green salad on the side."

She nodded, slapping open her order book.

"But coffee. A man's got to draw the line somewhere."

He ate his lunch in silence, and the chicken was good, the salad tasty. As Ike was finishing, the front door opened and Joe Mattick came in with two others: one school age; the other was Lester Colcox, a cowhand from one of the ranches, a decent hand when he was sober. Which he didn't look to be at the moment. Bad company. And Ike remembered how Purvis had balked at talking about Joe. He looked at his watch. One-thirty. Seemed a little late for a school lunch hour.

The chicken was bones on his plate. He considered a wedge of pie, reconsidered. Fran brought the check. He shuffled his papers into a manageable heap and started to rise, but her hand fell on his shoulder. Gently. Just a squeeze.

"How's Pattiann? She getting on all right?" She smiled, the corners of her mouth turned up nervously. She wasn't asking about Pattiann but about herself. She was a young, healthy woman. Trying to come to terms with betrayal. Testing the waters.

"Yeah," he said. "She's fine."

"Good." She dropped her hand. "Good. Just thought I'd ask." She stepped away, looked down at her shoes, over her shoulder, then back at Ike. "You let her know I said hi."

He nodded, but she was already off for one of the other tables. At the counter, the Mattick boy hunkered in his stool. Lester was humming under his breath.

"You on lunch break from school?" Ike asked Joe.

The young boy next to Joe giggled. "Suspended," he volunteered. "For the week." He elbowed Joe in the ribs, and Joe slapped at the boy's arm. Lester was singing an old tune made famous by Rex Allen, "The Last Roundup."

"Well, it's true." The boy was bright and fidgety. "Last Friday. For drunkenness." He giggled again.

"That right? You were drunk?" Ike asked.

Joe shrugged.

"Lester here didn't have nothing to do with it?" Ike reached over and snatched Lester's collar. The singing stopped.

The man's eyes slid over to the sheriff, widened. "Why, it's the sheriff."

The boy giggled again. It was getting on Ike's nerves. He blessed Fran for the quiet in his stomach. "You boys been into some of Lester's liquor?" he asked the youngster.

"We're clean," the boy said, his voice a squeak.

Ike turned back to Joe. "Saw Purvis. He says you're doing fine work."

Joe looked pleased. "That old Chevy's close to running," he said. "He thinks I'd make a good vet." Joe seemed as clearly confused by the logic of that as Ike was. "Says he'll let me help in surgery. Nothing big, just fetch instruments, prep animals."

"That all right by you?" Ike asked.

"Yeah. I guess so. Said he'll pay me."

"You could do worse," Ike said. He looked at Lester. "You got a job, Lester?"

"Lazy K. For now, for a while, forever." His head rolled on his neck.

"Good. Hate to hear you were out of work, just bumming, or giving kids booze."

"Gotcha," Lester said. "Milkshakes all around. Chocolate, right?" The boys nodded. And he took up another chorus of "The Last Roundup."

Chas dropped by Coker's feed mill. The clerk said Coker was "indisposed."

"Is that like he's hammered to a toilet seat with the shits?" Chas asked.

"Sir? I don't know. He's not here. Can I help you?"

"Sure. See that pickup out there. Why don't you fill the back with feed cakes." Chas tipped on his heels, scanned the aisles to see what was interesting.

"Is that for cattle, sir?"

"Do I look like a pig farmer to you? Or sheep?" He bounced forward on his toes. The boy backed up. Just a whip of a kid. Gangling and gawky.

"How many sacks?"

Chas thought on it, picked at his chin. "Stack them tight, make it twenty."

The boy smiled. His big sale of the day. "Cash or credit?"

Chas cocked his thumb at the speaker overhead. "Coker know you play that stuff when he's not around?" Chas shuffled an awkward dance step, gave up. "An abomination." He stepped toward the door. "You go about your business. Seems I forgot to bring cash. You tell Coker I said hi."

"Who do I say, sir?"

But Chas was already in the warehouse stepping toward the open bay doors. The sun was shining. It was turning into one of those bright days with the sun hooked high in the wide blue. He looked over his shoulder and the boy had gone back to the shelves, hips twitching to the music. Chas looked around. Feed. Feed and more feed. And then his eyes alighted on the thing he was looking for but hadn't realized until this moment. He snatched the small box under his coat and jumped off the loading ramp. He tossed the box under the seat. When he backed the truck out, the sun struck off the glazed windshield, a blinding white, and as quickly gone. But he felt like he'd been riven from the head through the heels by a bolt of lightning, bored clean in a single stroke of inspiration. If he opened his mouth now he would speak in tongues.

Chapter Seven

I n the kitchen, at the plank table swept clean with the heel of his hand, Chas sliced cubes of meat. Tenderloin. For each cube he slit a pocket, ran his finger back and forth inside, cleaning a nice tight space. He hummed "Rock of Ages," a tune his mama had been fond of. On the table in front of him was the box he'd lifted from Coker's mill. Twenty-five silver-foil packets of rat poison, stacked in fives. He unwrapped one, sniffed. Good enough to eat. He tucked it into a meat pocket, squeezed the opening shut behind the treat, and set it aside. He worked at a leisurely pace.

"Big dogs, little dogs. Here, Fido." He practiced whistling, imagined a dog, any one—fat-bellied, long-legged, parti-colored—creeping up to filch the treat, gobble it down. He tucked two in for good measure. Set it to the left, earmarked for a big dog, a very big dog.

He thought of Taylor's yapping little mutt. Coker's heeler on a short chain. The assorted town dogs. One night's work.

He had no use for dogs, nor did his father, who also had no use for cats, women, or children, though he'd saddled himself with a wife, and with her fathered a child. What delight in that? Like feeding poison to a dog. Only draw it out over years. He pictured his mother, the sincere, ineffectual woman· she was—hope-chest linens bleached and soured, bleached and soured—taking Avery into herself like every hurt he ever doled out.

Until the hundred daily doses took their toll, and she walked with her hands cupping her stomach, as if they held a cancer. Though by nature a tidy woman, she became meticulous, windows glossy with polish, the corners of the wood floor picked clean. He supposed he should have known by the way the bun of hair at the nape of her neck was strung tighter and tighter, until the hairs pulled loose from her temples, trailing down her back or over her shoulder, and she snatched them out and burned them in the woodstove, a stinging stink that marked the hours that last day.

He shook his head. He should have known that in the deep night she would steal herself away to the barn, so that in the morning, when he went out to chores, Avery would find her hanging plumb from the rafter.

Chas set another large dose aside. Some creatures were born to be martyrs: cattle, hogs, sheep, goats, dogs, chickens, women. When he'd used up the last of the silver packets, he slung the prepared meat into a paper sack.

Outside, the night was black under the new moon and the stars pulsed with a light so clear and close that when Chas put his head back, it seemed as though the heavens were falling, and his arms spread out to check his sudden dizziness, the paper bundle in his hand swinging back and forth until Chas tucked it close to his side, as a hand might steady a racing heart. The truck windows were sealed with frost and he waited in the cold while the defroster raged, his breath building a white rime on eyelashes and brows. He planned a route. He'd save most of it for the town dogs, but with nearly two dozen doses in hand, he could afford to be generous.

He wheeled down the highway in a state of near giddiness. It was not the act of killing itself that enthused him, but the sense of purpose once again, direction, if even so fleeting as for these brief hours. He'd found again an urgency that set the clock moving forward on real time, and wasn't that what terrified him most these days, how he'd discovered his life to have become nothing more than a string of odd moments that turned into hours that turned into days that amounted to nothing? Sometimes he felt like the dead in waiting.

Outside of town, Chas turned his headlights off and angled down side streets. He parked in back of Truman's shop, the town's mechanic, always a changing group of cars and trucks awaiting maintenance back there. No one would notice another vehicle. Chas set out on foot, found he could generally pitch the meat the distance to where the dog was chained. He came across a stray in the grocer's back lot, foraging at the base of a Dumpster. A midsized long-haired mongrel, asymmetrical white and black coloration—heeler cross, maybe. It padded up to Chas with its nose narrowing in on the bag. Chas moved into the building's shadow. The dog followed. He told it, "Sit." The dog sat, tail wagging. "Down," he said, and the animal slumped to its belly. "Good boy." Chas patted the wide dome of its head. Its dark eyes were raised, trusting. Chas reached into the bag, pulled out a cube of meat. The dog sat up. Chas drew the meat back. "No," he said. "Down." And the dog complied.

"Better," Chas said. He stroked the striped black and white brows. The dog's breath warmed his knuckles and the tail gently thumped the asphalt. He cupped the jaw in one hand, held the meat at a level with the dog's eyes. Chas could almost swear the animal smiled. "I believe it will be fast," he said, surprised at how much that sounded like an apology. No difference, he told himself, one death or another, cattle or dog. Still he held off and the moment passed into another and another, longer yet. Just minutes ago, two blocks away, it had been easy enough tossing the meat over a fence, staying to hear the gabble of a chained hound as it wolfed down the treat. And it wasn't as if he were foreign to the sound of dropping bodies, and despite the reasons he might give others or himself on a more resourceful day, he *was* aware of his own part in the *cause* and *manner* of his cattles' deaths. The dog rested its head on its paws, eyes steady on Chas. Finally, it was all about the killing itself. Because he could. Because he wanted to. For although they might believe him a fool and helpless, still he was, after all, not really *harmless*.

The dog shifted, creeping toward the bag on the ground, masking its motives with a gesture of affection—it laid its head on Chas's knee. Chas smiled. It was in the nature of dogs to be fools for man. He ruffled the dog's neck, feeling a keen sense of regret. He wished there was someone he could talk to about it. "Stay," he said, and perched the cube of meat on the dog's nose. The dog sniffed delicately, but held in place, its eyes alert on the meat. It would be a matter of self-determination. "You be a good boy now, and we'll just see . . ." He took his hand away from the dog's muzzle, the meat floating in the dark on top of the dog's nose. "Stay," he ordered. He would give it a minute, maybe two more, and if in that time the dog held faith . . . well, then . . .

Chas crouched back on his heels admiring the way the dog balanced its split nature—heart against gut. The temperature was dropping and Chas flipped his jacket collar up, muffled his hands in pockets. A hoar frost was building, and over the parking lot, beneath the arc of a street lamp he could see a shimmering mist rising in the light, like powdered glass. By morning the overhead wires would bristle with frost and the scrub brush, the tumbleweed and sage would thicken, grow coats of crystal, like coral conceived in a sea of air. Chas lifted his face, closed his eyes, and imagined the utter stillness, the long night of dreaming it would take to grow a coat of ice. It was so quiet, he believed he could hear the crystals forming and that he could hear the shush of tires on the highway miles away, the bang of a pot in a kitchen nearby. And then the distant bark of a dog roused him like an alarm, and when he looked down to the dog at his feet, it lay there waiting patiently in the dark with its eyes trained to Chas. The chunk of meat was gone.

"Good boy," Chas said, and felt neither joy nor disappointment, but relief as if the dog's willful act were an affirmation of Chas's own. One way or another we were all made to swallow our own death.

Ike left the office midmorning. He'd called the courthouse. No word from Stubblefield and the judge wasn't about to rush it. Ike parked outside Purvis's barn, let the heater warm him before stepping into the cold. He was getting soft. As a kid, he'd worked long hours outdoors and in the barns with January temperatures averaging in the single digits and snow to the eaves. But here, the difficulties were of a different nature. Here, in the open, snow traveled, always shifting, and with no buildings as referents you didn't know how deep until you were in it. So easy to become lost. It all came down to getting lost. You were or you weren't and he felt himself continually stumbling between the two. A hell of a thing to admit if you're sheriff.

Ike found his friend in the pole barn. There was a row of dead dogs, assorted by size, muzzles clenched over teeth, tongues distended. "Been coming in all morning," Purvis said. "Joe's out, picking up more." He nudged a stiff terrier with a toe.

"What's going on?" Ike asked.

Purvis peeled back a dog's lips—a shepherd gone fat and too soft to ward off that last unfriendly hand. "Strychnine. Not a pretty death. Run-of-the-mill rat poison. Whole world's gone cockeyed. Nine dead dogs and more on the way." He stopped for breath, gripped his stomach. "And I haven't had breakfast yet."

Ike led the way into the living quarters. He opened the refrigerator with a familiarity, already knowing what he'd find—plastic bags filled with the odds and ends of animals. Tissue samples in wafered slices. Vials of blood and urine. "Purvis," Ike said, "no wonder you don't eat at home."

"What?" He turned with his hands dripping, reached for a towel, smelled it first, then wiped his hands. "Perfectly safe. They're all contained. I keep the semen in the freezer." He joined Ike, brought out a dozen eggs, a quart of milk, two pork chops, and some leftover green beans which Ike pitched into the garbage.

Ike fried the chops, salvaged some potatoes for hash browns, and topped it with four eggs. They cleared a space at the kitchen table and sat to eat. Purvis made the coffee so Ike drank water.

Ike spooned up more eggs and potatoes. "Joe's been suspended from school, you know that?"

Purvis nodded again. "He told me."

"For drinking. Been hanging out with Lester Colcox."

"Didn't tell me that."

Ike took a bite of the pork chop, chewed it slowly. "I thought you might like to know is all."

Purvis finished the plate of food, shoved it back. "Thanks," he said.

He looked to the door that led to the surgery and the barn. "There's more out there than a man wants to know or can deal with. You know, Joe could do well. He could be a vet. Or a lawyer, or doctor, or I don't know what, don't really care. But he could *be* someone, given a chance."

"You sure he wants one?"

Purvis looked down at the empty plate. "Best breakfast I've had in this kitchen. I don't know. He comes around, we work and talk. He's got my Chevy running. Did I tell you that?"

"No." Ike smiled. "When's the unveiling?"

"Spring. When the ice's off the roads. I'm going to buy a Panama hat and a good cigar, and I'm going to drive Main Street on a warm night with the windows down and wave at everybody, like I was my own parade."

Purvis rubbed his belly. "Maybe I'll drive clear to Illinois, pull into Leroy's Custard stand, order a double thick malt, cheeseburger, and fries, and be the envy of every sixteen-year-old there."

"You miss Illinois?"

Purvis smiled. "Sometimes. When I'm picking cheat grass out of an animal's eyes and there's not a quarter of shade for miles and the water tastes like piss. But mostly when you come around asking questions like that. You got a case of it, don't you?"

"Winter blues is all."

"Well, I put myself here and I'm bullheaded enough to stick with it. And truth is, I've come to love it. Imagine that, come to see a whole lot of nothing as beautiful." A truck pulled up outside. "That's Joe," Purvis said, rising from the table, and they both went to see what the boy brought.

He looked young but comfortable behind the wheel–driving ranch rigs since twelve, licensed at fifteen. They pushed young boys to adulthood out here, Ike thought, or maybe elsewhere they were coddled too long? Who was to say? He didn't understand children and maybe that had to do with being an only child. And maybe that had to do with his discomfort about having children of his own. But now, come fall, it looked like Justin would be moving in, turning tables every which way.

And here was the old bachelor, Purvis, taking Joe under his wing. What was it that made middle-aged men believe they could raise a child better than they could have as a younger, fitter man? Discipline. Reserves of patience. Or something more selfish? A last stab at making a difference.

There were two dogs lying in the back of the truck—a heeler and a border collie. "Picked this one up just outside of town. Coker's dog," Joe said.

Ike prodded it with a finger. "How do you know?"

"Saw him dump it." He turned to Purvis.

Ike lifted the dog off the truck bed. Joe carried the other dog. Purvis opened the door for them and Joe moved up alongside Ike.

"Hard to believe somebody would do this." Joe shook his head. "Think it was someone we know?"

Pattiann pulled into her parents' drive, four miles of frozen road, snowbanks scalloped by the wind. She didn't remember a winter with this much snow. Good for the soil come spring. They were still a long way off on the water table and it would take years of good snows, wet springs to make up for it. A beneficent decade or two—and that's the way you had to see it out here—a generation spent keeping even, or catching up for your children's time on the land.

A kestrel on the fence, neck feathers ruffled, watched for movement—mice bulldozing snow tunnels, a system of veins bulging on the otherwise flat white surface. And if she stepped out of the truck and walked across the snow, she'd see where mice had rooted up to the surface, their small freckled prints. Or maybe she'd see the scoring of wings where hawks and prairie chickens made their floundering takeoffs. And jackrabbit tracks like exclamation points. Pockets where elk bedded. Fox spoor. Raccoon—a pestilence of them these past years, decimating the prairie chickens. What had tipped the balance, upset the numbers. Something new, a crop, fertilizer? Or was it a matter of accretion? Because somehow, each minor change seemed to snowball. Take out the buffalo. The wolves, ferrets, fox, hawks, eagles. Introduce roads and towns, fireweed, cheat grass, cattle, people, and garbage, and watch it all turn topsy-turvy, slowly, over a hundred years, until it never seemed to be anything other than it was right now and you're confounded by the way prairie dogs colonize in numbers out of proportion and raccoon invade and there aren't enough bullets, traps, or people on God's green earth to answer for it. But it's always been tough out here, and at least, by God, you don't have the wolves to contend with. And here is where she was torn, because this was all she had ever known, and didn't want to see it change either, could not bring herself to leave, could not argue for the return of wolves and buffalo and unpopulated grasslands because she believed herself as native as the trees and rocks and snakes. It was not something she could undo. She had tried.

Rob's truck was parked next to the barn, but the horses were out, so she assumed they were checking the herd, fence, or both. Or bringing the cows down for calving, short weeks away. And that was what she'd enjoyed most. Late nights alone in the barn. The warm pen. The cow's grunting, the crick of wood. The first earnest pushes.

She set her foot on the driveway, found the familiar strange. It had been a long time since she'd come to her parents' house. Anger? Avoidance? Or just more comfortable to leave things where she'd left them.

The door was unlocked, as always, even when they drove into town. *A hell of a way to drive for little enough worth taking,* her mother'd always said. The living room was unchanged, though less managed. A quiet dishevelment. Rugs needed vacuuming, tables dusting. Her father's spot was neat, papers folded, his reading glasses clean and on the table where he'd reach over and swing them up over his nose, screw them down tight on his ears as if he faced a brisk wind. She pictured him, feet in a pail of Epsom Salts water, *Rancher's Quarterly* or *Horse and Tack* or his private addiction *Field and Stream* propped open on his lap, though she couldn't remember the last time he'd taken off for a pack trip or fished. She supposed it had to do with her mother's health, his own aging.

As a younger man, twice a year, he'd take a four-day weekend with friends: Bill Baxter, Charlie Potts, Blair Oliver, Jason Fales. They'd meet at the ranch, horse trailers loaded, supplies tarped down in pickups, and they'd plan in the kitchen while it was still dark outside, stewing over maps they knew by heart. Her mother packed lunches and waited for them to be gone, for her own vacation to begin, one less mouth to feed—two when Rob got old enough—and time in the evening to read, put off the dishes until morning, or drive herself and Pattiann to Lewistown for dinner, a movie, and a night in a motel where someone else made the bed. A second-rate adventure for Pattiann, who had wanted, more than anything, to be with the men on horseback in the mountains.

Pattiann called out, hoping it wouldn't startle her mother too badly. She called again, and from the bedroom her mother answered, "Be right there. Give me a moment."

When her mother came into the room, she acted as if her daughter stopped regularly, as if years were days. "Got some coffee on." She headed into the kitchen. Pattiann poured, cut the cake, and served them on the unchipped china—*company* plates. "I was just driving by," she said.

Her mother nodded. She wouldn't question it any more than she'd believe it. "Your dad and Rob are bringing the cows in. There's going to be a bad blow yet. Something's coming. You laugh, but I can feel it. Don't I sound like one of the old men? Age makes you a believer. We're never far from the clay God formed us from." She sipped the hot coffee. She set the cup down gently. "I'm hardpan gone to gumbo. You'll have to excuse the mess." She thumbed toward the dishes, stacked and waiting. "I get to them, just not as quick as I used to."

"You could use a dishwasher," Pattiann said.

"Never as clean as hand-washed. And work keeps a person motivated. Damned if I'm going to do less than I can. And I *can* do it. Just not as quick."

Their coffee cooled. Tenderness had never been an easy thing between them.

Martha tapped a finger on the table. "Ike's well?"

Pattiann nodded.

Martha smiled. "He's a good man for a hard job."

"Husband or sheriff?"

"Ha," Martha shouted. "When you were a baby, you gummed my teats like you wanted it all—milk and meat." She leaned forward, propped her chin on a hand. "Never lost that appetite, did you?"

Pattiann waited.

Martha looked around the kitchen. "My mama would have said I had it all. Married to the neighbor boy, properties buddied up. Deeded over the home place day after my father's funeral. Now don't go mistaking me, I loved your daddy, would have married him land or no, but it pleased my mama to see the place grow. The day we bulldozed the homestead, she stood with us. Said she wanted to see the place as she'd first seen it. 'Prettiest piece of land in God's good eyes,' she said, 'before we put up that butt-ugly tar paper shack.' The same shack she raised me in, addition by addition.

"Right up to the moment the last wall fell, she seemed pleased. Walked in the cat's treads where the living room used to be. It was the strangest thing I've ever seen come over a person. There was my mama, her feet planted on those rocking walls, crazy happy one minute, and then you could see her whole body shift, at odds with itself. And her eyes wandering like they'd lost their focus. As if she didn't know where she was anymore. The land had reclaimed it all—her place and history. Just that easy." She snapped her fingers.

"I must have thought about that day a hundred times since. Imagine discovering you can be wiped out so easily, so completely. Or that the one thing you believe you want out of this life can undo you. The house was gone and then so was she." Martha picked at her cake with the fork.

"I wish I'd known her," Pattiann said.

"Well, hell, you're enough like her. She died just before you were born, and sometimes I've thought, if there is such a thing as reincarnation, she didn't wait long or look far."

Pattiann laughed, but Martha stared down at her cake and took a small bite. "Ike's a good man," she said again.

Pattiann nodded.

"Hasn't been easy for him, making his way in here, being sheriff and all. You appreciate that? I mean, sure Art booted himself out of his job, but Ike's earned it. Isn't a person out here knows him or of him and doesn't speak well of him. That's no easy chore."

"It could change," Pattiann said. She slid her plate to a side. Refilled her cup and her mother's.

"Is changing," Martha said and nodded. "Stubblefield. I may be old, but I still get around. I've overheard."

"And?"

"Nobody's pleased. But Stubblefield comes from a long history of not making friends. His daddy, Avery, was a step below coyote in the social register. His daddy, they say, was mean enough to starve the animals for spite. But Chas? They think he's been forced into it by the banks." Martha snorted.

"Chas got in too deep with the banks," Pattiann agreed. "But it was of his own choice."

"I believe that's what your daddy said."

And that surprised Pattiann. Her father taking Ike's side, the law's side, the bankers'. It went against grain.

"Anymore, the small ranchers have trimmed to the bones or sold out. Chas's father doomed him years ago. Chas took on Avery's debt and added his own without a lick of sense. Without an inkling of what was coming down the hi-line.

"These days, ranching's a business, not a way of life. Probability forecasts and money management. Rob's facing it, and I pray to God he makes it, but I won't lay odds, not over the long haul, not for Justin. Maybe it's for the best. I don't know." She reached across the table for her daughter's hand. "But I don't want to be here when the bulldozers wipe it out again. I don't care what the land looked like without us. Is that selfish?"

She shook her head. "The others feel sorry for Chas. But mostly they're thinking it could have been them, might be yet. And that makes it personal. I feel sorry for Chas. It's only natural." She reached up and touched her daughter's cheek, an uncommon gesture between them. "It's going to be harder for you." She lowered her hand. "To know what it is you feel."

Pattiann cleared her throat. Wanted to speak. But it was not something she could put that easily into context, that mix of feelings, love or friendship, pity or guilt.

Martha sighed and ate her cake in silence. When they did talk again, it was of safer things: the ranch, the coming spring, tidbits of town news, the grandkids, and when the kitchen turned warmer with late afternoon sunlight, Pattiann rose from her chair, stacked the dishes. "I've got to go," she said.

"You could stay for dinner. Your dad will be home soon; he'd hate to have missed you."

"I don't think so." Pattiann carried the dishes to the sink. Her mother stayed seated. The dishes in the sink were a reproach. It would have killed her mother as a younger woman to have her kitchen seen this way.

"You don't give your father enough credit. He loves you, always has. He's just not a vocal man."

"I remember him being pretty damn vocal," Pattiann said.

"I remember you could be pretty damn deaf."

The two women looked at each other across the kitchen. Long shadows tilted across the floor, over the checked linoleum still buckled at the doorway. The refrigerator hummed softly. Pattiann suddenly felt the poor daughter; she was the stranger she'd always thought Harriet to be. She lifted a clean dishrag from a drawer. "You want help with these dishes?"

Martha waved her off. "I can do them later. I can still do for myself."

Pattiann smiled down at her hands. It was never easy. "You want me to stay?" she asked. "Then give me a reason."

"All right." Martha labored over the words, as if chipping them out of hardpan. "You wash. I'll dry."

By the time Pattiann drove out, the sky was a bruised light paling to gray. When her father'd come back with Rob, he hadn't seemed surprised to find her there, or the dishes cleaned, the floor mopped, and the house tidied. And that was like him—more likely to question the ways of

God than women. Pattiann took her leave before she could be talked into dinner. Easy enough. She used Ike as an excuse. "He'd starve without me," she said, which was unfair to Ike, but her father seemed to find that idea reassuring.

She wound out through the private road, onto county, flicked the headlights on. In this twilight, with the roads straight as furrows, distances were abbreviated, the sky and land fused gray on gray. The temptation was to let the rig steer itself down the straight and narrow. She could drive this road in her sleep. The bump of tires over cattle guards, then the quick hitch over Beaver Creek Bridge where as a child she'd caught carp and hell from her father for calling them trout.

She thought about her grandmother watching the bulldozer wipe the slate clean and herself with it. And then she was approaching Stubblefield's and found herself slowing. As a family, they'd had little to do with Stubblefields, though their proximity might have dictated otherwise, would have in any other case. What did she remember of Chas as a boy? Not much, a kid riding fences. She thought she remembered the mother, a tall, slim woman, snatching clothes off the line. A blur as they trundled past in the old pickup, she and Rob piled in back, shouting open-mouthed into the wind.

And then like a memory called up, there was Chas, his truck stalled on the side of the road, and he was waving her down. She hit the brakes even as she knew she shouldn't. She came to a stop twenty yards farther on. Stubblefield loped up.

He leaned against the closed window, hands cupped around his face. He smiled, and there was the boyishness she'd always found so attractive. He tapped the glass with a forefinger. She rolled down the window.

"You need help, Chas?"

"I need to see the judge on business, and my truck's down. You headed to town?"

She paused and saw this amused Chas.

"Just a ride," he said. He hooked his fingers over the door, the nailbeds scoured and red.

"Why don't you phone?"

"It's turned off. Thought you'd heard—my life's gone to shit and back."

And he did look lost, befuddled by the calamity his life had become, and Pattiann felt a twinge of guilt, a certain culpability in how she'd abandoned him. But no, that wasn't the truth of it, was it?

"Jesus, but that heater feels good," he said. "You going to give me a ride? Honest to God, I'm going to drop with cold if you don't say yes." He crossed his heart, and the gesture struck her like a blow. That old joke between them. She reached over and unlocked the passenger door.

Chas bolted around the front of the truck, slapping the hood so that it banged, the sound still jolting through Pattiann as he clambered in. He slid his left arm over the bench seat to rest behind her neck. "I am not a prosperous man, but in friends. I'll tell you what—" He opened the door again, swung his legs out. "You wait. I got something." And he was running toward the house.

Out in the yard a knot of cattle stood, sides stoved in, and she realized that in all the times she'd driven past his spread she'd avoided looking, and even now it was just a glance, as if at a shameful thing she had a part in, something nasty. She shifted on the seat, tapped the wheel with her fingers. She could leave. Yank the door shut, throw the truck in gear, and haul ass. Which was only common sense. It would be dark before she got to town. She was thinking of driving down the highway alone with Chas. Her foot dropped the clutch, she slipped the stick into gear— the path of least resistance—but then she was back in neutral. She couldn't just leave. Mostly she didn't want Chas knowing he had disturbed her enough to send her running. Again.

She looked across the yard with its covey of junk to the house with its boards weathered to a dark gleaming. It might have been a nice place at one time, a trim little construction with generous windows bracing either side of the door and fronted by a covered porch with many of its spindle rails missing, a gap-toothed look that was strangely charming. The door opened and Chas swung it shut behind him. He jumped off the porch, tripped, slid to a knee. He limped to the truck door, his cheeks a high red with cold and embarrassment. He raked a hand through his hair, tossed a wrapped parcel on the floor, and stepped in. "Meat," he said. "Sirloin tips."

"Thanks, Chas, but—"

"I got more beef than I can eat." He laughed and looked out at the pen where a few cattle milled. The horse pawed at the snow, moved on. "They ain't much to look at," Chas said, "but they're all mine. Raised every mother one of them. You got a minute? You want to meet them? Pay your respects to the dead?"

"Look, Chas—"

"Your husband does that, you know. Comes out late at night to visit that old horse out there, feeds it when he thinks I'm not looking. Even offered cash for it—down to three legs with age and less with hunger—imagine that. Only neighborly to turn him down. Good thing he's a sheriff, your husband, don't know shit about livestock."

"Ike?"

Chas nodded. "Wants my horse. Maybe the whole spread. You'd like that. Always wanted a place, didn't you?"

She looked stung. "You don't know what I want, Chas."

He slung his arm back over the seat. "Knew you once," he said, and his hand bundled her hair gently. "Know you still." He rubbed her hair between his fingers like coins.

Pattiann didn't move. She could feel his hand on her neck, and the heat rising in her face. "You'd better step out," she said.

"No." Chas shook his head. He released her hair, moved his hand back to his lap. "It's a cold, cold walk to town, and no telling when someone else might come along. I got business with the judge—news he and your husband have been waiting on. Now I understand that we've got some unfinished business you might be uncomfortable with, so you *could* order me out of here and get along with your life . . . or you could help me get this over with."

She punched in the clutch, put the truck in gear, and pulled out. Chas settled his hands on his knees. "Nothing like a proper truck," he said. "Mine's a good old heap. Runs all right, except now and then."

They drove in silence.

Chas shifted, toed the packaged meat to a side. "It's good meat, you know. Fried some up for myself the other night." He whistled softly, stopped. "Damn," he said, looked out the side window. "I find myself with a shitload of time now, you know?" He turned to her. Her face was grim. "Find myself thinking on the strangest things. Things I haven't thought on for years—like you. We're two of a kind, you and me. Two sides of the same coin—your daddy trained you for what you can't have, and mine left me what he didn't prepare me for." He fidgeted in his pocket, pulled out a dime. He flipped it, let it drop. "We'd have made a good couple."

Pattiann flicked him a sidelong glance. "Chas, we made a lousy couple."

Chas turned back toward the window. His legs were splayed and the one kneecap was dark with wet and dirt where he had fallen. It was touching, like a dirty knee on an errant child. She wondered if the skin was scuffed beneath. She looked away, up the road for the town lights she knew were miles and miles away yet. The sky had darkened and the road spun out broad and white in the headlights.

"Well, good or no, it's always been a mystery what brings two people together. I used to wonder about what my mother saw in my father. She was a woman of no particular talent, except faith, and maybe that was enough. You know, faith sets you up for things like that. Believe long enough in the fall and, by God, you'll fall. Head over heels for a man who hit rock bottom and liked it there. What is it Satan says in *Paradise Lost*—better to rule in hell than serve in heaven? Think he had Montana in mind?" He rolled down the window, bent his head into the cold air. His hair, bright as flax, whipped from one side to another as he turned his face to and fro. Then he pulled back in; he looked up at the overcast sky. "Not a star in sight. Clouds. More clouds." He closed the window.

They turned onto the highway and Pattiann relaxed, drove a bit faster on the plowed pavement.

"Want to know what I've decided to tell the judge?"

He surprised her with that. And, yes, she did want to know, but didn't find it in herself to ask.

"No? It's no secret, leastways it won't be. Hey, say what, I'll tell you a *real* secret and then you give me one. Like best friends."

"I don't think there's a thing I could tell you, Chas."

"No?" He scrubbed at his cheeks with the palm of his hand. "What to tell?" Then he slapped his hand back on his knee and took a deep breath. "One time, when I was about five, I found this cat. A small scruffy thing. My daddy was gone for a few days, cattle sale, or some such excuse, so I carried it home to show to my mama. She says we'd keep it, *just for the time being,* because we both knew he wasn't going to stand for no cat. But after a day or two, she'd taken a real liking to the animal, and so when my father returned, we kept it hid, she and I. For a day and a half, we fed it leftovers, tucked it under the quilts with me at night." His face lit. "By God, she liked that little beast, though by then I'd about come to hate it, the fleabites and claws. But that seemed a small enough price to pay. She wasn't happy often, and it was a thing to see.

"Until my father smelled it out. He had a nose on him; I give him that. He could smell out anything. Told me once, he could sniff out my mama's woman parts in a whorehouse. 'Sanctimonious,' he'd call them—'the smell of God with dirty hands.' " He looked over at Pattiann to see how she was taking it. He wished he could see if she were blushing, but she stared at the road, concentrating as though the highway might veer where it never had before. And that seemed reasonable to Chas. Having seen firsthand how the familiar shifts and cants under your feet—one day prosperous, the next day a hundred less cattle, no two mornings alike no matter how many you woke to. "Now," he said, "I hope you're not offended, but the hard part about secrets, you understand"—he leaned toward her, rested his hand on the space between them—"is that you got to tell it all or nothing."

She nodded.

"Anyway, by the second morning, he found the cat in my room, hauled it out by the scruff of the neck. I've never been able to figure it, I mean, it had clawed me often enough—but in my daddy's hands it went limp as a hung man. And even when my daddy shook it in my face, all it did was blink. 'Where'd you get this?' he asks me.

"To give my mama credit, she said, 'No, Avery,' maybe once, twice. But he was not a man to be deterred, and so he asks again. I can hear the cat panting. And then he lays his other hand on the back of my neck like he does the cat."

He paused and in the silence there was the hum of the tires on the highway and her steady breathing with which he willingly fell into step. The indicator lights in the truck dash gave off a dim, green glow that buffed the knuckles of Pattiann's fingers, the point of her chin and cheekbones. The highway markers closed in the dark behind them. He pinched his eyes shut. Opened them and picked the story back up.

"My daddy's hand tightens on my neck, cricks my head over to a side. I hear the cat yowl.

"Then I hear a snick from his left hand and the cat stops blinking. He hands me the body. 'Bury this.' And I did. Took the cat to the manure pile, dug a space with my own hands, and stuffed it in. I wasn't about to question my daddy ever again."

Chas took a deep breath, eased it out between his teeth. Pattiann stared ahead. She reached over, turned the heater down. He thought he could smell sweat and perfume, wondered what it would be like to take her in the cab of the truck, or in the flatbed, the cold iron against her back tempering his heat. He wondered if she'd feel different now, all these years later, wondered if her bones had grown longer, or looser, if her flesh were still dimpled so sweetly over her ass. He looked out the window so she wouldn't see it on his face, but he slung his arm once again over the back of the seat, his fingers behind her neck.

"That old man kept things lively." He laughed. "The old coot. Lived longer than he had a right to." He paused. "Wasn't about to give the ranch over to no one, especially not me. But then there he was, dead at last. Do you have any idea what it feels like to find the thing you've stopped believing can happen, suddenly has, and the porch you're standing on is yours, and all the land becomes particular to you, every stone and shrub, and all the creatures on it, and even the Goddamned stars are at attention and the night's not big enough? And I wouldn't have been more surprised," he said, "if the sky had opened up and trumpets sounded." He giggled. "I half expected the world to end."

"But it didn't," she said.

Chas leaned his forehead against the side window. "No," he said softly. "Not then." He watched the road wheel away beneath them. He looked over at her, saw in the tilt of her head, the way her face softened, something reminiscent of that time between them, and it moved him so that he believed he could risk asking. "Why'd you leave?" His voice nearest a whisper. "Run off like that? Sometimes I think if I had a chance at all in this world, it was with you."

Her hands tightened on the wheel. She shook her head. "Damn you, Chas."

He had stung her and there was a pleasure in it, not exactly happiness, but something deeper, more integral, like releasing a long-held breath.

Her voice was calm. "This is a pretty time to dump this load of crap on me. All these years later. I've got to wonder if you're remembering the same time I am. I mean, how do you see us as being so *good* together? Because we could drink each other under the table, and we never hurt one another beyond a slap or two. I guess that's on the plus side."

She swiped at her face, as if some microscopic bug pestered her, a nervous habit that usually signaled the beginning of a blowout between them. It was a gesture he'd come to hate, seeing himself as that invisible gnat flinching about her face.

"But what were the good times, really? When we rolled the car and neither of us remembered who was driving? How about the time I came to in my own vomit, on the side of the road, twenty miles from town, and you were gone and so was the car? I mean, this is all just so much crap—if you cared to be honest at all, you'd admit the only thing we were good for with each other was trouble. And that has a pretty limited appeal in the long run."

"We were young, reckless," he said. "It would have changed, if you'd given it time."

"No," she said. Her eyes narrowed. "You think if we'd stayed together, everything would be different—your ranch intact, your cattle healthy. But the truth is, had I stayed, it would have still turned out as badly as it has, because all we had between us was an interest in self-destruction. As long as we could hurt each other or ourselves, we got on fine. But it couldn't stay there, between us, could it? That kind of hurt spreads."

She cracked the window a moment, let the air rouse her, then cranked it shut. "My secret," she said. "Why I left in such a hurry."

Pattiann downshifted for the curve in the highway and the engine whined. This was something it had taken her years to let go. Except in dreams. And sometimes she woke up sweating, heart pounding, the air thick as smoke. It had been a long time since she'd allowed herself to think about those years—her drinking, the hurt she heaped on her family. And taking up with Stubblefield. Mostly to get back at her father. How he'd laughed when she'd asked which half of the ranch would be hers. *Honey, you know* the ranch will be Rob's. *Hell, someday you'll have a husband with his own spread, and if he's any part smart, you'll be his right-hand man.*

"You and I, we'd been to the Stockmans' earlier on, bought a bottle and drove out to my folks' place."

He nodded, grinned at her. "You were wearing jeans and a shirt with little flowers, blue ones."

She tried to call that evening to mind with a clarity that matched his. But it was difficult. She'd spent so much time trying to forget.

Chas started in again. "In the wheat," he said. "Same place I'd first bedded you, back of your pa's place, south field. Damn, but we were eager." His voice was almost reverential, as if surprised at the ambitions of the body, the heedless way the young take in life like air into lungs. "Barely time to unzip."

Pattiann's eyes were focused on the road. Her jaw worked, clenching and releasing. "We fucked. We finished and I left. Not a pretty sight."

Chas laughed. "Not half so bad, way I remember it. You shed of your shirt, walking away wearing nothing but sex, sweat, and the night air." He wanted to tell her he'd kept the shirt. For the long six years she was gone. And even the first year she was back, like a token, a promise, as if she'd return, if not for him then for that thing she'd left behind—a shirt with small blue flowers on it.

"Drunk or no, I managed to stumble home, right into the house in front of Rob and a couple of the hands, and my mama," and she could see Martha as she was then, staring at Pattiann's breasts, gaze sliding down to the dirty knees on her jeans, the wheat chaff stuck to skin. "Didn't say a word."

"And your daddy?"

"Sent Rob and the men outdoors. Then he walked right up to me, not really looking at me but over my right shoulder. He was making this noise, like his wind had broke. Then he was talking about killing you, and Mama was wrestling with him. I stood there laughing until they stopped. And then he swung back his arm and laid me flat."

"And so you ran away," Chas said.

"They locked me in that night," she said. "I was still higher than a kite and strong. Proud because my dad had knocked me flat and I'd stood back up. Middle of the night I climbed out the window, went to the barn, then walked back out to the south field."

"What'd you get in the barn? A gun?" He raised his head, sniffed intently. "Gasoline," he guessed, and smiled.

"You were gone. It was me and the wheat—the crop I'd helped plant. Before that moment I'd have never believed I had it in me. It was midsummer, the crop still green but filling out. I splashed the gasoline around, struck a match, and it blew me off my feet for the second time in a night."

He threw his head back. "Whoowee," he said. Rubbed his hands together as if before the fire. "It must have been something," Chas said.

"Fire took a good hold for awhile. And then the lights were coming on in the house—I could see them: bedroom light, hall light, living room, kitchen, porch." What she hadn't seen, she knew, her mother at the phone and Rob stumbling into jeans cranky with sleep, scared, and her father loading wet burlap sacks into the back of the pickup and hustling the men to ready the tractor, plow a break around the fire. And in awhile men from other ranches arriving to help, to contain the blaze before it reached the barns, the house.

"I was drunk and sick and scared. I left before they got out there, holed up with a friend for a day, pulled what savings I had, and hitched a ride out."

"And nobody ever knew how the fire started."

Her parents had known. And perhaps that was the thing that had really chased her from her home and town, coming to the realization that her father had always known what she was capable of. Had, in fact, been right to give the ranch to Rob, because when it came right down to it, she'd risked it all—livestock, crops, land and buildings, her family's home and history—in a drunken tantrum. And she'd seen then, the long years she and Chas had been feeding off each other's anger had less to do with love and much more to do with ambition—a staging ground, bolstered by their petty violences, for just such an act of meanness.

They hit the outskirts of town, the first homes snug with light in the kitchens and dining rooms. Ike would be waiting dinner. She had no appetite left. "I burned the land," she said.

"Yeah, well," he said. "You were drunk."

She gripped the wheel, downshifted to the speed limit. She had no answer. Her act was an offense against land, family. But Chas would never see that—his heart as flawed as hers. She stopped at the courthouse. The building was dark. "You could leave a note, I suppose," she said.

He shook his head. "No. I got to see the judge. I'll walk over to his house." He laughed. "Maybe he'll invite me in to dinner."

Pattiann snorted at the idea.

Then Chas was reaching for the door and then he stopped, his hand on the handle. He turned the palm of his free hand up. "None of this talk will change things. You're married now and I understand that." He looked out the side window, then back at her. "But I'm not willing to let it go as easy as this either." He leaned over, spoke softly next to her ear. "We had *some* good times," he said. He buffed her cheek with a kiss. "I remember how you would cry out in my arms." He winked at her, pushed the door open. "Need to thank you, Miss Pattiann, for the ride and talk."

"How you getting home?"

He shrugged, tipped back his hatless head, and studied the sky. He pointed out the North Star. "I'll direct my feet and hike my thumb." He closed the door, bent down into the open window. "I'll threaten to camp out on the judge's sofa. Bet he'll find me a ride then." He stood back, slapped the hood with his hand. He started walking away, turned. "You tell your husband, I'm handing the cattle over. He might forgive you the ride." He turned on his heels and walked off.

Ike came home to an empty house. It was beginning to feel normal. Like everything else in this Goddamned place, a dozen dead dogs, Harley whining because he was on call, and then the only woman deputy complains about sexual innuendoes made by another deputy, Jim Parker—a man Ike's age who sprouted a handlebar mustache, wore his Stetson like a second crop of hair, and lived in another Goddamned century.

"I was just being nice," he'd said, slumping in a chair. He perched his hat low over his eyes. Ike's office door was closed, but shapes congregated outside the frosted glass for an earful.

"Telling her she should go braless so you can see her titties better."

"Maybe I didn't say that."

"Then what?"

He shrugged. "I don't remember." He was smiling now. "Nothing I said ain't been said a hundred times."

"Not by my officers," Ike said, and Jim snickered, so Ike knew he had an afternoon ahead of him with the men. One of those man-to-men chats about respect for fellow officers and workers, one of those friendly commands to stow their juices or he'd have their badges. "You're suspended. Two weeks without pay."

Jim sat up. "You can't—"

"The hell I can't. You're just damned lucky she's not pressing charges, because I'd back her up. *Do you understand?*" Ike kept himself in check. He was angry and you didn't mix anger with discipline.

Jim stood. "Two weeks?" he said. He walked to the door. "Maybe I'll check out the bulletin board for openings elsewhere."

Parker was a good deputy, knew the county, the people, better than any other on the force. Ike didn't want to lose him, but if he pushed it . . . Ike sighed, shrugged.

"You ain't making friends," Parker said. "People here know me."

Ike was tired. He had paperwork to finish. "Two weeks."

Which left him the rest of the day, tied to the office—a flubbed robbery out in Shono, vandalism at the elementary school in Derby, and some drunken boys picked up for driving down the wrong side of the street, and finally, a late afternoon call from Parker's wife calling Ike a sonofabitch and "Just how the hell do you think we'll make truck payments, mortgage, and groceries without two weeks' pay?"

Which finally sent him home, that last call, with his back and head aching, and hungry and in no mood to turn on the lights as he walked through the empty house. So he didn't. He sat in the dark, sipping Dickel, getting lightheaded on the way to drunk if he didn't eat soon, but he wasn't inclined to find his way through the dark for cold chicken or old cheese and bread.

When the phone rang, he was tempted to let it ring. It might be Parker's wife again, or another dead dog. But he picked it up, because it might be Pattiann, and drunk or no, he couldn't leave her out in the dark. It was his mother, long distance from Florida, where she'd moved after marrying Raymond, a retired colonel from the armed services. She'd been thinking of Ike these last several days, and it was probably her turn to call, though who was counting?

Ike lowered into his chair, rested his head against the back, and sipped the whiskey, nodding into the dark, saying yes and fine when necessary.

"Pattiann's not there? You drinking, Ike?"

"Some."

"You want her to find you that way?"

"Yup."

He could hear her breathing into the phone. "Maybe you think I should take it elsewhere?" he said, and thought he was drunker than he'd known. His dad had been a binge drinker who liked his privacy. And yes, he'd loved his dad, but it was his mother he'd believed in. And now he'd hurt her, too. Chalk it up to the fitting end of a perfect day. "I'm sorry. Listen, everything's fine. I had a difficult day at work," he said.

"That's no excuse," she said, as tough at seventy-five as she'd been at forty-three, or thirty-two. He could picture her hands spidered around the receiver, her left leg bouncing as it always did, setting the floor, the ground quivering. As a child he'd found it comforting, and wasn't that a queer thing, the way he could feel her presence alive and leaping through the floorboards, while his father was a quiet absence. "Listen," she went on, "I didn't mean to scold. This is obviously not a good time to talk. Just wanted you to know we're well."

"Good to hear that, Mom. Listen, I'm sorry, too. What say I call you back in a day or two, my nickel."

"Give Pattiann our love," she said and was gone. Always the efficient one, even at good-byes. He thought about filling his glass again, but he wasn't in the mood anymore. As a young man, on the rare times he drank to excess, he was always careful to do it away from home. Like his father before him. His family hadn't been so different from folks out here. What you didn't see, you didn't have to deal with. It made for polite company. He was woozy and closed his eyes, and when he opened them again, perhaps he'd slept a bit. He felt stiff and his tongue thick. There were sounds in the kitchen.

"That you?" he called out.

She peeked in the doorway. "You were asleep, thought I'd wake you for dinner. Got some nice beef."

"Surprise, surprise," he muttered. A cattleman's daughter. He pushed himself out of the chair. His headache stirred and he made his way blinking into the kitchen to douse the beginnings of a hangover. He drank a glass of water at the sink in a few large gulps, came up panting.

"Celebrating?" she asked.

He seated himself in a kitchen chair, poked at a wrapped package. "What's this?"

"Some meat," Pattiann said. "Beef. Chas gave it to us."

"Stubblefield." He hefted the unopened package and studied it. "Giving us gifts now." The package was solid in his hand and he lofted it, trying to guess the weight. Substantial. His mouth had gone dry. He found he had to ask, "You two getting chummy again?"

"For Christ's sake, Ike. He needed a ride, and I was there."

"Convenient." Even as he said it, he knew it was petty. Trite. But his head was pounding and so was his heart and he believed he recognized in her eyes something that hadn't been there that morning. She was avoiding him. He moved in on her, the meat still chilling his palm. He meant to crowd her, push her. Into what? An admission of guilt? Confession?

She cocked her chin high. "How bad do you want this fight?" she asked.

He balanced the meat in one hand, looked at her, then walked to the back door and lobbed it like a football, a long pass into the dark. He heard the thump as it hit the dirt, could see the pale wrapping turn end over end into the bushes. There was the snapping of small twigs and then nothing. The night air was cold on his skin and the shock of it was invigorating. Like a cold shower. Like a good fight. There was silence at his back, and then he heard her long, exasperated sigh.

"That was good meat you just threw to the neighborhood dogs, Ike."

"The neighborhood dogs," he said, and turned back toward her, "are dead. Long live the coyotes." He closed the door. She was standing with her back to the sink, the distance of the kitchen between them. A careful space. And he suddenly believed, as he hadn't to this point, that not only was he was capable of losing her but was capable, in fact, of driving her away. Right into Stubblefield's arms. Again. Maybe that had already happened. And that realization started like a small tic in his gut, a sudden need for caution, that triggered instead something more resembling anger. A part of him was alarmed, how quickly it had escalated to this, tried to clamp down even as another part of him wanted to let it get out of control. Wanted to hurt her in whatever way it took to put her as much at his mercy as he was at hers. With all his years in law enforcement, he believed he understood the attraction of violence, the satisfaction of it, how you became submerged in the act, became the impulse. He did not think himself a violent man, but knew he was susceptible to it, the way the game face you put on before kicking in the door *became your face,* violence begetting violence. And sometimes Ike believed he could smell it when cuffing them, or transporting them away from the scene, could smell it on himself as well, a musk on the skin, a sweetness that quickly turned bitter and soured after the fact.

"What's wrong?" she asked, and touched his hand, and his arm startled out from under her fingers.

He settled his hand in his pocket to cover his surprise at how she had crossed the distance to him in his distraction, and at the same time he tried to resurrect that edge he'd been so carefully walking. "What's wrong? I have the original day from hell and come home to an empty house and you ask what's wrong. Somebody's poisoned half the dogs in the county, I have to suspend my best officer who's threatening to leave me in a lurch in the middle of this . . . this dog killing." He hooked his thumb toward the yard. "And Parker's wife wants to know who's going to pay for groceries and maybe, just maybe, we ought to take that hunk of meat and give it to them." He walked past Pattiann, sat heavily at the table. He was more sober than he wanted to be.

"You suspended Parker?"

"Fuck Parker."

Pattiann stepped away, put the kettle on to simmer. She busied herself at the stove and then she stopped as if to say something, shook her head, and took the lid off the kettle to prod at the contents with a long fork. She tried again. "In case you're wondering, we're having stew, tonight." She waited, put the lid back on. "If you'd turned on a light and read the note I left, you'd know that. It was in the fridge. All you had to do was pop it on the stove to simmer."

"No," he pointed a finger at her. "All I had to do was sit in an easy chair and unwind from a day at work while all you had to do was be here and pop that Goddamned stew on the stove. Instead, you're off wandering around with that half-cocked psychopath, Stubblefield, who's giving you presents now, meat off his half-rotted cows."

He thought she'd blow, and he looked forward to it, an honest fight, some good clean anger to settle the air between them instead of this skulking about. But she eased back into a chair, blinked into the overhead light, and then crossed her hands before her.

"I spent the day at my mother's," she said. Her voice got smaller. "I haven't been much help to her."

And that was so Goddamned unfair of her. Turning him upside down. Making him feel the lout, and worse yet, never intending to. He dropped his head into his hands, felt the headache bloom, the day's frustrations, Parker and Harley. And Stubblefield—the one who made the whole thing personal as the law was never meant to be. "We got any aspirin?" he asked. She brought him two and another full glass of water.

She sat across from him after he swallowed the pills. "I was coming home when Chas waved me down. His truck was stalled on the roadside."

She got that look in her eyes that came at rare moments, so that they lit a little sharper and her brows drew tighter. She took a deep breath and leaned back. "And I knew you wouldn't like it, but he *needed* a ride, so I gave him one, and as a thank-you, he gave me the meat. Nothing more, nothing less. He's going to turn the cattle over. He came in to tell the judge." She waited.

Tomorrow would be no better, he thought. Except that maybe they could begin to put this Stubblefield business behind them. He wanted to reach across the table, take her hand in his, but he didn't trust himself yet. "How's your mama?" he asked instead, and, "When do we eat?" Though he wasn't sure he could swallow a bite.

As it happened, the judge patted Chas on the back. "Good, good," he said. "Better this way."

Chas said how happy it made him to come out a hero in this sorry mess. They stood in the foyer. Over the judge's shoulder a door opened on the living room. Beyond that, in the next room, was a table laid out in dinnerware. "Well, I just wanted you to know there ain't no hard feelings. Smells good. Pork?"

He could swear the judge cringed. Chas smiled. "Got beef at home. Good cuts. A little on the lean side, but only does the heart good, right?" He slapped the judge on the shoulder and the old man rocked. "But it's a cold night, and a hell of a walk on an empty stomach. Truck broke down, had to hitch a ride in. Don't know how I'm getting home. Maybe I'll hang till morning, find a *neighbor* with a spare room. Surely God will provide for His stray lamb? Though this being cattle country, *our* God don't abide sheep. Pork, you say?" And that was when the judge made the phone call. Moments later, a squad drew up and Chas was on his way.

The ride home was silent. The thin-lipped young deputy, Harley, insisted Chas sit in back, behind the cage, beyond reach of the shotgun, and maybe that was a smart move, because Chas was feeling churlish, up to his craw with bigger-and-better-than-thou types, and Harley was just another example, fiddling with the radio, rolling through stops and flipping on the overheads at the one traffic light in town, as though this were a real emergency. God suffered more fools than He had a right to.

At home, Chas moved the horse into the barn, gave it the last of the feed cakes. As for the cattle, they were out of his hands now and there was nothing left he could do for them, except maybe put a hole through somebody's head—Sam Coker, or Taylor.

He'd resigned himself to what would inevitably happen. When the sheriff and his helpers came, they would find what they'd find—cattle good as dead anyway, anemic and developing coughs that laid them lower than hunger did. Cattle that had long ago stripped the jack pines, needles greening their tongues, to abort their fetuses. What protein they burned came from the liver, spleen, and muscles. Did Parsons know this, that they stop pissing after awhile? What was spared was the heart and brain. Nature's questionable taste in jokes—the heart keeps beating so the brain takes it all in, all the hope and pain.

The piebald nickered, snuffing the bare floor for more feed, rocked against the stall. His daddy's old horse. Down to its last legs anyway, but fitter than the rest of his stock. The sheriff had kindly seen to that. And that was why Chas hid the horse now. Call it one small blow. Let the nag starve. He still had that right. He'd given them the cattle, but the horse was his, and in case they meant to argue it–what they didn't know they wouldn't miss. He leaned over the stall and the piebald crooked its muzzle toward him. "Now you get hungry, you let me know," he said to the horse and laughed. He walked to the house. The sheriff would take the cattle out of Chas's hands in a day or two. He would take another piece of Chas's life away, even that last piece, and call it humane, and then he'd go home and warm his feet against Pattiann's back cheeks. And that picture proved too much to imagine, so that Chas could not use it, not even to prick his anger. Instead, he thought of her riding the long miles in the truck with him, how, willingly or not, she made him feel as if there was still something left for him. And he did not know whether he meant to thank her for that or curse her.

He stopped in the doorway. He turned to the yard, gazed out over the bones of cars, rusted fenders and gaping doors, discarded balers, an old wagon bed, the odd hubcap eyeing him from the shrinking snow. He lifted his sight, beyond the corral where the steaming breath of cattle fogged the air, to the open land that appeared, even now, as it had the night he'd held his dying father, to invite dreams, so generously expansive it was. Enough land to make a man itch with possibilities. *It could have been,* he thought. He stepped in and closed the door behind him. *Could have been,* but for all the things in this world beyond a man's knowing, all the slights stacked up against him. No. This was no accident, no casual catastrophe of nature. It was a trail of culpability: the mill, the bank, the government. And by whose higher hand the drought, then winter? It was provoked. And it occurred to him, that if there were any *real* justice in this world–if God were a man, He'd come down again, just so Chas could put a bullet in His head.

Chapter Eight

It took three days to arrange and another two days stalled by bad weather, but on the sixth morning the sun shone whole and faultless in the blue. People waved to each other from the streets, and raised their fingers on steering wheels as they passed on the highway, cracked windows to the air and shucked coats. Ranchers tuned in futures markets, plotted crop strategy, and anticipated rolling up their sleeves in the calving pens. Soon. Everything about this morning said *soon.*

It seemed a curious contradiction to Ike, standing in Stubblefield's feedlot, everything around him quickening to life again while he watched the front-end loaders make tidy work of it, the buckets scraping cattle free from the ice and snow, lifting another carcass, or a half, a quarter, to be stacked in the waiting trucks, WESTERN BIPRODUCTS, wide red letters. It wasn't that Ike could hear the bodies being snatched free over the whine of hydraulics, diesel, the rumble of tracks grinding up the ragged turf, but somehow his mind supplied the details, the chew and tear, bone and muscle—everything still frozen, nothing liquid anymore.

The judge had had the papers ready, his only questions being cost and who got charged? And so Ike knew the judge was covering his ass, had talked to the commissioner's office, assayed the economics of moving and disposing of nearly two hundred head of cattle, sniffed out the potential voter response, and scrubbed his hands in public. Ike reassured him. The rendering company had been only too glad to take the problem off their hands.

They'd hauled off the first three truckloads. The hands from his brother-in-law's ranch were there. Ike had phoned Rob to call in a favor—men to ride the back pastures, locate cattle, lend a horse so he could ride out with them. He would do what killing was necessary. That was as it should be, wasn't it?

Pattiann was with them. She'd insisted. Still, Ike wished he could send her home. Protect her. No, be truthful. Protect himself, from how she would see him, clumsy in the saddle, exposed in all that land and shooting another man's cattle. No better than a rustler.

Purvis had trailered his own horse to the site. He'd brought along cattle markers—fat, colored grease sticks—to mark the cattle with a bright red X like a stand of trees to be thinned. But the herd was too far gone. They'd given up marking them. "Ah, Jesus," Purvis had said. "They're standing on dead wood—not enough protein to keep the blood circulating. Come a good thaw, the legs'll turn black and rot. What a waste." He looked away.

Harley was in the far corral helping load the cattle. In a passing cruelty, Ike wondered what Harley would say about his day to the dispatcher tonight.

Chas had yet to put in an appearance, and though Ike supposed he should be grateful for that, especially with Pattiann here, perversely enough, he wanted to see *them* together, to hear her voice, see if she ducked her head with annoyance or blushed with pleasure. Chas's house looked peaceable, squat and square. The windows were corniced with snow and a plume of smoke pulled out of the chimney. Just so damned domestic and sensible-looking. Ike warned Harley to stay put, keep his eyes open, mouth shut, and his temper in check.

They rode out the north fence line, over Beaver Creek, past the cut banks and buffalo jump, to where the trail climbed the rising hills to a high plateau. They took it slowly, single-file, staying to the high ground where the winds had blown clear the snow, and alternating leads in the hollows, sparing the horses who plodded through it, heads lowered, as do all good cow horses. Ike thought about the piebald. Had they found it? Hauled it away while he hadn't been looking? Would they find it yet, out here? Or had it turned like the other animals to frozen turf? He thought of that first night in the field, that graceless beast with its honest face and how it had followed him. He was ashamed he'd forgotten the animal. Maybe it would have been the one thing worth saving. The animals they were riding were groomed and well fed. They snorted into the sweet wind.

"Chinook," one of the men said and opened his parka.

Pattiann rode ahead. Her back was straight, her seat tucked well into the saddle. He envied her ease and he was proud of her. She'd once told him, as a child she used to ride out where no one might see, ride her horse *breakneck and far from chores*. Her words. Until one of the hands saw and told her daddy. He took her horse from her. Ground-tied her to the house, cooking for ranch hands, working with her mother, a sullen union that held for nearly five years. "Two women in the kitchen," Pattiann had said. "Better he should have beat me."

At the top, the men rode off to plant flags where they found cattle submerged in snow, and already the draws were dotted with bright scraps of red perking in the chinook. The surviving cattle were too far gone to herd down, a number of them blind with starvation, bumping into each other or the horses as they milled a moment before settling into a sullen stillness. Ike sidled his horse alongside Pattiann's.

"You shouldn't have come."

"I won't embarrass you," she said, and tugged her horse clear before he could tell her it was not *her* competence he feared. And then he was not sure he could have said that anyway.

Fewer than thirty cattle still stood on the high plateau. When they walked, the hooves clacked against each other like a chorus of wooden spoons. They would never survive a drive down to the waiting trucks. Ike pocketed his gloves, curled and uncurled his fingers, wiped the palms on his jeans. He unsheathed his Winchester 30.30.

He looped the reins over the horn. "Easy, girl," he said to the horse, and hoisted the rifle to his shoulder. It was a mercy, he told himself. He concentrated on a small patch of hide, the soft area behind the ear. Black Angus had damnable bony heads. He *could* risk a shot between the eyes, just below the frontal plate, but he imagined the trajectory of the bullet slowed through bone, shredding, imploding–the agonizing damage. No.

Behind the ear and out through the eye. One shot. A neat snick and pop, the cow dropping, that easy, and damn Chas Stubblefield. He worked the lever action, snugged the maple stock into his shoulder, held his breath, and sighted on the small flap of flesh.

He focused on the black, the snow burning a frame for the animal. He squeezed. A recoil against his shoulder and the cow dropped. The horse flinched but stood steady. "Good girl," he said, and kneed her forward lining up another black scrap. He cocked the lever, aimed, squeezed. The spent cartridge flicked waspish into the air. He didn't have to hear the cow drop; instead, he listened for the bang winging out over the plateau to where coyotes denned, and beyond where the land dropped to the valley floor and cottonwoods grew in a snarl on the riverbank. By the fifth shot, the horse no longer flinched. A tenderness set into Ike's shoulder. By the tenth, the ache was bone deep. He changed rifles. Still Ike distanced himself from the cattle, imagining himself instead down in the breaks where the sound of the killing would have long faded, following the distant river, listening to the water's muffled current beneath the icy shelf where trout flashed out of the deep.

By the eighteenth shot, his shoulder felt compressed, his arms sore. He could no longer trust the careful shot behind the ear. He resorted to the point between the eyes, his attention wrenched back to meat and bone. He heard the concussion like a blow to his head and he lowered the rifle to his lap. His shoulder had numbed and his cheek tingled. There was a ringing of brass in his head. He stopped to let the commotion quiet.

Pattiann approached. She reached over and touched his knee. The men were scattered about the plateau. Purvis looked politely away. "I could take over," she said.

He *wanted* to hand it over, but this was his work. It no longer mattered how he'd come to it. Good intentions or not. There was a penance here he'd meant to inflict and it had come back on his own head. "No," he said. Then he touched her fingers. Sheathed the rifle. He dismounted and dropped the reins. He waded through the snow. Slipping the handgun from his holster, he approached a cow. It turned to him with eyes that were wide and unfocused as if in a rapture. Ike aimed and shot.

There was nothing distant anymore, it was up close and personal. He was surprised to find how little he felt besides gratitude for not feeling more. He shot them. They folded. One after another.

Pattiann and the other hands worked on around him, planting flags like a flock of cardinals on the snow, marking the buried carcasses for the rendering crews that would join them after they'd finished below. Purvis sat astride his horse gazing over the valley.

The actual killing took less than an hour. In the end, both Pattiann and Purvis helped. Purvis had been the first to step in. Pattiann had followed. Some of Rob's hands rode out farther, to check for animals still standing. What few were left were fodder for the coyotes, their numbers small, and nature was meticulous: coyotes, buzzards, magpies, beetles.

None of the riders had seen a piebald horse. "It's pretty damned big out there," one had said. "The only thing moving is slinking."

Pattiann and Purvis stayed on as the hands turned their horses back down the trail. The three of them stood in a loose group, surveying the flags, the downed cattle. "It was a mercy," Purvis said.

"Once before," Pattiann said, "I've seen it this bad. A blizzard—lasted two, two and a half days. My dad lost cattle. They all did. But Goddamn it, he tried so hard. Blamed himself for years because he wasn't stronger than the weather. But this . . ." She turned her back to them. "Can Chas sleep at night? You have to pity him."

Ike wanted to tell her she should save it. Chas had gotten off easy. But he kept his quiet, looked at her across the distance of a few feet. Her hand raised to her horse's chin strap, fingers looped through it.

"Pity?" Purvis said. "Maybe I'm just too sick of this business to think properly. I *want* to believe I'm a man who can turn his cheek if the occasion calls for it." He lowered the reins, lifted his foot to the stirrup, and hefted himself into the saddle. The leather creaked and the horse huffed as Purvis shifted the saddle under him. "But at this moment, Pattiann, if you can talk about pity, you're a better person than I am." He swung his horse toward the trail at a slow walk.

Ike scanned the area one last time. He raised his foot into the stirrup, bounced twice on his standing leg, an embarrassment that he couldn't do it in one faultless swing like Pattiann, or even the older Purvis. He headed down after Purvis and soon he heard her coming up behind.

The snow in the low spots was already pooling from the chinook. They caught the odd jackrabbit lapping at the standing water. In less than a month, barring another heavy storm, the snow would be gone. The range would turn to gumbo, followed by lush green shoots, and the ranchers would breathe easier with calves coming in, cows and the range both freshening. Ike lifted his face to the breeze, let the reins swing with the horse's nodding. *Soon.* All spring and summer would stretch ahead as if it had no intention of ending, except in the designs of men who plotted crops and planned from the lessons learned this winter and all the preceding winters. And he wondered how long could a man learn, unlearn, and relearn before he came upon the thing that undid him? Storm. Drought. Age. The market. One year you're at home and the next—a stranger to the place you'd made for yourself. And maybe the best you could hope for in those instances was to find yourself, like Chas, still young enough to start over at something else.

When they got back down, they found the rendering crew in good spirits. This was a windfall. Meat for the taking, enough to make it worthwhile. The lower feed yard was cleared, scraped. Workers milled around machines. Harley was in the cruiser, on the radio. He clicked off when he saw Ike. A half-dozen cars and pickups lined the roadside, people sitting in cabs or bunched by the fence. Spectators. Neighbors with a nose for misfortune.

"Harley," Ike called. "Tell them to leave."

"I tried," Harley said. "Don't get pissed at me. I kept them behind the fence, didn't I?"

Fred Timbers was there, Ben Joust, Paul Lange and his wife, Letta. Old Tom Millan stood by his truck. Still carrying his grudge with the IRS and probably seeing this as just another example of big government squeezing the little guy. Ike could read it in their faces. A lynch mob. Who they wanted to lynch remained to be seen.

"You see a horse?" Ike asked Harley. "A piebald, white face? Stubblefield's horse?"

Harley shook his head. "Shit. I've seen more cows today than I ever wanted to see in my life, but no horses other than what you rode in on."

"Check the barn," Ike said.

Harley looked at his watch. "I was hoping to get out—"

"Then it's a good thing I'm only asking you to check the barn."

"Guess so," Harley said. He smiled.

"And while you're at it, check the shed." He pointed to the far corner of the yard.

Ike handed the reins to Harley and approached the gathering of bystanders. He seated his hat, nodded to Letta still in the pickup. "You men here to help?"

Joust snorted. "Don't seem the bank needs any more bully boys than what's here already."

"That how you see this, Ben? Hired guns? Just like the bad old days, huh?"

"Government kill-ers," Millan said, his voice breaking on the last syllable.

"Tom," Ike said, holding up a hand, "this is me, Ike Parsons, and that there is Harley, and Purvis, and there isn't a soul here you don't know by first name."

"That include Stubblefield whose cattle you just killed?" Joust asked.

Ike nodded. "He signed the cattle over to dispose of as best we could, a merciful act, don't you think . . ." He held his hand up, tipped back his hat. "But you all know that already, and have come in a good community spirit, to support Mr. Stubblefield in his time of need. I'm sure he appreciates it, watching as he must be from his window, knowing you all came out of friendship and not out of a need to gawk and gossip."

Letta laughed from inside the pickup cab. "Right between the eyes," she called. Paul leaned down and hushed her. "Ha," she said, and again louder, "Ha."

"Now, if you got any questions, I'm in my office, regular hours." But Ben was already stepping up into the cab.

They pulled out one by one. Tom Millan was last to leave. "Blood-sucking government," he called out.

"Yeah, Tom. You drive careful."

Tom smiled, waved as he pulled out onto the highway and rumbled off in his Studebaker pickup. Ike turned, looked over at Stubblefield's house. Blank-faced windows. No chickens, cats, or dogs. Machinery rumbled in the yard and men called to each other. He could hear Harley laughing. Pattiann and Purvis were loading the horses, and once it was done, all the trucks and men with their noise pulled out, Ike tried to imagine this place. There would be nothing. Just Stubblefield. And all the silence he could ever hope for.

Pattiann rode back with Purvis. She would have stayed until the last truck left, but she sensed Ike didn't want that. He wanted her far from Stubblefield, and maybe from himself as well. She'd stepped in it for sure. Pitying Chas, but there it was. She wasn't about to take back the truth. Purvis drove slowly, checking the trailer in the sideview mirrors. The horse shuffled, leaned to a side, and the truck hitched and meandered over the line. "Damn cob-headed beast," Purvis said.

"Your horse likes to lean," she agreed as the truck wandered a few feet left.

"I'm talking about the truck. Not made for hauling something more determined than it is. But it'll settle down in awhile."

"The truck?"

"The horse. Always spooky the first couple miles. He'll get a comfortable lean—I'll compensate—and sleep the whole way home. The horse, not me."

"I'm relieved."

"You're tired. You want, you can rest your pretty head." He patted his shoulder. "Take a nap."

"No," Pattiann said. "I'm tired, but not sleepy." She watched the road spindle away in the sideview mirror. It would be dark soon. How was it, she wondered, that in fall the days shortened so much more quickly than they lengthened in late winter. Or maybe winter days were so gray, it seemed like dusk from dawn to nightfall. But today had been brilliant, the chinook making you believe the end was at hand. Perhaps her mother had read her bones wrong and they were done with the worst, the last big blow come and gone. An early spring. Something they never tired of praying for. She rubbed a cramp out of her thigh. She hoped Ike would be home early. She wanted to make it up to him.

"You think Ike's upset with me?" Pattiann asked.

Purvis ducked his head. "You know him better than I do."

Pattiann laughed. "You believe that? Or just dodging the question?"

"Both." He corrected for the lean. "I think Ike's out of sorts with the world right now, understandably, and you stand front and center in his attention, always. It's a condition of marriage—to judge the weather by each other. I'm not saying you're responsible, but he sees you pitying Chas, he reads you as the community. *They* see you pitying Chas, it feeds the fire."

"So I shouldn't care?"

Purvis sighed, hunkered down in the seat. "You confound me, Pattiann."

"Chas hasn't got a friend in the world," she said.

"He's got himself," Purvis snapped. "Fitting company."

Purvis stared at the road, his hands fixed on the wheel. Pattiann looked out over the snow, the small pools of meltwater cupped on the surface that shone a deeper gray, like so many tossed coins. How the hell could this have happened? Really? A bad year for snow, yes. And last summer, yet another summer of drought. But others had managed, laid away feed, sold off stock. And that was the pinch. She could imagine it as Chas must have. More land, turn it over to pasture for quick profit, turn the profit into more cows banking on a mild winter, banking on God Almighty, a last-minute miracle.

Not the God Pattiann knew. Her God was a distracted presence whose attention wandered, did His best work over millennia. She did not pray for miracles. Her God was larger than a last-ditch miracle. And if it was true that in the early days God walked with man, He'd long since grown bored with their questions.

Purvis broke the silence. "So maybe I'm wrong. Maybe you know something about Chas I don't?"

Pattiann shook her head. "Who knows Chas but Chas, or any of his family? No one cared to know Avery, and that was fine with him. I barely remember Chas's mother, Abbie. I do remember she was a seriously religious woman, and I don't mean the type who wears it like a new skin." Pattiann looked out the window. "She was"—she looked over at Purvis—"what's the word?"

"A fanatic?"

"She was too *distant* for that, know what I mean? Always staring off at some other place, or plane. Not that we saw her that much. Maybe my mama knew her best, and if you asked her she wouldn't claim much more than a passing acquaintance. Otherworldly, that's the word."

"Died young."

"Suicide."

"And Chas must have been what, about twelve? That's a lot for a young kid to bear up under. Then of course there were all those years alone with Avery." Purvis leaned his head back, closed his eyes a moment, and when he opened them again he gazed up into the rearview mirror and held his focus there, as if at himself. "But isn't there a time when a person has to say, all right, now this is the *rest* of my life? And I'm accountable for that?"

He looked over at Pattiann. "Chas was offered help. He *chose* not to take it. Now you can shrug that off to pride, some people might even admire it, 'Well, he come on hard times and wasn't a man to take what he couldn't pay for,' that sort of thing. But then he wasn't the one starving, was he? He ate the dead like it was his just meets, and maybe it was. Point is, I can't look into his soul. I got only his actions to judge by, and if there was suffering in his past, that's not what I see now. He's taken a pleasure in this business."

"Is that the way you see it?" Pattiann leaned over to Purvis. "Christ, maybe he's just trying to find his own damn way."

Purvis's foot lifted from the gas pedal. He shifted and the engine whined down. He pulled to the roadside, sat with the truck idling. The horse shuffled awake in the trailer, the truck jolting softly. Purvis pulled a cigar from his jacket pocket, slid the cellophane wrapper clear, nipped the cigar end, and lit it. He inhaled, held it, exhaled. "You're pretty touchy when it comes to Chas."

"So I should just shut up and keep house."

"Damn it, woman, I'm not saying that. Now if you insist on pitying Chas, all right. But it's a thing any self-respecting man would detest. Now, *understanding* is another thing." His cigar bobbed in the darkening cab. "Compassion. Yes. And I think those require a right-minded thinking. A considered and deserved emotion. But pity—"

"Semantics," Pattiann said.

"Hell, yes, semantics. It occurs to me, you haven't examined what you're feeling or why—pity's what Chas is tweaking right now—self-pity and no thought about those animals, or what he's done to this community. Pity is mindless, invoked by the self-pitying. It's an emotion that calls for no direct action. We are *salved* by pity—'nothing I can do but feel sorry for the poor bastard.' And you, soft-hearted as you are, and mind me, I'm not saying I'm not in favor of that, God spare me the hard-hearted woman, but he's taken you in hook, line, and sinker."

His eyebrows raised, cigar smoke curling through his hair and drafting out the window. Purvis clamped the stub between his teeth, put the truck in gear, and pulled out slowly.

"I'm not saying you're entirely wrong in this," she said softly. "But I think Stubblefield's hurting. And if someone had been there earlier for him, this wouldn't have happened."

Purvis clucked his tongue. "This is the worst kind of spilt milk," he said. "Whatever you did or didn't do, you can't take back, and no amount of beating your breasts is going to make Stubblefield any more or less than he is right now."

"So we let it ride?"

"For now. This passes, hopefully, and we offer what help he'll accept." Purvis shuffled his cigar to the other side of his mouth. He blinked in the smoke, eyes watering.

"You know, one day, smoking's going to kill you."

"You worried or hopeful?"

"I'm thinking how there wouldn't be a soul left in this world to lecture me."

She studied him in the last light, a graying man, his chunky fingers wrapped around the cigar, who did his work quietly and took his friends seriously. Good humor and a true heart his only defense. The sides of his hands and jacket sleeves blackly inked by grease sticks. Got more on him than the cows. She turned away, looked out the side window at the last miles before town.

It was dark by the time they drove the front-end loader onto its trailer. "You need help again," the rendering company foreman said, "give us a call. You ever in Helena, stop by for a beer. Want a tour of the plant, we'll take you through. It's a good setup. Clean. We feed the nation's dogs, feed yours—you got one?—no? Well, we do good work. Hell, we ain't ghouls," he said, spreading his hands like an apology. "It just looks that way."

He smiled and shrugged, and after he'd driven off, Ike stood in the exhaust and the scraped yard believing he still smelled death and wondered if that man carried it home with him to his wife and children, set it at the table alongside the aroma of potatoes and green beans. Ike sniffed his own hands, his jacket. Gunpowder, all in all a clean business. The last semi trucked down the road, the crews gone off for beers and home, and still no sign of Chas, though a light had come on in the house, moved from room to room like a hand-held kerosene lamp, and Ike wondered if Chas's power had been cut, too. But no, the yard light was on and it sketched intricate shadows amid the tangle of old car parts and machinery.

He stood in the scoured lot, turned his head aside from the wind that brisked across the field. First time he'd smelled death, it was back in an apartment building, apartment 4D, Sutter Street, Milwaukee. Mid-August, ninety-eight degrees. Humid. He was twenty-two, and it was his first bad one. A retired school principal who'd lived alone, dead four days when a neighbor complained. At the scene, just outside the apartment door, his partner Bassette lifted his nose into the air, sniffed, and stepped back. "This ain't going to be amusing," he said, and signaled Ike to go first.

The apartment was clean. Everything in a predictable place. That was the first thing that struck Ike. All the lamps had ruffled shades and the tables had clean tops. The sofa was chintz-covered and there was one worn cushion, as though she'd lived her life in that one spot. It was an orderly apartment but for the corpse that had bloated until the skin had split. Her dress was hiked up over wallowing thighs and it seemed indecent to Ike so that he started to rearrange the skirt when Bassette stopped him. "Leave it be. Ain't nobody embarrassed here but you. We make the report first, call in the coroner." They wandered through the apartment, waiting for the meat truck to arrive, and when it did, the attendants gripped their noses with one hand and folded her into a rubber sheet with another. She was fluid. She rolled like jelly, emitting great vaporous farts. Bassette seemed disappointed that Ike didn't get sick, but afterward, in the shade of the oak-lined street, he said, "You did good, kid."

Ike stood in the lot, staring at the fields, the fences, the house cozied into the night. It came to him like a premonition that it was not over, a foreboding that rooted him in place until his skin burned with cold, felt as raw and scraped as the yard around him. And then he was crossing the lot, passing through the gate he no longer bothered to close, and stepping onto Stubblefield's front porch. He knocked twice. He wasn't sure why he was standing here, except he knew he couldn't steal away into the dark. There was a reckoning he hadn't made yet, but what it was he wasn't sure.

Stubblefield opened the door a crack, peered out. He gestured with a cupped hand, turned his back, and disappeared. Ike followed. To the side, he could see a light in the kitchen, but Stubblefield moved into the dark of the living room where he settled into the shadows. Ike seated himself on the sofa adjacent. A bar of light from the kitchen doorway sliced across the back cushions and over his lap.

"Thought you'd want to know we're done." Ike nodded toward the door. "It went quick. Purvis said there was nothing to save—"

Stubblefield sighed, a sound like the last breath issuing out of a corpse. Ike waited. He should have let matters ride. He should have driven off and not looked back. He spread his hands out in the slab of light and the gesture seemed clumsy, as if his hands had become out-sized in the small room. "I just thought I should tell you."

"You want a drink, Sheriff? I got a last bottle here somewhere." There was the chink of glass, then Stubblefield leaned into the light with a half-emptied bottle.

Ike took a sip and handed it back. Stubblefield drank deeply before settling back.

"We are, all of us, a sorry lot." Chas paused. The sound of liquid sloshing, another dark swallow. "Last year, when I was still young, I believed I would make this land and it would make me."

It got so quiet, Ike thought Chas had fallen asleep, but then he said, "I had ambitions." He giggled and then it turned softer, more like a kind of crying and perhaps it was.

"Whooee," Chas said when finished. "I'm on my way to drunker. Care to make a night of it, you know, like old friends, partners in crime?"

He pushed the bottle into the light, but Ike shook his head. He should get back. He should get on to doing what he'd come here for. But that escaped him still, what it was he expected of himself. He pushed for-ward, perched on the end of the sofa. There was a pair of clean socks bundled in the corner of the couch, and in the dark, Ike thought he could make out a line of shapes—shirts with arms up in surrender, pants, underwear. And although it must have been there all the time, only now did he hear the *drip, drip.* Ike smelled detergent and bleach. Laundry.

"Maybe you could start over," Ike said.

"Sure, sure," Chas said. "Work cattle for someone else, save up. Buy a few head, find some land, hit my old buddy Taylor up for a loan at the bank, buckle down, pull myself up by my bootstraps, marry well. Any number of things could happen. I am a man rich in potential."

"Do something else," Ike said. "People change their lives all the time."

"Attaboy," Chas said. "Reborn—a grocery clerk." He got up, walked over to the window where the moonlight broke over him, his pale skin tinted blue as new snow. "What do you want? Really? Ain't neither of us interested in holding the other's hand. What *more* do you want?" He pressed open palms to the window, leaned his head against it, stared out.

Ike looked down at his own hands. What did he want? His assurance that this was the end of it. That it stopped here. But Ike could not find the words, or maybe he was just unwilling to give Chas the pleasure of knowing how much he disturbed Ike.

Chas looked over his shoulder, his palms still spread on the cold glass. "Fact is, I gave it over to you years ago."

Ike sat still on the sofa, waiting to see what turn Chas would take next. He gripped his knees with his hands.

Chas slouched against the sill so that he was back-lit, a pale corona blueing his hair, the moist palm prints shining from the window on either side of his head. "When Pattiann first came back home, I thought all I had to do was give her time. Just bide my while and she'd come around." He was laughing and shaking his head. He looked across the room to where Ike sat. "Can you believe that?"

Ike found himself shaking his head. No. Pattiann would never be the first to come back around. Ike knew her better than that.

"And by God, I *knew* her better than that," Chas said.

Ike sat back. His own thoughts echoed by Chas in a voice tender with grief, a level of intimacy he didn't want to share, and just as suddenly given an insight into the couple they'd once been, and maybe it wasn't just haphazard fucking, or the youthful wildness Ike'd wanted to believe, but something deeper that had more to do with the territory of love than lust.

"Queer, isn't it? Here's you and me talking like old friends, and all we got in the world to hold us together is dead cattle, and the same woman."

"No, Chas," Ike said. "She's not the Pattiann you knew."

"Hah!" His laugh came out like a bark. "You think you know her differently?"

Ike shifted to the edge of the sofa. He kept his hands on either side of his body, locked on the cushion. This was going bad. He could feel his heart laboring as if his blood had thickened, though his arms and hands felt strangely light and he gripped the worn cushion tighter. The butt of his gun goaded him in the ribs. He was a professional, he told himself.

No room for the personal in his job. Ike stood, rolled his hat brim in his hand, stopped.

"I didn't come here to talk about my *wife*." He felt angry and just as suddenly foolish for being pushed into this by Chas, the man who had, after all, lost everything, who spent his day doing laundry while another man shot his cattle. It was pathetic, really. And just as suddenly Ike was aware of what it was he'd really needed to say, even though it would be a bitter thing. "I'm sorry. It's what I came to say. I'm sorry it had to be this way."

Stubblefield moved. The bottle landed on the floor, rolled the small distance between them, and stopped. Chas giggled again, the pained little sound. "Want to know what I learned?" he asked. "What I learned is there ain't enough time left us in this world to be sorry for all our transgressions. Little ones, big ones, cattle, *friends,* fuck 'em all, I say." He leaned into the light. He giggled. "That means fuck you too." He fell back into the dark.

There was a snicker from the shadow and Ike left the house feeling he'd wear that sound on the long ride home, but the clear air made him feel buoyant again. He drove to town strangely unburdened and he drove quickly, the window open so he could savor the last of the chinook.

He stopped by the diner after checking in with the office. He told himself it was because he was hungry. Just a bite, another hour before going home. He didn't examine it too closely. He took a corner booth. There were five people seated at a table near the front and a couple at the stools. He could smell the special—fried liver and onions, a dish his mother had made him eat until he'd acquired a tolerance. He hadn't eaten it since.

Roy was in the kitchen, singing a monotone "Stairway to Heaven." Fran was working the front alone, and when she came to his table she smiled as if it cost her.

"Long day?" he asked.

She glanced over her shoulder at the table of five. "Three hours to eat three specials, two fried chickens, a swill of black coffee, and a quick run through the dessert list. They'll pay their bill and leave. No tip. Every Wednesday night. This ain't home. Does this *look* like home?" She sighed. "But my shift ends in ten minutes. What the hell." She stripped her apron off, tossed it onto the seat. "Cup of coffee?"

She brought a pot and two cups. She looked serious about relaxing, propped her feet on the seat next to Ike, pulled out a pack of cigarettes and lit one. The five were shuffling to their feet, pawing through pockets and purses. "Have a nice day," she called over her shoulder and took a long pull on her cigarette. "You look pretty done in yourself. That Stubblefield business? Heard about it."

Ike nodded. "The usual malcontents?"

"This Goddamned county is malcontent. It's the winter. Brings out the worst at a time when you don't want to see it." She made a face. "I should have brewed us a fresh pot." She poured in a dollop of milk, added sugar. "Am I being crabby? You don't need crabby." She waved the cigarette at him. "How'd it go?"

And he found himself telling her. He told her about the cattle. He told her about his bruised shoulder, the ringing in his ears. He imagined he could tell her damn near anything and she'd make sense of it. He told her about Stubblefield.

"Well, there's reasons enough in this life to get drunk. Having your herd destroyed is one of them," she said. "Having to do another man's job and shoot that herd's another one. But here you are, drinking coffee. You did your job, you'll do it tomorrow and the day after. It's what separates you from Stubblefield." She sipped her coffee and paused, looking at the window where they sat stiffly reflected in diner light. She picked up her cigarette and snubbed it out.

She stood up. "This coffee's terrible. No wonder I don't get tips. I got to get home. Sitter's waiting. Want to walk me?" She stood tableside, bunching up the apron in a hand. She looked small, hanging on to the strings.

"You get ready," he said. "I'll finish this. Bad or not, it's the first warm thing I've had today."

She smiled and stepped through the kitchen door.

A few minutes later she returned, wearing a coat and mittens. Her face looked pink and scrubbed. She breezed out the door ahead of him, throwing a good-bye over her shoulder to Roy, who grunted from the counter. He nodded to Ike and Ike could already imagine the word spreading through town, but that was unfair because Roy was a man of few words who kept his nose in his own business. The streets were empty, scrubbed clean by wind. Water from the day's warm spell glittered in a frozen runoff down the gutters. Fran lived two blocks west, a block south, the small residential section.

Fran kept in step with Ike. "This is kind of you," she said. "You got your own troubles and here I hand you mine as well. But in all this town there isn't a soul I can talk to. It happens. You grow up with these folks, make a fool of yourself at their parties, fight and get past it because who the hell else is there? But tell them something and you live with it the rest of your life."

Ike knew what she meant. Sometimes he thought even their faces came to resemble one another's as married couples do over a long time. Cottonwoods lined the street, spindly limbs fretting in the wind. He lifted his coat collar over his ears.

She slowed her pace. "You know how I told you I thought that Dave was seeing Jolene, on weekends I couldn't get home? Well, he moved her trailer onto our back acreage, out of view of the house. He called a couple nights ago to tell me. Said he was just being neighborly. The poor girl *can't make it on her own,* but don't take this wrong, understand? Just being kind. He thinks we could be friends. Thinks I'm that kind of fool. And why not? All this time and I didn't say a word."

It felt at that moment as if Ike were cursed to spend his life apologizing for sins he had no hand in. "I'm sorry," he said.

"Ah, don't be. There'll be enough of that once word gets out. You know the thing that absolutely beats me? When I told him I knew he'd been shacking up with her off and on for the past five years, he didn't deny it. He said, we could work it out. Like it was a sliver. And then the sonofabitch cried. In fifteen years, I never heard him cry and now . . . *now* he cries."

"What will you do?" Ike asked.

"Get a divorce. Raise the kids and try to be out of the house when he picks them up. Isn't that the way? You know what *really* hurts him—all those tears—this is going to cost him big time, he figures. He's afraid he'll lose the ranch."

"The courts won't ruin a man," Ike said, but then he thought of Stubblefield. The laundry dripping in the dark.

"They can come damn close. He knows it, and I know it, and right about now he probably thinks I'm angry enough to go for his throat."

"But you're not, are you?"

"Oh, I'm angry enough. But he's still the kids' dad and I can't destroy that, can I?"

They walked the last steps to her house. Lights were on throughout the first floor. They stood in the dark of the street.

She tipped her head. A tinny sound came from the house, voices and music. "Why is it kids turn up the volume so they can hear it all over the house, like they'd miss something otherwise? It's all so much garbage. Garbage in, garbage out. I wish we'd called it quits earlier, but there were the kids and there was the ranch. I hate that he thinks I'd sit out there with his girlfriend and take it, but mostly I'm relieved." She laid a hand on his arm. "And scared, I'll admit."

He folded his hand over hers. He touched her face, wiped the tears with his thumb, and he imagined kissing her cheek and then imagined her lips, and in the quiet of the familiar street, under the honest cottonwoods, the strangeness of her mouth would be exciting, shocking, and he wished he could forget who and where he was. So easy, he thought, and then he stepped back.

She smiled, glanced over at the lit house. "I'd better get in, turn down the television before the neighbors call the sheriff." She leaned into his ear. "Thank you, Ike," she whispered. "You tell Pattiann, hi." Then she pivoted on her heel and crossed the walk to her front door. She waved good night and disappeared inside.

The house was spotless. Pattiann was restless and it translated to washing the kitchen floor, scrubbing counters, tables, cleaning the glass on the pictures that hung in the hallway. She tried a book. Turned the television on for background, turned it off. She settled into the kitchen to make spaghetti, something that would keep late and heat easily. She shaped meatballs, sliced onions, tomatoes, peppers, seasoned the Dutch oven and thought about Ike.

It was a nasty job and no rancher relished it—putting down the odd steer that broke a limb, or the old cow that prolapsed or wouldn't freshen, destined for the canning jars—a meat gamey with age and pressure-cooked until it was chewable. She'd been raised on it. On those mornings her father would sit at coffee a little longer before he'd slap his hat on and suggest Martha check her jars. And Martha would not have to ask which animal—she knew the stock as well as he did—but would instead kiss him on the cheek and thank him for his work, suggest the meat would taste good come winter. When they were ten years of age, the children helped dress the animal out. At fourteen, Pattiann was handed the gun.

"Make it clean," he'd said and she had. There was no lecture on respect beyond what she'd witnessed all her life—ranchers gave their lives over to the care of livestock, and the meat was a kindness returned.

She set the sauce on at a low simmer, threw her coat over her shoulders, and stepped out onto the porch. She perched on the top step and pulled the coat closed. The street was quiet, and she leaned from under the porch roof to see the stinging points of starlight in the black. The snow had disappeared, save a few baleful patches against garages and in ditches. In a month or less, the air would smell new with rain and thaw. Children would scramble in spring games in the school yard while the town people resurrected flowerpots.

A cat stalked the curb, a large gray and white tabby, its paw fishing the gutter. When she moved, it crouched and then startled off into the dark. Pattiann rested her back against a post; she looked up the street. Small town. Down the block, windows glowed. The half-dozen houses rucked up against each other, boundaries picked out by split-rail and picket fences that children hurdled and adults tended as though fearful their neighbors might break free to range elsewhere. She wondered at her being in this place, tucked in among houses and neighbors instead of coulees and breaks. Married to a town man, who liked the orderly lawns and fences, the streetlights. She thought of the midwestern cities with all the confinement of a side rail feedlot. On sidewalks, streets, the ceaseless movement—she knew a herd when she saw one and she'd ridden them too long to become part of one. She eased back on the step to brace her spine. There was comfort to this house, and as far as compromise went, it wasn't a bad one, but sometimes even this small town seemed to close in on her, and then she found herself dealing with it the only way she knew how, retreating deeper into her own territory, spending more time at the ranch, longer hours on the road between here and there.

The cat was back, playing with its own shadow. She called to it and the animal stopped, moved nearer on the points of its toes. It sidled within inches of her outstretched fingers, and then a door slammed down the street and the cat was gone.

By the time Ike came home, the sauce was done. She hoped the fragrant house made him feel welcome. He hung his coat up, washed at the kitchen sink as he preferred, a holdover from his youth, and she found that endearing, as though she were seeing him as a young boy again, ladling water over his neck. He raised his dripping face. Pattiann lifted the towel from a rack and pressed it to his cheeks, then his nose and eyelids, his forehead and the tuft of hair that always fell unchecked over his brows, dried them all carefully. "I'm sorry," she said. "What I said earlier . . . about Chas. It was thoughtless of me."

He stood with his face in her hands, then he put his arms around her. She could feel his wet palms through the back of her shirt, his thumbs cradling her wing bones. He smelled of horses—unfamiliar on him but comforting to Pattiann. "It's been a day for apologies," he said.

"Sshh." She tamped the towel over his lips, followed it with a kiss, and she wanted him to be ardent, to clench her blouse in his hands and bury his mouth in her hair, but he was tired and hurt and she was, according to her nature, a practical woman, so she sat him down in a chair and spooned hot spaghetti onto two plates. He ate slowly at first, but after he cleaned the first plate, he served himself another the same size and finished that as well. She pulled out an apple cobbler, scooped ice cream onto it. When he worked the spoon into the cobbler, she asked, "Did it go all right after I left?"

He nodded, swallowed a bite. "Didn't think they'd get it done. But it was a good team, and they were grateful," he said. "Invited us to tour the plant, have a beer with them. Can't think of anything I'd rather do, can you?" He smiled. "Chas stayed away." He stopped eating. "Stayed in the house. From another man, I'd believe he was embarrassed and hiding, but not our boy, Chas."

Pattiann sat waiting. She'd flinched over the way he said "our boy" with a tenderness she hadn't expected. She was embarrassed by her own surprise. It was one thing for the town to believe Ike did his business without feeling, it was another for her to do so. She knew how much the law meant to him. She also knew how much he labored over the consequences it dealt to people's lives. Sometimes, she thought, he was too human for his job. But of course, that's what made him right for it.

"I stopped in afterward, to let him know we were done. He was on his way to drunk. Offered to take me along."

"You must have felt ready for one," she said.

He stopped eating. He shifted his eyes away from Pattiann's. "Well, I didn't." He pushed the plate aside and stood up. "Think I'll go to bed."

"Want someone to join you?" she asked.

He shrugged. "If you're tired."

He was walking away and Pattiann wasn't sure how to stop him, so she followed. He climbed the stairs like an old man and she wanted to offer her arm, say something that would lift his steps or his heart, and it always came to this, she thought, this simple loss of words, some tenderness lacking in her.

"I'll turn down the bed," she said, and he closed himself in the bathroom. When he came back, she was tucked in and waiting. He turned off the light and felt his way to bed. "We could use some time to ourselves," she said.

He didn't answer. She moved over to snug at his side. "You've been working too hard."

154

He sighed, moved an arm under her head. "Is this what you wanted? From your life?" he asked. "This place? Me?"

She reached up for his hand, pressed it against her cheek. "I don't know what else to ask for." She should say more. Do more. She wanted to wipe the day away. Take him into her body and rock him as she would a child in her womb. She ran her finger down his arm, felt the muscle tight beneath the skin. His shoulders were bunched and she wanted to knead them, straddle his belly with her legs and stroke his chest, feel his cock grow erect beneath her. She raised on an elbow. She should take him, tired or no, pull him inside of her and carry him to someplace beyond this room, this small house and town, let him feel how the land grows large beneath your feet and the sky crimps at the edge of your heart. She should do all this with her body as she never could by speaking of it. She wanted him to know how much this place was a part of her and he a part of it all now.

But he was tired. The small furrow between his brows eased; his breathing deepened. His foot kicked as he struggled into sleep and she eased herself down beside him. She moved her arm over him as if she could safeguard his dreams, cradled her ear to his chest, and closed her eyes.

Chas had watched the sheriff pull out of the drive, taking his sad act of guilt and repentance off somewhere where it might do him some good— to bed with his wife maybe. There was not a thing in this world Chas felt required to grieve over. Certainly not the cattle. They were raised to die. Chas flipped on the lights, stoked the woodstove fire with paperwork from a generation and a half of ranching. His father's accounts, printed in his crabby script. What would that old man feel? Not surprise. Proved out, that's how. Proved out and gratified to see it. There wasn't anything that old man liked more than being right. "Pleased to oblige you, Daddy," Chas said, and fed another stack to the fire. He slipped on his coat, strung bootlaces, and walked outdoors. Smoke purled down from the chimney. A hot, dirty smoke—paper, ink, ambition.

He drew a bucket of water at the pump and carried it into the shed. He'd move the horse back into the barn tomorrow. There'd been a moment this afternoon when Chas thought he'd been found out. Harley had come snooping around, had headed for the shed. It had been close, but all he'd done was stand in the lee of it and light a smoke, so God-damned full of himself, just feet from the piebald, the last living thing on this spread save Chas himself. And then again when the sheriff stopped in. Chas had waited for the question, *Where's the horse?* but nothing came of that either. And so it was still here, alive for now and safely his. Wasn't no one coming anymore, not until spring, and then it would be bankers, auctioneers, and acquaintances who would ring him around to say, *Sorry to hear of your trouble,* and, *Yes, I'll take that tractor thirty cents on the dollar.* And the banks would be distressed to have to take such measures, but appeased. And his neighbors and friends, oh, they'd be sorry to do it, but you understand how tough it's been.

His father used to say, "You're a fool if you think you can get rich in this business." But Chas had come close. What? Three, four weeks short of a break, a damned month or two of feed and he'd have had cows calving, then summer pasture, a crop of steers and the market for it.

Well, he'd made a killing all right.

He turned on the overhead light, a single bulb screwed into the plank ceiling. The shed was a tight fit with the horse in it, discs and harrow, rake and baler, and in the far corner, the horse bumped tight against the wall. An ugly thing, but his. "You are the last word in the argument," he said to the horse. "And I spoke it." He set the bucket on the dirt floor and the horse nosed over, snuffing at his pant legs, dropped its muzzle to the water, and drew in guzzling draughts.

"Fill your belly," he said. "Suck it up till you slosh like a canteen, then drink some more because it's all God's provided." He laughed. He felt good and knew it was the booze, but more than that it was a curious feeling of relief. His life reduced to this last knowable thing.

The horse nosed the bucket over. Water dribbled out and beaded on the dirt floor. The shed was a history of ranching details: bailing twine, a roll of double-barbed fencing, a broken ax handle, posthole digger, wire stretcher, an old milk crate filled with empty oil cans, and a coffee mug with its handle broken off. Shovels, pick and hoe, wedge and ax hung on the wall, and below, in the corner, there was a hole where a pack rat had burrowed in, lived its life, and deserted or died. Chas had to admit a begrudging fondness for the creatures. Given a chance, the little thieves would steal the buckle off his belt while he slept. He cursed their thefts with an animation born of admiration. He'd set out poison and traps, collect the carcasses like a tithe, fling them into the manure pile where they festered in the heat or froze in winter.

But there would be no more of that. And no more pulling calves, breaking ice, honing harrow blades. He could see it. The house gone, the well seized up, the fences lapsing back into the land. And himself? He squinted as if he could see beyond the canting clapboard, the hoes and rakes, the barren fields, to some place where he walked in cleated heels on concrete, past houses and cemeteries, beneath skyscrapers where pigeons cooed and swooped alongside the clatter of trains, the hump of turn buckles, following the endless lines of freight to some other place where the dirt was red and crusted his face while he worked another man's land with nothing he could call his own but sweat. But he could not *see* it. Could not call to mind a tangible future. He was a hole in the city, a lapse in some other man's bright red earth. He was nothing, beholden to nothing. Accountable to no one. A wisp. A puff of air no more substantial than the breath of this horse.

He wondered what he would do tonight. Tomorrow. The next day and the next. There was nothing left here but this last piece of work. What he had been was no more and what he would become was mystery. He was, it seemed to him, a piece of God's whimsy. But if he was no more than a whim, look what a whim could do: fire, flood, hurricanes, drought, tornadoes, disease, plague. God made man to have something to destroy. He fashioned man's will to bend it. And *then* came the kicker—after all was said and done, the judgment rung in, He exacted eternal praise from this lot He'd buggered from cradle to grave.

Chas picked up the bucket and the horse snapped its head away from the swinging metal. The handle creaked and sawed, creaked and sawed.

He watched the horse and the horse watched the bucket swinging in smaller and smaller arcs.

"Hear that?" he asked the horse. Its ears flicked toward him, settled back. "Might as well be a clock winding down. And maybe all the time you got left in this world is the swing of this bucket." He stopped it with his free hand, set the bucket down. He laid his hand on the horse's belly, lowered his ear to the stomach wall and listened for the rumbling, but it was still. Quiet as the shed and the reaches beyond it. He stayed that way, and after awhile, the horse crooked its neck over his back and rested its head on Chas's flank, as it would a companion horse in the fields.

Chas listened for the thump and lub of the horse's heart. Waited for the small squeezings of stomach or intestine and imagined the landscape within, awash with water, feeding on itself while time spindled on and on. That was all that was left. Time. He would have whole days to take account, rack up the scores against Providence and man. Given enough time, whimsy brought down buildings, rearranged the land, fed the flames, triggered fear, grew bold and terrible.

The piebald shifted and Chas stepped away. And just as suddenly, Chas doubted what it was he planned to do. He thought of the sheriff and his fondness for the old sway-backed animal. He thought of Patti-ann and just as quickly pushed her from his head. Amazing, how she could still evoke in him feelings he could no longer afford. Hope. Salvation. But that was flogging a dead horse, wasn't it? And he laughed, a harsh little sound that surprised even him. The horse snorted, lowered its head to the empty feedbin that would only get emptier. Chas turned his back on the animal, shut the door behind him, and stood on the threshold of the land. He had never much liked the horse, all that white, like God Himself had laid its face open to blame.

Chapter Nine

S even in the morning and Ike was at the Brandt place—trailer home on a thousand plus acres of low-yield scrubland. Lila Brandt had called in a shooting. She was the daughter of the lately departed Asa Brandt, lifelong practitioner of subsistence living. Fifty head of cattle and a three hundred square-foot pole barn. Also a believer in the theory that homes didn't build barns, but barns built homes. So a year ago he died at the age of fifty, finally having achieved his dream of a respectable barn and still living in the trailer house at the door to which Ike now stood. In the front yard, her new boyfriend mourned his motorcycle.

She was telling Ike about her former boyfriend, Eddie Bacon, of Absorokee, who worked for the Millers. A round-faced man, barely twenty; Ike would have thought he lacked the imagination for this.

"He came rapping at the door, six a.m., with a rifle under his arm." She nodded at the man in the yard. "Henry took one look and shut the door."

"He's armed," Ike said.

"Didn't I just say that? Shoots a hole through my porch roof, jumps onto his horse, ropes Henry's motorcycle and drags it around the yard. Hollering." Her face turned thoughtful.

"He shot my bike," Henry said. He had a small voice, out of place in his large body. He wore tight jeans with pockets worried thin and an under-shirt stained in the armpits. He toed the sprinkle of chrome and glass, what remained of his headlight. "He dragged it around the yard, then he shot it in the head. Took off on his horse, leading a fresh one."

Ike had an outlaw on his hands. Getaway horse and all.

He caught up to the desperado where the road hitched north. Ike hit two short blasts on the siren and picked up the mike.

It was a short, spirited chase. When Eddie dismounted, he looked a little chagrined, and proud. Ike was amazed by the willful naiveté of it all. Eddie, the young fool, romantic and in love, reverts to the silver-screen cowboy, the West's own Don Quixote lassoing motorcycles on the lone prairie.

"You going to cuff me?" he asked.

And there was Eddie, five foot seven, trying to look bigger than life, wearing a long-rider coat, Mexican spurs that clanked when he walked, cowboy hat with a white neckerchief, for Christ's sake, knotted around his throat. The horse shook its head and the bit chimed. Ike stared over Eddie's shoulder, to the land that ran low and level as if it couldn't get to the horizon quick enough. How could you not half-admire this? All the grandiose schemes it hatched in people.

Eddie wanted to be a legend in his own time. As if there weren't enough already. A pain in the ass. That's what legends were, a pain in the ass.

"No," Ike said, and walked over to Eddie's rifle. Ike picked it up and put it in the back of his Bronco. "You've been enough of a damned nuisance. You take those horses home, get a ride down to the office by early afternoon, or I'll issue a warrant."

As Ike pulled away, he could see Eddie mounting. He'd turn himself in first thing. Ike had no doubts about that. Eddie would make his apologies and pay the damages. He'd see his story in the newspaper and hope his mother didn't read it, and if she did, she'd mention it once and never again. The other hands would make his life hell for awhile with jokes, but he would survive that. Someday, when he married, he *might* tell his wife. He'd never tell his kids. Because by then, of course, he'd be an upstanding member of the community.

Ike called dispatch. The Brandt woman and Henry could come down and file charges. He'd be in soon. Had some things to check on first.

He headed out toward his brother-in-law's place where Pattiann was helping, bringing the cows into the lower yards, preparing for calving. He'd be seeing less and less of her for a few weeks and he remembered resenting it early on in their marriage. But the resentment had passed until now—and he wasn't sure what he'd feel this spring calving; indifference? some—but truth was, he still loved Pattiann, and he wanted it to be as easy again as those first fumbling nights back in his small apartment, where crowding with Pattiann was a delicious kind of constraint, a hand-to-hand combat so that they fell into each other more deeply, heedless of the close wall, the single bed. And what had come of those early days? Only this—the certain knowledge that all the room he'd ever needed was in her.

He turned onto the county road, the snow mostly gone, and slowed the car, cranked down the window hoping to hear geese overhead, or the drum of prairie hens mating, some indication that they'd turned a corner into an early spring. But the air still had the edge of snow in it and the wind whistled aimlessly. He found himself speeding toward Rob's ranch, wanting to put the miles behind him, see this place in a different light, discover he still gave a damn.

The Stubblefield place shunted past. It had been close to a week now since they'd cleared his yards of cattle and no one had seen or heard from Chas. Partly the reason Ike drove out this way, he supposed. There was no sign of Chas. He felt a small regret when he thought about the horse. Nobody had seen it, and he wondered again if the crew had scooped it up from the snow, or if it had ranged off onto higher grounds scrabbling for food, or fallen to coyotes, and that seemed the most likely scenario and so he'd let it go—just another guilt he couldn't afford to live with.

In the distance, the seamless land ran helter-skelter to the breaks and beyond to where the Little Rockies were etched clear against the sky. A few more miles and he'd be at Rob's, for no other reason than he wanted to see Pattiann.

Harriet was on her knees scrubbing the kitchen floor. "You can come in," she said, waving the sponge at him. "It's dry. I'll be done soon." The kitchen was warm, and Ike could smell chicken in the oven. "You'll stay?" she asked. "All my recipes feed a troupe. Anymore, off season or not, I can't seem to cook less. They'll be in shortly, I'm sure . . . chores always manage to end around an empty stomach."

"Who's working?" Ike asked.

"Bill, Rob, Pattiann, Justin. Martha's in the barn to see the new horse Rob bought Angela. She drags everyone she can out there to see the beast. Ugly brute, a gelding with a head like a bass fiddle." She shrugged, pushed her hair back, sopping the ends with soap. "I meant to go rescue Martha myself, but"—she threw the scrub brush back in the bucket, water sloshed and stilled—"maybe you could? Make sure Angela hasn't worn her down?"

He was glad for the excuse. He liked Harriet, but she was a woman who spoke in abstracted segments, her attention wandering so that you were never sure if you were talking just to hear yourself talk.

The barn was fragrant with hay and droppings—musky with fresh manure and urine, the feral hints of cat, rat, starling, and magpie. Back home it had been barn swallows and pigeons. The pigeons flapped wings with a slap like dealt cards and cooed garbled messages his father translated. One afternoon, he'd pulled Ike to his side and said, "Hear that? That's the plump one. Imagine being raised in *her* downy breasts. Then one day," and he booted Ike gently in the seat, "out of the nest, into the wide, cold world and all your life you wander, seeking a nest as sweet as the one she fashioned. Someday . . ." His eyes raised to the hard window of light, the single shaft spilling over the loft's slotted floor, and his father had stood there in the shattered light and dust, hands sunk into the breasts of his bibs, eyes lit with a look between glory and grief so that Ike did not know from which to turn away.

He could hear Angela prattling, her small girlish voice piping clear. "Don't you think he's handsome?" she asked. "I learned this in 4-H."

Martha was in the aisle, seated on a milking stool. She looked frail in the half-light, her spine curved, ankles crossed one over the other. She was studying the wide rump of a horse across from her. In the far stall, their milk cow shifted from foot to foot, its ears cocked to the young girl's voice. Ike took off his hat, slapped it gently against a thigh. Martha looked up over her shoulder, smiled, and nodded toward him, and he could see Pattiann's vigor in her, but also a quiet he'd never yet seen in his wife. She was strength and heart where her daughter was still nerve. Ike longed to believe that in the years to come, Pattiann would find a similar sweetness of her own and that he would be with her to see it.

"Ike," Martha said, and beckoned him over with a finger, "come take a look at Angela's new horse. He's a big one, but she can handle him."

"Oh, he's kind, Uncle Ike. Even you could ride him," Angela said, and turned back to curry the animal's coat.

Martha reached up for his hand, gave it a squeeze. "Good to see you, Ike. What brings you out?"

"I heard you were in a cold barn at the mercy of a young girl in the first throes of love. Thought you could use rescuing. Harriet's about done with the floor, lunch is heating. I'm invited."

"Angela, you're going to wear a patch on that horse's back before you ever put a saddle to him. Why don't you see if your mother needs you?"

Angela blew out a gust of air that flopped her bangs off her forehead. "You just want to get rid of me."

"Yes," Martha said.

"Brother," Angela said, but put her tools away. She rubbed her horse's forehead one last time and slowly walked to the barn door, looking back over her shoulder twice. She paused at the door.

"I forgot—"

"Your manners. Your horse will be here after lunch. Go on."

"But isn't he beautiful?" she asked.

"He's a rare, beautiful beast," Martha said. The young girl shut the door quietly behind her.

"Pattiann was just as bad," Martha said. "Pull up a sawhorse. Can't stand to have people hovering up there." Ike sat. "Been meaning to ask how you're doing," she said. "I worry, you know."

He waited, unsure what she had in mind. He ran the brim of his hat through his fingers. She plucked it away.

"You look like Rob used to when I caught him taking shortcuts with chores. This Stubblefield business. Isn't over yet. You know that?"

"Haven't heard a thing from him in almost a week. Looks over to me."

"There's talk. Always talk. Here and there. Won't say much to us, you being related, but I hear it and you ought to know. People are saying Art would have handled it different."

"No doubt." Ike smiled.

Martha picked at her jeans. "Oh yes. Art had a way. What he didn't know about . . ."

"And if it had been brought to his attention?"

"Oh, he'd have slapped Stubblefield around a few times and called it even. He could get away with that. You could have, too. Slap a man around for being a jerk and they'll say he had it coming. But take away his cattle?"

"I didn't take them. I shot them."

"Yes, well." She leaned back on the stool, her hand propped against her spine. She stretched. "Someone, I'm not saying who, but *someone* with maybe an eye on your job is saying there might have been money involved."

"Jim Parker."

She crooked her mouth in a tight smirk. "You didn't hear me say that."

"It'll blow over."

"Maybe. If the weather turns and folks get busy with other matters. Then Stubblefield will be forgotten and so will the rumors and Parker will be back as your deputy and glad for it. And maybe in a year and a half he'll forget this barb up his ass and not bring it up in a bid to defeat you."

Ike eased his buttocks on the wood, braced both hands on the beam. "Assuming I don't hand the whole shitteree over to him or someone like him before then and skip town with all that money I made off Stubblefield's scrawny herd."

"That isn't funny." She shook her finger at him. "Parker's a good old boy from way back and if he hadn't felt Art's scandal a little too closely he might have run for the job and gotten it."

"And he might have done all right by this community. Do the jobs they want him to and ignore the ones they don't. It's what they want. A homespun boy who'll spit with them and wrangle the pesky cayuse when necessary."

She sat resolute on the stool. "Do we look that small to you?" She studied her feet, kicked them like a schoolgirl. "I suppose we must appear unworldly sometimes. But don't mistake that for stupid." She pointed a finger at him. "You're a good sheriff and we've needed one. That'll sink in. Give it time . . . and a little judicious self-defense right now. Sue the sonofabitch for slander."

He sighed and leaned his elbows on his knees, his hands clasped in front. He looked around him. "Maybe I'm not cut out for this place."

"You thinking of leaving?" She crooked a fist and rubbed her lower back. "She won't follow. It's not in her."

"You know your daughter that well?"

Martha stood from the stool and offered her hand. "Let's start up to the house. Used to be," she said, "I could outstride any cowhand on the place, outwrangle, outride. You should have known me then. Pattiann got the best of me and her father, that one. And the worst."

They stepped out into the bright afternoon light. Martha squinted against the sun. Her skin was freckled, liver-spotted, tanned, and worn fine. "This is what Pattiann wanted." She waved her hand over the ranch. "And the hard truth of it is, she could have done it. She had it all: smarts, talent, drive, stubbornness—a whole lot of that. At ten she killed a rattler that bit her, hung on to the damn dead thing the whole ride in to the doctor's. Bill couldn't take it away, not the doctor or the nurse. I didn't try. Why? Because I knew her that well. She wanted us all to know—the family, the town, God, and the snake—that she'd gotten the upper hand." Martha slowed to a stop, took a deep breath. "If there was one failing in that child, it was a lack of humility. Took her until her early twenties to learn that. And then she left."

"She came back," Ike said.

"She came back when she was ready. After she'd met you and come to realize there were other possibilities to life, even out here. Before that,

she was a young woman going to seed who ran off every eligible bachelor in a hundred-mile radius, to hang with that worthless Stubblefield.
And I knew what was behind that, too." She crooked a finger at the
house. "Harriet's a good woman, don't get me wrong. She's what a
rancher needs. Keeps house, helps out, raises a brood of kids, and generally stays out of the way. Pattiann wasn't about to set herself up for
that. She didn't see it could be any other way. So she picked Stubblefield,
the one man it wouldn't happen with." The focus in Martha's eyes softened. "Pattiann didn't get to see me in my glory days."

"You must have been hell on a horse."

She tugged at his arm. "And don't you forget it." She stopped and
looked over her shoulder. "This is not something a mother should say,
but I'm going to. Whether you go or stay, Pattiann will survive. She'll
work the ranch for a hand's wages, move in our house when we die.
She'll be a canker in Rob's side, and you, dear boy, will be well out of it.

"She's a survivor. I'm not saying I like the picture I painted. What I
want to see is her having a decent life with you. Some kids to keep her
occupied; she'll wean herself away from here, given time. Maybe the two
of you will find your own small spread and it'll be hers. Not mine or
Bill's or Rob's. Her own." Martha picked at his hand, shook it hard.
"You should stay. It'll get better. It's just this damn winter gets to folks."

He ushered her onto the back porch. "And you want me to stay."

She perked her head into the wind, listened a moment. "Misery loves
company, son." She opened the door, stuck her head into the kitchen.
"Get the food on the table, Harriet. They're back."

The first head of cattle made their lowing entrance into the feed yard
and behind them the young Justin, looking older on his mount, then
Rob and Bill, and trailing them all, Pattiann. Clear across the yards and
the milling cattle, the tired, dismounting men, Ike saw the smile that
spread across Pattiann's face at the sight of him. Her wave was light-
hearted. He thought he loved her more than he could bear, and as he
turned away, he saw that Martha, standing at the side of the door, had
read it on his face.

Purvis sat on a stool in the empty garage. The Chevy was gone. He'd had a full surgery, pets. They carried his business through the slack winter months, before tuberculin testing and calving and the usual assorted ailments of working, range horses. There'd been a cat with ringworm that had dosed a passel of children.

There'd been some distraction with the one case of indiscreet digestion in a Great Dane. They'd lumbered the animal up onto the X-ray table, he and Joe, while the owner, Lois Varner, wrung her hands and baby-talked: "Oh my precious, my sweetie-umpkins." The dog snarled, snapped at Joe.

Purvis twisted the hindquarters up for a side view, told Joe, "Throw a blanket over sweetie-umpkin's head so he doesn't take your arm off."

The woman swore the dog was gentle and a finicky eater. "He won't touch anything but what we give him in his doggie bowl," she insisted. "He's a good boy. But such a picky eater. You don't know what I've gone through to bring him to size. It's a tumor. I just know it's a tumor. Cancer runs in my family," she said.

The dog's stomach was belled with bloat, and before operating, Purvis wanted to see what the dog had gotten into and if the spleen was still in place or had rolled under the stomach. Bloat wasn't uncommon among dogs that ran free on large spreads. They ate whatever presented itself until their stomachs swelled and rolled with gas, twisting the stomach, intestines, and displacing the spleen—if not corrected surgically, the animal died. He'd read about a case of it in humans once. Fellow ate so much roast corn, it packed the stomach walls, then brewed enough gas to float him like a buoy. Ruptured the stomach. Corned to death.

They snapped two plates, side and belly-up. A real feat. When they put the film on the viewer, the owner sucked in her breath and sidled up to it. She fingered the illumined stomach contents—traced one bone and another, her finger filling in the details. "He ate one of my goats. *He ate one of my goats.*"

Purvis remembered then, her State Fair, grand champion, dwarf

Nubian goats. And yes, here one was, the tiny skull still mostly intact and curled against a fetlock as though it were asleep in its mother's womb.

"Jesus," Joe whispered. "Would you look at that." He glanced over at the bloated dog as if it were a miracle. "He swallowed it whole."

Purvis steered the woman away from the picture. "Let's get you out front," he said. Then, to Joe, "Put her on the couch. Set her feet high, her head low. Get her signature on an operating form, then come back and help prep."

The dog survived, but with a newly acquired taste for Nubian goat. In all, a day of small emergencies among the mundane. Joe left the clinic before five. Purvis had come out into the garage after dinner to bask in the glow of his carnauba-waxed, fully operating car, to find it gone.

He'd walked around the garage, as if another angle might reveal the car. He sidestepped the grease-spotted concrete. He sat. He didn't want to think it was Joe. But Joe had a key. Purvis had the other one in his right hand. So this was what it was like, he thought, to be a parent. Your best shot rolling down the highway behind the wheel of a stolen '57 Chevy. What could he have been *thinking*? How could he explain what he'd seen in the Mattick boy that had sounded off him like an echo of himself at fifteen, that made him want to see in himself the kindness, the steady hand and level heart of his own father? And perhaps to be given one last chance to save something in this world besides some goat-eating dog.

He scuffed his heels on the cement, snatched up an oil rag and rubbed his hands on it. Still trying to resurrect the hog. His wife Babs had recognized it early on, threw up her pretty little nineteen-year-old hands after a quick year of marriage, and absconded with his favorite Stones album and a jeweler's apprentice for the good life far away from veterinary schools and one-room apartments. And what the hell, she'd been right to go. He was a budding young doctor, not the real kind, but the kind fit for animals, who would scrimp and save and work his whole damned life to cash it in on a small clinic in the badlands of Montana.

"Good for you, Babs," he said. Got out long before it came to what it would have between them, this moment where he'd want more out of his life and turned to her for it. It was more than a person could ask of another, a wife, a friend, or a fifteen-year-old boy named Joe Mattick. Had Joe ever *said* he wanted to be a vet's assistant, or a vet or an auto mechanic? Hadn't Ike warned him, hadn't he?

His stomach tightened. He should call Ike. His chest hurt and he sat quickly back on the stool, tried breathing through his nose.

He could see the chase, the car rolling down some bank, end over end, a dull *whump, whump, whump*. Purvis was shaking. He didn't give a shit about the car. He just wanted to know he hadn't done something irreparable this late in life.

He stood, turned a slow circle around the garage. What he should do is call Joe's parents, or get in his truck, go looking for the boy. He wadded the oil rag and flung it at the far wall, but the cloth billowed open and fell short and soft. Goddamn it. Give me something I can do.

Just after a late dinner with Pattiann, Ike's phone rang. "More dead dogs, Purvis?" he asked, half hoping that's all there was to it. "We're still working on it," he said, and they were, sort of, a low-priority investigation. He'd given it to Harley.

"Forget the damn dogs. This is about Joe."

Ike waited, could hear in the pause how reluctant Purvis was, and at the same time how desperate. "What?"

"The car's gone. Joe's got a key. He needed one, you know, working on it . . ."

Ike could hear Purvis blaming himself, and hadn't Ike known somewhere down the line it would come to this. "Maybe he's just out on a test drive."

"No."

"You're sure it's Joe? Have you called his parents?"

"Yes, yes, of course. They thought he was with me. I told them not to worry, I said I'd talk to you. I told them you'd make sure Joe was all right. You will, Ike, won't you?"

"Cripes." He looked up at Pattiann, who was near; she perched herself on the edge of the dining table. "I'll do what I can. I'll have the officers keep an eye out."

"I'm just asking you, no high-speed chases, okay? Let him ride the damn thing out of gas."

Dan Roehe was a rookie on the sheriff's force. It showed in his work hours: graveyard shift on backcountry roads, worked in tandem with the Highway Patrol. The local drag strip, lover's lane. The straightest route between reservation bars. He spent his nights running people through the DUI drill. Walk a straight line, backwards, heel to toe. Say the alphabet slowly, distinctly. Arms out, touch your finger to your nose alternating right and left. Close your eyes and stand with one foot raised. The other. He stocked Breathalyzer kits by the caseful.

But a good portion of the night, especially this time of year, after the worst of winter, he spent hours daydreaming into the dark fields, or spotlighting coyotes, the occasional elk herd, an antelope and his harem. His favorite, oddly enough, were the jackrabbits, leggy, mule-eared beasts that bumped their way across the land in vast numbers. Once or twice an evening he liked to open his squad door quietly, then slam it, and a hundred heads would jerk up into the night, ears lifted in surrender. On a really good night, when the ground was pounded hard with cold, he'd turn the car into the field and part the sea of rabbits, like Moses delivering the Jews. He'd cut the engine and roll the window down to hear the stampede. The small thundering of a thousand paws. He'd have liked to pick a few off, but the sheriff was fussy about spent bullets. Like they came out of his own pocket. Accountability, he called it. But what the fuck was a guy supposed to do out here, at night, with nothing but time on his hands, and rabbits?

The car blew past him before he realized it. And then it was just a streak of taillights fading. He looked at the radar. He tried to keep it at a distance—everybody knew the damn things gave you cancer. It registered ninety-five. The old adrenaline kicked in, and he fought for calm. He turned on the engine, switched on the headlights, checked the rearview mirror, and gunned it onto the highway. It was a lovely machine, zero to sixty in no time at all. He checked his seat belt with one hand and then leaned back and floored the accelerator. The taillights grew closer. He was cruising at eighty-five. The car ahead slowed. He switched on the overheads and startled himself—a hangover from his pre-force days. That little kick of fear when you see rolling blues hit the road.

There were two, maybe three in the car. A classic, '57 Chevy. Some kids out for a joyride. *Well, it'll cost you boys.* He hit the siren, two short blasts. The car pulled away; he could smell oil and exhaust as the driver hammered the accelerator.

Sonofabitch, they were going to make a run for it. He set his jaw, felt the first nervous ticking in his chin. He felt like a kid himself again, dragging down this highway or another one very much like it. He might have a girl alongside, Bernice, or better yet Adrian, sweet Jesus how she loved speed, and they would run until the road won. It always had, with his old secondhand cars throwing up smoke that greased the windshield. But he had the car for it now. He had the excuse. He had all the time and road in the world and these kids were going to learn one hell of a lesson before he was through.

He goosed it, called dispatch. "Yeah, I'm in pursuit. On Frazier. Maybe ten miles to Baptiste, heading south. '57 Chevy, license plate number . . . hold on. No plate. Dark red chassis, white roof." He left the channel open, heard the dispatcher call the Highway Patrol as backup. He was doing ninety-five and still cooking. The road was sweet and clean, straight as the day was long. They were topping a hundred and five and the engine was just coming alive. Jackrabbits slewed in a blur from the road. He nosed up to the Chevy's fender. Two in the car, hit the siren again, saw the passenger, the smaller one jerk in the seat as if hit with a cattle prod. The Chevy inched away, hauling hard now. It was a classy rig—what he wouldn't have given for one like it as a kid, a lot of muscle, but old, and he could smell the oil.

Ahead, he thought he could make out a flash and sweep, blue lights like heat lightning, coming down in the distance, and he inched around the vehicle. He wasn't sure what he was going to do, maybe just take a good look at the kids, maybe swerve at them a little and scare the beje-sus out of them. Or maybe it was just the sheer joy of the engine hum-ming under him and the road a level sweep and help just moments away that turned it all into a sort of reckless game, and Ike would have his skin for it, but that didn't matter. This was his collar and those kids were going to know it. He glanced over at their window, grinning. He could pick out the dip of cowboy hats, chins, and jutting noses. The passenger, just a young kid, white-faced and out of his league, and Dan almost felt sorry for him. And then they were swerving off, braking and skidding in a glaze of dirt and hard grit, sliding into the field, and he looked ahead in time to see *it* in the headlights and he thought as he caromed up, how beautiful—with head lifted into the lights, eyes luminescent and full rack grazing the hindquarters, and then it was levitating, lifting into the air, swimming in the air that was all light and glass, and it hit the windshield, the glass spidered, buckling in like a net, as if he were casting into water and hauling in some huge glittering fish, and that was all Dan knew as the legs drove through the windshield and a hoof took him in the neck, snapping it at an angle so that his head bumped on his shoulder like a baby who hadn't learned to lift it yet. The elk plowed through the cab, hindquarters slewing through the passenger seat, toppling into the back where it hung up, and the cruiser careened into the field, hit a rock, canted, rolled onto its side. It flipped onto its roof and smeared a path through sage and cactus, broadcasting bits of metal and glass until it planted itself hood-first into the gouge it had shoveled out. And after a small pause among the startled stampede of jackrabbits, it rocked back down onto the flattened roof and rested with a final settling of bolts and joints, the wheels spinning as if there were road yet to travel.

Ike got the call shortly after hanging up from Purvis. He drove out to where Fred Elrose sat stunned in his cruiser and the Highway Patrol set up detours. Elrose was shaken, said he'd gotten the call and being close by had responded quickly. He'd seen two sets of headlights heading down the road toward him, and then the one in the right lane swerved and shortly after that the left, and then he could see the left bumping and airborne it seemed, and then there was this. He'd gotten here as fast as he could. He didn't know what happened to the other car. He hadn't seen it after it had headed right. Maybe it cut across the field. Maybe it headed back down the highway. He didn't remember. He'd run out into the field, looked into the cruiser, and found himself sitting in the dirt with his eyes shut. There was Dan—and all that meat and blood—and then Fred was lowering his head again and breathing through his mouth.

It had to have been Purvis's Chevy. Everything happening, Ike reasoned, even as he was talking to Purvis. Dan was already dead, his neck snapped, the car flipping and stopping. All in the span of a phone call. Or no. It would have to have been earlier. Time enough for Elrose to arrive, witness the scene, recover, and call it in. The dispatcher getting over her first shock, calling Ike. There was an APB out on the car. An officer was dead.

It was all so senseless. Dan had been a good man. Ike would have to drive out to Dan's folks, tell them their son had died in the line of duty. They lived a good eighty miles away, on a small ranch that Dan had bragged himself lucky to escape—the small life, the boredom. And now he was dead and his parents, early in their middle years, would wake the rest of their days and know the relentless taste of grief as sharp and cold on their tongues as metal on a winter's morning.

The wrecker's winches growled and the cruiser bumped up while pieces—a fender, glass, some bits of metal—sprinkled down like a curious rain, and then the car was slowly rotating back onto wheels that had stopped and would never turn again. The ambulance stood by, its lights strobing red, crisscrossing the multiple blues that swept from the parked cruisers so that the entire area had a carnival aspect, even among the somber-faced deputies who stood in small packs at a distance and the wrecker crew trying to avoid looking inside the vehicle but unable not to, the rescue team studying how best to retrieve the body, and the ambulance attendants who had seen it all before, leaning against their van, smoking cigarettes, waiting for the door to be prised open so they could bag it and be gone, back to the tail end of their shift and home to wives or parents. And he tried to imagine how Dan's parents would take it, gowned and robed, in the living room politely waiting for the sheriff to speak, or by then sitting, though they would have known when they first caught sight of him at the door. And he wished he could spare them that—he on the doorstep under a lone lightbulb, sheriff's hat in hand, the truth already sinking in, limbs turning insubstantial, and realizing that *our Dan is dead*.

They fired up the Jaws of Life and the gas engine cut a swath through their voices. The attendants snuffed cigarettes. Ike moved just behind the rescue team, believing it important to witness, a friend among strangers. He had a fleeting image of Dan in his crisp uniform, all bluster as the others teased him about his spit-shined shoes. It was hard to make him out in the tangle, human and animal, and disconcerting the way his head rolled across the chest as they lifted him out. Elrose stood with his back to the scene and Ike was torn between doing right by the dead and dealing with the living. The attendants were skilled, already folding Dan into the body bag, and there were no jokes about the elk as he'd half expected, the size of the rack wedged between windshield frames, no death-site humor, so he went to where Elrose was looking out over the reaches as though he expected someone to come walking out of the dark. Elrose spoke. "I'm all right," he said. "I'll be fine." And Ike realized Elrose was speaking to himself, assuring himself his legs still worked and his heart still beat, and barring further catastrophe, would wake on the fortunate side of his bed in the morning.

"Go home," Ike said. "Can you drive?"

"Yeah," he said. "Sure. Slow as hell, you bet, but I'll make it all right." He shoved his hat back on his head, held his hands to his ears to warm them. Elrose's hands were trembling and he confined them to his pockets. "It's not like I haven't seen this kind of thing before," he said.

Ike gave him a moment. He glanced at his own hands and was surprised to see that they didn't hitch or jump, that other part of him taking over, inspecting the scene, distancing itself, preparing for the rest of the night.

Fred was nodding. "But this one was rough. I was so damned close," he said. "And Dan—what the hell was he doing? I mean, I was close. We could have run him to ground between us."

He blew a thin breath. "When I first shined my light in there, I didn't really expect to find him alive. Not with the mess, the speed they must have been traveling. I thought I was ready for it. But there was all that fur and bone. I mean, the Goddamned elk was glaring at me and Dan's head cheek-to-cheek with it so you couldn't make out at first what was what. Scared the hell out of me. Took me a moment." Elrose laughed softly. "I mean, I didn't expect *any* of this. And then this *thing* happened—like I was looking in a mirror and it was me hanging there with my neck broken, in my uniform, in my cruiser, and then I was just sitting and it was dark and"—he laughed again—"it was dark because I had my eyes closed, and when I opened them, I was sitting in the dirt and Dan was Dan and I was alive."

"I imagine it felt good," Ike said, laid his hand on Elrose's shoulder.

"You can't imagine."

"Yeah," Ike said. He looked around. "I'm going to send you home with one of the others. I know you're all right, you're fine. I'll send someone back out for your car. Lock it up, give me the keys, take a ride home and get some sleep."

The ambulance and rescue team pulled away. The wrecking crew was chaining the squad up to be loaded onto the flatbed. In an hour there would be nothing but the roadside scorch of flares, a scooped-out place in the dirt, some trinkets of glass and metal the pack rats would covet. In daylight, buzzards would feast on the elk carcass and a magpie might weave the hair in its nest. Ike made arrangements for Elrose's ride home, battened down the details before hitting the road himself. He had bad news to deliver. It was quarter past midnight.

The sheriff's office was buzzing when Purvis stepped in and then the noise fell to a hush and then silence. He felt it coming, something awful, like the news of his father's death, like the time Babs walked out on him and everything he did turned to shit. He braced himself in the chair.

Ike told Purvis the story, explained the wreck, his drive out to Dan's parents' place, and how later, in town, they'd found the Chevy and Joe Mattick.

"Oh God," Purvis said.

Ike rubbed his hands over his face. "Don't start wringing your hands now. I have put up with enough shit for one night. Joe's asking for you. His parents are with him now, and a lawyer. He claims he blacked out. Doesn't remember anything. If you're his friend—and he believes you still are—get that boy to talk."

Purvis nodded. He felt old, as if he'd just outlived his own life.

Joe looked small behind bars. A kid, on the point of being sick. His legs swung forward and back, one, then the other. The lawyer sat on a chair to the side, a yellow legal pad filled with scribbling on the floor next to him. Ike let Purvis into the cell, positioned himself next to the door. The kid looked up and quickly back down at his feet. His eyes were red and ringed with a sheen. His nose ran so that he swiped at it with his sleeve. Purvis offered his handkerchief and Joe took it.

Joe turned away, stared at the graffiti on the wall. *Hank was here.* Biblical quotes: *Bring my soul out of prison, that I might praise thy name.* And *Merry Fucking Christmas, December, 1984.* Purvis wondered what this young boy thought. He tried to see what it was in the kid he'd believed in.

Chas seldom drove into town now. There wasn't much to warrant it but boredom. He always drove past Taylor's house, kept an eye out for the wife, the tiny yapping dog. He'd idle past Coker's store, honk if he saw him and grin. They wanted to think him done with and over. He liked to think that too, sometimes. He wondered if Coker'd gotten a new dog yet.

Of course, he always watched for Pattiann. She'd been alongside her husband that day at his ranch. Chas had watched from the kitchen window, wringing his clothes in a basin of rinse water, while the sun picked out colors like blooms: blue sky, green jackets, gray, brown, a splash of red on Pattiann's shoulders where her hair wandered loose. Something satisfying about that. Watched her work the horse from a distance, a big gray. He'd wondered what she was thinking. If she thought of him at all, or watched for him as he watched for her, something inside her wringing each time he twisted the cloth in his fists.

He parked the rig next to the grocery. Foolish, but it was where he'd come across her before and that seemed enough reason to believe it could happen again. He stretched his legs and leaned his head against the window, squinting into the gray half-light this season was painful for, everything the hue of an unattended corpse: sidewalks, streets, cars and trucks, cinder block buildings, windows glazed like banks of sightless eyes. He felt immersed in gray, and looked at his pallid hands and believed if he could look through the flesh down his chest, he would see the cage of ribs dirtied to the bone. He felt chilled and thought of the store, its banks of fluorescent lights that hollowed eyes in people's skulls and spread its uniform blandness over the gaudy cans of food, the winter fruits, and the store's back wall with its coffin of meat brighter in dismemberment than in life. He stepped out of the rig, closed the door behind him, and waved himself into the store through the electric eye.

Johnny Cash groused through the overhead speakers—gone and shot another woman, Delia this time. Chas dipped his hat at the checkout girl, a woman of fifty who never raised her eyes from the conveyor belt of food but kept a running conversation with the customers as though she knew them by smell, and he could swear her nostrils flared and pinched as he walked by. She tolled the charges while a young housewife tried to look casual, fiddling her purse clasp like a thief fingering a combination. The owner, Ray Weldert, stood behind the customer service, watched the store's sole stock boy punch new labels over the old. Chas walked the abbreviated aisles: shampoo, hand soap, racks of makeup with packages sporting pouty women and slutty eyes. The end of the

aisle was a comedown: douches, pills for bloat, feminine hygiene prod-
ucts—a mountain of cotton wadding a woman would straddle before she
turned old. He picked up a package of tampons and tucked it under an
arm. He turned the corner and even as he did, he knew he would see
Pattiann. But there was only an old woman. Her head twitched toward
him, and she smiled in a way she must have imagined as coy. She
dropped a can of coffee in her cart and pushed it, one front wheel
thumping at a right angle to the others. He slipped the tampons in
among the instant coffees, snatched up, instead, a box of Earl Grey tea.
Tea with Pattiann. He would feed her orange slices. Then he was in the
pet section with its collars and leashes, flea powders, rubber bones, Kitty
Litter. Dried food, canned. He hefted a can of dog food, turning it over
in his hands.

His own good meat.

He laughed, could picture the neat slices of Alpo quick-browned in a
skillet. His own good meat on clean white dishes instead of slipping
down the gullet of some dissatisfied mutt who would blow a rank fart
that the owner would smell and never imagine what was behind the
smell: the sweet fields, grama grass and buffalo and sage. Never imagine
Chas of a summer night, standing in the field watching his cattle like so
many dark stars.

He made a circuit of the store. He was tired of it, thought Pattiann
selfish to keep him waiting in the aisles as if she must know they were to
meet today. At the end of his third walk through, before he passed the
customer service desk yet again, he tumbled the items in among the
refrigerated butter and eggs and walked through the register with a pack
of smokes. He paid out the price like he was pissing it, one coin at a
time. The checker said, "Have a nice day."

He stepped into the cold, looked up and down the street in hopes of
seeing Pattiann. No kids around, must be a weekday, school. Mostly
women, a stray one here and there. And it seemed to him they moved as
if in mourning, their coats buttoned to the neck, hands weighted with
packages, and still they stopped to stare in store windows, one blank

gaze meeting another, and maybe one sucked in a gut while another turned away like she'd seen more than the day allowed.

But no Pattiann. He could call her and that seemed reasonable. There was a phone booth across the street and he thought of dialing her number, out in the street, and he cut a diagonal across to the bar where there was a phone in the back hallway.

It was early, so Barry sat with his feet propped on the bartop. He read a book under a goose-necked lamp. The gray daylight filtered through the window in careful sips. Chas nodded, ordered a tap beer, and crossed through the room into the back hall. He filched out a quarter, fed it into the slot, and hung up when he realized he didn't know her number. The phone book dangled on a chain. Its upper edges were worn, a brown stain down the side. He flipped through: Ableson, Dilling, Latouse, Miller, N., O., P. He ran a finger down the directory: Pamier, Pape, Pappet. Parsons. Ike and Pattiann.

He committed the number to memory. He heard the coin drop, hit bottom. He moistened his lips, punched the number. She answered on the third ring.

"Yes?" she said.

"Yes," he agreed and cradled the phone on his shoulder.

"Who is this?"

And he was sure he could answer her, yet he didn't; he waited instead to hear her voice again. The open circuit hummed and the wall heater gave off a smell like burning hair. He should have had a beer first. And there was a dial tone. His quarter was gone and so was his stomach for it. He picked up the day's paper discarded on one of the back tables, drank the beer slowly, paid and left the bar.

He didn't know what he intended, but he drove to Pattiann's house, parked across the street. He imagined her in the kitchen, or showering, or making the bed. He sat with his hand on the truck's door handle. It would take a little push, a shove. Up the sidewalk, knock on the door. She would want to know what he wanted.

Good question.

He imagined her surprised at first, but then she'd invite him in. They were friends, after all. And maybe that was true. He approached the house, held his finger above the doorbell, enjoying the potential—if he did, if she were—and then he tried the door, unlocked, as he knew most doors in this small town were. He opened it a crack, and warmth eased out. He took in the first deep breath of her place: woodsmoke, lemon oil, bacon, something flowery, leather. He crossed the threshold, listened. He stepped into the hall, glanced in the mirror over a small chest in the entryway where he saw himself and the living room behind him reflected, rippling in the old glass as he moved from foot to foot. When he faced the room, its precision surprised him. The room was neat, snug with overstuffed furniture, a rocking chair with hand-embroidered seat covers alongside a fireplace. He tried to imagine Pattiann in the rocker with a sewing basket, and knew even as he thought it, that was not Pattiann. No. At the room's threshold was a boot tree, the hardwood floor scuffed where heels had clattered into the crotch. He vised his heel against the wedged back and pulled gently. The boot resisted and he stopped, stepped clear, and entered the living room.

He set the rocker in motion. He guessed the recliner was Ike's and so he settled himself into the plushy cushions, braced his heels on the ottoman. He tipped back his head and inhaled. He believed he could smell Pattiann, just like his daddy claimed he could his wife. Where was Pattiann anyway? On an errand? Or here, in the house? He hefted himself clear of the chair, whisked at the dirt newly smudging the ottoman, spat on a finger and rubbed the cloth, gave up with a shrug. He stepped quietly across the floor. The best part of it, he thought, would be surprising her around one corner or the next, an expectation that clenched him up in ways he hadn't known for awhile now. Not since the night he'd done the dogs.

In the kitchen, he could still smell the morning's bacon, and the coffeepot was half full. A cup was next to the pot and he ran his finger over the stain of lipstick. He raised the cup in a salute and sipped. Still liked her coffee black. He drank as he stepped off the kitchen's perimeter, opening drawers. He liked the mild disarray, towels mixed with dishrags, a potholder scorched but clean. The sink was chipped in a corner, and next to the sink was a thick cutting board. He picked up a filet knife. This too would be Pattiann—her tools in good order. He might have predicted this. He pressed the razor edge to the callused side of his hand, the skin lifting like a dull scale, an opaque sheet on the knife's shining surface. The clock above the sink ticked, the furnace blower kicked in with a hum, and sunlight through the window skewered his hand, the knife glowing and the skin curling over the blade, and then there was a noise upstairs. A squeak, shift, and back into quiet. He cocked his ear toward the ceiling. It was so still that he might have doubted himself had he not been sure from the start that *she was here,* as she was *intended* to be.

He set the knife down, and then he found himself on the stair and then in the upstairs hallway where he paused to study the portraits grouped on the wall: Pattiann as a younger woman, astride a horse; with her brother, branding calves. And Ike. His family farm. A young man milking a cow, forehead pressed to the ribs of the animal, face tilted toward the camera and smiling. Chas leaned closer. Parson's father, and Chas tried to imagine what it must have been to have lived Ike's life—the neat barns in the background, the cozy pens, the attention of the man in this photo. How delicately the fingers framed the cow's udder. Chas shook his head. He walked down the hall, glanced into the spare bedrooms, the bathroom, and at the head of the hallway he stopped before easing through the door. Pattiann was stretched out on the bed, fully clothed and sleeping. He waited in the doorway, just taking it in. He moved to the bedside and stood over her, as though he had the right.

The house was quiet, even the hum of the furnace had cut out, and sunlight sluiced through the window over her bed, kindling her hair, warming his skin. It was enough, he thought, to just stand here awhile and then leave—no one the wiser for it. He bent over, saw how the chenille spread dimpled her cheek, ran his hand over the still-warm depression from where she'd turned over. He sat on the edge of her bed, her body tilting with his weight. He stroked her cheek with a finger. She stirred and he could see how she rose out of the deeps of dreams, like a fish breaking the surface, her eyes flicking beneath the pale lids, the beginnings of a smile shaping itself on her face, a slow lovely gesture. Her eyes fluttered, opened, and grew larger with recognition and surprise, then narrowed. She lay still.

"Pattiann," he said.

She closed her eyes as if to send him back to the dreams she must believe she was still in. But when she opened them again, he could see the resignation there. "Chas," she said. She tipped up on an elbow, looked him in the eye. She held him with a stare for a long moment. He tried to read her.

He traced a ridge in the bedspread with a finger. "This don't need to be anything more than what you make of it," he said.

"What I make of 'it' is an invasion of privacy. Ike might give it another name—breaking and entering—you think of that, Chas?"

"Door was open." His finger followed the spread's fold to where her knee lay and he drew the finger back again. He folded his hands together in his lap. It was not a customary gesture and how strange—to find his hands so committed to nothing, so idle in his lap and primly posed. He crossed his arms, uncrossed them and let his hands drop.

"I didn't plan this, if that's what you're thinking," he said. "I didn't plan anything." He looked over the headboard, out the window to the gray sky, the blur of black branches against the gray, the scramble of twig and limb as the wind tussled the treetops. "Not even coming to town, or leaving the ranch, but here I am and if you asked me why, I couldn't say, except"—he rubbed a pant leg with his palm—"that there's *nothing* there at home. No one thing I *need* to do anymore."

"And so you just walk into my house, into my bedroom like that's the next natural thing?"

He studied the hand he was scrubbing down his pant leg, the palm reddened. "Yup. Go figure," he said.

She swung her legs off the other side of the bed, sat with her back to him. "Chas." Her voice was weary. "I am not now, and have not been a part of your life for a long time."

"Bullshit." He reached across the bed and grabbed her elbow. "Enough a part of your life you had to come out to the ranch and see for yourself. You may choose to think otherwise, but it was still a part of me you aimed for when you sighted on my cattle." She tugged her arm and he let go. She stood, brisked a hand down her shirt as if shaking off dust, and faced him. "All I want to know," he said, "is what I did that you should hate me so." He stayed seated on the bed, opened the bedside dresser drawer, looked in at the oiled rag neatly folded there. "Now, your husband, I can understand that, and that's not to say it was right, or just, or forgivable." He lifted the rag, sniffed it, tossed it back into the drawer. "Like two dogs staking out territory. I lift a leg, he lifts his a little higher." He smiled. "I had you first, but he has you last. Doesn't he?" he asked with his back still to her, his voice softening. "Doesn't he?"

"Oh Christ." Pattiann walked to the door. She crossed her hands over her chest. "This is an unlikely role for you: 'Oh no, honestly, it's really not about starving cattle, or even bad advice, but something much larger, something almost noble. Why, it's a struggle for love.' " She shook her head, nailed him with a finger. "Now we're really talking bull-shit." She turned her back and disappeared down the hallway.

He followed.

Her voice trailed as she stomped down the stairs. "Ike saw your cat-tle and did what he had to. It's not a pissing match, Chas. But I suppose it's easier to live with if you think it has to do with something other than your own mistakes." She turned the corner into the kitchen.

He stopped short of the doorway. "What would you know about *my* mistakes? For three years"—he slapped the doorframe on either side— "you've lived the snug little life of the sheriff's wife. You keep a clean house, work your brother's cattle when you get bored. How nice for you." He clapped his hands. "No mistakes for Miss Pattiann, no siree. No sir-eeee." He walked over, and she stood her ground. "No mistakes. No dirty hands here." His fingers wrapped around her wrist and raised it to eye level.

She curled her hand into a fist. He folded it in his free hand, the small bones balled tight, felt the urge to crush them, compress bone on bone until it and the distance she kept folded in on itself like flesh. He leaned in toward her ear.

"Yes," he said. "I have made *mistakes*. Some of them . . . Listen, I have done things you would not want to hear of," he said. "And things . . . have not worked out as I *imagined*." He backed off, laughed softly. "Maybe," he said, "this is all just a failure of imagination. I look out my windows. Nothing. I walk the feedlot. *Poof.* All gone." He smiled. "Everything. Like a dream." He released her hand and it dropped slowly back to her side, the fist intact. He tugged at the fringe of hair over his forehead. "And so here I am, and by God, there you were, dreaming in the middle of the day."

She didn't answer and then he saw a softening come over her, a looseness of the neck, perhaps, or the way her cheeks suddenly appeared less drawn, and her eyes lowered and looked away. She turned on a heel and walked to the door. She stood with her hand on the doorknob. "You have to leave, Chas. You can't do this again."

He shifted from foot to foot, rocking in place so that the floorboards beneath him ground like old bones in a socket. He could feel the sag and rise, the flooring a gray and white checked linoleum, the old-fashioned type—one solid sheet—that dipped in a well-trod swale in front of the sink and window. The curtains fluttered briefly as the furnace blower cut in and the warm draft brushed across him. And only then did he realize he was already sweating under his heavy coat, the rank stickiness of fear and anger and embarrassment rising up through the layers and folds, lifting into the air, into the room, taking up residence alongside the work and sleep and rut of this couple. Just another breath in the house.

He crossed the kitchen and she was swinging the door open so that the chill flushed his heat and stink and he supposed he should be angry at how easily she rid herself of him. But it was all becoming so ordinary, so expected, almost boring. *Poof.* He's gone. Just like the cattle. He turned in the doorway, cupped a hand to the back of her head to stroke her hair—bright enough to heat his palm, he thought. Her feet were planted on the threshold and her eyes locked over his shoulder. He dropped his hand and turned to see Purvis standing at the roadway, watching. He smiled. "Your day for company," he said, and was gratified to see her composure slip. And then her head gave a tight nod toward the street, as if to a dog, as if to say *scat*.

It had taken awhile to convince Purvis to enter the house and sit down to a cup of coffee. "I'm not bothering you?" he kept asking. "I didn't mean to interrupt anything. . . ." That and other leading questions. But it was not in her to explain or defend what he'd witnessed. She was weary of men and their expectations, tired of being forced into a corner, one way or another, just because she was a woman. He would believe in her, or not. They were friends enough for that trust. Or not. She made fresh coffee. Purvis seated himself at the kitchen table, his gaze jumping over the counters, his shoulders tight. She sat across from him and they drank the first sips in silence. Purvis looked as if he were going to speak, but each time it was as though he'd lost track of his thoughts or the ability to shape them into speech. He sighed largely, once and then again. "Forgive me," he said. "It's been a hard morning."

And then Pattiann remembered. Dan was dead. She remembered Ike's grief, the loss of a good man and a friend—and having to inform the parents. And of course, there was no appeasing the loss of a child. But you could blunt it, for a while, maybe, by providing an honorable purpose to the death—*in the line of duty*—and arranging the police escort and graveside honors. It helped the family, he said. What he hadn't said, but she already knew, was it also helped that someone was in jail. The slowest healing, Ike always claimed, were the families and victims who had no one to fix blame on, finally coming to hate everyone and no one in specific. Or in some cases, ladling blame on themselves—*if only I'd been there, if only I'd warned him, if only I'd stopped him*. Providing answers to victims was part of his office, and mostly satisfying. But this time the answer was Joe Mattick.

Ike had stayed out all night, finally calling her at five in the morning, weary and stunned. "I wouldn't be surprised," he said, "if Purvis comes to see you." It had been offered as a caution. Preparing and then coaching her. "He'll need help. Some kindness."

She'd hung the phone up disappointed. He believed he had to tell her to be kind. What did he imagine her to be? What did he see when he looked at her?

But then, after all, there'd been a measure of accuracy in his doubt. Here Purvis was, and all Pattiann could think of was her own small difficulties, Chas's visit, her embarrassment. But then, it had always been the small acts of kindness she was most awkward at.

Life, as she understood it, was not kind. You never gave in to tears or asked for someone else's. It had always been that way. Rope burns, the come-along latch that snapped back, windburn, sunburn, frostbite, snakebite, insects, accidents. Keeping your hands to yourself was safe. Keeping your concerns to yourself was safe, because you had enough Goddamn troubles of your own. Silence was safe. Keeping your heart in your own hands was safest. And if a marriage or friendships worked, it was because you were responsible for this or that and you didn't interfere. Sometimes that translated to an unwillingness to risk any more than you had to. Even in love. Staying power was all.

So be it.

She found herself scratching circles on the oilcloth.

"You've heard about Joe?"

She braced the cup between both hands. "I'm sorry," she said. He looked older, used. She wanted to reach across the table and touch his hands. He was breathing as though he couldn't fill his lungs sufficiently. She became slowly aware of other sounds: the drip of water from the faucet, the wind at the windowpane. "I'm lousy at this," she said.

Purvis nodded his head. "Yes," he said. "You are." He let out a sigh and shrugged. "I sat across from Joe in his cell, and damned if I could find a way to make it easier for him. But then, wasn't that the problem? I made it too easy for him, and now he's in there because I trusted him, and somewhere inside I knew better. Shit." He rubbed his chin, a rasping sound of stubble against palm. "Ike warned me," he said. "I should have handed Joe over that first time, when he stole that money. But I let him off, so the next time he stole a car, and now a man's dead."

Pattiann tipped back in her seat. "No guarantee though that Joe would have gotten more than a slapped wrist. Or he might have done his time in juvenile and come out with no better prospects than what he'd learned from the other reform school boys." She found herself growing impatient. Her day had taken an off step somewhere, maybe by napping in the middle of the morning, giving dreams a foothold on the waking hours, and those hours becoming more and more unreal. First there was Chas who couldn't take responsibility, and then Purvis who couldn't let it go. And each of them coming to her as if she were the final arbiter, when what they really wanted from her was the very thing they couldn't find in themselves—a middle ground that found its logic outside of reason, that could love in spite of what they did or didn't do. Someone who could show them how to love themselves again. She thought how angered Purvis would be, to find himself compared to Chas, and how laughable Chas would find it. She would find it laughable herself, if the grief hadn't been so plainly written on both their faces. And of course, she did love them, in spite of it all. Chas and Purvis. And Ike.

She shook her head. "Damn. What could you have been thinking of? Taking him in after school to help around the clinic, showing him the prospects of real work and a paycheck, a way to make himself something other than a low-rent cowhand floating his way from job to job, season to season like his good buddy Lester. Jesus Christ, you ought to be horsewhipped." Her mouth snapped shut on the last syllable.

Purvis lifted an eyebrow at her.

She ducked her head, glanced to where sunlight buttered the counter surface. She looked back at him. Gave it a count of three. "More?" she asked, turning the coffee cup in her hands.

He leaned back in his seat, and his back and shoulders loosened. "Sometimes a good scolding cuts the crap," he said. "Women know that. My mother knew that." He got up, went to the counter, retrieved the pot, and poured them both fresh cups. He set the pot in the center of the table, then walked over to the sink where he stood looking out the window. "The thing is, there he was in jail, just a kid, wearing the same clothes he'd wear to school and saying he couldn't remember. But the keys were in *his* pocket and the car parked just down the street from where they found him." He turned around. Leaned against the sink. Pattiann watched him over the rim of her cup.

"What I can't really seem to get around," he said, "and maybe it's just me trying to pass the buck, but where's the justice? Who or what pits a fifteen-year-old boy against a world so much bigger, older and savvy? I mean, where's the mercy?"

Front-page news: OFFICER DEAD IN CAR CRASH AFTER CHASE. Chas imagined Ike laid out, meat for the renderer. There was some pleasure in the thought. He sat at the kitchen table, reading the paper he'd lifted from the bar: the sports pages with their petty ambitions and the classifieds—all the wants in the world. He imagined Ike dead, Pattiann grieving. He would console her. He would walk back into her life, like he'd walked into her house. That easy. And then he looked up, at the uncluttered room, thought about the empty feed yard. No. What he once had to offer her was gone.

He looked at the picture of the dead deputy and set it down, wondered if the guy had had any intuition of it the morning he'd waked. Did he feel God's hand shoving him through the day, directing him to *the* place at *the* time; did he notice the subtle realignment of landscape— moon here, barrow ditch there? An elk? God pulling the old sleight of hand—now you breathe, now you don't, and hiding behind scripture: "He maketh me to lie down," when what He really meant was *He maketh me to take it lying down.* He was a sucker for blood, a little sacrifice: lamb, sheep, goat, cattle.

Or your own son maybe. Like Chas's father holding him by the neck, next to the cat. Or like Abraham—You want this boy dead?

No, just testing, but would you have done it?

Of course, wouldn't You?

He fed the newspaper to the stove. He put on a coat, his hat, slipped into boots, and filled a bucket of water at the sink. It sloshed against his thigh and rang with a roiling chime against the jamb. The air was moist. The warmed fields steamed in the night air like a winding sheet. All the husk and meat gone. *Poof.* Just so much vapor. The night was gravid, his lungs packed with breath. Overhead clouds lowered the sky. Dark and darker. When he walked, he felt the new resilience of soil. Soon, there would be scrub feed on the ranges. He saw it as an impertinence—the first signs of reprieve so close on the heels of his cattle dragged to the waiting semis. A glut of warmth, rains saturating a land already gorged on snowmelt, turning the fields to soup, raising the reservoirs and creating of the hollows and low-lying fields a mirage of blue. And over his land the greeny growth would spread. A luxuriance of green. A wasteland of green. A spendthrift gesture like coins on the eyes of the dead.

He fumbled with the barn door and when it opened it was to a pitch darker than the night. He struck a kitchen match off his jeans and the flare was a bright hole he winced from. He lit the kerosene lantern next to the door and the flame glowed a weak amber through the sooty chimney. He was like a creature out of a fairy tale, a night visitor bearing gifts, his shadow stretched behind while a pale circle of light sketched his hands and lit the dirt at his feet. In the rafters there was a skittering. Wood dust bored by weevils fell like talcum on his clothes. He stopped, cocked his head, asked, "Where are You?"

He raised the lamp to the far corner, to the bolted stall that looked empty. But there was a wet breathing from the far corner, a cough and wheeze and then a heavy fumbling in the dirt and the slats of the stall thumped and groaned. It felt as though the air were an upwelling of expectation, the lamplight brittle, the birds salted to their perches.

Chas saw the wide blaze on the horse's face, its black eyes. The head slung over the door. The animal wheezed and finding its footing stood quiet as the accused in a witness box.

Chas set the pail down and the horse sniffed the air and nickered. "You." Chas said. He lifted the hat from his head, flagged it at the horse asking, "You in this horse?" The horse swung its head away from the hat, its nose jerking high in the air while its eyes rolled white. Then the horse lowered its head, pressed against the stall door, pushing at it, trying to get at the water. When it tired, it lowered its head so that the poll rested against Chas's chest. Chas spoke into its ear. "See, the way it really is, it ain't personal." He hefted the water pail over the half-door and into the stall. The horse backed up, then lowered its head to drink. "It's all just a pecking order. The sheriff's over me, *and* the judge *and* the bankers." He paused, looking about the barn.

"So if you think about it, it's not just me . . . and, of course, we can't be forgetting God—that sly old coot. Talk about dominion. Huh. You and me, we're all just jerking around at the end of our strings down here." He twitched a hand in the air, floated it up and down before his face. He took a couple of deep breaths and cupped his hands. He breathed into the hollow of his palms, stared into the dark there. "But in all that order of peck and pecked—you are the one thing left me."

The horse drank deeply, a sound issuing from its throat like an underground stream.

"You ain't listening to a thing I'm saying. Why do I bother, huh?" He draped his arms over the stall door, hung there idly. He thought of Patti-ann. Her neat little kitchen. How for that brief moment in the doorway her face had turned tender and he'd believed he was that close to getting back some of his own, but then she'd shagged him from her house like a dog. And now, here he was talking to a damn, spiny-backed nag. He clapped his hands against the stall door just to see the horse shy. The animal pivoted and swung into the corner. "Now I got your attention?" It watched Chas from the dark, the whites of its eyes shining.

"She wants responsibility . . . and by God, I can do that." He opened the door, stalked up to the horse, and the animal stayed riveted to the corner. He reached up, snatched its jaw in his hand, and pinched it between his fingers. With his other hand he grabbed the forelock and pulled the head down. "You don't know the meaning of hungry yet," he said. And then as if the anger in him were as easily calmed as the horse, it flickered and ebbed, and he leaned his forehead against the forehead of the horse, and he stood there like that a long while. And when he left the stall, it was as if the horse had understood him, and having given up hope of food had turned its back instead.

He hefted the lantern, blew it out, and let his eyes adjust to the dark, the trim square of starlight in the doorway. Chas stopped. The fields were heavy with permanence. It was the house that seemed insubstantial, a pale light moored in the darkness. His for a little while yet. He had no way to imagine it. This place separate from him. The cleft in his hand, the creek trough, the flat of his chest, the high pasture—the plat of the land like a map of his body. In the distance under some safer sky, he knew men dreamed of tomorrow. They fell through their days as they fell through sleep, heedless of God's inconstancies. He looked out over the far dark night, over the waking clay, the sage clumps where prairie hens clutched in sleep next to cattle bones. He looked to the far horizon he could not see.

Chapter Ten

The limousines, sheriffs' cars, Highway Patrol, and visiting delegates from other regional police enforcement wound slowly through Main Street, their overheads spiraling red and blue. People on the street doffed hats, bowed heads; the flag on City Hall hung at half-mast. As good a day as any to hold a funeral, better than some. Intermittent sun. Graveside, the mayor spoke, and then Ike, followed by a twenty-one-gun salute. Jimmy Matovich, in American Legion uniform, played Taps on a trumpet. The parents stood side by side. Dan's father accepted the folded flag, held it to his heart. To the side of the group ribboned flowers stiffened, their meaty petals turning translucent about the edges. Pattiann raised her eyes to the horizon and the Little Rockies. Her coat hung open. They'd turned a corner. She was sure of it. It *would* snow again, but it would be as transitory as the flowers on the grave. They'd come through the worst, and she felt guilty with relief, here, on this side of the grave while across from her Dan's mother's hands hung as though emptied of work for the last time. It was something perverse, this feeling that one woman's sacrifice spared another's, as though Pattiann had been given another chance.

The funeral director was inviting family members up for a final farewell. Pattiann leaned into Ike's hearing, whispered, "I'll see you at the hall," and picked her way through the mourners. She preferred to walk: through the old churchyard, and down two blocks to the Grange, where the town women were setting out food. At the outer edge of the mourners, Purvis stood alone. When she caught him by the elbow, he startled. "You should have stood with us," she said and hadn't meant to scold, but it sounded that way and she said more softly, "I'm always glad for your company."

He patted her fingers, turned to walk with her. "I know," he said. "I was late." He read a headstone. "Chambers," he said, and then another, "Samuel Walters and wife Christina." They found their way around the plots, some with short, spiked fences, headstones of granite, or sandstone, the oldest inscribed with origins from Scotland, Germany, Wales, like hopeful mile markers.

"Sometimes," he said, "I regret not having become a real doctor"—he waved his hand over the graves—"who might look at old Samuel back there and think, now there was a fine pain in the ass. Imagine seeing all the babies you'd delivered. It would give you hope." He put his hand over hers, squeezed it. "But when I was young like you, I didn't think of such things—hope was a given."

He led her into the shaded corner of the cemetery, behind the chapel, in a grove of stunted Russian olives. In summer they would rustle silver, drop their mealy fruit into the cheat grass and broom. Dogwood shrubs bordered the plot, their red canes a stab of color against the brown grasses. Purvis stepped carefully. "Right about here is Abigail Stubblefield."

Pattiann was hesitant to follow, though she was curious. It was the sorry back patch of the graveyard reserved for the poor, the abandoned. But the small white clapboarded church lent them some dignity. Purvis stood scratching the back of his head, his greatcoat shrugging up and down. "Here, I think."

"No marker?" Pattiann asked, but of course there wouldn't be one.

"Was one, once. I hadn't lived in town long at the time, but I used to take walks here. I suppose I thought the dead were easier to get to know back then. Found Avery here one day, pounding a cross into the head of her grave. A slapped-together thing. He resembled Chas, though thinner."

She picked her way through the sodden grass, past the odd stones with names and small concrete plat markers.

Purvis stepped around the area, checked the angle of the olive trees over his shoulder, and then the church window. "Picked up the shovel and drove it in up to the cross arm so that it made an X, like X marks the spot. Said, 'That ought to keep her,' and stalked off." Purvis kicked around in the weeds. "I'm glad it's gone."

"Hung herself, you know."

His eyes flitted from the grave to the trees. "I never know what to say to the dead. I can only trust they don't expect much."

"Doesn't look like anyone's been here in years. She must have hoped for better."

He took up her arm again, led them away from the grave site. "Well, hope's not enough in this world. The fact is I didn't become a medical doctor because I didn't have the stamina. And I wasn't a husband to my wife—yes, don't look so astounded, I was married for a brief time—but I wasn't a husband to my wife because I believed in the next day and the day after that, and all the time in the world, and what I didn't get done that day would surely get done the next. I was a dreamer. Back when I was young and immortal."

He wagged a finger in her face. "Oh hell. I should have, would have, could have. Moot points all of them. I've got to resign myself to the life lived. Surely there comes a time when a person can give over *wanting* and find some joy in what's been given?"

They stood at the crosswalk. The wind was picking up. Down two blocks and a short left was the Grange Hall where Ike and her family had filled plates with baked ham and rolls and potato salads, relishes. They'd be gathering in small groups, speaking in low voices, telling stories on one another, and soon there would be quiet laughter, because the living can't stay daunted by the dead for long. She buttoned her coat, knowing Purvis waited for an answer she didn't have. It seemed she only knew how to want as well. He nodded good day and turned away, but she snatched his sleeve and held him there.

"I don't know," she said. "Maybe it's in our nature to want more than we have." She looked up to where cirrus clouds scrawled across the blue. And she was struck by how much of her life had been determined by discontent, how at odds her dreams had always been with reality. She wondered if she would have been any happier had she gotten the ranch. She took a deep breath, let go of his coat.

He knocked a clump of dirt off his shoes into the curb. "My first muddy shoe of the season." He lifted his head and shook it. "It's all so damned human, isn't it? Here I am talking about resigning myself to the present and I can't help but think of spring." He lifted his nose to the air. "Do me a favor? Give Ed and Myrna my condolences. Tell them I'll come visit in a few days."

Pattiann tucked her hands in her pockets. "Ike's doing all he can for Joe."

Purvis nodded, and walked away.

Ike hated public speaking. Funerals were the worst. Give a man his due in ten minutes, console the family, heal the community, and call it duty. It was a good speech. He'd spent a long night writing it, but all through the delivery what he saw was Dan in his office a month prior, sitting awkwardly at attention in a straight-backed chair while Ike read him out for giving a young woman a "pleasure" ride in the cruiser. Though the office was cool, Dan's shirt leeched sweat under the armpits. There was chew in the young man's lower lip, and he swallowed his spit. He apologized, said it wouldn't happen again, ever, and confessed he was afraid of dismissal or suspension, of shaming his parents. "It'd kill them," he said. He was young enough to believe that, and new enough to not realize this was a perfunctory warning Ike had been compelled to give young men any number of times. Ike nodded tightly, said, "See it doesn't." And when he offered his hand, Dan shook it. "Yes, sir," he said, "yes, sir." And it seemed with the twenty-one-gun salute popping in his ears Ike could still feel that damp hand in his.

There was plenty to eat, and though he had little appetite he filled his plate respectfully. In its practical way, the community offered what it could to stave grief: hot ham and biscuits, linked sausages, sliced beef with gravy, chickpeas, corn, wax beans, string beans, maple muffins, dilly bread, enough food to stagger a man. There were town people here, and ranchers who had traveled the length of the county toting covered dishes. And better than eulogies or twenty-one-gun salutes was that first bite of warm bread—acceptance for what is given as well as taken. It's what they do best, he thought.

Among the mourners, Jim Parker shook hands. Groups of men gathered to hear his lowered voice. Parker's bait to the commissioners had failed, quietly and quickly. The commissioners, old cowmen themselves, knew the state of Stubblefield's cattle. As Brett Handover one morning in his office had told Ike, "Parker's pulled his pants down on this one, but you might want to watch your back." And so the commissioners and by now most of the county knew Parker was making a bid for sheriff come the elections.

Let him. Ike didn't know how seriously he wanted the job anymore. He seated himself at the end of a long table, talked to fellow officers from neighboring townships, picked at his food between conversation. He sat next to Fred Elrose, who looked steady enough. Ike thought of the man as he'd seen him the night of the accident, still shaken and bewildered by the sight of the mangled car, elk, and body. When the table's attention was directed elsewhere, Fred said, "I wanted to thank you."

Ike speared a slice of ham onto his fork. "We were all shook that night."

"No," he said. "For talking to the captain. You must have called pretty early."

"I had a long night."

Fred nodded. "Me, too. He gave me a couple days off with pay to sort things out. I split wood, fixed the bathroom sink, talked to the wife and played with the kids. Read the help-wanted. By the end of the second day, I was ready to come back."

But he wasn't sure he'd done Fred a favor. It was getting to Ike—that responsibility for other lives, other families. The names on duty rosters

197

weren't faceless. You felt their handshake for days after. They confessed their fears like sins in the after hours. They believed in you, and you were too human to qualify for that kind of trust, and sometimes the worst happened, and if they were young like Dan, you questioned your judgment in sending them, or if they were seasoned, you blamed yourself for not sensing the strain, and ultimately it didn't matter who it was, they were *all* at risk. And he was tired of it. How many dead did it take to bury you? He set his fork down. His plate was filled with food, the ham neatly sliced—*when did he do that?*

Ike felt Pattiann enter the hall before he saw her. He wondered why it was that he could sense her presence, lifting his head to see her suddenly appear in the quiet of his office or on a busy street, as though he knew her step that intimately, or the timbre of her breathing. It was one of the things he found most comforting, how love announced itself in familiarity.

She was making her way to him, hair tousled, and she raked through it with a hand as was her habit. Her cheeks were a high color and as she said her hellos to friends her eyes made contact briefly before moving on. She hesitated at the edge of a group that included Harley, several deputies, a few town people, and Jim Parker. Her back stiffened and to the side of her Harley shook his head. Then Harley was pushing his way into the center and Ike saw Pattiann extend a hand to stop Harley and then drop it at her side. Ike excused himself from the table.

"That's bullshit," Harley said, and at a nearby table the men turned in their chairs to see who spoke while the women frowned nervously or dipped more earnestly into their food.

Ike approached the group, looking over their heads to where Pattiann stood.

"You calling him a liar?" And Ike couldn't see who'd asked the question, but Parker backed up.

"I'm saying—" Harley's voice raised and Ike put a hand on his shoulder.

"Trouble, Harley?"

The deputy nailed Parker with a glare. Ike turned to the group.

"Maybe we ought to take this discussion outside, or hold it later. None of us wants to intrude on Ed and Myrna's grief."

"That's right," Parker said, stepping forward. "This is better discussed elsewhere—"

"Well, you brought it up," Harley persisted.

"Harley," Ike said and tightened his grip. He looked up at Pattiann, saw the stricken look.

"He's blaming you for Dan's death." Harley snapped off the last word.

At the surrounding tables cutlery stilled. Voices at the far tables droned on and children bolted from their seats to run outside. He wished he were out there himself, or fifty miles down the road and driving, and at that moment he was *willing* to leave everything and everyone. He saw Dan's father at the far edge of the group. The man was studying him, a slow appraisal. He met Ed's eyes and felt there was a reckoning coming that might be, finally, the thing that would send Ike on his way, out of this town and these lives. Nothing left to hold him in place. He'd welcome it. He angled his way toward Ed, felt Pattiann in the wake of people behind him.

Ed waited for Ike. He blew out a couple deep breaths, stared down at his feet. "My son," Ed said, cleared his throat. "He did good for you those years?"

"I never had a complaint," Ike said.

Ed nodded, tucked his hands inside his suit-coat pocket so that the corners pulled down and Ike could see the coat was one he didn't wear much, the material good but old, the narrow lapel resurrected now as stylish. He was ill at ease in the suit. He must hate it. "At the grave," Ed said, a hand gestured vaguely, "your words helped." He looked around. When he looked at Ike again, his focus was sharper. "I don't know what's all being said"—he glanced around the group—"but all those years at home, Dan was a good hand. And I may have given him more than he could handle, but I never gave him *less*. I like to think he respected that. I know he respected you." He jerked his head down, his face knotted above his tie. "That's all I got to say. Good day, Sheriff."

And he turned on his heel and worked his way to where his wife sat with friends, and as the group around Ike dissolved, he watched Ed offer his arm to her and lead her from the hall. And then Ike was alone and he felt Pattiann at his back. When he turned, he saw Harley was still there, red-faced but appeased. Parker was gone. Ike put Pattiann's hand off his sleeve, told Harley to stay put, and walked to the back door where he knew Parker had ducked out.

By the time Ike stepped outside, Parker was already nearing the far end of the parking lot. Ike walked briskly. A light wind spun grit and bits of litter around the cars. In the open bed of a pickup, a cow dog lifted its head, nosed into the wind, and yawned as though to eat the air before sliding back down into the bed with a grunt. A pop can rattled across his path and wedged against the tire of a '61 Oldsmobile—Paul Tinsley's car, and Ike wondered briefly if he'd gotten the taillight repaired. Parker turned.

"I don't like what you're doing, Jim. You got an ax to grind, bring it to me first," Ike said.

Parker smiled. "You offering your own neck? Or you got some other young kid like Dan to take it for you? Maybe that fool Harley."

"Take your complaints where they'll do some good—or, if you prefer, Joe Bridley at the feedlot, or Ben, Hank, Tom, and Arty chewing fat over at the elevators. The commissioners must have been a disappointment."

Parker prodded a finger into Ike's chest. "You don't know jack shit about us. We don't stay fooled for long."

Ike stared down at the finger, the plumping digit, the smooth nailbed that poked at his uniform coat. He was surprised by his lack of anger. He turned away from Parker, looked at the sky breaking blue, the clouds clumping like scattered thoughts. Or maybe he just didn't give a good Goddamn anymore? He could almost see them as the town must, squared off against each other. The dog snored in the truck bed. He cricked his neck to a side, said, "It's a damned beautiful day." He looked at Parker over his shoulder. "Why do funerals come on days like this?"

Parker's hand stopped fussing in the air, dropped to his side, and he stared at the sheriff, and then he lifted his head as if for a moment he too was struck with the incongruity of it. "Spring's coming," he said, and mumbled as an afterthought, "none too soon."

"Longest winter I've ever lived through." Ike scrubbed at his face with a hand. All he wanted was a clean pickup to lay himself down in in the sun. When he looked up, Parker was still there. "Why do you stay?" he asked. And as he asked Parker this, he knew he was asking more. He was asking why all of them stayed, through bad crops and indifferent weather, accidents and divorce, when all the country stirred around them changing households, cities, states, packing the roads with U-hauls and semis, industry shifting, leaving potholes in cities where rats flowered as suburbs grew like benign cankers and people rose from restless sleep to change beds, families, neighborhoods, and jobs, until change for its own sake was reason enough. Why did these people stay?

Parker smiled, a small shrug tilted his shoulders. "That's just the way it is." He inclined his head toward the sheriff. "What's your reason?"

Ike stooped to pick up a piece of paper that lodged against his shoe. It was a grocery receipt. On the back someone had scribbled: *pick up kids from dentist.* He hoped she'd remembered, been on time.

"Honestly? I don't know." He nodded good day and turned back to the hall.

As he neared the door, he realized he couldn't go back in. He saw Fran standing at the corner. She lifted a hand in a small gesture that might have been a wave, or a catch at the scarf that snapped in the wind. She was smiling, and he thought briefly of Pattiann before walking over.

"You look like you could use a drink," she said.

He tucked his head down and shook it. "Some fresh air maybe."

She led off. "It was a good speech. I stood in back. Dan would come into the café once in a while. He was polite. Left tips. I guess that's all it takes to ingratiate a person to me." She blinked as a quick gust flicked her hair across her eyes. She restrained it in her hands and tucked the ends into her collar. The scarf dangled from her fingers. "You all right?"

They stepped from the curb, turned away from the town center. A bell hammered from the single-story brick schoolhouse and there was a simmer of noise from inside and then the doors banged back on hinges and a stream of children boiled into the school yard, their noise mightier than their numbers. Girls with jump ropes swung them over their heads like lariats, and boys ran the length of the lot bunching fists in the air and shouting.

Fran scanned the playground, perhaps to see her own children and discover who they were when not with her.

"Your kids all right?" he asked.

"Yeah," she said. "Not much has changed for them. They live with me, see their father on weekends. They think of Jolene like some kind of older sister to keep clear of." They walked past the schoolyard, turned down a side street. "Were you the one took the papers out there?" she asked.

Ike nodded, thought about when yesterday he'd rung the bell and Jolene had answered the door, not slovenly as he'd hoped, but pert in a gingham apron which her hands kept brushing in a nervous gesture. She'd called Dave and he'd come into the living room with shaving cream still dappling one ear. Ike could smell dinner cooking, and to a side in the dining room he saw the flicker of candlelight. Dave seemed inordinately pleased with himself. Jolene appeared embarrassed.

"Delivered the papers late yesterday afternoon."

"How'd he take it?" She didn't look at Ike when she asked, but studied the pavement where the sidewalk had buckled over the cottonwood roots.

"Fine," he said. There had been that moment—Dave accepting the papers and his smile wearing thin before lifting a hand to Jolene's shoulder, squeezing it gently. He looked bolstered by the small woman, calling it finally "a relief" and joking, "thought you'd come to shoot my cattle."

He couldn't tell Fran this. How Dave had taken the paper and how his hand had rested on Jolene's shoulder. How happy they looked and how Ike, even for Dave's joke, couldn't dislike the pair—their happiness transparent as gingham and shaving cream.

"Well." Fran sighed, stopped where she stood as though she'd meant to be here, as far removed from her orderly day-to-day life as she was from her previous life on the ranch. "I guess that's the best of it. He's got what he wants."

"And you?" Ike asked.

They walked two blocks in silence, turned the corner, and found themselves on her street, standing opposite her house. "I make a good cup of coffee," she said. "Better than the diner's."

She was nervous. Her fingers picked at the coat buttons. But it was not in her nature to play Jolene's role, nor in his to be the man sitting across the table in candlelight, with shaving cream on his ear. That kind of love would be ponderous. "I would love a cup, Fran, but I'll have to pass."

"Well, then"—she pulled the scarf up about her head—"I'll see you at the diner sometime. Or in church maybe."

He watched her walk away, wondering why his feet refused to move.

Pattiann waited for Ike, but he didn't return. She helped with dishes while men stacked folding chairs and dropped the cleared tables with ricocheting bangs, carried them back into storage. Children were called in with yells and whistles, loaded into cars among the leftovers, and the numbers in the hall dwindled to a dozen and then a handful, and then there was finally only herself and the funeral director—keeper of the Grange Hall keys—who locked the door behind them. He stood on the step next to Pattiann trying to make conversation, and curiously, everything he said sounded like consolation, even his comment on the fine weather.

"It was a nice service," she said. "It's hard when they're so young."

They stood in the open air. He inhaled deeply. He smelled of cosmetics, powders and rouge.

"Would you like a ride?" he offered, the limousine at the curb.

He waited patiently as Pattiann did not answer, and then she asked, "Do you think there are deaths a person can't survive?" She looked at him, and she had the feeling he wanted to shake his head and walk away, an unfair question after all, but he steadied himself with a deep breath.

"I think there are some deaths we *believe* we cannot survive."

They stood near the hearse, beside the tinted windows where she saw reflected the roof of the Grange Hall edging up against a sky, bluer for the tint, and clouds that held still though the wind tumbled her hair, the world skating across that glib surface. She watched her hand gather the hair and shrug it into her coat collar. The undertaker looked away as if he'd witnessed something too private.

She turned from him. "I should be going," she said.

He fidgeted in his suit, as if wanting to say more, or ask what loss *she* believed she could not survive, but offered his hand instead. When she took it, he laid his other hand on top as though consoling her, as though it were her child who lay in the ground. He stepped off the curve, into the glare of sunlight on chrome, and dipped into the driver's side of the hearse. The big engine hummed alive, and Pattiann watched it pull away, and then she was alone and heading home.

She could drive to the ranch, saddle a horse, and ride out farther than the day's light would permit. But once home, she found herself doing odd chores, stopping now and again to lift the phone, to dial Ike's number at work before setting it back on the receiver. She polished furniture: the birch writing desk her father had given her as a young girl, the oak wardrobe Ike had found at a secondhand shop and refinished over two and a half years of "spare time," the dining-room table they'd bought together at an antique shop outside of Billings with a set of four cane chairs, worn in all the right places, as Ike liked to say. She worked in silence, as if all the creakings of the house were suspended so that the pipes did not rap and heaters did not tick and the wind outside avoided the eaves, and the only sounds were the small grunts as she wiped down the turned table legs, the pop her knees made when she stood suddenly. She was too restless for music. It was an irritation with herself she worked on, on her knees at the furniture, as if by becoming intimate with the chinks in the joints, the wood grains and inlays, she would understand what she and Ike had made of themselves.

She squatted on the living-room area rug that had been rubbed down in places to the weave beneath, a thing she was fond of for the graceful way it had withstood the abuse of years. Like people surviving in a land-scape that did not welcome them. Like losing the land that was never yours. She rubbed the oiled rag over her fingers, slid her wedding ring above the knuckle so that she could see the pale circle beneath.

She remembered Ed and Myrna graveside, neither touching the other, as if the air between them was a wedge as deep as the grave. They were strong, by God, and stood on their own two legs. Admirable. Ter-rifying. The stuff of everyday lives.

She looked about the living room. She settled herself into Ike's chair, the deep recliner where he rarely found the time to rest between work and community business. And of course, there were all the times she wouldn't have been home to see him, busy as she kept herself on her brother's place. Even now, she felt the old restlessness, the urge to get up and drive away. With Chas it had translated to a wildness that she was paying for these many years later. Wasn't that what had really drawn her to Ike? His solid, midwestern nature? A most ordinary man, who'd done a most extraordinary thing. A full year after she'd left the Midwest, he'd shown up on her doorstep wearing clean jeans and a shirt still wrin-kled from the traveling bag.

"You must be surprised," he'd said. "And maybe a little alarmed." He kept his distance across the threshold from her, his weight spread evenly on his feet, his hands composed at his side.

She'd studied him a long moment. She could see he watched her like a suspect, reading her body language, and in that quiet span of time she understood she'd never really stopped loving him. She saw that the root-edness within him did not depend on the familiarity of the ground he stood on. It was a quiet, unperturbed steadiness, even as he waited at her door like a supplicant, and she came to love him again, though it felt something more like hope.

"You missed me," she'd said, and he nodded. "You don't know what you're getting yourself into," she'd said. He shrugged, suggested that that was the case with waking up in the morning. He added it was prob-ably what made each day doable and how the the term "blissful igno-rance" had been coined. She suspected he was only half teasing. She'd thought on it a moment longer, then said, "Bliss." She cocked her head toward him. "Think we can manage that?" And then she'd invited him in and he'd accepted. They'd married shortly after, and she'd never regretted it. She wondered if he had.

Pattiann pushed herself up and out of Ike's chair, feeling the need to move about. She put her house in order, working through the changing light, the shadows of household objects shrinking, pivoting, stretching. She moved into the kitchen late afternoon, watched the last bit of sun ease over the backyard. She set a meal in the oven as though Ike would come home from work as he always did, trusting his love, and when, finally, the back door opened and he stepped in, she blessed again the ordinariness of the man, the habits that determined the smallest of his actions, like coming home, like hanging up his hat in her kitchen.

They ate between bits of conversation. He'd worked the rest of the day. There were some interesting results on the fingerprint tests they'd done on Purvis's car. He'd say no more until he knew more. A few of the visiting officers had stopped in after the funeral, compared similar accidents on their watches. They meant to be kind, he said.

"Did it help?" she asked.

He shrugged. "Maybe tomorrow, or the next day. Right now," he said, and looked down at the plate of food he'd been picking at, "I want to sleep, but I'm not tired."

Pattiann cleared their plates. He sat, rubbing his head with his hands, his eyes closed. She cleared the table, flipped on the stove light and turned off the overhead light. She moved behind him, bracing his head in the cleft of her breasts, moved her hands down to his neck, his shoulders, loosening the knotted muscles. "We don't have to stay here," she said.

He grunted softly as she found a tender spot. "We could go upstairs," he said, misunderstanding her meaning, which was to leave this place, this house and town, this land, but found she was relieved he'd taken it wrong, her heart hammering. She followed him, turning off lights as she went and enjoying the old comfort in knowing her way through the dark, following the sound of his steps through their house. It was a good house, she thought, generous in spite of her.

He sat in the dark on the edge of their bed. He looked surprised when she knelt on the floor, took each foot in her lap, and eased the shoes from them. She turned a sock back, down, and off his foot, cupped the foot in her hands. The skin was dry and strangely soft, and she could feel his embarrassment, at first, that she would take his feet and explore them with her fingers, the arch, the wide ball, the hollow beneath the toes, between each digit. But he gave over to the comfort, her fingers practiced from long years of kneading strained muscles in livestock. As she worked, he gathered her hair to his face and she felt the touch of his lips so lightly pressed she could not be sure, and when that ceased he sat perfectly still over her, his head suspended over her head in the dark with his feet in her hands, and she worked on until each foot was pliant and his breathing eased.

When at last she set his feet down, he touched her elbow, lifting her, drew her legs up and onto the bed, and laid her next to him. They let their eyes adjust to the dark—deeper than the starlit fields beyond the window, and his shirt a lesser black than the sweater he lifted over her breasts, the paired aureoles of her nipples dim as new moons against the pale skin, and his buckle a dim twinkling.

It was a marvel the way her hands revealed him. And how she had come to this place, after all these years, to find his body new—the cock in her hand, this shifting flesh that she had taken into herself countless times before and would again with such familiarity, having the same comfort as knowing a house this well, or the land whose ditches and hummocks only surprised you by their constancy and the stones you kicked over now were those same stones you had turned over as a child, and the earth itself was a skin that you wore on the soles of your feet, taking you into itself even as she took him, now, clothes turned back and down, wrung around their legs and arms, tangled in each other, her hips rising to his, the muted slap of flesh, and beyond the listening walls of the house the wind grew hushed in the fir bows, the croon of cats was silenced, the town extinguished beneath the brilliance of stars.

For the next week, Chas stayed on the ranch. He had no call to leave. He spent his waking hours between the house and the barn, and all the hours seemed waking now even when he slipped into his bed, the covers shedding like a snake's skin as he turned and turned, rising in what he believed were dreams only to discover he'd not been sleeping. He lived on the last of the flour mixed with water—a gruel that crusted and recrusted the kettles like highwater marks, and when it ran out he found that was okay too, having lost the taste for it anyway. He lived in what clothes were available—odd-paired socks, a shirt balled under the sheets, pants draped on doorknobs or kicked into the corner. He took on the smell of his clothes and his clothes the smell of him and the house was rank with it as though he wore the house as well. He chewed his fingernails, browsed the empty cupboards, spent long hours in the chair by the window. Each morning, he delivered a bucket of water to the horse, and returned with another in the evening. He idled the days between house and barn, and with the lack of sleep and food often found himself rising from his bed with no memory of having left the barn the evening before. One day he mistook sunrise for sunset and thought it a good joke when it took him hours to figure it out. Sometimes he thought he heard voices, or got dizzy if he stood up too quickly. The world became peculiar, and the peculiar became ordinary. There were few terrors left for him.

He stood in the barn, looking out the door at the land that was as empty and quiet as his own shriveled stomach. And that was a curious relief—how his gut no longer griped. He wondered briefly if the horse felt the same, or if it heard voices, too? If for the horse, the moon tracked backwards so that the sun set instead of rose? When he turned back to the interior, he heard the sound of small feet scrabbling about the loft, across the rafter. He stared up at the hand-hewn beam until his neck cricked, though the small pain proved a pleasant distraction now against the greater numbness.

Was this how his mama had come to feel, out here in the barn studying the rafter, all sensation bled from her limbs like her belief in Him, for wasn't that what her suicide was about? Despair. Having finally despaired of Him, or believing He had despaired of her—daughter of a preacher, granddaughter of a preacher. She with her missionary's heart; what a plum Avery must have appeared to be.

Better yet, he wondered how his father had felt coming into the barn, in the early dark, to the surprise awaiting him. Chas remembered. A spring morning. A Sunday. And he was a bare twelve years old, shuffling out of the house, wrestling his way into a jacket, when he saw his father coming out of the barn. He was leading the saddled piebald, the broad door banging shut on his heels. How many times had Chas tried to remember his father's face? His expression particular to that moment, having just saddled his horse in the shadow of his wife. Chas looked across the space. Not very wide where he'd have had to lead the animal past her. Did the horse nose her, or shy? He could almost see it. The horse bumping her, the stirrup catching her skirt. And the rope twisting, winding right and right, then slowing to a stop. The body beginning its slow spin to the left.

But what was it in his father's face? Nothing that would suggest what he'd seen. His face was as still, his focus as removed from Chas as it ever was. He'd handed the reins to Chas, told him to check the fences in the high country. "Be back before dark," he'd said. Nothing more, but sparing Chas the sight of his mother, or of the sheriff cutting her down. And just maybe that was the most merciful thing Avery had ever done. Albeit a cold kind of mercy.

In the stall, the animal drank, pausing often with the effort. A wind kicked up, gusted through the door, and Chas opened his jacket, letting the breeze air him out. He supposed he could clean the stall, but then we all died in shit, didn't we? The body purging itself as though dropping the ballast that kept it connected to the earth.

Then again, there was no need to die in more shit than necessary. He wasn't uncaring, after all. He chuckled. And what else did he have to do? The wind was moist with thawing earth, though the few grasses it ruffled in the feedlot were still reluctant and brown. The horse nickered, coughed, and as Chas turned, the animal lifted its head over the stall door and into the wind. It almost looked lively for a moment, a shake of head and mane before lowering again to drink. Chas hefted the pitchfork, tapped his way across the dirt as a blind man uses a cane, and as happened fairly often now, the distance became elastic, the stall and horse moving away from him, as if viewed through the wrong end of a telescope. "Whoah, there," he said, and staggered to a stop. When the dizziness eased, he walked forward, thinking to count the paces to the stall. But he as quickly forgot that idea.

The horse waited. And he wondered if the animal comprehended it was going to die? And if that were the case, how did it pass these moments? Biding its time, Chas's own good time. "You still here?" he asked, and he gathered by the lack of an answer that He was. Waiting, biding His time, which was no time and all time, and Chas believed now, finally, he had an inkling of that trick, how a moment stretched to breaking, and next thing you knew it was dark of the next day, or maybe next week, and what did it matter because it was all pretty much one and the same thing. The horse dying here was already dead, and his cattle had always been just food for Taylor's dog.

He knocked the wood handle against a center post and the rap sounded clear and hard. "You here?"

He set aside the fork and entered the stall, prodded the horse's ribs with the wood handle, as if tapping at a door. The horse swung to the side, haunches swooning into the stall slats so that the head turned to look at its hindquarters as if they were just so much meat pieced together.

Chas scraped at the horse's shit, loose and black, packed into the dirt flooring. The smell of ammonia stung his eyes. The horse's piss was the color of straw, bright yellow. "Seems you're all the entertainment I got left."

He tossed the pitchfork over the stall, crossed to the horse. He studied it, how the ribs labored like a bellows, the bones rising and floating in the skin. The coat was rubbed in patches down to pink skin. Its tail was a club of piss and shit. He leaned up to the horse's eye, stared into the pupil, large and black. He tried to see into the horse, past the glazy surface down into the hole of the horse where its stomach puckered like the empty sack of a castrated dog, to the intestines that shed skin and blood because it did not know how to stop pushing—he tried to see all of this and beyond it to that thing in the horse that was horse, some elusive, shining thing. He peeled back the eyelid with two fingers and the white rolled and flashed and Chas squinted so close that their eyes moistened with the nearness of the other, and the iris flickered and widened like a shutter, an aperture that opened on the dark of the barn, to the opened door beyond where shadows yawed over the muddied lots, and then, as if the two eyes had changed places, the lens pivoted on its axis, it was, he saw, the horse looking into him and he saw as the horse did—his own laboring heart and lungs, organs and bone, and he felt trapped there, squeamish with his own curiosity, and even as Chas jerked back from the horse's head, the horse raised its head to clamp teeth on his arm and held until the flesh tore and the teeth shivered across bone. Chas squeezed the bloody arm with his good hand and watched as the horse backed away.

And he heard that voice again, as he had off and on these last several days. *"Do you see?"* the voice asked.

Chas closed the stall behind him, walked out of the barn. "I'm not listening," he said.

Chapter Eleven

Across the table from Ike sat the young boy—a nervous tic in one eyebrow. The nape and sides of his head were neatly trimmed. His hands were on top of the table, clean and clenched together. Bobby Acklin—Joe Mattick's best friend. Ike was in the boy's kitchen with the mother and father sitting at opposite ends of the table. A pie cooled on the counter and a puppy, the new family dog replacing the one they'd lost last month, paced the kitchen pausing now and again to lift its nose toward the dessert. They sat in silence, except for the occasional caution to the pup. The mother drummed her fingers. Ike had informed them the prints from Purvis's car included their son's. He'd been in trouble before.

The father, Kevin Acklin, rubbed his face in his hands. He was a rancher who ran a solid operation, a member of the Rotary who played fiddle with a small band at weddings and community dances. When Ike called, he'd been interrupted from practice for the Grange Hall dance to be held later that week. The fiddle sat on its back on the table looking outlandish, a delicate bracing of wood, gut, and wire on the white Formica top. "What the hell's next?" he said.

Rose stopped her fingers, looked from her husband to her son. "Tell me you didn't do this," she said.

"No," Kevin said. "Tell us what you did."

"Nothing," the boy said, and glanced over at the gangly-legged shepherd pup nosing the counter again.

Kevin stood, crossed the kitchen, and booted it away. "Go lay down," he said softly, and the pup retreated to a corner where it curled its nose into its tail and watched with nervous eyes. Kevin stood behind his son. The boy sat at attention. "You think I don't know a lie when I hear one?" Kevin asked.

The boy flinched and Ike found he had to look away—the mother shaking her head, the boy rigid in his chair. It was getting late. He had a long ride back and he was tired.

"I wasn't driving," the boy said softly.

"I can't hear you," Kevin said.

He repeated it louder. "I never planned on going," he said. "But we were drinking a little—"

"A lot," Kevin corrected.

The boy shrugged. He looked to Ike to save him. "I didn't know what I was getting into. Lester said we'd just take a short ride. Get the car back early."

"He gave you the alcohol?" Ike asked.

The boy nodded.

Kevin walked around the side of the table, sat at the head again. He pushed the violin aside; it wobbled on its back like a distressed turtle. He leaned across to Ike. "You nail that sonofabitch, you hear?"

"Who drove?" Ike asked. He wanted to hear the boy say the name.

"Lester. Found the keys on Joe. Joe passed out early on, in the back of Lester's truck. He can't hold his liquor," the boy giggled and stopped. He looked at his mother, but she kept her eyes averted. He did not look at his father.

"Joe was with you in the car?"

The boy shook his head. They'd driven around town, Lester stopping to pick up beer and then heading out toward the reservation. "Wanted to do him an Indian," Lester'd said, but Bobby confessed he didn't know exactly what Lester meant by that and they'd never made it onto the reservation. "And then there was this cop, and Lester tells me to hang on. I told him to stop." He turned to his mother who sat with her forehead in her hands. "Honest." He looked over at his father, who sat unflinching.

"A thief," Kevin said. "A damned thief."

The boy started to cry and neither parent moved to comfort him. Ike shifted in his seat. He waited for the boy to calm down. "So then what happened?"

The boy sighed. "Next thing I know, the cop's next to us and then Lester turns right and the car takes a ditch, bottoms out but keeps on going across a field, and then we're back on a road and I can't see anything behind us. No cop. Nothing." They'd driven back to town, parked the car, and hauled Joe out to the street where they left him with the keys in his pocket.

"Lester said to keep shut about it. Said he'd kill me if I talked."

They sat in silence again. The dog yawned in the corner and shut its eyes. Rose studied her son. "What happens now?" she asked Ike.

"Up to the courts."

Kevin sat back, shook his head. "He does time, you hear?" His finger moved across the table, pointed at his son. "By God . . ."

Ike pushed his chair back. "Can't say. I'll have to file a report, bring Bobby down for more questioning, and Joe."

"And Lester?" Kevin asked.

"I pick up Lester."

"Well, you'd better find a deep, dark place to put him, because if I see that sonofabitch, I'll shoot him."

Ike stood up, feeling strangely weary for the relief this should have been. "Mr. Acklin, I'd hate to have to jail you too. I'll take care of Lester."

Kevin stood, looked down at his son. "See you do." He spoke over his shoulder as Ike crossed to the door. "See you take care of that sonofabitch."

Rose held the door open for Ike. He looked down at her, his hat in his hand. "Good night, Mrs. Acklin, thank you for your hospitality."

She closed the door behind him without a word.

They had their first taste of spring, and while none of them was naive enough to believe it would last or that winter was done with them, still merchants had stock boys out on the sidewalks sweeping litter clear of their doors and the churches vied with seasonal quotes, the reformed church from New Testament, Mark: *So is the kingdom of God, as if a man should cast seed into the ground; and should sleep and rise night and day, and the seed should spring and grow up, he knoweth not how;* and the less forgiving from Old Testament, Proverbs: *The sluggard will not plow by reason of the cold; therefore shall he beg in harvest, and have nothing.*

Cattle were brought into the calving pens and children chucked outdoors to play. The days stretched and nights quickened. Men stomped the ground to hear how far the frost had receded. The cattleman's association prepared for its annual dance at the Grange Hall. It looked to be a good turnout, if the weather held, a last-ditch Canadian arctic system stalled north of them. They'd shake off winter, tipple away the cold. It was a chance to talk cattle and crops and be among the survivors again.

Ike was no different. It wasn't that he enjoyed dancing, but he liked the laughter, the easy bumping into folks he knew on the dance floor, the relief everyone exuded even in their tight-fitting best clothes, because the worst was past and any groundhog worth his spit knew that there were always six more weeks of winter and that was as it should be, and out here you could count on ten or more, but they'd come near the end of even that dour forecast, and the season's change was inevitable, and the people had come to the point where they could believe again.

He was an early arrival because Pattiann had been enlisted to help set up. She was spreading paper cloths over tables, lighting votive candles on each, and he liked to see the match flare, the way she touched light to the wicks with such single-minded concentration and how the glasses took on a glow until the room had a dozen or more flickering lights on white-cloaked tables.

The stage was a riser of boards and plywood that someone had covered with indoor/outdoor carpeting years ago. Two men on ladders were aiming spotlights, replacing gels—blue and red. His nephew Justin was testing the mikes, *check, one, check two,* and thumping the head with a finger. Ike watched the boy a long moment, wondered what it would be like when he moved in with them next fall, for they had agreed to his staying with them through the school terms, had told Harriet and Rob just a couple days ago. When they had told Justin, he'd taken it with his usual quiet good manners. "Thank you," he said, and then, "I won't be much of a bother." Ike had told them all how Pattiann had already been sizing up the extra room, moving furniture, clearing out the closet. He shook his head. "Next thing you know, she'll be sewing curtains," he said.

Pattiann had smiled, a lopsided grin. "Serve you right if I did," she said.

What he didn't tell them was how they'd both come to anticipate the idea of Justin living with them, the house snugging comfortably about the three of them. "Maybe it's time we learned how to make room for someone else in our lives?" Pattiann had said and Ike had begun to believe just maybe, she was right.

Justin moved to the next mike, waved to his grandfather who was off to a side with Kevin Acklin and Pete Wolfgram, tuning up their instruments.

Pattiann slipped up to his side and leaned down as if to tell a secret, hiding a kiss in the gesture before moving off. He fingered where her kiss had touched his cheek. What was he to make of it? This new Pattiann. They talked more. "Making up for lost time," she said. She was like someone coming out of a sleep, and when he told her this, she laughed. It was not as if she neglected her brother's ranch, but she rode out there less driven. He began to believe if he had to leave this place, it would not be alone.

Overhead the heating vent chuffed, and Ike leaned back, hands laced behind his head. The alternate banks of lights flicked off or dimmed, ceiling stains, pipes, and vents receding. There was a solitary clapping and Ike saw the room softened by candles, the blue stagelight brittle on the chrome drums. There was the chink of glassware as the bar opened on the far side of the room away from the temperate punchbowl the church deacons guarded.

He could name these people, recount their graces as well as sins, and it was a heady feeling, coming through the worst of it, a witness to their lives and they to his. How could he not feel new? As transformed as the hall. He thought he was close to laying a finger on what he needed, to be . . . content . . . and perhaps it would come to him in a moment longer, or a day, a month, an understanding of this place and these people in his care. And the truth as he saw it now, sitting in the Grange with the people filing in through the doors and the musicians tuning for the first set, he did not want to leave, would do what was in his power to stay. Let it be. Let it be spring, let the rains come and the grasses grow, let the wounds heal and the graves settle.

Before an hour was out, the hall was stifling, the old boiler throwing jets of hot air so that the dance floor smelled of Old Spice, Stetson, Canoe. Men shed suit coats and women piled their hair up. The fiddlers sawed, handkerchiefs bundled on chin rests to absorb the sweat, paused only to call out the tunes. Ike danced with Pattiann. The prettiest wife in the county, he called her.

"What about the single women?" she asked.

"Can't hold a candle," he said, tucked her closer, and they slewed out into the center of the floor where couples jigged the two-step and around the perimeter others processed clockwise, side by side, arms locked about waists.

Purvis showed up in a red suit coat, gray pants, and a bright yellow vest. "Christ," Ike had said. "All you need is a tuba and epaulets."

Purvis grinned, slapped Ike on the back. "I am a man of fashion."

"You're a bloody peacock."

Purvis nodded. "Damn right. I've decided to take my courting seriously, fan my feathers, jiggle my tail." He lifted a lapel. "Red's my color, don't you think?"

And now, from the dance floor, he could see Purvis still reclining by the bar, lifting his head back in guffaws as the men joked about his attire and the women contrived to get a closer look. Ike hoped it worked. It was good to see Purvis back on his feed now that the Mattick boy was home. Bobby Acklin would do time, but it would be minimal, Ike suspected, probation most likely, and he knew Purvis had already made an offer to the court to provide the boy with community service at the clinic, should the court feel so inclined, which Ike also suspected it would.

He nestled his hand lower on Pattiann's back, edging his finger nearer the crease of her buttocks. Her head snapped up in surprise, hitting his jaw. He drew his hand away to rub his chin. "Sorry," she whispered, but he could see she was amused. When the set ended, they joined Bill and Martha at a table. Purvis pulled up a chair and tipped a whiskey back.

"You going to dance with me, Martha? We could make out like Rome on fire while your husband fiddles," Purvis said.

Martha cocked an eyebrow at him. "Purvis, even if I could dance anymore, that coat's enough to give a woman the staggers."

"You like it? My father wore red long johns to bed. My parents enjoyed a long and fruitful marriage. He used to say, 'Red warms the cockles.' I misunderstood him for years."

"I think it's handsome," Pattiann said, and touched his sleeve.

Purvis waggled his brows at Ike. He leaned back in his seat, took a deep breath, and looked around. "Just what we needed," he said. "Good to see people when they're not on the far end of a cow. How's the herd, Bill?"

"Shop talk," Martha said, shaking her head.

"Might do all right, do better when the grass greens up." Bill paused. "And that's saying we get rain, the sun shines, and we don't get kidney-punched—"

"Listen to him," Martha said. "I for one have had enough, and if it means getting on the dance floor with Purvis to avoid it, I'll do that. Moreover, if God should see fit to strike me dead in midstep, at least I'll have gone out dancing." She pushed herself to her feet. "Where's the music?" she called out. She stood, looking down at her husband.

He finished his drink. "Order me another one, son," he said to Ike. "And you . . ." He leaned down to Purvis. "I'll be watching."

The band gathered. Bill, plucking up his fiddle, started playing "Waltzing Matilda" in a slowed tempo, the others picking up the tune as they joined him on stage. He kept them to that slow pace, his eye on his wife and hers on his, as she stepped into Purvis's arms and danced carefully. She was small and no longer nimble, her steps circumspect, and the other dancers on the floor kept their jostling to themselves, cutting them a space like the eye of a storm, upon which the lead fiddler smiled.

And when the song ended and Purvis escorted Martha back to the table, the company took up a romp, skirts bunched in hands, and boots beat a tattoo, couples changed partners, and some few abandoned the floor to the heat and sought the bar, or moved to the sidewalk in front of the hall and stood under the street lamps, their bodies steaming in the cold night air.

No cars moved about downtown. It seemed as if the entire county must have parked their rigs in the parking lot and down the long street. Businesses were shut, gas pumps locked. Down side streets, in well-lit homes, baby-sitters guarded sleeping children, an easy ten-buck night. Taylor's house was dark, and Chas Stubblefield walked up the back steps, tugged on the door. A small barking erupted at the side window. He waited but no lights came on. The dog chattered against the glass. Chas stepped next to the window, leaned his forehead against the glass. He could feel the heat of the house, and the small dog backed away. Chas pushed at the pane and the window eased upward. The dog crouched and whined.

"Hey, pooch," he said. "I should have brought you a treat, hmm?"

The dog, a small rag of an animal, whined, wagged its tail. Chas extended his hand and the animal sniffed it cautiously before twitching its tongue over the fingers. Chas snatched the neck, hauled it squealing over the sill by its scruff. The dog hung in his fingers, the whites bulging around the black of its eyes. He raised the dog to his face, sniffed. It smelled of canned food and shampoo.

He hung the slack-mouthed dog in front of his face. "Where's Daddy?" he asked. "Asleep?" He pounded against the side of the house with his free hand. "You in there, Taylor?" But all that came to him was the strangled breathing of the dog.

He shook his head. A fellow comes calling, nice and neighborly, and no one's home. Wouldn't you know it? "Even got cleaned up," he told the dog, then he lowered his arm so that the animal swung at his side. The night air was turning colder. Over the trees he saw the sky bit in half by a bank of clouds. Storm, he thought, and wished it so, believed he saw a flash of light, waited for the rumble. Seeing things. He felt light-headed, his body's hunger a distant distraction. Didn't remember when he'd last eaten. Days. A week? More? A fire would be nice. Kitchen curtains, carpets, furniture, drywall. His knuckles rapped down the clapboard side. He imagined squatting by the fire. He and the small dog. But Taylor wasn't home. Not him, not his wife. He raised the dog up and shook it. "I killed better dogs than you." And the dog seemed to agree, lolling from his bunched fist. He swung the animal back over the sill, closed the window behind it.

What had come to him these past days, in the silence of his fields and house, in the horse's complicated wasting away and his own gutted flesh, was a singular clarity of what and who he was—a man absolved of every last thing that held him bound to this earth or to the laws of man. And to God he neither spoke nor listened anymore.

He walked through the yard, turned down the street toward town, pausing now and again to peer into windows at hand-painted ceramic table lamps, walls with framed sunsets, the trophy elk or deer with their unconvincing glass eyes. He felt apart from this race who lived in tidy houses and bore children with sound teeth. He supposed he'd always been so, only now he knew it. He ticked the streets off on his fingers and kept an eye to the clouds stalled against the tide of stars. Working his way to the center of the town, he crossed the footbridge over Deer Creek where he stopped to listen to the water, heard music instead, and the sound of voices niggling through the air.

He followed it. He heard his own boot heels clapping off the brick storefronts as if they were another person's and looked over his shoulder to see who followed. Across from the Grange, he glanced in the bank windows, at his reflection—hair washed and combed, shirt and jeans cleaned for the occasion.

Beside him were parked cars, and across the reflected street, knots of men in red shirts and green, striped and checked. He breathed through his nose, watched as they talked or broke away to re-form new groups. When he turned to see them across the street, they looked nearer than in the glass. He stepped off the curb. He brushed past the men in front of the hall and he could tell they were grateful to be ignored. He stepped into the room and felt the wall of heat and noise roll over him like a weather front. Tables had been pushed back along the wall to enlarge the dance floor. When he walked in, it wasn't as if the seas parted, but he caused a ripple. A nodding of heads, a curt hello or two; more telling was the concerted effort not to acknowledge him. But how could they deny him? There came a crude lowing sound from a young teenage boy, and the call was taken up briefly by others in his circle until someone stepped in and silenced them. Chas walked heel to toe, between the tables. At the bar, Taylor froze mid-drink, but Chas looked through him and kept walking toward the dance floor. *Too big for his Goddamned britches* and *They shot the wrong one,* but he didn't pause to locate the speakers.

The dancers milled in a circle, colors all wrong in the blue and red light so that skin and clothes looked the same, and he could hear their breathing like the breath of a congregate animal. He stood at the edge and leaned on his toes, his grin loose and slipping on his face, and then someone was at his side, fingers on his sleeve, and he eased back on his heels and turned to her.

"Pattiann," he said.

"Chas?"

He bumped his head up and down. "Yes, yes," he said. He looked over his shoulder, didn't see the sheriff. "Come for my dance. Like the old days," he said. He tweaked a smile at her.

When Pattiann had first spotted Chas, she'd not recognized him. He looked hollowed out, like a child playing dress-up in clothes too large, or one of his own cattle lost in its skin. He moved like someone sleepwalking, his eyes moving back and forth. She touched the cuff of his shirt-sleeve, believing she could do this necessary thing, and it took a moment for his eyes to focus on her. "I haven't danced," he said. "All these years."

He turned to her, took her hand in his, and laid his other on her waist. He moved them out onto the floor. They stood there. "Am I doing all right?" he asked, and she nodded though they barely moved.

His hand was hot through her dress, and she thought he must be running a fever. "You been sick, Chas?"

"Sick?" he asked. "Yes." He shuffled to the side, his feet bumping hers.

The number of couples on the floor dwindled. Pattiann tried to ignore it, suggested they sit the dance out, and Chas nodded yes, but continued in the tight square he'd framed on the floor. "Nothing to it," he said. "One step in front of the other, just like I've moved my whole life." He stumbled and winced. "And sometimes," he said, "you step on someone's toes and that's nothing new either." He held her out in his arms. "Thought there was more." He stopped, looked around at the tables and the couples who had shuffled to a stop, and let go of her hands.

"They're staring," he said to Pattiann, giggled. "Must be I dance like shit. Must be I forgot to zip my fly," he said louder. There was a small commotion at the back of the room, and then a path opened and Ike was coming toward them.

Ike had been in the men's room, wiping a wet paper towel over the back of his neck trying to cool off, when Harley found him. He smiled into the mirror. There was a flaw in it, a black stain where the silver backing had corroded, leaving a thumb-sized hole in the reflection. Harley shifted.

"Hotter than Hades out there," Ike said.

"Getting hotter," Harley said. "Chas just come in."

Ike's hand stopped and water dripped over his collar. He tossed the paper towel in the wastebasket. "Trouble?"

"Hard to know, he's such a Goddamned spook. Might be drunk, wasn't walking real straight."

Ike tucked his shirt in. "What's he doing?"

"Dancing."

"No crime in that."

"With your wife."

Ike smoothed the hair down at his neck. "Not at gunpoint, I trust?" He patted Harley's shoulder. He saw the young man breathe easier and wished he could be as easily reassured. He just wanted the evening to go on as it had. A knot formed in his gut.

On the other side of the bathroom door, Taylor was waiting in a short queue that included Sam Coker and curious onlookers.

"That sonofabitch killed my dog," Coker was saying.

"Fuck your dog," Taylor said. "He junked my car." He turned to Ike. "You throw that sonofabitch out."

"Back off," he said.

"You don't tell me to fucking back off." Taylor leaned his face into Ike's. "I can break you, you sonofabitch–" He wagged a finger in Ike's face.

Ike snatched the finger, folded it back. "Get in line," he whispered. He dropped the hand, stepped past the group of men. An aisle opened to the dance floor where he saw Pattiann, her hair redder in the lights. She stood at arm's length in Chas's hands, staring at her feet. Ike strode up the opening, nodding to folks as he passed. Purvis appeared, and Ike urged him back with a firm hand to his elbow.

The back of Ike's neck felt sticky. The music never broke stride, and on stage the musicians watched even as they played. Chas had dropped Pattiann's hands. She looked tired, but brave, and he was alternately angry and proud of her.

Chas looked spit-polished. A slide guitar whined, drums gunned, and Ike thought it felt like the floor had turned slick. Chas sidestepped clear of Pattiann.

"How you doing, Chas?" Ike asked.

"Passable." Chas nodded his head slowly. "Passing queer, though, how this floor cleared soon as I got on it. Must know something we don't, Sheriff."

Ike tried to read the faces of the crowd. He knew the ranchers' feelings–the law had gone where none of them wanted to see it go, onto a man's property—but what Stubblefield had done was cruel. Worse, it was shoddy work, and they did not take that lightly. He had shamed them.

And there was fear, because it didn't take much—poor judgment, weather, accidents. He saw in those who refused to look at Chas a denial of that shameful possibility in themselves.

Ike wiped his forehead with a hand. "Hot in here." He looked over at Pattiann, jerked his head toward the hall's far end, then he turned away, cutting her off, focusing instead on Chas.

"Just dancing," Chas said, "and all of a sudden, *poof*, gone. Like so many cattle." He moved as if to follow Pattiann, but Ike's hand caught him gently by a cuff. He turned back to Ike. "I must carry the smell of pestilence," he said, and slapped his thigh. "You and me, Sheriff," he said. "Lepers. One of God's least amusing diseases. Weeping sores, bad breath."

He looked around him, then leaned into the sheriff's hearing. "But you got a temporary condition. Me? My fucking nose is falling off." He tweaked at his nose. He was suddenly steady on his feet and his words distinct.

Ike nudged at Chas's sleeve and he followed, across the floor. People shuffled aside. "You want something, Chas?" Ike asked.

Chas paused, considered. "A bell," he said. "Like they used to wear around their necks. Small ones for all the little lepers. A big one for you, me, and a fucking anchor for God."

Ike moved him on, through the hall, out the door, and into the cold night air. There was a sudden hush as the door shut behind them. "You drunk?"

"Haven't had a drop. Can't afford it. Pathetic, ain't it?" Chas nodded. "Nothing worse than a pathetic man. You know where my cattle are?" He stepped across the porch, settled a hand on the banister, leaned over the railing. The bank of clouds had closed in, low and black. The air smelled of moisture. "You know, some nights I see it—the trucks rolling across Montana, and Idaho, a convoy of meat high-balling to Spokane where they're chopped to meat and cooked down to feed somebody's dog. Think of it . . . my cattle—all of them, just yards on yards of little-dog shit." He reached over and squeezed Ike's arm.

"Christ, Chas, they were coyote food your way, what's the difference?" Ike asked.

"The difference," Chas said, "was this was all just so neat, wasn't it?" He clumped down off the porch. His feet wobbled in his boots. "You must feel clean when you go to bed. Your wife must like the smell of you." He danced off a few steps. "Nice music, huh?" He stopped, cocked his head to one side.

"You got something new to say to me?" Ike wanted to return to the warmth of the hall. Sweat was freezing in his armpits and down his back. His collar had frozen in a vise around his neck, but Chas was there, strung tight, contained for the moment; Ike couldn't release that inside. Not with his people in there. His wife.

"What's the difference, you say? Dead is dead, and my cattle are dead. So's my mama, and her husband. So's your deputy and tonight any number of people will die in their sleep, or while humping their wives or being humped. Fact is, we are populated by the dead and the about-to-be, so where's the difference?"

"Chas—"

"Parsons, you don't know *shit*." He squeezed his eyes shut. "The proceeds of your goodwill is just so much dung in Taylor's backyard." His eyes opened. He looked up at Ike on the steps. "Tell me, Sheriff. When you shot my cattle, did you look in their eyes first?"

"This is sick, Chas."

"No," Chas shouted. "Because if you had, you would know that the cattle, you, me, each fucking breathing thing is just so much meat for the Renderer and His big old meat hook in the sky.

"We are deceived," he added quietly.

"Deluded," Ike answered.

"That too," Chas agreed. "Fact is there's no real choice about it. We are handed our ends as blindly as we are handed our lives." Chas walked off a step, looked down the long street to where the blackness implied the vast sweep of land better than sunlight could. "I believe it's going to blow up a hell of a storm. One last stab at winter."

Under the streetlight, Chas was a man whittled to stick. He shook his head, looked up at Ike with a smile, and Ike was reminded of how after his father had sold the farm, he would come home from the factory, his body jangling with the noise of it all, and how he picked at his dinners, growing slight and slighter, his heart fodder for the machines, but still that same sweet smile had persisted. And Ike found he wanted to do something for Chas as he hadn't been able to do for his father, but Chas stood apart, under the solitary breach of light in the darkness as though he preferred it, or knew something beyond Ike's ability to know, even as Ike's father had seemed to before he died. And it came to Ike that Chas was as dead as his cattle.

Chas nodded, as if he'd read the sheriff's thoughts. His eyes were unblinking. "Still some final business left. Some loose ends," he said. "Paperwork, bills, forwarding address, things you can't imagine. But don't you worry, Sheriff, I'll have them cleaned up quick. Be gone in no time. Will you grieve to see me go, Sheriff?" He waited a beat. "I thought not."

Ike nodded. "I'm sorry, Chas," he said.

"Hell, yes," Chas agreed. "We are a sad and sorry lot, each last one of us."

Ike turned away and he heard Chas make a clicking noise with his tongue. "Hey, Sheriff," Chas said, and when Ike turned back around he saw Chas standing there, his finger pointed like a gun at Ike's head. "Bang," he said. He unfolded his hand, held it palm up. "Meat," he said. "Just that close to meat."

"That wouldn't be a threat?"

"No." Chas shook his head. "Just a friendly reminder."

Ike waited until Chas turned the corner. He stood on the porch debating whether or not he should follow or post someone to keep an eye on him. But then he thought of Chas under the light, how pathetic he had looked, and Ike knew what had become of the man was, in good part, Ike's own doing.

And Ike was a boy again, at the close of a summer's day, the light wan as a drawn-out sigh. His father was with him, outside the door of the milk house, sitting on upturned crates, scraping his boots. And Ike was a sixteen-year-old boy stuck in what he'd always known, while the world changed, the war ending in Vietnam, and his friends moved on to bigger lives somewhere out there. He was a young boy who felt caught in his father's life, trapped like the tic in his father's cheek.

And Ike made it his business to explain what it was his mother feared, dairy prices falling, the conglomerates pricing the family farms out of the market. His mother was the strong one, the levelheaded, the no-flights-of-fancy woman—sell the land to developers before the bottom drops, before the saturation of housing, none of them able to foresee there would *be* no saturation point, that family farms would continue to turn belly-up as the fields had once to the plows.

But logic and money talk never cut it with his father. "Don't you love us?" Ike asked instead. And that was the thing that still stung.

His father sat with his back against the stone walls, but his frame seemed to collapse on itself, and of course, he had agreed then, yes, he'd sell the farm. And Ike remembered how the nightjars kited through the great doors of the upper barn, and from within the lower barn with its damp fieldstone walls and its concrete catwalks and chain-scrubbed gutters, the cattle lowed in their stanchions, the sound rising like another moon that his father turned his face to, and that sound cutting of him a new silhouette as the moon does shadows, and what was it his father had said? *Was there ever a sweeter sound? Like the cry of angels.*

And Ike saw with an awful clarity that keeping the farm might be the ruin of them all, but losing it would be the ruin of his father, and how he could know this he could not say except that his father sat straighter, his bones knit tighter somehow in the wake of the cattle calling.

Ike looked up into the sky over the town, to the underbelly of a cloud dimly threatening. And now Chas. Purvis had seen it. That day Ike had driven with Purvis to see the animals and Purvis had suggested Ike turn his head the other way. Had there been another way around this all? Had he gone so far in service of the law that he'd overlooked a greater service underlying it?

The door opened behind him, and Pattiann stood there. "You all right?" she asked.

He looked down the street for Chas, but he was gone. Ike tugged at his shirt collar, stiffening in the cold.

Pattiann joined him. She gripped the railing. "I'm sorry," she said. "I didn't know what else to do."

Ike put his arm around her. She was shivering. He had the sudden urge to take her away from here, take her home where he could hold her for however long it took. Tell her how he had *seen* Chas in that brief moment under the streetlight. How he'd heard something in Chas's voice that had been so resonant that Ike had thought instead of his own father.

She was looking down at the porch floor, her brows drawn with worry. He smoothed the crease in her forehead with a thumb. "You did fine," he said. "You were kind." He pulled her to his chest and held her tight. "More than I can say for myself."

"Want to leave?" she asked.

He stroked her hair. Thought about the town people inside the hall. Waiting for his reassurance. He shook his head and gathered her elbow in his palm.

In the hall, Purvis tried to read Ike and Pattiann's faces. They'd reentered with arms about each other, smiling at the people who stood waiting as he did. Ike was putting off questions. Elsie Lager, a pert seventy-year-old who baked cakes for a hobby, said, "Shame on that boy," and wagged her head. Ike said he was eager to dance, and he was convincing enough so that Purvis thumped Harley on the back and offered to buy him a drink.

Harley countered, "I'll take that drink and raise you one."

They nursed their whiskey ditches at a table. Purvis watched Pattiann and Ike dancing. Times like this he thought of how it might have been for himself and Babs. Had they not married so young. If he'd known her now. Or if he found someone else. Times like this he almost believed he was not past having it yet.

Harley leaned into Purvis's arm, tugged on his sleeve. "Purvis, I'm in love," he said.

"Goddamn, this coat does wonders," Purvis said.

Harley slapped Purvis on the arm. "Not with you." He laughed. "You ain't got tit enough."

"A tit man? My father used to say, the only thing you could trust a tit man to know was where the milk came from. Not that he meant that disparagingly. He was a tit man too, my father. Admired the hell out of my mother's. But me, I prefer a good leg, I think. With a strong back and a weak mind."

"Purvis," Harley whined. "I'm trying to be *serious*. I'm thinking of popping *the question*."

"To whom?"

"Our dispatcher, Michelle Bonne Chance."

"Good luck."

Harley's brows beetled.

"Drink up, boy." He bumped Harley's elbow. "You owe me one."

"What if she says no?"

"You're not drunk, are you?" Purvis asked.

Harley shook his head.

"You've thought this over, deliberated soberly and judiciously?"

He nodded.

"Want to borrow my coat?"

Harley spit back some of the whiskey he'd sipped.

Purvis slapped him on the back. "You love this girl, you take her out on that dance floor in front of a hundred people, get on bended knee, and ask for her hand. Declare your undying love and undivided attention." He pulled Harley closer. "And then you live up to those words. Raise a passel of kids and send them to me for shots."

"My kids?"

"No, their pets. Every kid's got to have a pet." He hefted Harley to his feet. "Where is she?"

"Over there." Harley pointed vaguely.

"Well, go to it, boy. Go on."

They shook hands. Harley hitched his pants up and left. Purvis stayed long enough to watch the young man fumble his way to a table, speak into the ear of an honest-faced woman, then Purvis made his way to the door and out. He stood in the cold, wrapping his bright red coat tighter about him. It was, after all, a glorious night. He smiled to himself and crooned a few bars of "Oh Lonesome Me," before stepping down onto the sidewalk.

Chas retraced his steps to his truck. He rummaged about in the cab, grabbed a handful of oily rags. He hauled a can of gasoline from the back of the pickup. When he approached the house, the small dog yapped twice at the window, and when it saw who had come to call, jumped off the sill and retreated to its hidey hole under the stove. Chas tried the overhead garage door. Locked. He walked around back, wrapped his hand in the rags, and put a fist through the back door garage window. He let himself in, pressed his ear against the door connecting to the house, and smiled at the silence. "Good dog," he said.

He was still cold, though he no longer shivered. He sprinkled gasoline over rags and cardboard he found stacked in a corner. The small dog snuffled at the crack under the house door. Chas stepped back from the pile, struck a match, and dropped it. The *woof* of flames set him back on his heels and he snatched at the hair sizzling over his ears. "Oooee," he hooted, slapping at himself. "Damn near joined you, Mama." He crossed to the door, listened briefly to the fire's crackle before shutting the door and returning to his pickup. He pitched the empty can into a stand of brush, sniffed the gasoline on his hands, and started the engine. It would be satisfying to see the flames spread, better yet to have the luxury of waiting for Taylor to come home to a

231

burning house. The twelve-gauge, side-by-side shotgun lay across the seat. He had a full night's work ahead, and damn, it felt good having something to occupy his time again. He drove slowly down the street. He would save the sheriff for later. Coker: that was the ticket. He watched Taylor's house dissolve into the dark of his rearview mirror, imagined the garage, the fire melting bike tires, gutting out the insulation, eating into the house. The little dog scrabbling at the window to get out. He hummed a tuneless song, and the wind gusted dirt at his lights. Overhead the stars had gone out, the cloudbank lowering with the temperature.

He didn't have far to walk, and the cold sobered him. Purvis shoved his hands into the sports-coat pockets, clenched and unclenched them. Down two blocks, past the mill and grain elevators, cut through the alley and across the cemetery to home. He'd fill the tub with hot water. He'd bundle up in his ratty bathrobe, light a fire in the woodstove, and contemplate his feet. He picked up to a jog but stopped when the cold made his lungs ache. Dirt lofted into the wind and he narrowed his eyes against it. The last dregs of winter. It would not be denied. Come spring rains, he would curse the gumbo mightily, but right now, by God, even that would seem like a blessing.

He laughed. His teeth chattered and he clamped them tighter. A red sports coat and yellow vest—always rains hardest on the peacock's tail. He was alone on the street, and he paused. He could turn around before he got any farther, warm himself with a woman's sweat on the dance floor and beg a ride home later. And then he saw someone over at Coker's mill, a pickup idling in the grain elevator yards. He ducked his head against the gritty wind. Maybe he could hitch. Though by then he realized the strangeness of it—a man on the loading docks, this time of night, everyone at the dance. Some fool kid, he thought, and Joe came to mind.

Purvis buttoned his coat over his belly and jogged down the street. He did not think what he would say or do. He tried to keep an eye on the man. The chill deepened. He was too old. Too nosy. His legs ached and his wind was short. By the time he got there, he'd be in no shape to do more than pant in the man's face. He slowed and recognized the pickup at the same moment the first flames erupted on the dock. "Stubblefield," he shouted, and the man turned.

It was the queerest thing. How the fire trickled a path across the dock. Not bright and leaping, but blue and low, as if tamped down by the cold, and then it reared upward with a *whoosh* into a stack mid-deck, and sent runners like a living thing, a branching tree, until there were four bright stacks lit against the walls and the walls themselves were fueling the fire. The wind huffed and the fires wavered and grew larger, and Stubblefield's figure rippled before them, as though the man himself had become part of the conflagration.

As Purvis ran toward the dock, the grain elevators bobbed up and down, a row of sedentary sentinels become animate, and he imagined he could already hear the suck of heat, the explosion from container to container taking out the homes around it. He could see Stubblefield in detail now—the curious smile on his face, *how nice to see you*—and the gun rising even as Purvis couldn't find it in his body to stop, as if he'd been lockstepped to this gravel lot from the first time he'd seen Stubblefield's cattle. In his coat, he looked like a stray flame in the dirt. He thought of the work he'd not gotten to. The work that never ended, cattle, calves, horses, the family dogs. He stopped short of the dock. He could feel the wave of heat and he withdrew his hands from his pockets and looked up at Stubblefield as if they shared a joke.

Stubblefield stood on the top step, his feet planted wide apart. A sportsman's stance. He tipped his head at an angle, sighted down the barrel. It should be Taylor, he thought, and for a moment willed it so, but the red coat kept tugging him back to the ridiculous vet, his country doctor ways. "Hot enough for you, Purvis?" he asked.

The wall of heat moved upward. There was a canopy of blue flames overhead. Chas took a step down, the gun barrel gravitating to the yellow vest. He flexed his shoulders and kept his attention on the spot pinpointed by the barrel, *like the finger of God,* he thought. And then there was a wail from the town's fire siren, long and protracted, while a wall behind Chas buckled, and the vet stood in the fire's light with his hands stretched out as if to warm them and the siren's wail raised higher, then fell, and rose again.

Purvis seemed relaxed and then he smiled at Chas with a dreaming look on his face, and Chas fired, and the body bent backward from the knees and toppled. The bright coat fanned open and the yellow vest turned black. Chas lowered the gun, jumped down from the last steps, and swayed on rubbery knees. He stood over the body. He lifted the hem of the jacket with the shotgun barrel, and wondered if Purvis had had some inkling when he put it on that he was dressing for his own funeral. Across the street, a young girl stood on the porch, outlined by the light of windows behind her. He waved her back into the house, and in the fire's parade of shadow and light, it looked like the porch she stood on was moving and she waving as if from a float. The siren halooed into the night, and soon people would be arriving. He felt the satisfying grab of heat, stack on stack of feed, straw bales, chemicals, and there was a small explosion behind him that lifted him to his toes and rocked him over Purvis's body, and standing on tiptoe, his arm wheeling for balance, hovering over the body, he saw Purvis's face and the eyes, empty as they were, shone in the firelight. He found he was trembling and he pivoted on his heels and fled across the parking lot to where his pickup idled. He threw the gun in on the seat and was pulling away before he'd closed his truck door. Down the block, he saw the first men running toward the fire. He turned his truck in a tight circle, headlights failing in the brighter glow of flames, and he had a quick glimpse of the red coat just before the truck bumped over the railroad spur and down a dark side street.

The dock fire spread quickly into the central building, warehouse, and retail shop. High winds rushed the flames across the roof, sparking down into the brushy lot, the tinder grass sizzling and popping. Children were the first on the scene. From across the way, the baby-sitter, who had called in the alarm, wrestled with a handful of her charges. She maneuvered herself between the children and the body. When the eldest boy at seven pulled free to look, she slapped his cheek, the sound lost in the popping fire. She hauled the startled boy back under her arms and moved them off the lot in a wedge about her body.

This was the sight that first greeted Ike: the building in flames, the children being herded back by a girl not much older than her charges. He helped the sitter move the children to safety across the street. She pointed to the gravel lot. "A man," she said. "In a old green Chevy pickup. He shot . . ." Her arm wavered. The fire trucks, hook and ladder were arriving, volunteers in party clothes, suiting up. The town hall siren had stopped but squads howled through the streets and trucks of volunteers squealed to the curbs. He looked where the young girl pointed, and from the corner of his eye, Ike saw the bit of color in the gravel. "Get the children out of here." He shook her gently, drawing her attention away from the gravel lot. "To the Grange Hall. You understand?"

She nodded.

"They'll help you out. Don't stop. Just get the kids there." She took a deep breath and straightened her back. She snagged the youngest boy by the back of his jeans and started moving off.

"An old green Chevy?" Ike shouted after her. She nodded. "Did the driver have dark hair?" he asked, and she shook her head. "Light," she shouted. "Blond hair," and then hustled the children down the street.

He covered the parking lot at a run, saw the scrap of red in the gravel, knew who and what it was before he approached. He felt for a pulse, found nothing. It had to have been a quick death. Parker arrived on Ike's heels, and Ike was grateful for the man's presence.

Ike released Purvis's hand. "We need to move the people out of these houses," he said. When there was no answer, he turned to Jim. "You hear me?" And then he realized that Parker had nodded but not spoken.

"I'll get on it," Parker said, but he remained staring. "Oh, Jesus," he said.

Ike squatted next to the body. "Get Harley, Turner, whoever else you can rustle up. We need a door-to-door. Evacuate them to the Grange, or churches, friends, anywhere outside of this perimeter. If the grain elevators go—" He tried to estimate the proportion of a blast. "Make it three square blocks."

Parker nodded. "Anything else?"

"We need to act on this fast. That's first priority. But keep an eye out for Chas Stubblefield. Armed and dangerous."

Parker jogged across the lot to a waiting squad. He snatched Harley on the way, waved Turner over, spoke a few words to each. They split up.

Teams of men beat at the grass with wet sacks in the back field. The wind frisked across the lot and the stream of water from hoses turned at a right angle. Ike studied the scene, tried to memorize it. Imagined the gun aimed at Purvis's chest. Imagined Stubblefield aiming the gun.

Ike sat back on his heels. He'd cordon off the body, put out an all-points, put his own men on it as soon as they'd evacuated the area, and made sure the fire was controlled. The wind and cold would make it tough. He needed photographs. When he looked up, Pattiann was there.

He rose from his squat. He didn't touch her, but spoke into her ear, his face buried in her blowing hair. "He's dead, Pattiann. There's nothing you can do here," he said. He put a hand under her elbow and braced her arm. He could feel her shaking. "I want you to go with your folks. Stay at their place, or Rob's. Are you listening?"

She nodded.

"I don't want you alone. Can you do that?"

She nodded again.

"You find someone to walk back to the hall with you, or I'll get you a ride."

"No," she said. She stared at Purvis's body. "It was Chas, wasn't it?"

"I can't be sure," he said. "Seems likely."

"I could kill him," she said. Her voice cracked. "I could."

"Stop this. Go to Bill and Martha, now. Let me know you'll be okay, so I can get on with my work. You understand? I can't do my job if I'm worrying about you."

She pushed away.

"I don't have to lock you up for safekeeping?" He could see she was angry now, but relenting. He cupped her elbow tighter in his hand.

She nodded.

He turned away, called over a deputy, spoke to him, and as he met with the fire chief, he watched Pattiann make her way out of the lot, heading back toward the Grange.

She walked. Or at least her feet moved, one then the other. She was shaking. Maybe it was the cold that was settling deeper and deeper. Purvis was dead.

She crossed the street, stepping to the heartbeat in her ears. The town looked strange, glass and brick fronts rosy, the sky an outraged orange. She tasted wood ash. She could see the lit hall, the first of the children being led inside. "Puff the Magic Dragon" was being played, and she could hear children singing along, and she pictured it—the small faces pleased with the night's adventure. She stood on the stairway and tried to make sense of it. She looked over her shoulder at the bright corona in the night sky, and down at the blank windows and in the black glaze the tidy yellow squares of warm light reflected from the Grange. She felt remote. Culpable.

She couldn't imagine walking up those last two steps and going through the door, or talking to people. Telling her mother and father about Purvis. She could hear her father playing for the children, fiddling to keep them calm. Her own heart raced. She stepped away, down the street, angled across fenceless yards toward her house. They would need blankets, pillows, extra bedding at the hall. She jumped Deer Creek, slid, and soaked a foot. She'd change into jeans, boots, bring extra winter gear. She imagined tucking the children in, brewing coffee for the firefighters. She hoped the fire was contained, but found herself bracing for the blow that could come at any moment, the repercussive wave of hot air that would level her, make knives of every window.

She ran up the walk, opened the door, and locked it behind her. It was cool in the house. She turned the thermostat up and ran up the stairs, flipping on lights as she went. She gathered blankets, stripped the bed, and dumped the pile in the hall. She pulled on jeans, snugged a wool sweater over her head and arms. She pushed away the image of Purvis. She put on a down jacket and gathered the bedding in her arms.

It was good to have something to do. She wasn't ready for grief, wondered if she ever would be. Coming down the stairway she was surprised by the cold, wondered if the furnace pilot light had gone out. A newspaper fluttered on the sideboard at the base of the stairway. She hugged the bedding tighter. The back door was open.

And then she could smell the gunpowder. When she stepped off the riser facing the living room, he was there, in Ike's chair, waiting. The gun in his lap.

"Pattiann," he said.

"Chas," she answered. She dropped the bedding.

"I knocked," he said. "Knocked twice. Thought I might run into your husband before you."

"He's not here," Pattiann said.

He looked around, sniffed the air. He stood. "You disappointed in me, Pattiann?"

"Oh, Chas." She shook her head. She backed away, toward the kitchen, turned and ran. A chair fell behind her and there was the sound of heavy boots. She made it to the backyard before he caught her. He threw an arm around her neck, tackled her tight to him. He smelled of smoke and gasoline. "My truck's over there," he said, pointing with the gun in his free arm. She could see it parked on the dirt road off the corner of their lot. "You drive," he said, quirked a grin at her and lifted the gun higher. "I'll ride shotgun."

He directed her down back roads. He sat with his back braced against the passenger window, the gun angling up across his lap. He reached over, turned on the heat.

The fire's glow had lessened in the rearview, and she hoped it meant the worst was over. But there it was again—full blown in her head—Purvis dead. She was next. Her hands tightened on the wheel. What could she do? Wreck the truck? Wrestle the gun away? Shoot the sonofabitch? Was it in her to do such a thing? What was it she'd said? *I could kill him. I could.*

"Not a fit night," he said. "Damn." He slapped the dashboard and she jerked like a fish on a line. "Sorry about that, but I imagined this differently. Turn left, here." He nudged the gun toward her.

It was a gravel road, well off the highway. "Where are we going?" she asked.

He shrugged. "It's not like I planned this."

"And Purvis?"

"I didn't invite him to my bonfire. No. But it was fate, you know." He wagged his head. "God *will* stick His hand in where it don't belong. Best I could have hoped for, it would have been Coker, or Taylor." He paused. "Your husband maybe. Turn here again, right."

She slowed, did as he said. "This is all just getting worse, Chas. What are you going to gain by taking me?"

"Your sweet company, little girl. Like it used to be." He pushed his hair back, wiped sweat from his forehead though it was chilly in the cab. "Anyway, can't get much worse." He rested his elbow on the dash, his hand still snagged in his hair. "Killed a man . . . if only your husband had minded his own business."

"You *made* it his business. Goddamn it, Chas, Ike didn't make you kill Purvis. Ike didn't even kill your cattle—you did. You starved them until they were dropping dead in your fields."

"Well, he said that very same thing this evening, and all those fine, fine people in the hall straining to hear." Chas shook his head, clucked his tongue. "I know what they think of me," he whispered. He eased back, opened his jacket, tugged on the shirt at his neck, until the top button jettisoned, lightly banging off the windshield and falling into the dark at his feet. He settled the gun butt on the floor, his hand on the barrel, and the barrel alongside his cheek. He pointed to the next turn, and said, "What I do not know is what *you* think."

"I think you murdered Purvis."

He waved that away. "It wasn't as if I meant to." He looked out the side window, then back at Pattiann. "He was just there. Come out of nowhere, dressed like a clown. I warned him, I said, 'Is it hot enough for you, Purvis?' but he just stood there, warming his hands by my fire. Now don't you think that's a sorry-ass thing to do?"

"He didn't believe you'd shoot him."

"Oh, he *knew*. If you'd have seen his face . . . he was already dreaming of the other side, his smile kind as Christ's own, for all the good it did either of them." He leaned his head back against the glass, looked down on Pattiann.

The wind tugged at the car. She thought she saw a flash across the road, and then a few drops spattered the windshield with a slushy mix of ice and water and she heard the delayed rumble. If things could get worse, she thought. Freezing rain. A sleet storm. "It's going to get bad," she said.

"Pattiann," he said. "It's bad already. Don't you know that? Don't you know it's been bad forever?"

Pattiann took a firmer grip on the steering wheel, settled her left foot against the floorboard. She felt the rear end break loose, grab, and then she floored it. Chas was thrown back into the seat, and she grabbed the gun barrel with one hand and jammed it up toward the cab ceiling.

Chas reached across with his free hand, caught her by the collar. The truck wrenched to a side. "Brake," he yelled. He squeezed down on her neck; her hand on the gun was rammed tight against the dash. She kept her foot down. The tires gripped and slid, and then his leg was wedged between hers, his foot punching down on the brake pedal, and the engine screamed while the brakes locked, and the truck was skidding sideways toward the ditch. She hauled on the wheel and straightened it out, her foot lifting off the gas.

The truck slid to a side and swung two full circles before it jounced to a stop. He was still pressing down on her neck. The cab grew dark, darker. She could hear Chas at a distance but could not see him. She let go of the gun and wheel to pry at his hands. And then her head was rocking back, bounced against the side window. She heard the slap after the fact.

When she could see again, his face was close. "I've never given you reason to do this," she said.

"As if I needed one."

"I won't make it easy."

"Woman." He swung his head side to side. "There *is* nothing easier. All that keeps you suspended in the here and now is this thin skin of yours." He put his hand on her left breast, held tighter when she pulled back. "And this heartbeat."

He let go of her breast. He pushed back in his seat, lifted the shotgun into his lap. "It is *easier* to kill than you can imagine."

"Chas, you have no reason—"

"Reason? We put too much Goddamned almighty trust in reason. Why . . . why reason's just a justified whim, like lending money or not, shooting cattle or men. It's the *desire* that counts. There ain't a reason to keep on breathing day to day but that we desire to. And you don't need any more reason to kill than that you want to. Purvis knew that." He swung the gun barrel toward the road. "Now why don't you just drive on?"

The warehouse was gutted and a column of white steam bloomed over black boards. They plied water over the buildings and grasses, and sleet joined the barrage until fantastic ice shapes grew in the dark, stalactites and pillars and in the core of some the coals ebbed and glowed like small hearts beating. The men turned hoary with ice, gloved hands fused to firehoses, and others used their fists to break them free. They labored in shifts of quarter- and half-hours, de-icing gear, warming themselves with cups of hot coffee delivered from the Grange Hall. They bided their time at the fire and it would raise itself from time to time, flame jutting from a blown window or door, so that any number of false tongues wagged in reflection on slags of glass and ice.

Ike stayed until Purvis's body was removed and the homes surrounding the elevator had been evacuated. He regrouped his deputies in the hall's back office. Outside, the sleet kept falling—they could hear it on the boards and window. The highways and roads shone as if lacquered and Chas wouldn't get very far. Nor, of course, would they. He'd called in a vehicle description to the Highway Patrol, but they'd yet to report seeing it, and it was unlikely they would. Chas would keep to the little-traveled county roads.

In the room, chairs were banged open and scraped across the floor. There was a restlessness that transmitted itself through a hum of small movements. Men tugged at coats and raked fingers through their hair. The buzz was that Stubblefield had tried to burn Taylor's house as well, but Taylor had a sprinkler system in his home installed just last week. He'd come home to find a charred circle in the flooded garage interior.

Ike closed the door, shutting out the noise of children and a three-piece lullaby. Until the roads improved, they would keep the search down in numbers. Harley, Parker, and Ike. Work the back roads to Stubblefield's place. "If he goes to ground, it'll be there. Better chances are we'll find him spun off in a ditch. No heroics." Ike eyed Harley. "You spot him, call for backup. Just keep him in sight, that's all. Take foul-weather gear, blankets, a thermos of hot fluids. If you get stuck, it'll be a long night. Radio in and stay put." He ordered a rotation on dispatch and deputies ready to respond.

After he dismissed them, it didn't take long to discover that neither Bill nor Martha had seen Pattiann. Ike would not let himself be nervous, but he gathered his gear, made a radio check with the other units, and turned toward home. He kept his speed down, the Bronco holding a stable path on the streets. It would be slow going, torturous, and he could not imagine Chas's old pickup making any great distance. Tree limbs and powerlines already sagged under the ice. On the outskirts of town and nearing his home, it was quiet, no movement but for the downward sluicing of sleet. Ice filled the windshield well, the wipers skidding over the jelling mass. He pulled into the driveway and saw, with relief, the houselights were on.

He stopped just inside the front door, felt the cold. He believed he could smell smoke and gasoline and he hoped it was his own clothing, but knew it wasn't. He found the pile of bedding on the floor by the stairway, cut through the kitchen at a clip, and out the opened back door. He called her name. He stood in the yard, trying to see out to the street where Chas's truck might have parked, where he hoped it was still. When he turned back toward the house, the grass shattered under his feet.

He called it in to the dispatcher, to Harley and Parker. "He's got my wife," he said. And silence answered and then a muffled cursing from Harley, and a seasoned reassurance from Parker, and then Ike was inching his way out onto the roads, the house and town falling behind him.

"You just keep driving straight, unless I tell you. But you're doing real good." They'd been driving awhile now, though it was hard for Chas to say how long, everything seeming to be quick and slow at the same time with the ice crusting the side windows so that the world was a dark ripple and what was left them was the narrow beam of headlights, sleet falling into it as if the dark had quills. How could a body tell time in this elastic night, when all of Chas's life seemed a drop in that larger moment when he'd fingered the trigger and Purvis had dropped dead? He closed his eyes and played the moment out as he knew he would, again and again, for whatever time was left him—Purvis smiling and falling. Falling. Then there came a flash across his eyelids and a boom that startled Chas back to the here and now, but it was only lightning, and there was another fork of light and a lesser concussion and in the brief flash it seemed the land had turned to glass.

He looked over at Pattiann. She was focused on the road. Her eyes looked hollow in the dashboard's light, her lips a thin line. Her cheeks were dry. "You know what I find really strange?" he asked. "I don't think I've ever seen you cry. Not ever. Not back when we were together. Not now with your best friend dead . . . and you next, for all you know."

He smiled. "Not that I don't admire that," he said. "But strange, don't you think? You being a woman and all." He nudged her arm with a finger. "Don't pray either, do you?"

"What do you want me to say, Chas?"

"The truth."

"The truth," she said, her voice breaking, "is with the roads like this if you don't kill me, *I'll* probably kill us both."

"Hah!" he shouted. Lightning coursed across the sky and Chas slapped his thigh on the heels of the thunder. "That was a good one. Well, and I'd take over driving, but then you'd have to hold the gun." He grinned.

"Chas, if you cared for me at all—"

"If I did . . ." He looked out the side window, pressed his forehead against the glass so that the cold burned a path through his head. "Why," he said, straightening up with a smile, "I'd probably want you here with me. Right up to the end." And then his smile disappeared and he snatched the gun up, the barrel swiveling to her hairline. He pressed the bore against her temple. The truck hitched and slowed, and coasted to a crawl. The black night sealed them in, a shell forming around the doors and over the roof and hood, the antenna sheathed in ice, and they were pocketed in the green glow of dashlight while the wipers scratched at the windshield with a sound like a small animal at the back door. The gun bore eased up. "Just like a kiss, ain't it?" He slid it away.

"Keep driving," he said. "Did I tell you to slow?" And the truck eased forward. The cab silent except for the sound of slush in the wheel well, the hard pelting of sleet on the roof.

He lowered the gunstock to the floor again, his hand gripping the barrel like a divining rod. "I never asked for this, for any of this. The bankers, with all their money—*just take it,* they said—*this country's on the rise. Let us help you,* they said. Until I really needed their help. Until the drought settled in and the market bottomed out. Until I had more range than hands, and then more cattle than range, and there wasn't a soul I could turn to, not them, not God." He turned to her. "Not even you."

He was silent a long while and then Pattiann answered, "Purvis was right. You are a self-pitying sonofabitch."

He looked over at her, his eyes widened. "He say that?" He laughed softly. "Shit. I should have killed him twice."

244

She didn't have time to answer. There was a shape in the road, rushing out of the dark, large, square, and black, and she slammed on the brakes and as slow as they were traveling the truck swung in a pirouette once and then again, and they were sliding sideways past the cow and she could see its startled eyes, its head swinging to watch them pass, and then its kick before it bolted across the road and she thought she could see other cattle gathered in the field on the side of the road as the headlights circumscribed a wide circle and then the truck was canting sideways into a ditch and the front bumper slammed against the embankment, the wheels coming to a stop, and she was recoiling into her seat, feeling the punch of steering wheel to her breastbone. They rocked to a stop.

"Whooee," Chas said, and let go the dashboard. He leaned his head against the back window. He ran a hand over his face and neck, checked it for blood. "You think that was a real cow, or one of my own come back to haunt me?"

The headlights were a hot glare in the ditch. The truck had stalled and the last of the exhaust smoked over the light and vanished. "Start it up," he said.

The truck started. The wheels spun. She tried reverse. "Try rocking it," he said. The tires spun.

"You stay put," he said, and pulled on the door handle. The door was frozen shut. He hefted the gun out of the way, hunched his shoulder, and drove it into the door. There was a cracking sound as the ice shattered, and he was spilling out into the air.

He settled the gun in the bed and skated to the front wheels, holding on to the truck for balance. She could hear him pounding on the hubs, breaking the ice to lock them. She tried her own door. Frozen. Her chest throbbed. Chas was crossing in front of the headlights. He looked tidy, composed even, with the sleet beating on his face, his hair clinging to his scalp. He looked up at her through the windshield and bared his teeth in a grin. He mouthed something and then he was bending to the last hub. She heard it click in place. She threw the truck into compound gear and revved it forward, threw it into reverse, grinding the gear, back in compound, and Chas was beating his fist against her side of the door. She yanked on the wheel, eased off the gas, then down again, and the truck reared and she believed she would break free, but it was only shunting to a side, settling deeper in the ditch, and Chas was scrabbling over the ice on all fours, and then the truck tilted and held.

Chas picked up the gun on his way back. He opened his door and hauled himself into the cab, slammed it shut.

"We're stuck," he said. "We'll just have to wait."

She wondered for what, or whom, and she hoped for and against it being Ike. She began to appreciate how the storm had kept her attention elsewhere, her hands and mind occupied. Now she had time and more time, as much as Chas would allow, and the cab felt smaller for it so that she found her hands fussing at her coat and the seat belt. She fixed them on the wheel, ten and two, and waited.

Chas wrung water from his hair. Small clumps of ice dropped to his lap. "Cozy, huh?" he said, and looked around him as if the truck had changed in the short time he was outside.

Pattiann focused on her hands. "Why don't you let me go?" And then she looked out the windshield at the iced fences and grass.

He shook his head. "Boot you out into a storm like this? Damn. You wouldn't last an hour." He rubbed his hand down his pant leg. "It's been a rotten winter. Shit. It's been a craphouse life. Can you tell me what the attraction is? I mean, what keeps us living—besides being too scared to die?"

She lifted a hand from the wheel, ran it through her hair. She looked at him, and he was staring back. "Is there a point in my answering, Chas? Will it make you put the gun down? Turn yourself in?"

Their breath fogged the windows, and Chas wiped a clear circle, palm squeaking on the glass. "Never can tell," he said. "Can't hurt now, can it?"

A minute lapsed. Another. He clucked his tongue. "What is it about you, you got to make everything so difficult?" he asked.

She turned away, rubbed a clear circle on her side of the window, pressed her forehead against it.

"Maybe you can't help yourself? Maybe it's just in your nature to be obstinate. Some people are—like my father. Too stubborn to die. God damn. I thought he'd live forever." He laughed and it trailed off with a sigh. "My mother must have thought the same. For her, I think it just got to be more work to live."

Chas fell silent. He cranked down the side window, and as the glass eased into the door panel it left a pane of ice in its place. He rapped on the membrane. He pressed his face near, broke off a piece, and slid it into his mouth. He rolled the window back up. He sucked on the chunk of ice awhile and then said, "I never saw her cry either. Like you. A woman of few words . . . but a lot of prayer. She prayed for a sign, anything to let her know that He was still top dog. She made me pray along sometimes, but my heart wasn't in it. And to tell the truth, God wasn't speaking those days. Unless you count her hanging herself." He sighed again. "Aah, shit. She deserved better than that."

"And Purvis?" Pattiann asked. "Didn't he deserve better?"

His eyes were closed and his hand was gripping a knee. He shook his head. "God damn, but he looked the fool." When he opened his eyes again, he stared ahead at the windshield closing with ice. "Killing's easy. Doesn't take much. Point and squeeze." He rubbed his knee. "It's damn shabby, this body. Takes so little . . . effort. You know what you see when you look in the eyes of the dying?" He leaned closer to her. "I could *kill* you," he said. "And that terrifies you, doesn't it?"

She gripped the steering wheel. "Is that what you want? You want to frighten me, Chas? You want to see me cry?" She shook her head. She *was* scared. Terrified. But this was different from what she'd have expected—no rush of adrenaline, that first energy having deserted her now when she most needed it. Rather her arms felt weighted, her heart a brick in a chest too narrow to fill properly with air. Her mouth was dry. She wished she had the energy to break open the window as he had done. To suck on a sliver of ice until it melted, as if she were a child again, idling away thirst on a summer day. She became aware of how her hands cramped around the wheel, and she was amazed that he did not see, even in the dark of the cab, how her wedding band glowed against the unnatural white of her finger. "I don't . . ." she said. "There isn't . . ." she said. It pained her to realize how much time she'd spent, idling over the past, consumed with it, reinventing old grudges, distancing herself from family, from her husband. She thought of Ike, and longed for his gracious calm, the single steadiest, most precious gift he could have offered her, that quiet biding that *risks* everything, that offers itself with open hands and *demands* nothing. She looked over at that other ring of metal, the bore of the gun with its dimmer gleaming, Chas's hand white against the gunstock. Chas had been headed this way a long while, she realized. Only he'd never found his way out of it; he'd never found, as she had, another person who could turn the pain aside long enough for him to heal. No. He hadn't brought her here out of love, or regret, or even revenge.

She knew what it was he wanted, and she realized how alone he was, how utterly, devastatingly alone. "Chas, don't do this," she said. "Don't take me with you." And she saw how accurately she'd read him by the way he studied her face.

"Tell me why I shouldn't?"

"Because you don't have to," she said. "Because it's equally in your power not to do this." She took a deep breath. "Because," she removed her hands from the wheel, folded them in her lap, "I'm happy with my life." She waited a moment, then turned to see how he'd reacted. His cheek was resting against the gun barrel, his eyes staring out the side where he'd punched the hole in the ice, and that space already closed in with a new skin, a lighter wrinkling against the dark like an old scar. He rubbed his cheek up, then down the barrel, and it seemed to her that he was nodding to some voice she didn't hear and she heard his breath catch and realized how thoroughly cocooned they'd become in the ice, how the fierce wind and sleet drove soundless over the glassy surface.

When he finally stirred it was to throw his shoulder against the door, and the sudden noise and action startled Pattiann back against her own. And then he was lifting the handle, throwing his weight against the seal again, and the door opened. Sleet drove in the crack. "You stay dry," he said, a smile as if he'd told a joke on himself.

It took her a moment to react and one of his legs was already out the door. "Where are you going?" She reached across the seat, her hand stopping short of his.

He looked at her, at her hand. The sleet drove in with the wind so that she lost her breath, drenched in the chill. He shook his head. Shut the door behind him.

She watched him, gun over his shoulder, stumble up out of the ditch and into the field. She forced her window down and a sheet of sleet toppled into her lap. "Chas," she called, but the wind snatched her voice. She called again. She could not see. Icy water ran down her hair, her face. She swiped at her eyes with drenched hands and then raised the window against the cold and wet. She sat in the truck. She had a half tank of gas. She was shaking, as if all the cold and terror had just now taken hold, and her fingers fumbled at the ignition. She prayed the engine would catch, and when it did, she turned the heater on. She stared into the dark. There was nothing to be seen of Chas. Just the falling ice, the glazed fields.

It was Ike's old nightmare—every crossroad a decision and any one wrong decision carrying him farther away. He closed his eyes, breathed deeply, trying to lay out the land like a grid and imagine the turnings a madman might direct toward home. The other units called in with no news, and each time the radio stammered back into silence, Ike's heart stilled with it. Ike loosened his jacket. The ice and dark diffused the headlights and the sleet kept coming and he had to make another choice on which fork to take, and chances were that it would be the wrong one, that he would miss them, aiming parallel to them, or maybe the pickup had already stopped, or wrecked. He turned right.

He blamed himself for getting involved. The cattle were as good as dead before he'd gotten in the middle of it. What had he gained putting them down? "A mercy," Purvis had called it. And now Purvis was dead. And Pattiann? He concentrated on the road, invoking a discipline as old as setting one foot in front of the other.

When he first saw the truck in the distance, brake lights red in the ditch, he'd turned off his own headlights. He feathered the brakes, the Bronco's chains skittering, but the vehicle stopped several hundred feet short of the pickup. He'd work his way along the high end, well away from the truck lights, and hope to get a better view of the occupants. He prepared quickly: extra ammunition, gun loaded, safety on.

It was slow going, half crawling and sliding, and yes, it was Stubblefield's rig, and he couldn't make out anybody in the cab with the windows iced, but exhaust billowed. He eased his way toward the back of the truck, down the ditch on the driver's rear side, sliding hard, the shotgun punching into his ribs so that he lost his breath, and then he was on his hands and knees and the brake lights flashed again and the engine cut. He sat, collecting the calm he'd need. He kept his head low against the truck bed until he could see into the rear window. It looked to be one person. He thought he could make out Pattiann in the driver's seat. He eased up to the cleared side window, saw she was alone.

He rapped gently, and she startled, spread her hands on the glass as if to touch his face. Then she called through the ice and glass. "The door's frozen tight," she said. She pointed to the passenger's seat. "The other side . . ."

He slid around the front of the truck, eased himself into the seat next to her. He held her briefly, touched her wet cheeks. When he was convinced she was safe and well, he asked, "Where's Chas?"

"Gone," she said, pointed into the dark. "Out there. Somewhere."

Her hand snatched at his and he squeezed it gently. "You all right?" he asked.

She nodded. Her breath was a gulping and he knew she was close to hypothermia, shock, or both. He led her out, back to the Bronco where he pulled out the emergency blankets, dried her face and hair, wrapped her in their warmth. He studied the color of her skin, listened for her breathing to come back to normal. He wanted nothing more than to hold her. He cupped her face in his hands, pressed his forehead against hers, kissed her eyebrow. "You all right?" he asked again.

"Yes," she said, though her voice was small. So unlike her. She was trembling.

"How long's he been gone?" he asked.

She shook her head. She was crying. "Not sure." Her teeth still chattered and he snugged the blankets around her. "Maybe twenty minutes."

He reached into his pocket, pulled out keys and handed them to her. "There are more blankets, a thermos of coffee, some emergency supplies. A dry parka." He called dispatch, for backup, and then he pulled on a dry down-filled parka. He tucked two road flares into the inside pocket.

"You're not going?" She set down the thermos of coffee.

"Stubblefield's out there."

"Then wait for backup."

"That could be hours."

She shook her head. "No. Listen. You don't have to . . ." She wiped at her eyes, looked at her hands as if surprised to find tears, and he realized she'd been crying without knowing it.

He put his hand on the door handle.

She grabbed his free arm. "Goddamn it, Ike, he's still got the gun. He's half out of his head and wandering around. Don't you know, he's as good as dead out there?"

"Not if I find him first."

"Why? What do you gain? Revenge? Is that it? Because of me? Because of Purvis?"

"It's my job."

"Fuck your job." Her hand tightened on his wrist. "I'm sorry. I didn't mean that. But sometimes what's right and what's the law isn't the same."

Ike shook his head. "I can't just ignore what he's done, Pattiann." Ike flipped the hood up over his head. He grabbed the door handle.

Pattiann clasped his free hand. "He could have killed me, but he didn't. That should count for something." She squeezed his fingers. "Let the range take him. It would be a mercy, really. I'm not just pleading his side anymore. You don't know what it's like out there." She held tighter to his hand. "You go out there, it's not Chas you'll have to worry about. Chances are you'll never even find him. You'll wander around out there, get lost, die for nothing." She let go of his hand. "God damn it, what makes you so bullheaded?"

Ike smiled. He leaned over, buttoned her jacket closed at the neck. "A man less bullheaded wouldn't last around you." He fingered her cheek. "You know I *have* to do this."

She turned away to look out the side window. The door handle on his side clicked and the wind drove in.

"Ike," she called.

He leaned into the car one last time.

"The animals that survive keep moving. They outwalk the storm, keep the wind at their backs. Chas knows that."

Ike nodded, stepped back.

"I'll be here," she said. "Right here."

Chas slid and walked, and clods of ice built around his feet. He lowered himself between barbed strands in fences, his clothes cracking as he bent, spears of ice falling. He wished it was a clear, cold night. It would be nice to have the moon or a star to guide him.

But then, he was going no place in particular. He walked and walked until he couldn't feel his feet, nor most of his legs or his hands. When he tried to blink, found he couldn't. He'd walked for hours, he thought. Or minutes. It was that old shell game of time.

When he opened his mouth, he felt the ice crack across his cheek and jaws. He laughed, and it came out a muffled *mumph, mumph*. He kept the wind at his back. Like cattle, he thought, always moving ahead of the storm until they came to a fence and stopped. He was thirsty and he lifted a hand to his mouth and sucked at the crust that rimed his fingers.

"You here?" he asked, and listened to the wind, and then realized it was not the wind he heard through plugged ears but the booming of his own blood. He tried to nod, but his neck would not bend. Quite a night. He paused, looked around as if to get his bearings. Yes. Quite a night. Pulled out all the stops—killed a man. He laughed. That red coat, so absurdly bright—like a joke at a funeral.

He stumbled, slid to his knees, and thought his legs would snap. He teetered back on his haunches. He brushed at the ice that balled from his brows and hair, looked up. Not a damned star up there. "Couldn't give me that, I suppose?"

In the air around him there were creaks and groans and snappings, as the ice settled, layer over layer, and tiny fractures bloomed below and the crowned heads of sage shattered with weight and the wind skittered the tinkling shards across the glassy surface. He sat until his knees grew into painful knots. In the morning, he thought, he would see the sun rise through eyes frozen wide. He made a lowing sound deep in his throat. He felt the corners of his eyes sealing and could not tell if it was sleet or tears.

He believed he was warm, though he understood it was the numbness, and so he pushed himself back up to his feet. Moved on.

He still carried the gun, barrel pointed down, though almost certainly by now sealed tight over the chambers and the shot tucked within. He could have cast it away, but he did not. He kept it now simply because it had become a part of him—his hand fused to the stock.

The world was growing dimmer through the ice, and he closed his eyes, imagined it as he best loved it—the light coming over the fields. He was a boy again, flat on his back in the greening land, chewing the sweet stems of grama grass. Then he was a young man, and Pattiann was there with him, plucking wheat chaff from his hair, in the bed of straw where they'd just made love. And then he was a child, in his mother's arms, inhaling the earthiness of her skin, her hair. It smelled of iron and salt and a sticky sweetness like blood, and he saw Purvis, his eyes fixed and shining.

Chas discovered he'd stopped. "I'm cold," he said. "Tired."

Sleep.

"No," he said. There was something more. Some thing not done. He pushed himself. He thought of home. And when he looked up again, he saw that he was not alone.

Ike followed the iced track that led away from the truck. It was hard to see in the dim flashlight beam and driving sleet, and the tracks were filling in, glossing over. In another hour, maybe less, they would be gone. He looked up, to the far horizon, where he thought he could see a break in the storm, the glittering edge of stars. But it might have been wishful thinking and he trudged on, sliding and skating, his back wrenching with a missed step. He drew the parka's snorkel tight around his face. Kept his revolver pocketed and dry, the shotgun barrel pointed down and a canvas draped over the mechanism. He was warm and better prepared than Chas, though turning into the wind, that didn't make him feel any more assured. He stopped, looked back over his own tracks breaking through the ice, and somewhere, already out of sight, was the Bronco and Pattiann. What was it she had said? *Let the range take him.* Ike looked out over the level land. A dispassionate place. It just *was*. It gave you all the rope you could ever hope for with a vast, incomprehensible indifference. Ike skated his feet forward—the way he'd learned to walk the icy lakes back home as a kid—shuffle, shuffle, slide.

He remembered the ice storms of his childhood, every few years they would get hit with sleet, maybe once in a decade it would be as severe as this one was. Noise. That was what he remembered most vividly—the bang and concussion of maples exploding from the inside, the skreel of shredding limbs, or when the winds hit, the overhead shattering like wreckage in a glass shop. But here, it was so quiet—the small muttering of ice, the crunch of his feet breaking through.

He was scared. He could admit that. But he could not let that turn him aside. Why not? Revenge? And he believed he could honestly say, no. Though when Pattiann had asked, he'd doubted himself. His friend dead in the gravel. And his fear for Pattiann? So, wasn't at least a small part of

this pursuit inspired by something less than noble? He felt a cramp beginning in his fingers and switched the gun over to his other hand, flexed a
fist, relaxed, flexed. He had a right to anger. He tried to see farther into
the gloom, imagined Chas out there, trudging a path ahead of him.

But he had his duty as well. He was a man of the law. It was what he
knew—as his father had known cattle. As Pattiann knew this land. The
law. And wasn't part of the law justice, retribution? Punishment.

Jesus Christ. He could hardly stand to listen to himself.

He'd walked for a long while, or so it seemed to him, though when
he checked his watch it had only been a little over a half-hour. Still he
could see the storm was moving, the sky clearing, the faint points of
stars swimming in the waning sleet, and at the skirt of clouds a brighter
smudge where the moon must be. He cleared the ice from the flashlight
lens, tracked the light's beam over the faint trail, though of course, he
realized, it could very well not be Chas's at all. But perhaps a game trail.
Or had he doubled back on his own? He could not afford to think about
that. Instead, he opened the snorkel on his parka, took several deep
breaths, and knocked off the clots of ice that dangled from the rim of the
hood. He ran a check over his body, flexed his fingers. His hamstrings
ached and the calves of his legs felt stretched, but all in all he was in
pretty good shape. No lightheadedness, no dizziness. No major numbness, though his feet felt, he thought . . . distant.

Certainly no worse than Chas must be feeling. Assuming Chas was
still on his feet, that he hadn't found someplace to hole up—a shed, a line
shack, or old homestead.

He struck out again and for the next ten minutes he covered a fair
amount of ground, believed the track looked fresher, as if he were gain-
ing on who or what it was that walked ahead. And why not. Starved.
That's how Chas had looked—hair slicked back, cheeks sunken, pants
leashed tight. Hardly up to a trek like this. And then Ike's feet slid from
under him and he landed hard on his hip and back, the air woofing out,
the gun breaking free of his stiff fingers and clattering across the ice until
it rucked up against a rock. It took a moment before he could start
breathing again, and as he curled up onto his elbow he felt the bloom of

pain at the back of his head and down his spine where it had hit. He rested a long minute, letting his vision clear, the pain ebb, and his breathing resume to normal. He checked his limbs, only now becoming aware of how close it was—a concussion, a broken bone—how deadly. He raised himself to a kneeling position and closed his eyes, waiting until the nausea subsided. And when he opened them it was to a world transformed, the moon sailing clear of the clouds, laying a roadway of light on the ice. And to the right of him the sleet was a storm of moonlight, silvered streamers pulling back in a curtain over the blackness. And maybe it was the hurt, the tailspin of emotions, or the brightness of the glazed fields with their faceted heads of sage and rocks, the spired bluestem and fused tumbleweed—a cathedral of light—so that he pinched his eyes against the sudden tears and a deeper confusion seated itself like a pain in his chest: loss, love, anger. And he felt the tingling in his legs, the ache in his hip, the nerveless absence of his toes. He plucked ice from his brows and rubbed his cheeks until they burned. What was it he'd come out here for, really? The end of a long ugly business? Justice? Not for Purvis—long past caring—nor for Pattiann—*Let the range take him.* For his own sake, then? For that thing done to him, back when Ike saw Chas's face transformed by a too familiar despair, and took pity.

And taking pity, turned him loose.

When he looked again, to the left he could see the triple strands of barb, sagging from pole to glittering pole stretching out and down into the shallow swale ahead where shadows inked against the indigo light, and he thought he could see a cluster of blacker shapes, up against the fence line, and listening he heard a dull thud and still another. He retrieved his gun and eased forward, until he could see the crisscrossing fences, and he could make out a half-dozen cattle stalled in the corner. And moving among them, he saw the smaller form of a man. His pale hair iced with light.

Confounded by the storm at their backs and the barbed wire in front, the cattle had stopped in a loose group. Chas moved among them as if he were caught in some recurring dream, back and forth he moved, between one cow and another. His first impulse had been to warm himself against their bulk, but they were sheathed in casings of ice like the carapace of outlandish beetles, their legs and hooves locked in place, their noses fused to the ground. A huffing steam rose through blowholes, like small thermal pools of warm breath. Their eyes were sealed. He used his fist on a cow, but it had no effect, and he could not feel his hand and so did not know how hard or soft his blows were. He tired and leaned over the back of a cow as if it were a bartop, his elbow skidding out from under him, so that finally he laid his cheek directly on the iced back where he could see air bubbles trapped among the hairs. When he felt strong enough he lifted away from the cow, and his clothes stuck, gave with a tearing sound. He patted himself as if expecting to find his skin exposed and then looked at his other hand, frozen to the gun. No pain. And for that matter, he realized he'd been relieved of his body in general, his feet, legs, thighs. His trunk just a dull presence. He punched the gunstock into the ice next to the cow's head, chipped away at it, the icy sheath shattering from the gun's mechanism, his own hand bleeding from the blows. He felt nothing, so he kept at it. He moved around the cow, moved on to another, and another, then back to the first. They were well sealed, and it didn't take much to exhaust him. He slid down next to the cow's head, rapped on the sealed eyelid, thought he saw the ear twitch beneath the ice.

"Now you're done for," he said. He pressed his cheek against the cow's. "But I don't blame you. Sometimes a fence is excuse enough." He leaned his head back. Easy enough to let go, here like this, use the fence as his own excuse. But it still seemed as if he'd misplaced some *thing*, some *purpose* that had been clear enough when the night had begun. Long before Purvis. Back in the barn with his father's horse, the last thing he owned on this earth beside his own skin. The dark had just begun settling into the window frames, and over the fields. In a short while, he would be gone, the door bolted from the outside, and already he could imagine the rats congregating, the coyotes circling the locked barn and abandoned house. He'd stood listening to the barn settle into the cold with creaks and groans like an old man hobbled to the lands. The air smelled burned clean.

The horse lay prone against the far side of the stall, where the wood was raw as a canker from the horse licking its breath's condensation. It was a genuine curiosity, he thought, what that animal had become. Eyes moving as if in a waking dream. Nothing could save this animal anymore—its stomach fallen in upon itself, intestines gone blue and useless. But still it struggled to live, and he watched amazed by the heart's labor, the lungs' need to fill and empty—until he almost believed it would rise and stand again. And then, when Chas saw the inevitable film growing over the open eye like a first frost, when he knew no amount of willpower would ever suffice to raise this beast again, then the legs began to move, churned the bedding in a slow, improbable gallop, as dogs will chase in dreams, and Chas wondered if this was death, was the animal running to or from it? Its wide, white face nodding over the dirt floor, then, my, how the skin had settled into each hollow and the ribs spread like an opening hand, releasing . . . what? That thing there is in all of us that desires its own end as much as fears it? And it seemed he could hear again the last breath, as if it was his own as well, and for the first time he had a sense of what loss might feel like—a true grief—that was not the vacuum, the nothingness he'd fingered all his life like a sore waiting for the pain to tell him he was still alive. He lowered his face into his hands.

"Put the gun down, Chas."

He might have imagined the voice for when he raised his head, he could not see, but then he remembered to open his eyes. It seemed he was ready for sleep, after all. The sleet had stopped. He wondered when that had happened? A moon, too—capping everything with an icy light. Even the sheriff.

"Do you hear me, Chas? Put the gun down." Ike kept his distance. It had taken him awhile to work his way close, his approach slow and circuitous, but now he could see how bad off Chas was and it was clearly a different kind of risk. He cautioned himself against pity, again.

"Sheriff," Chas said and nodded. He eased the gun up across his lap and the sheriff raised his own. "Is it me you're aiming at this time, Parsons, or the cows again?"

"You're in trouble, Chas. Put the gun down, slide it this way, and I'll help you back."

Chas shook his head. He could feel the weight of it, the last thing left him to feel. He smiled. "You are God's own fool for mercy, aren't you? I kill your friend, kidnap your wife . . . What's it take, Parsons?"

Ike kept the gun level, but raised his head away from the sights. "I don't know, Chas. More than I'd have guessed. Put the gun away. Let's go."

"No. I don't think so." Chas leaned his head back against the cow's leg, looked up into the clearing heavens. "There isn't a thing back there." He wagged his head. "Not a person. Goddamn," he said, lifted his hand over his eyes, "but that moon is bright."

And yes, it was bright and the light was amplified by all the ice so that shadows stretched as if for late afternoon, and Ike began to notice other things, how the feeling in his legs had vanished and how his arms shook holding the gun to his shoulder so that he wanted to ease it down, settle himself on the ice, back braced against a post, a cow, his face turned to the moon as Chas's. He simply wanted this to be done with, this question of what he should do, or what he was capable of. He felt an enormous fatigue lay hold of him, understood that he was chilled more deeply than he'd acknowledged—edging into hypothermia himself. If it took much longer, how much good would Ike be to Chas or himself?

Ike took a step closer and Chas lowered his face. "It could be, Parsons"—he spoke slowly, trying not to slur—"that you've . . ." and he raised the gun, but it was only to settle the stock against the ice, lean his cheek against the barrel. "Damn. Forgot. You find Pattiann?"

"Yes. She's fine," Ike said, lowered his gun.

"Obstinate woman," Chas said, grinning.

Ike nodded. "Chas—"

Chas waved him off. "This is one sorry-ass predicament, ain't it?" He tipped his head forward. "I mean, here you are, and here I am, and neither of us getting any nearer where we mean to be."

"Where's that, Chas?" Ike took another step closer.

"Parsons." Chas wagged his head. "Back off." He settled the gun bore under his own chin.

Ike put his gun down, took a step back. "You don't want to do this, Chas." And then another step when Chas's finger stretched down over the trigger. "Chas. Wait. Remember that day we first met? In the corral?"

Chas nodded, and the gunstock followed, sliding back and forth on the ice next to his leg.

"What was it you said about the cattle?"

Chas grinned. "Just so much meat," he said.

Ike nodded. "Yes. Not worth this, surely?" he asked. And suddenly he was no longer just interested in stalling for time. "Just meat," he repeated. And he wanted to know how it all might have been different. "Should I have given it over?" he asked. "Should I have left it alone? Your cattle?"

Chas laughed. "Would Purvis be alive, you mean? You accepting blame—or taking credit? You really think you had more say in this than I did?" He laughed and his chin bumped on the bore, but he did not feel it. That was encouraging. "Pattiann knows better. Fuck, Parsons. I *found* my way here. You're the only one thinks I'm lost."

"Chas . . ."

But Stubblefield shook his head as if to say enough, and his eyes squeezed shut as his finger squeezed the trigger and there was a loud click like teeth hitting on teeth and then silence. He pulled the bore away. "Damn," he said, swinging the barrel up, sighting down on Ike. "Chances are," Chas continued, "that this one won't fire. Or chances are it will. But I try this other shot on myself, and it doesn't work you'll drag my ass out of here. You'll *save* me." He clucked his tongue. He sighed. "But I shoot you dead, then I get to sit here and keep you company for as long as it takes."

Chas smiled and it was the earnest smile of a young boy again. "I *will* kill you, just like I killed Purvis. You going to just sit there and take it?" He steadied the barrel on Ike's chest even as Ike's gun swiveled over Chas's heart.

Ike looked down the barrel, his heart banging in his chest where the other bore centered. He struggled for another way out, but everything had turned to glass beneath him. He thought of Purvis. He thought of Pattiann. It seemed in the moonlight that while the earth had gone hard, Chas's face had softened, gone dreaming.

"Do you understand?" Chas asked.

Ike snugged the gun closer, took a deep breath, and even as he saw Chas's hand tighten, the facing barrel ease away from his chest, he heard the concussion from his own gun. There was a flash and it felt as if someone yanked his arm back, but still he watched and saw Chas fall to a side and lie still. He heard the booming in his ears, though it was like a faraway bellowing that rose up from under his feet, and then he understood that it was not the guns he heard, but the struggling of the frightened cows, their panicked cries venting from the airholes as if the land itself were hurting. And he stood riveted the long while it took for the cries to slow and when it was silent once again he put his gun down. He did not need to check a pulse to know he'd killed Chas. He saw the shadow lengthening down over the body, and he saw the sightless eyes staring moonward. He lowered his arms, felt warmth seeping into the palm of his left hand. He turned away from the body, to where the moonlight fired a hard path to the elusive horizon and the stars . . . the stars.

He heard shots firing in the near distance. He fumbled in his jacket, pulled out a flare, lit it, and propped it up on the ice. He slid to a seated position. The flare's light sputtered a hot pink across the icy floor and over the spindled weeds and sagebrush. It hurt Ike's eyes with its brightness so that he looked away. He roused to his knees, where he hunkered over, breathing through his mouth. In the distance, he believed he could see a set of small lights moving across the ice. He took off his belt, bound his arm to his side, and grunted when he pulled it tight, though he didn't think he'd felt any pain. He raised to his feet, shuffled across the short distance to where Chas lay.

In the light of the flare, he studied Chas, the ice beading down his hair, the hair still parted neatly to a side. The jacket open at the neck where a button was missing. A boot toed inward. It always startled Ike to see how small men looked in death. And then he was reminded of his friend Purvis, the same dark pool widening over the ground, eyes locked open to the heavens like a last avenue of escape. Or refuge.

He felt an immense weariness descend that he could not give in to yet. *Soon,* he told himself. In a short while, they would find him, and tend to his wound. He would make his way back to the squad where Pattiann waited. She'd look at him and know without asking of Chas's death. She'd embrace Ike, finger the crust of ice on his brow, worry over his arm, though that would not stop him from holding her close the rest of the long night and all the nights to follow. He knew that over the weeks and months and years to come he would question this night. He would question justice. And mercy. Whether he'd shot out of self-defense or compassion. Or anger. And on most sleepless nights, when he found himself striving to remember, trying to order and reorder the sequence of events, the sound and the flash, it would be the moon and the ice he remembered clearest, and that too, finally, he would come to see as a kindness. He looked out over the vast ice-locked landscape. The flare was guttering, its fierce light subdued so that Chas's body was a darker spot that jiggled at the side of Ike's vision, and beyond that the columns of ice that were the cattle glowed and dimmed against the blackness like the embers of a fire. He turned to the cattle and set to work, as Chas had before him, breaking them free.